Praise for …

Blowing on Dandelions

"I loved *Blowing on Dandelions* for its wonderful characters, the variety and depth of the conflicts, and a storytelling style that kept me reading chapter after chapter. I've been eagerly anticipating this next book in the series, hoping it would be just as good. And it is! Ferrell is a master at writing complex, fascinating characters and at building suspense and mystery in her books in a way that keeps me turning the pages until I finally hit 'The End'!"

Roxanne Rustand, award-winning author
of *When He Came Home, Harlequin
Heartwarming,* and *Summer at Briar Lake*

"*Blowing on Dandelions* is a fun read with a beautiful setting in 1880s Baker City, Oregon. Ferrell has created characters you'll root for, and the attitudes feel appropriate for the time in this tender romance. The relationships of mothers and daughters in this story speak deeply of the need for acceptance, love, and respect from one's parents."

Susan Page Davis, award-winning author of
the Prairie Dreams and Texas Trails series

"As soft and gentle as the wisps of snowy seeds for which it is named, *Blowing on Dandelions* is an achingly tender love story that will lift your spirits—and your heart—high on a gentle breeze through the Oregon mountain valleys."

"Miralee Ferrell's writing style is always a delight, even as her stories are captivating. *Blowing on Dandelions* is no exception. From the opening scene the reader is drawn into Katherine Galloway's life, and we care about her from that moment on. This is more than a heart-tugging romance—though it is that; it is also a mind-challenging read that will leave us in a different place from when we began."

"In Katherine Galloway, Miralee Ferrell has created a woman who models grace. As the story unfolds, readers see Katherine's faith lived out in a way that is authentic, challenging, and encouraging. A book you won't want to put down … and a story you won't want to end."

"In *Blowing on Dandelions*, Miralee Ferrell gives us an engaging story with strong characters who have hidden depths. The theme of the story is universal and will touch hearts and help heal longtime hurts. As with all of her books, Miralee weaves a satisfying romance through these pages. What else could a reader ask for?"

of the 2012 Selah Award winner *Maggie's Journey, Mary's Blessing*, and the 2011 Will Rogers Medallion Award winner, *Love Finds You in Golden, New Mexico*

"Miralee Ferrell's *Blowing on Dandelions* is a deeply inspiring story about family conflict and the transforming power of rekindled love. A richly written story chock full of nuggets of divine wisdom, this book was, for me, a genuinely satisfying read."

Walt Larimore, bestselling author of *Hazel Creek* and *Sugar Fork*

"Miralee Ferrell delves deeply into the issues of bitterness and family discord and shines a bright light on God's path to reconciliation for every hurting heart. You won't be able to read this book without shedding a tear as you identify with one or more of these true-to-life characters."

Louise M. Gouge, award-winning author

"The relationship between a mom and her daughter can be complicated. In *Blowing on Dandelions*, Miralee Ferrell writes a compelling novel about a single mother trying to raise two girls even as she works to mend the relationship with her own mother. Miralee's story takes place more than a hundred years ago, but the poignant themes of friendship, healing, and forgiveness will inspire readers today."

Melanie Dobson, award-winning author of *Love Finds You in Liberty, Indiana* and *The Silent Order*

"An interesting combination of the classic Western and prairie romances. No cowboys but a hero who loves his son and a heroine who loves her daughters. Mix in a boardinghouse, a mysterious boarder, and two matriarchs marking their territory. Katherine Galloway is a heroine to root for! And Miralee Ferrell is an author to watch!"

Lyn Cote, author of *La Belle Christiane*

"With characters who will both delight and dismay, Miralee Ferrell's compelling style has created a story that explores relationships and the deeper emotions behind the conflicts of ordinary people in extraordinary circumstances."

Martha Rogers, Texas Christian Writers Conference 2009 Writer of the Year

What people are saying about …

Dreaming on Daisies

"I love Leah and Steven's story. They were wonderful characters that I wanted to root for. Miralee Ferrell paints a picture of the past and makes a reader feel she is right there with the characters. *Dreaming on Daisies* keeps you reading to the very end."

Margaret Daley, author of the Men of the Texas Rangers Series

"Miralee Ferrell once again takes us to the Oregon wilderness in *Dreaming on Daisies*. Filled with familiar characters as well as new ones, this book will delight readers and fans of the series. In a heartwarming story filled with misunderstandings and miscommunication, Leah Carlson and Steven Harding overcome their differences and rise to the challenge with courage and determination in a story that will touch your heart and keep you turning the pages."

Martha Rogers, author of The Winds Across the Prairie Series, Seasons of the Heart Series, and Homeward Journey Series

"*Dreaming on Daisies* is a compelling tale of family, faith, and forgiveness. Rich characterization and vivid descriptions enhance this story of reconciliation and romance. Miralee Ferrell has penned another engaging story that is sure to tug at your heartstrings."

Vickie McDonough, bestselling
author of more than thirty books

Praise for …

Wishing on Buttercups

"A family tragedy, a woman scarred for life, a chance meeting, and a charming ensemble cast blend together to make Miralee Ferrell's *Wishing on Buttercups* a story that runs the gamut of emotions, from enthralling and heart-wrenching, to the enjoyable, satisfying end."

Vickie McDonough, award-winning
author of the Pioneer Promise series

"In *Wishing on Buttercups*, Miralee Ferrell invites us to enjoy the charm of the Oregon wilderness and a boardinghouse filled with fascinating characters. This romance will speak to many as a beautiful young artist struggles with mystery, pain, and shame from her past, and fears to step into a future filled with promise. Will she find the will to overcome her reluctance to trust again? *Wishing on Buttercups* is filled with enough questions, twists, and turns to satisfy the most demanding of readers."

Hannah Alexander, award-winning
author and author of *Keeping Faith*

Dreaming on Daisies

Love Blossoms in Oregon Series

Blowing on Dandelions

Forget Me Not

Wishing on Buttercups

Dreaming on Daisies

MIRALEE FERRELL

A NOVEL

Dreaming on Daisies

Love Blossoms in Oregon

David C Cook

transforming lives together

DREAMING ON DAISIES
Published by David C Cook
4050 Lee Vance View
Colorado Springs, CO 80918 U.S.A.

David C Cook Distribution Canada
55 Woodslee Avenue, Paris, Ontario, Canada N3L 3E5

David C Cook U.K., Kingsway Communications
Eastbourne, East Sussex BN23 6NT, England

The graphic circle C logo is a registered trademark of David C Cook.

The website addresses recommended throughout this book are offered as a
resource to you. These websites are not intended in any way to be or imply an
endorsement on the part of David C Cook, nor do we vouch for their content.

This story is a work of fiction. Characters and events are the product of the author's
imagination. Any resemblance to any person, living or dead, is coincidental.

Scripture quotations are taken from the King James
Version of the Bible. (Public domain.)

LCCN 2014945715
ISBN 978-0-7814-0810-3
eISBN 978-0-7814-1242-1

© 2014 Miralee Ferrell
Published in association with Tamela Hancock Murray of The Steve
Laube Agency, 5025 N. Central Ave., #635, Pheonix, AZ 85012.

The Team: Susan Tjaden, Ramona Tucker, Carly Razo,
Ingrid Beck, Amy Konyndyk, Karen Athen
Cover Design: Kirk Douponce, DogEared Design

Printed in the United States of America
First Edition 2014

1 2 3 4 5 6 7 8 9 10

073014

Acknowledgments

I decided when I started writing that each book must point readers to God in some way, and I hope and pray this one won't be an exception. I write for Him first. If He's satisfied, I know the rest will fall in place. All glory goes to: God, my Father; Jesus, my best Friend; and the Holy Spirit, my Guide and Comforter.

My biggest thanks goes to my family—most especially my husband—for being patient as I work toward my deadlines, while being supportive of all it takes to bring a new book into the world. My children, Marnee and Brian, and Steven and Hannah (who provided me with a baby granddaughter last year); my mother, Sylvia, who is one of my closest friends—all offer encouragement and support. Also a special thanks to my church family, who pray as I write each new story and eagerly awaits the publication of every novel. You are special to me.

The writing of a book is never completely about the author; it takes a team working behind the scenes to bring it to life. First are my critique partners, Kimberly Johnson, Vickie McDonough, and Margaret Daley, who also offer brainstorming help. Judy Vandiver also read and critiqued my manuscript when it was finished. Kimberly Johnson, Vickie McDonough, and Judy Vandiver spent time on the phone brainstorming parts of the story line, and a number of friends gave me title suggestions. I love all these wonderful ladies who are an integral part of my team.

Early in the writing of this book, I put together an amazing group of ladies that I call my Street Team. Each of them is a strong champion of my work, and each has become dear to me this past year as they work hard to spread the word about my books and pray for me as I write. Thank you each and every one. You girls are wonderful!

My publishing team starts with my agent, Tamela Hancock Murray, who champions my work and helps find it the best possible home. Tamela, a friend as well as a business associate, works diligently to make my career succeed.

This is my third book with David C Cook. They graciously accepted my request to assign an exceptional editor, Ramona Tucker, for this entire series. I'm so blessed to partner with Ramona and value her professional expertise and editing, as well as her friendship. The Cook team welcomed me from the start, and I've loved working with Don Pape, Ingrid Beck, Karen Stoller, Caitlyn Carlson, Tonya Osterhouse, Amy Konyndyk, Jeane Wynn, and Michelle Webb, as well as the sales and marketing team. I look forward to interacting more with these quality people.

And, last, to my readers—I value every email I receive, as well as the posts on Facebook, Twitter, Goodreads, and Pinterest, and I'd love to have you drop by. Thank you for your faithful support!

- My Facebook Fan Page: https://www.facebook
  .com/pages/Miralee-Ferrells-Readers-Group
  /203176599584
- Twitter: https://twitter.com/#!/MiraleeFerrell

- My personal website: www.miraleeferrell.com. My website opens at my blog page, and you'll find a form on the right-hand side where you can sign up for my newsletter. I'd love to keep in touch! View pictures of my book research and travels, family photos, upcoming speaking event updates (via my blog link), and find announcements about future books.
- You can also drop me a note at miraleef@gmail.com.

Chapter One

One mile outside Baker City, Oregon
Mid-March 1881
Leah Carlson kicked a wicker chair out of her way and stormed off the porch, angrier than she'd been in years. Well, years might be a stretch, but at least weeks. Or perhaps several days. Maybe riding to town and finding Pa would be a good idea.

She glared at the ground, her mood not improved by the thick mud clinging to the bottom of her boots, and scraped it off on a horseshoe nailed to the bottom step. March her least favorite month— always felt somewhere between winter and spring, with none of the benefits of either.

She trooped up the steps and righted the chair. Not the chair's fault Pa had gotten drunk again and stayed all night in town. Buddy, their aging ranch hand, had seen Pa go into the saloon when Buddy had headed home from the mercantile last night. At first he hadn't told her in hopes that his boss would return at a decent hour, but that hadn't happened.

Leah wrapped her coat closer around her shoulders. Now most of the chores would fall on her, Buddy, and Buddy's wife, Millie. With Buddy's back giving him fits, she couldn't ask him to do the

heavy work, although his pride would force him to try. Why did Pa
keep falling off the wagon whenever hope set in that he'd finally beat
that horrible habit?

Empty promises, that's all she'd ever gotten. Promises he'd
change. Promises he'd do better. Promises he'd broken ever since Ma
died nine years ago. And lately it had only gotten worse. Leah had
gone from a child at the tender age of fourteen to a caretaker and
ranch foreman almost overnight, and to this day she still felt robbed.

At least the ranch was safe as long as she worked hard to pay the
bills—as long as Pa didn't try to use it as collateral for his drinking
debts. But something needed to change. Maintaining this place was
too much for her and Buddy alone. Pa had to stop drinking. Of
course, he appeared to think everything was fine and even bragged in
town about his successful cattle and horse business.

She plopped down into the righted chair. Over the years she'd
done her best to cover for him, but he'd had enough "episodes" lately
that she knew people were talking. All she could do was keep up
appearances and find at least one more hired hand—the sooner the
better. Digging up some extra cash and increasing her herd of horses
by a couple dozen wouldn't hurt, either.

Dragging Pa home and shaking some sense into his noggin
sounded very tantalizing. But knowing her father, he would ignore
her efforts or embarrass her in public. No, accosting Pa in town
wouldn't work. Somehow she had to beat him at his own game and
bring him to his senses. She had no idea how, but she'd find a way, if
it was the last thing she did.

The front door creaked on rusty hinges, and Millie poked her
head outside. "Girl, you goin' to sit there all day starin' at nothin', or

come in and get ready for that weddin' you've talked about for the past two months?"

Leah bolted upright and jumped to her feet. "Oh my goodness. I can't believe I forgot Beth's wedding." She brushed a strand of hair out of her eyes. "How much time do I have to get decent?"

Millie gestured at her mud-caked boots and stained trousers. "Not near enough, from what I can see. Guess you could stay at home. It's not like you're close friends with either the bride or the groom."

Leah shook her head. "I promised Katherine Jacobs I'd help with the refreshments since they're entertaining a few close friends at the boardinghouse after the ceremony. Besides, Beth has attended our quilting group occasionally since Christmas, and we've become friends."

She stepped past Millie and headed for the stairs leading to her room. "If Pa comes home while I'm gone, see if you can make him stick around, will you, please?"

Millie grunted. "Can't nobody make that man do nothin' he don't want to, girl. You should know that by now, especially if he's been drinkin'. But I'll try."

She waved her hands when Leah paused. "Get on with you. Nothin' you can do here, anyhow. It's about time you had some fun before you're old and gray like me. Who knows? Maybe some good luck will rub off the bride and land on you." She wrinkled her nose. "There's got to be at least one man in this world who's marriage material that don't irritate you."

Leah grinned. "Of course there is, but you snatched him up years ago. I'm destined to be an old maid the rest of my life and live here with you and Buddy, so quit trying to fix me up. I'm perfectly happy the way things are."

"Hmmph. Likely story." Millie crossed her arms and scowled, the creases beside her mouth deepening. "We're not going to be around forever, you know."

"You are too. Neither of you have permission to leave me alone." Leah choked on the last word and fled to her room. Millie had been the closest thing to a mother she'd had for more years than she cared to remember.

Steven Harding hauled on his horse's reins, his heart galloping so fast he thought it would burst from his chest. Had his horse trampled that man lying in the road? He set the brake and wound the reins around the handle, then leaped from his buggy and ran forward.

The man seemed almost burrowed into the mud, his shoulder muscles twitching and right leg jerking. He lay flat on his back, eyes closed, with one arm flung over his forehead. A guttural groan broke from his parted lips.

Relief swept over Steven. At least the man wasn't dead. But where had he come from? The busy streets of Baker City were behind Steven, and the boardinghouse where his sister and mother lived was only a few blocks away on the outskirts of town. Had he been daydreaming and not noticed the man crossing the road?

He leaned over and touched the man's arm. "Are you all right, sir?"

The fallen man mumbled before rolling to his side and pushing to a sitting position. He swiped a filthy hand across his cheek, flicking away a glob of mud and blinking his eyes. "Wha' happened?"

Steven recoiled as the stench of alcohol hit him. It was only midmorning. Surely no one started their day drinking enough to be intoxicated at this hour. He pulled his thoughts back where they belonged. It wasn't his place to judge, especially after he almost ran over the fellow. "I'm not certain. I didn't see you crossing the road in time to stop. Can you get up? Nothing's broken, I hope?"

The man groped for his hat, resting on a flat rock a short distance away. He clutched it in his hand, then jammed it onto his head, covering the ring of gray hair. "Don't think anything's broken. I don't remember what happened. I need to get home and do my chores."

Steven gripped his arm and hoisted him to his feet. "Let me give you a ride. Unless you have a wagon or horse nearby?"

"Don't rightly remember if I do." He gazed around with a bewildered stare and took an unsteady step. "Reckon I can walk." Taking another stride, he staggered, his boot plopping into another section of mud, sending a spray of dirty water only inches from Steven's clean trouser leg.

Steven sprang forward and caught the man with one hand before he pitched onto his face. With his other hand, Steven took out his pocket watch and gave it a hurried glance. Two hours before he had to pick up his sister, Beth, and his mother for the ceremony. "Do you live far?"

The man shook off his grip. "'Bout a mile or less. My ranch is the closest one to town. Don't need no charity from strangers, though."

"I'm headed that direction, so it's not charity. Please. It's the least I can do."

Bloodshot eyes met his. "Guess it won't hurt nothin' if you're headed that way."

Steven stayed close as the older man lumbered into the passenger side of the buggy. He'd have to scrub out the mud before taking the womenfolk to the church, but it couldn't be helped.

It was possible this individual was already lying in the mud when he came along. That would account for Steven not seeing him until he was almost on top of him. But it didn't matter. He wouldn't drive off and leave anyone needing help, whether his fault or not.

The ride to the ranch was silent, and Steven kept his gelding at a hard trot, intent on making the best time possible. He drew to a stop in front of a two-story white house sadly wanting paint and repair. After setting the brake, he leaped from the buggy and hurried to the other side, determined to keep the man from falling as he disembarked.

His gelding dropped his head and nibbled at a clump of soggy grass near the base of the hitching post. Steven halted on the passenger side and lifted his hand to the man still sitting inside.

The front door of the house slammed nearby, but Steven kept his attention on the fellow climbing unsteadily to the ground.

The older man ignored Steven's extended hand. "Don't need no help, mister. I'm right as rain." He grasped the handrail next to the seat and swung his legs over. Planting his boot on the step, he edged down, but as soon as his feet hit the ground, he lurched forward, almost into Steven's arms. Steven grabbed the man's arm and held him upright.

"Pa? What in the world?" The feminine voice was accompanied by a light patter of steps on the porch. "I see you finally decided to come home and got another one of your cohorts to bring you."

Steven loosened his hold on the man's arm and pivoted, arrested by the undercurrent of anger tingeing the words. He turned slowly and his heart jumped. A young woman who looked just a bit younger than him stared at the man she'd called Pa. Her emerald green gown matched her bewitching eyes, but the glow emanating from them certainly wasn't warm or friendly. "I beg your pardon, miss, but I think you've misunderstood."

The fiery redhead stood with her hands planted on trim hips, her green eyes shooting sparks. "I doubt it. You aren't the first man to bring my father home in this"—she shot an irritated look at her parent—"condition." She nearly spat the last word. "I appreciate the ride, but I'll thank you next time not to buy him any more drinks when he's had more than enough."

Steven's heart sank, and he took a step back. The last thing he wanted was to add more sorrow to this woman's life, but he hated that she thought him responsible. But did it really matter? He wasn't likely to see her again. He tipped his head. "Sorry for the trouble, ma'am. Now that he's home and safe, I'll be on my way."

Leah gritted her teeth to keep back the words threatening to spew out as the handsome, dark-haired driver picked up the reins and clucked to his horse. This one was certainly younger and better mannered than her father's other cronies who had delivered her inebriated parent to their door in the past.

Anxiety struck her as she remembered the crisp white shirt beneath the suit jacket and the stiffly starched collar. What were the chances he'd come from a saloon dressed like that? She'd probably stuck her foot in her mouth again with her impetuous accusation. Someday she must learn to think before she allowed words to blurt out.

She swiveled and glared at her father, who was tottering up the path toward the porch. "What do you have to say for yourself, Pa? I've been worried sick, not to mention having to do most of the chores myself. Was that man who brought you home drinking with you at the saloon?"

"Who I drink with is my own business, not yours," he tossed back. "I told that fella I didn't need his help, and I'm tellin' you, too. If you already did the chores, I'm gettin' a short nap."

"Pa! We need to talk."

He squinted red-rimmed eyes at her. "Done talkin'. I'm hungry, and I'm tired. Millie can fix me a sandwich; then I'm goin' to bed for an hour or two. Nothin' to talk about, anyhow." He waved a dismissive hand. "Go on with you, and leave me alone."

Leah moved closer, barely containing her frustration. "There is a lot to discuss, Pa. Starting with your drinking. It's getting out of hand, and it needs to stop or you'll put this ranch and everything we've worked for in danger."

Pa reached for the newel post at the bottom of the short flight of steps leading to the porch, clamped his hand on top, then maneuvered himself onto the first step. "I won't tolerate no daughter of mine preachin' at me about my responsibility or my sins. It's my ranch, so I'll do what I see fit with it. I've worked hard makin' it what it is all these years. You got no call to tell me what to do." He headed for the door. "Now leave me be whilst I get somethin' to eat. My head hurts, and I don't wanna hear any more."

Leah looked at the chair propped against the wall, wishing she could kick it again and allow some of her irritation to escape. Better that than allowing the tears building behind her eyes to spill over.

Charlie Pape plunked into a kitchen chair and slid the plate holding his sandwich closer, happy Millie had fixed it and left. The last thing he needed was another well-meaning female trying to tell him what to do or insisting he change.

He picked up the sandwich and took a bite, working hard to hold on to his annoyance toward his daughter. The girl had no right to tell him what to do or how to live his life. It was his business if he drank, and nobody else's. And she was dead wrong thinking she knew better than him how to run this ranch. It had been his for years.

A thought pricked at his conscience, but he pushed it away. It *was* his ranch, and he intended to make sure it stayed that way.

Leah was a good girl and meant well. He couldn't fault her there. But she was too much like her mother. Always trying to fix things to swing her own way and not taking into account what he might want. Of course, Leah wasn't his child by birth, but he'd taught her all he knew and was plumb tickled that she seemed to love the ranch as much as her old pa.

The girl had been raised here since Charlie married Leah's ma
when Leah was only a baby. He'd always figured he and Mary would
live their sunset days here, and then Leah and whatever man she
married would take over for him. Not once had he considered that
the unthinkable might happen, leaving him alone with only his misery to keep him company.

Steven Harding paced the parlor at the Jacobs' boardinghouse and
took out his pocket watch for at least the tenth time since returning from dropping the stranger at his ranch. Ten minutes after two
o'clock—only a minute since he'd last checked. He would have
wagered a guess that much more time had passed. Did his sister want
to be late to her own wedding?

Women's voices mingled not far down the hall. Moments later
Beth's adopted aunt, Mrs. Wilma Roberts—or, rather, Marshall,
since she'd recently married—and her friend Mrs. Cooper swept into
the room, arms entwined and faces aglow. They came to an abrupt
stop, and stared. Then both erupted in snorts of laughter.

He tugged at his tight collar. "What seems to be the problem,
ladies? I can't imagine what could be so amusing."

Mrs. Cooper's grin broadened. She shook her head, and a gray
curl slipped loose from under the brim of her dark blue hat. "A
stranger might assume you are the groom, if your distraught appearance is any indication. Are you terribly nervous about accompanying
your sister down the aisle this afternoon?"

Mrs. Marshall patted his shoulder. "Why don't you sit down,

Steven? It won't do any good wearing a path in the carpet. Beth will be down soon, and my Caleb will be back to pick up Frances and me."

"I'm not nervous at all. I simply don't understand what's taking so long. We still have to drive to the church. Mr. and Mrs. Jacobs and their children left long ago, and I'm sure Jeffery has been there for hours."

"Caleb drove my daughter and her family over early to ready the sanctuary for the wedding. And your mother is putting the finishing touches on Beth's hair. Your sister is going to make a beautiful bride, and Jeffery is blessed to get her. I am quite certain she will be worth whatever amount of time he must wait."

Mrs. Cooper pointed at a chair. "Sit. You are making me nervous, pacing like some caged animal."

"That's exactly how I feel." He plopped into the seat indicated and ran his fingers over his closely cropped hair. He glanced at Beth's adopted aunt, a woman he'd only known for a few months but had come to respect. "How can you be so calm? You weren't even anxious when you and Caleb married at Christmas. And why aren't you upstairs helping? I'm sure Beth wants you there."

Mrs. Marshall frowned. "I don't know what you have to be fretful over." Her face softened. "Beth asked me to stay, but she should have this time with her mother. Isabelle has missed so much of Beth's life these past years, which I was privileged to enjoy while raising her. I won't rob your mother of an instant alone with her daughter on this special day. Besides, the ceremony doesn't start for almost an hour, and the buggy will get us to the church in plenty of time."

Steven nodded but didn't reply. He was happy for his mother and sister but longed for this day to hurry to a close. Maybe once

Beth was married to Jeffery Tucker, life would return to normal. Finding Beth again after an eighteen-year absence had been exhilarating, but he'd struggled to find his place in the family with the ensuing changes.

He'd been the only child after Beth disappeared when he was eight years old, and while he rejoiced at their recent reunion, part of him longed for the time when Ma leaned solely on him for advice and support. Then, suddenly, he was ashamed at the direction his thoughts had taken. More than anything, he was lonely. Steven had thought his sister's return would unite their family. It hadn't happened that way. With Ma living at the boardinghouse to be near Beth, and him living in a mining shanty on the outskirts of town to be close to work, he didn't have much time with either of them. But Ma was happier than he'd ever seen her, and he couldn't begrudge her that. It was high time he moved on with his life. He'd better get used to being alone.

Chapter Two

Leah relaxed in the wooden church pew, thankful she'd made it to the wedding ceremony only a few minutes late and tiptoed into the last row. She'd barely slipped into her dress when the buggy had pulled up with her father on board, and she'd rushed downstairs to find him with that stranger.

Millie had enough to deal with keeping the house clean, meals cooked, and laundry done without tackling a cranky man with an overabundance of pride like Pa. With his present mood, it was a good thing he'd decided to take a nap, or she'd have felt guilty leaving him in Millie's care.

She came to attention with a start. The short ceremony had ended. Jeffery leaned over his bride and touched her lips with his, lingering a little longer than customary even for a wedding. The gesture birthed conflicting emotions in Leah.

Pure joy for Beth that she'd attained a goal longed for by so many women. Along with it came envy, a petty word Leah hated to allow into her thoughts. She strove to douse the simmering embers. Being jealous of her friend's happiness wasn't an option. Somehow she'd have to find contentment in her friends and work.

Beth and Jeffery stepped apart a few inches, but he kept a firm hold on her hand. Now that her veil was removed, the beauty was there for all to behold. Her blue eyes shone with a radiance that eclipsed all else in the sanctuary.

The pastor motioned toward the congregation. "May I present … Mr. and Mrs. Jeffery Tucker."

The two dozen or so people attending the nuptials broke into light applause, and Jeffery gazed once again into Beth's eyes. Leah melted at the raw passion evident on his face. Would any man ever care for her like that? Highly unlikely, since she'd reached the ripe old age of twenty-three and remained single.

She was not a candidate for marriage, living the rough life of a rancher's daughter and rarely attending social events in town other than the quilting group at the church and Sunday services. She'd yet to find an eligible man who caught her eye.

If only she could meet someone like Jeffery. Not exactly like him, of course, as Jeffery would never be content to live on a ranch and work the land. An image flashed of the man who'd driven the buggy and deposited her father a few hours ago. But she'd vowed never to give a man a second look who touched alcohol in any form.

That was one promise she'd never break. Of course, she had no proof he'd been drinking with Pa, but her father hadn't denied the man had accompanied him from the saloon. Why else would he have taken the time to bring Pa home?

Leah had seen firsthand the pain alcohol caused a family and the financial devastation it could bring, and she'd never willingly take that risk. Besides, she hated the changes it wrought in her father's behavior. Her mother might yet be alive if it weren't for some of her father's choices.

But this was no time to dwell on such gloomy thoughts. It was a joyous occasion, and she must put on a smile, no matter her personal feelings. Beth's aunt Wilma had stood up with her, while Leah assumed the man beside Jeffery must be Beth's brother. She'd heard he'd come to town not long before Christmas, but she hadn't met him. His back was turned to the congregation during the ceremony, but his stance and coloring seemed vaguely familiar.

He pivoted slowly, reaching out to shake Jeffery's hand and give his sister a hug before the couple made their way out of the church.

Leah craned her neck, hoping to set her mind at ease as the niggling curiosity increased. People stood and readied themselves to leave, and she had yet to glimpse his face. She tugged her cloak around her shoulders. A select group would assemble at Katherine and Micah's boardinghouse soon. Beth's family would be present, along with Jeffery's parents, who had traveled from Ohio a couple of weeks ago.

She eased from the bench and headed toward the back door, where the newly married couple stood with arms entwined, greeting each person as they departed. It might be best to head to Katherine's to help set out the food. With her friend's baby due soon, Leah didn't want Katherine to overtire herself.

Beth caught Leah's eye and waved as Leah slipped around the tight cluster of well-wishers. "Don't leave yet. I want you to meet someone."

As she moved closer, the man standing next to her met her gaze square on.

Beth patted the arm of the man who'd stood up with Jeffery. "This is my brother, Steven Harding. Steven, this is my friend Leah Carlson."

Leah's heart fluttered as she stared into the startled eyes of the man she'd so recently given a dressing-down.

Steven skirted the group of people in the Jacobs' sitting room but kept his gaze trained on the striking redhead standing behind the refreshment table. When presented at the church, he'd mumbled incoherently and made his escape, but not before he'd registered the shock and withdrawal on Leah Carlson's face. What could she have against him? All he'd done was to be a good Samaritan and deliver her inebriated father to her door. It didn't make sense that she'd think he'd been the cause of her father's condition, but since arriving at the Jacobs' home, she'd done her best to avoid him. On the other hand, he hadn't gone out of his way to correct her impression, as he'd never expected to see her again.

Firm hands gripped his upper arms. "Young man, you really must watch where you are walking." Frances Cooper, Katherine Jacobs's mother, eyed him. "Why are you staring at Miss Carlson? Is anything amiss?"

He shook his head. "Not at all."

"Have you met her yet? Perhaps I should formally introduce you. She is quite an attractive young woman, even if she does have flaming red hair."

Steven quelled the chuckle threatening to escape. "You have something against that color, Mrs. Cooper?"

She sniffed. "If you must know, my second husband was a red-head and quite mulish when it suited him. I have had occasion to get acquainted with Miss Carlson over the past few months. She is a delightful young woman, but she can be decidedly headstrong." She wagged her finger at him. "Mark my words, that tendency will land her in trouble if she is not careful."

He took a step back, more than ready to find an avenue of escape from this uncomfortable discussion. "I'm sure I wouldn't know, ma'am, but thank you for your warning. Now, if you will excuse me, I think I'll speak to my sister and her new husband." He pivoted and made his way through the crowded room to where a glowing Beth stood beside Jeffery.

She extended her hands and gripped his. "Steven. I've been look-ing for you."

He drew her forward and kissed her cheek. "You look beauti-ful—quite the loveliest bride I've been privileged to see." He leveled a stern gaze at Jeffery. "If you don't treat her right, you'll have to answer to me, you know. My little sister was gone for too long for me to allow anything to happen to her."

Beth gasped. "Steven! Jeffery loves me very much. I can't imagine why you'd say such a thing."

Jeffery produced a wry smile. "I admire your brother for speak-ing. I'd do the same with any man my sister chose to marry, regardless of the esteem with which I held him." Swiveling to Steven, Jeffery clapped his hand on his brother-in-law's shoulder. "I promise I'll take care of her. If I ever give her cause to come to you with a complaint, you have my permission to throttle me."

"Much appreciated. And I wasn't overly worried, as I believe you to be an honorable man." Steven lapsed into silence, letting his gaze rest on the redhead across the room.

Beth touched Steven's arm. "Is there something else bothering you?"

"Before I joined you, I was speaking to Mrs. Cooper. I suppose I'm still not used to the lady's straightforward personality."

Beth giggled. "That's a very kind way of saying she speaks her mind plainly without regard to where her words land. You should have seen her and Aunt Wilma when we first moved here last year." She smiled up at Jeffery. "Do you remember?"

He nodded, his eyes never leaving hers. "I'll never forget. For a while I wondered if either lady would emerge unscathed from their verbal battles, but they ended up becoming friends. It still amazes me."

Beth sobered, and her voice softened. "What did she say, Steven? I do hope it was nothing unkind. She has a good heart, and I'm certain she wouldn't intentionally hurt anyone."

Steven hesitated, hating to generate gossip, but he'd opened the subject and could see no way of retracing his steps without arousing more questions. "Nothing about me, but she offered to introduce me to Miss Carlson. Before I could reply, she launched into a discourse on the young woman's hair color and supposed tenacious behavior. I made my excuses and escaped before she could drag me over and give Miss Carlson an introduction that might include *my* shortcomings."

"That was good of you," Beth murmured. "It's strange she'd point a finger at Leah, though. I thought Mrs. Cooper liked her."

"Oh, that wasn't the issue; she admitted Miss Carlson is a delightful person. I'm not sure why she brought it up, but I didn't want her to go off on a tangent and make matters worse."

Jeffery slipped his arm around Beth's shoulders. "Worse? What happened?"

The young lady in question was still serving refreshments and didn't appear the least bit aware she was the focus of their discussion. Steven certainly didn't want anyone to judge her harshly based on what he'd seen earlier that day. "I'm afraid she's unhappy with me. I'm not quite certain what I did to deserve it—although I can hazard a guess."

Beth's eyes widened. "Oh? I wasn't aware you'd met her before I introduced you at the church."

Steven proceeded to give them the details of his encounter with the man on the road.

Beth grimaced. "Mr. Pape. No wonder Leah seemed upset when she arrived."

"Pape?" Steven glanced across at Miss Carlson. "I'm not sure who that is, but the gentleman I'm referring to is Mr. Carlson, your friend's father."

Beth nodded. "That would be Mr. Pape. Her mother was widowed and married Mr. Pape when Leah was a baby, so he's the only father she's known. He didn't formally adopt her, and she still carries her father's name."

"Ah, I see. She's an only child?"

Jeffery shared a look with Beth. "From what I understand she has a brother, Thomas Pape, who's a couple of years younger. He apparently ran away a few years after their mother died. He's not been heard from since."

What a heavy load for any woman to carry. "I see." Steven stared off to the side, his thoughts bouncing from one memory of his own to another. Sometimes life wasn't fair, even when you tried your best to do what you believed was right. Look at their own family—torn apart and damaged so many years ago, through no fault of their own—but oh, how his mother and Beth had suffered. Truth be told, so had he.

Beth tugged at his sleeve. "But why do you think she's upset with you? That is, if your buggy didn't harm Mr. Pape."

"It didn't. But when Miss Carlson came out of the house, there was most decidedly evidence of anger toward her father and"—he winced—"distrust of me. She might have thought I was responsible for his drinking."

Beth's lips compressed. "That's ridiculous. From what Mother has shared, our family never indulged in drink."

"We still don't. I've never touched the stuff, and I don't plan to change. I've seen it destroy too many lives. Too bad Miss Carlson has to deal with a father who imbibes." He cocked his head. "But perhaps it was a onetime occasion?"

Jeffery grunted. "Afraid not. The man is gaining a reputation. It's a shame too. He has a wonderful ranch, a quality herd of horses and cattle, and a daughter who works her fingers to the bone to make it succeed. If he doesn't change his ways, he could lose it all."

Steven hazarded another look across the room. Miss Carlson smiled at a young girl, and his heart contracted at the sweet expression. "How so?"

"Talk has it he's spending money at the saloon that ought to go into his ranch, and that he doesn't pull his weight like he used to." Jeffery shrugged. "Of course, it's all gossip, and I shouldn't be repeating it. But I've been concerned, since Miss Carlson is a friend of Beth's."

"Leah doesn't say much, but she's worried," Beth confided. "I'm sorry you got off on the wrong foot with her. If you have the chance, Steven, be kind to her. Leah may be embarrassed when she learns she misjudged you."

Steven kept his own counsel, but he couldn't imagine the beautiful Miss Carlson being embarrassed about much of anything—least of all an error in judgment where he was concerned.

Chapter Three

March 16, 1881

Leah shook out her gray linen dress, eyeing the wrinkles. Why did Millie have to be in town when she needed her? Of course Leah had used a flatiron before, but she was handier with a branding iron than with using a flatiron to press wrinkles from cloth. The last time, she'd gotten distracted and burned a hole in the middle of her best skirt. That couldn't happen now. It was vital she make a good impression at the bank.

She looked out her bedroom window, willing their buggy to materialize. Several minutes passed, but the only thing that appeared in the road was Buddy's brown mutt, Rusty. He planted himself off to the side and stared toward town.

Leah chuckled. It appeared she wasn't the only one longing for Millie's arrival. That dog doted on the older couple and, while Buddy claimed the animal was his, Rusty swayed to Millie's side more often than not.

At least the rain had stopped a few days before Beth's wedding, and in the three days since, the deep mud had finally started to dry. This time of year they could still get snow flurries, but hopefully nothing would stick. Roundup would begin soon, and the dry weather would be a blessing. Nothing like roping a calf and trying to hold on to the slippery critter while tying its feet and applying a brand.

She draped the dress over her arm and headed for the kitchen. There was no help for it—either do the job herself or go to town in a wrinkled garment. After a while she replaced the flatiron on the shelf and returned to her room, where she slipped into the gray gown. It was plain and serviceable. After all, she didn't want to appear gaudy for her visit to the bank. Better to look like the serious, hardworking woman everyone knew her to be and make a good impression.

One last peek in the mirror stationed above her cherry bureau showed everything in place. She ran a hand over the smooth wood grain. Her mother had loved this piece. Pa had given it to her as a wedding gift twenty-two years ago, not long after Leah's first birthday.

He'd been the only father she'd known, since hers died shortly after her birth. Leah remembered laughter and hugs those early years of her childhood. Then, for some reason she never understood, everything changed. Ma withdrew, and Pa spent most of his time outside. That hadn't bothered Leah at first, as she worshipped the man and became his shadow, attempting to emulate his every action.

If only Ma's death nine years ago hadn't changed him so much. Something inside Pa seemed to die, and his drinking accelerated shortly after that. She tucked a wayward strand of hair into the knot at the base of her neck and grabbed her shawl.

It did no good thinking of the past when everything she loved was in jeopardy. Time to see what could be done to change the present, and hopefully some part of the past could be redeemed as well.

She stepped outside and drew her heavy woolen shawl close around her shoulders, knotting it across her chest. The wind coming off the Wallowa Mountains had a bite to it, and Leah was thankful for her warm gloves and lined bonnet.

Hurrying across the barren space between the house and the barn, she approached the barn and drew open the heavy door, wincing at the grating screech of the hinges. Another chore Pa had ignored that she'd have to tackle.

Why hadn't she thought to harness the horse to the extra buggy before putting on her good dress? She hurried to the stall and removed a rope hanging on a hook to the side, then swung wide the door. A shadow fell across her path and she started. "Pa?"

"What you up to, Leah girl? Dressed mighty fine for a trip to the barn, ain't you?" Weary eyes peered at her from under the brim of his hat. "You're lookin' pert today, whatever the occasion."

She wrapped her arms around herself. How long had it been since Pa had spoken to her in such a gentle voice? She glanced at him again, worried at the sight of the stooped shoulders and tired eyes. He must not be sleeping well, as she saw no evidence of alcohol. "I'm headed to town."

"Huh." He grunted and pivoted away, then grabbed the harness off a nearby peg. "Suppose you want the mare hitched."

Surprise wrapped itself around her heart. "I can do it. No reason to bother you."

"Ain't no bother. Hate to see that fancy dress mussed." He clucked to the mare, and she stepped forward, nuzzling his pocket.

Grinning, Pa pulled out a carrot stub and offered it on the flat of his hand. "Good girl. Bet you'd like to get out and stretch your legs a mite, wouldn't you now?"

He ran a hand over her forelock and stroked her face, whispering endearments too low to reach Leah's ears. Looking back to her, he scowled. "You didn't tell me what you're up to. Lots of chores to be done before the day ends."

Why was it that most of the sweet words he managed to utter were saved for the horses and dog? She turned away, regret and bitterness leaving a sour taste.

"Don't worry. I won't be long. There hasn't been a day that I haven't done my share of work and more." She bit back the rest of what she'd like to say, but Ma always told her to treat her elders with respect, even if they didn't always deserve it.

A few minutes later, Leah stepped into the buggy and took the reins her pa offered. "Thanks."

"Drive careful. The mud is pretty much gone, but the sky don't look good. Could get another storm before nightfall." He stepped back, lifting his hand. "Don't suppose it would do any good to ask you to bring home a bottle?"

Irritation at his request ate away every bit of the warm sensation in her heart at the earlier concern in Pa's voice. "No, sir, it would not." She slapped the reins against the mare's rump. "Get along there."

Why did his life have to revolve around the comfort he got from a bottle? She'd done everything in her power to make Pa's days easier since Ma's death, but it hadn't seemed to help. She'd given up asking him to attend church. In the early years he'd managed to find an excuse, but lately he'd simply said no.

Within thirty minutes of leaving, Leah stepped down from the buggy and wrapped the reins around the hitching rail in front of the First Commercial Bank. Hopefully she could speak to Mr. Hunt, the bank president, and get this over quickly.

She pushed her way through the heavy wood door with the engraved plate glass set in the center. This brick building had been the talk of the town when it went up a few years ago, but now several others had joined it, and it no longer seemed out of place.

There were still plenty of wood-framed structures, but fancy brick edifices had sprung up along the main street, and talk was that a wealthy man was thinking of building a large, ornate hotel, the like of which this city hadn't envisioned. The last she'd heard, the town had grown to a little over twelve hundred souls—more than she'd ever thought would be drawn to this area. Of course, that's what gold and silver did. It changed things ... and people.

The door thudded shut behind her, enveloping her in a hush. Two tellers spoke in low tones to their customers, and a man worked at a desk in a far corner, his profile slightly toward her. An office door beyond him was ajar, but Leah couldn't see inside. Hopefully Mr. Hunt would have time to see her.

She didn't relish driving into town again this week, even if it wasn't raining. That wind bit clear through her shawl and bonnet. She removed the bonnet, smoothing a lock, which seemed to have a mind of its own.

Leah crossed the polished wood floor and stopped in front of a teller's cage, then waited for the man to look up.

"May I help you, miss?" His dark eyes flickered over her face.

"Yes, thank you. I'd like to see Mr. Hunt." She removed her gloves and placed them on the counter in front of the barred window.

He raised his brows. "Is he expecting you?"

"No, but I'm sure he'll see me. My father does all our ranch business here."

"Is your father with you, then?" He leaned to the side and peered behind her. "What might his name be?"

"Mr. Charles Pape, and he's not with me. Could you please let Mr. Hunt know I'm waiting?"

"I'm afraid not, miss. He's not in right now. May I ask the nature of your business?"

"You may not. I don't care to discuss that with anyone but Mr. Hunt."

He shook his head. "You don't understand. I asked so that I may direct you to someone else."

Leah tapped her toe. "I'm sorry, but you are the one who doesn't understand. I don't care to see anyone else." She motioned to a row of chairs placed along the side of the room. "I'll wait until Mr. Hunt returns."

The clerk sighed. "Then I'm afraid you'll have a long wait. He's out of town until next week. You can come back then, but I can't guarantee how long it will take to work you in. Mr. Hunt is always on a tight schedule, especially when he's been gone for a time. Now, if there's nothing else I can help you with?" He glanced at the man standing behind her. "I have several other customers waiting."

"Fine." Leah kept a rein on her frustration. The last thing she cared to do was make a scene in the one place that could help her. "You mentioned directing me to someone else." She leaned forward and dropped her voice to a whisper. "I'm here to inquire about a loan."

The gate in the low wooden barrier between Steven and the clientele entering and leaving the bank opened, and he swiveled his chair. The clerk stepped aside and beckoned to a woman dressed in a demure gray gown. His gaze traveled to her face, and he stiffened. He'd know that red hair and those green eyes anywhere. "Miss Carlson to see you, Mr. Harding."

He rose and extended his hand. "Miss Carlson, to what do I owe this pleasure?"

She halted midstride. "I ... I ..." Turning, she beckoned to the clerk, who had headed to his station. "Excuse me, but I think there's been a mistake."

The man paused. "You want to see someone about a loan, miss. Mr. Harding handles the loans when Mr. Hunt is away, and ofttimes when he's here." He glanced from Miss Carlson to Steven. "Is there a problem?"

Steven shook his head. "All is well, Mr. Parker. You may return to your duties." He stepped aside and motioned to the chair in front of his desk. "If you'd care to be seated, Miss Carlson, I'd be happy to help you."

She appeared riveted to the spot. "Maybe I should leave."

Something was amiss here, and Steven struggled to decipher what that might be. "I'm not sure I understand. Mr. Parker said you were here on business. Did you change your mind?"

The attractive redhead hesitated, seemingly torn between the seat he offered and the front door. Then her expression softened. "I beg your pardon." She sat but didn't lean back against the spindles. "You surprised me, that's all."

"Ah." Of course. He should have understood immediately. "You thought I worked at the saloon, I suppose." A smile quirked one corner of his mouth, and he pressed his lips together to keep it from blossoming further.

A soft flush colored her cheeks, making her all the more attractive, but she didn't lower her eyes. "I imagine I had that coming. I hope you'll forgive my ill temper and poor manners, Mr. Harding."

Contrition bit at his heels. He didn't make a habit of jesting with women—he'd simply hoped to lighten the mood and make her more comfortable. She had responded like a lady, and his admiration raised another notch. "Not at all. I am the one who must beg your forgiveness for my uncouth remark." He placed his forearms on the desk. "Now, how may I help you?"

With a tiny smile, she settled into her chair. "Thank you. I'm here for a loan."

Steven stifled his surprise. It wasn't completely uncommon for a woman to request financial assistance, but from what he understood, Leah Carlson was single. "On behalf of your father?"

She stiffened. "Why would you assume that to be the case?"

He picked up a pencil and rolled it between his finger and thumb. "You aren't married, and you live with your father. However, I may have jumped to conclusions. Would you care to explain?"

"I want to borrow against our ranch so we can increase our herd and hire more employees. Since the land is unencumbered, that shouldn't pose a problem, should it?"

Leah stared into Steven Harding's blue eyes. How could she ever have thought him a ruffian? His clothing as well as his buggy should have given her pause when he brought her father home, but at the time her anger at Pa had blinded her to those details. Seeing him in his work environment, it was all she could do to mask her embarrassment and ask for his help.

"Well, now." He leaned forward. "I require a few more details. Is your name on the ranch deed, Miss Carlson?"

She blinked. "No, it's not. But I help my father run it. In fact, at this point I do many of the outdoor chores as well as care for the books."

He tapped his pencil on the desk. "I see. But you don't have a legal interest in the land, is that correct?"

Her hope was evaporating as fast as a raindrop on a hot skillet. "What does that have to do with my request?"

"Everything, I'm afraid." He placed the pencil carefully beside a stack of papers. "I wish I could help, but we would need Mr. Pape's signature to grant a loan."

"But I've lived there and worked the ranch alongside him my entire life. It will be mine someday."

"Be that as it may, it's still legally his property. We would have to place a lien against the deed, and we can't do that without his permission."

"Is it possible to acquire a personal loan?" She gripped her gloves and bonnet lying in her lap.

Sorrow or pity darkened his eyes. "Are you employed, Miss Carlson?"

Impatience touched her words. "I told you I work on our ranch. I have no time to work anywhere else. It's a full-time job keeping things running there, especially when Pa—" She jerked to a stop. Mr. Harding had already seen too far into her personal life when he'd brought her father home after his all-night binge in town. She needn't make things worse.

"I see." He leaned forward. "Do you draw a salary?"

Her heart sank as realization set in. "I suppose that's necessary, isn't it?"

"I'm afraid so. The bank would want assurance the loan would be repaid, and you must have the ability to do so."

"But if I had a job that paid a salary, I wouldn't be asking for money." Annoyance oozed from her voice, but she didn't care. "That is the silliest thing I have ever heard."

Steven Harding closed his eyes briefly and sighed. "I'm sure it seems that way, but it *is* bank policy."

"I've lived in this town my entire life, and my reputation is above reproach. You can ask any of the merchants where we do business. We pay our bills." She hesitated as a horrible thought hit. "Does this have anything to do with my father's condition when you brought him home? I assure you; he's a hard worker and cares about the ranch." Warmth stole into her cheeks yet again, and she had to steel herself not to avert her gaze. She would never have come if she'd known Mr. Harding was the person in charge of approving applications. If only he hadn't stumbled upon her father when he'd been drinking.

"This isn't personal, Miss Carlson. If it were up to me, I'd consider giving you a loan, but my hands are tied."

She rose swiftly. "Then it appears I was directed to the wrong person. I'll return when Mr. Hunt is available and take the matter up with him."

Steven stood and held out his hand. "Please. Give me another minute, won't you?"

Leah hesitated, then slowly sank back onto her chair. "Have you changed your mind?"

He winced. "Not exactly."

She started to rise again.

"Wait. I'll take the matter up with Mr. Hunt on your behalf next week. Since your father is a customer here, it's possible your request for a small loan will be approved, although I can't make any promises. Would that meet with your satisfaction?"

She studied him for a long moment. "It would." She allowed a small smile. "And I appreciate your offer to help. Shall I come back to see you next week?"

He shook his head. "I'm not certain when I'll have the opportunity to speak with Mr. Hunt. I do a bit of traveling to mines and ranches on bank business. Since I know where you live, why don't I swing by after I've spoken to him?"

Leah's mind raced. Did she want her father to know her plans? She hadn't thought the matter through that far. All along she'd simply assumed she could walk in and borrow a few hundred dollars—enough for a couple of good broodmares and operating money

to tide them over until they could sell the four-year-olds they'd finish training this summer. Never once had she considered her father
should be included. At one time she would gladly have consulted
him, but his erratic behavior no longer made that an option. "If
you don't mind, I'd prefer returning. I'd rather not have our ranch
employees speculating on why a banker is visiting."

"Of course." He rose and offered his hand. "Give me at least a
week, and I'll see what I can do."

Chapter Four

March 30, 1881

Steven pulled Mr. Hunt's door shut behind him and crossed to his desk, regret and frustration battling in his mind. Nine days had passed since Leah Carlson's initial visit. She'd let several more days pass, then had visited him again yesterday, to determine if he'd attained a decision from Mr. Hunt. At least he'd managed an audience with the man, but little good it had done.

He ground his teeth. Where was the joy that used to accompany this job? When he was in his teens, he'd longed to leave the farm and find a new start in the city, certain he could make a difference in people's lives. But from what he'd observed, his boss hadn't developed an iota of mercy in that regard.

The past thirty minutes had been spent laying out Leah Carlson's request and balancing it with the young woman's sterling reputation, all to no avail. John Hunt didn't give a fig whose pride he trampled on, regardless of the years they'd banked here.

Of course, as he'd told Miss Carlson, it was bank policy not to loan money unless the customer had a job or property as security, but he'd hoped Mr. Hunt might make an exception. Maybe he was the one being irrational, and he'd allowed the young lady to cloud his good judgment.

Steven intentionally relaxed his tight fingers. No sense in getting worked up over something he couldn't change and hadn't expected to happen in the first place. Would he have reacted so if it had been a man who'd requested the loan? He shook off the thought, surprised at the realization that a personal attraction to Miss Carlson might have prompted this response.

He could only pray Miss Carlson didn't arrive today. Hunt was in a foul mood over the loss of some mining business he'd hoped to acquire. Steven had barely escaped with a scathing comment concerning his lack of discernment in what type of people were worthy of loans.

Apparently the subject of Mr. Pape's proclivity for tipping the bottle had made its way to his boss's ears. It mattered not that Pape's daughter was cut from a different cloth.

Possibly the best option was to drive out and let her know. Then he remembered her request not to do so. He placed his head in his hands and concentrated. There had to be a way to help. He'd tackled tougher situations in the past, and this one was important. A vision of emerald green eyes and creamy skin rose in his mind. Yes, sir, he'd find a solution, if it was the last thing he did at this bank.

At that instant the quiet of the morning shattered as a loud boom rocked the building and rattled the windows. Steven sprang to his feet and bolted for the front door, joining the tellers and customers at the expansive glass window overlooking the street.

Mr. Parker turned a pasty face to Steven. The teller's lips were trembling. "What do you think? An accident of some kind? That surely wasn't thunder."

Steven winced. "It sounded like an explosion. I hope something hasn't gone wrong at one of the mines." He pressed through the knot of people and gained the entrance. Men in rough miners' garb raced down the street, all seemingly intent on reaching the same destination. Stepping outside, he flagged down a passerby and grasped the man's arm. "Any idea what's happened?"

The fellow's eyes darted from Steven to the men disappearing around a far corner. "A man rode through town spreading the word. He said dynamite blew in a small munitions shack next to the Quartz Lode Mine, on the outskirts of town. Took out several buildings around it. Not sure if anyone was hurt or not." He shook his arm free and sprinted forward.

Steven slumped against the brick face of the building. The one-room cabin he called home was located at that mine site, and if he wasn't mistaken, it was only a stone's throw from the shed where the explosives were stored.

Charlie Pape scratched his chin and stared at the messy barn. How had it gotten this way, and where was Leah when he needed her? A flicker of memory illuminated his fogginess, and he snorted. That ding-blasted bunch of women who worked on quilts at the church. He wagged his head and spat. Not that he had anything against the women, but making quilts for a bunch of heathens was a waste of time, if you asked him.

Wouldn't his gal be better off helping him on the ranch? After all, since Tom ran off so many years ago, he had no one else to leave it to when he passed on to glory. Or wherever he ended up. He scowled. He didn't plan on dying anytime soon, so it didn't much matter. The point being, the ranch had a lot of work needing done, and he was only one

man. 'Course, Buddy pulled his weight as much as he could with his
bad back and all.

But no two ways about it, Charlie missed Leah when she wasn't
around. He didn't plan to let her know that, how-some-ever. The last
thing he wanted was her getting a big head.

He plucked a pitchfork out of the straw and bent over the pile he
needed to move. Why had he ever thought to put it here in the first
place? Another memory niggled—spending an hour pitching all this
straw out of the loft onto the barn floor one night after he'd returned
from the saloon. He could hear Leah's chiding almost as clear as it
had been when she'd found him, accusing him of having too much to
drink and not knowing what he was doing.

At the time he'd bristled and stormed around, informing her he
was her pa, not her child, and, by jing, he did *too* know what he was
doing. As he gazed at the looming pile still planted right where he'd
tossed it, he wondered if that were true.

But it wouldn't do to start second-guessing his decisions, even if
they did seem foolish in the full light of day. And it surely wouldn't do
to let Leah guess he'd wondered a time or two if the drinking needed
to stop. But how to do that was the question. And what would fill the
void if he did?

Leah halted her mare in front of Baker City Community Church and
sat, enjoying the peace that flooded her. The building was so much
more than a one-story structure with a bell tower and a stained-glass
window.

These past three years she'd built a deep friendship and sense of family with the group of women who congregated here once a month to work on a quilt for a needy family. Occasionally they gathered more often, and each time Leah came away with her strength and faith renewed. Not that the women often delved into topics from the Bible or prayed together. It was more the unity and fellowship they enjoyed, as well as having a safe place she could bare her soul with sisters who loved her.

A shiver ran through her as a brisk spring wind kicked up. Even though it was one o'clock in the afternoon with the sun shining, the cold still penetrated. She climbed from the buggy and tied the mare, eager to see how many made it today. The group had grown this past year since Katherine's mother, Mrs. Frances Cooper, arrived, as well as Beth Roberts—no, Tucker now. Leah would have to make a conscious effort to remember Beth's married name, and her aunt, Wilma Marshall. Another change, but not quite as difficult, as she'd not been well acquainted with the lady before she married Dr. Caleb Marshall last December.

Hurrying up the three steps, she tugged the door open, eager to arrive in the warm side room where the quilt frame was set. She stripped off her gloves, hat, and coat as the heat from the wood stove penetrated and hung them all on a hook. Excited chatter emanated from within, and Leah stepped inside, glancing from face to face.

Katherine, her close friend and owner of the boardinghouse, sat on one side, her rounded belly evidence of the growing baby due in two months. Her face glowed as she leaned over the cooing baby in Ella Farnsworth's arms.

Virginia Lewis bobbed her head at something Hester Sue Masters was sharing, and a silver curl escaped her cap. Wilma Roberts, no, *Marshall*— Leah smiled, amazed that she'd gotten it wrong already—stood not far away chatting with her close friend and Katherine's mother, Frances Cooper. Everyone was here except Beth, but since she'd only been married a couple of weeks that wasn't terribly surprising.

She lifted her hand in greeting and waved at Katherine, who made a move to rise. "Please don't get up, Katherine. I'm guessing you've been on your feet enough today. How is everyone?"

Voices echoed from both sides, and Virginia enveloped her in a hug. The warmth spreading through her now lodged deep in her heart. She could always count on Virginia's tenderness, no matter the situation or person involved.

Katherine patted the chair beside her. "Come look at this darling baby girl. I think she looks like her mama."

Leah perched on the seat and leaned forward as a proud Ella sat the baby on her lap and bounced her. The little one wore a hand-sewn gown with a drawstring at the neck and smiled and cooed as the ladies crowded close. "She's beautiful. I'm so glad you brought her. We've missed you on the days you've stayed home with her."

Ella beamed. "Missy had a cold last month, or I'd have been here. I'm thankful we don't have to deal with colic anymore. But I've been goin' stir crazy not gettin' to see you gals. I'm sure glad she's doin' better and the doc said I could take her out of the house."

Frances clucked her tongue. "Poor dear. I remember when Katherine had colds as well as colic. I do not believe I slept for a solid week. That is one part of raising a baby I do not miss."

Wilma nudged her in the side with her elbow. "Be careful what you say, Frances. Since Katherine's baby is coming soon, you might well experience it again." She winked at Katherine, then sobered. "Not that I wish it, you understand. No mother enjoys dealing with a fussy child.

We'll pray little Missy stays healthy from now on, as well as the baby joining our household."

Frances smirked. "I wondered if you had forgotten that you will be within earshot of the baby, should she have a tummy ache or any other ailments that keep her from sleeping. In fact, I will be calling on you to help walk the child when Katherine and Micah require rest, so I would suggest you take those prayers seriously."

Wilma rolled her eyes. "I declare, Frances, you do beat all. Caleb and I won't be living at the boardinghouse forever, but I'll do my part with pleasure, until the day comes we find our own place."

She patted Ella's hand. "I'm glad she's better, and I imagine your husband is quite proud."

The first-time mother nodded and smiled. "He shore is, ma'am. At first he was hopin' for a boy, but now he wouldn't trade her for a dozen sons."

"I should say not!" Hester Sue interrupted. "I've raised both, and I must say girls are a sight easier when they're young—until they start noticing boys, that is. Then they go plumb loco." She rubbed her hands down the sides of her skirt. "Guess we should get to work. I reckon this quilt ain't going to finish itself."

Virginia pulled up a stool and patted it. "Katherine, you should stay off your feet. And if you get too tired, tell us. We'll quit early."

Katherine rubbed the small of her back and grinned. "It's actually more comfortable standing. This little one seems to enjoy kicking every time I sit."

Hester Sue ran her gaze up and down Katherine's frame. "I'd guess from the way you're carrying it, this one's a boy. You got two girls already, so that might be a welcome change."

Leah glanced at her friend, wondering how she'd take that comment. Katherine's daughters, Lucy and Mandy, were two of the sweetest children she knew. Of course, Hester Sue hadn't meant to be unkind. She was simply a little gruffer than most.

Katherine chuckled. "I'm not really caring if it's a boy or a girl. But if Micah had his way, it would be twins. One of each."

She shook her head. "He has a son, so he'd like a daughter, but I have daughters and have always wished for a son. But we'll be happy with either."

Leah threaded her needle and plucked her thimble from the basket. "There appeared to be some excitement when I drove into town. A lot of miners milling about the streets and smoke in the air at the far end of town. Does anyone know what happened?"

Several voices chimed in at once before Frances took command. "There was an explosion at a mine. That is why Beth did not come today. She and her mother wanted to make sure Steven was all right, since he lives somewhere in that area."

Leah's heart jumped. "How terrible!" She placed her thimble on the stretched quilt and gave Frances her full attention. "Was Mr. Harding or anyone else hurt? It would be terrible if the miners were injured. Beth and her mother must be worried sick about Mr. Harding."

Frances shook her head. "They do not think so, as the dynamite exploded when Steven should have been working, but he does visit the mines periodically as part of his business."

Wilma nodded. "That isn't the only reason. Turns out he's been renting a one-room cabin on the mining site, since it's close to the bank. There's not much to be found in the way of housing in this town with all the new people flooding in the past year or two. That's why Caleb and I are still at Katherine's boardinghouse." She clucked her tongue. "Rumor has it that several of the buildings blew up or burned."

Virginia poked her needle into the fabric. "We need to turn our attention to doing what we can for those who might be injured. Some of our fabric could be used for bandages if necessary."

"I agree," Wilma added. "Let's put a few rolls together, and we can drop them by the doctor's office on our way back home."

Voices rose in assent, and the quilt frame was pushed to the side as some of the women dug through the boxes of fabric to find remnants long enough to be of help.

Ella lifted Missy to her shoulder and patted her back. "Gracious sakes! Where is that poor Mr. Harding goin' to live? Since his sister and mother stay at your place, I suppose it would be sensible for him to come there. Do you have room, Katherine?"

"I'm afraid not. We're full right now and, with the baby coming, Micah thinks we shouldn't rent to anyone new if a room becomes available. His business is doing well, and we'd both like to spend more time with the children. And I'll admit, taking on additional laundry and cooking is more than I can tolerate right now."

Wilma nodded. "I agree. You've been doing entirely too much since Beth and I arrived, and you ought to rest. I practically forced you to let us stay, and it's high time that changed. In fact, Caleb and I will look for a home of our own. That would ease your burden somewhat, wouldn't it?"

Frances drew herself up as tall as her short stature would allow and glared at her friend. "Balderdash. You will do no such thing, Wilma Marshall. If anyone leaves, it will be me. I came without so much as a by-your-leave. Besides, that would leave room for poor Mr. Harding, and he could be near his mother and sister."

Leah glanced from one distraught face to another. Katherine's distress was evident, and Leah hurt for the two older women trying so valiantly to fix what they perceived as a personal dilemma.

She placed one hand on Frances's shoulder and the other on Wilma's shoulder. "Ladies, I can't speak for Katherine, but from what I've seen, you're both a wonderful help." She narrowed her eyes and thought. "As for Mr. Harding, I suggest we pray that God opens the perfect place for him, if he has indeed lost his home."

"Wise words, my dear," Virginia said. "It doesn't pay to rush in when emotions are high and try to make decisions. Things tend to work out with time and prayer, as well as a bit of patience." She held out her hands to Hester Sue and Ella. "The quilt can wait a few more minutes. There may be others at the mining camp who are injured or without homes. Let's ask the Lord if there's anything more we can do."

Leah started at the words. She'd meant it when she'd said they should pray that God would meet Mr. Harding's needs, but not once had it occurred to her that any of them should offer assistance. Her heart sank at the thought. Surely Virginia wasn't hinting that God would expect *her* to do anything in the way of offering the man a home?

The women knew she had plenty of room in the bunkhouse, but the last thing she wanted was a greenhorn city man getting in her way, even if he was one of the most handsome men she'd ever laid her eyes on. In fact, that was even more of a reason to keep out of his way. She'd never get enough work done with a man like that underfoot.

Chapter Five

Hours after the blast, Steven stared at the ruins of his home, steeling himself against the rising discouragement. The smoldering cabin had been too hot to deal with after the explosion, so he'd gone back to work for a while. When he returned, he was armed with a shovel and work clothes Jeffery had loaned him. Tendrils of smoke spiraled from the pile, and the stench drove him backward a step.

It wasn't the first time he'd suffered loss. At eight years old he'd lost his father and his sister, and for several years following, his mother's grief and guilt over his sister's disappearance put her in such an emotional state he'd practically raised himself.

Ma had finally found a man she could love again, but after nine years his stepfather had died as well. The loss of their farm and the necessity of moving to town had set Ma back—not to mention her poor health resulting from the cholera attack years earlier that killed so many on the wagon train. But Ma had Beth now and a home at the Jacobs' boardinghouse where she was comfortable and loved.

With the town booming and lodging scarce, he'd probably be forced into an expensive hotel room. He'd only recently begun paying for his mother's lodging, and with almost no expenses of his own he'd put away a sizable nest egg from his wages. But that would get eaten up if he didn't find reasonable accommodations soon.

But seeing the remains of all that he owned lying in a charred heap snatched the wind from his lungs. At least he'd had his mother all those years, even if he'd had to be more parent than son much of the time. Part of what had kept him going was the knowledge someone depended on him. That all ended when Beth came back into their lives.

What did that leave him? A job he'd thought he'd wanted in a town where he now felt a virtual stranger, and no ties to the farmland he hadn't realized he would miss. He pushed the ungrateful thoughts aside and grabbed a shovel. Now that his cabin was gone, his job was all he had.

He wouldn't allow foolish sentiments and yearnings for the past to put that in jeopardy. The first order of business was to sift through the rubble and see what he could salvage, then figure out where he would live. Dark would be fast approaching, and clouds were moving in. He'd better get to work while he still had light to see.

Someone tapped his shoulder, and he pivoted. Jeffery stood nearby, shovel in hand. "What can I do to help?"

Steven grinned, thankful his sister had married this man who accepted him like a brother. "Ma and Beth brought me a shirt and a pair of old trousers a few hours ago, but it's going to be messy. If you don't mind getting dirty, I'm hoping I can find something to save. But be careful as there are hot timbers."

They worked side by side for nearly an hour. Then Jeffery paused and wiped his shirtsleeve across his damp forehead. "I'm ready for a breath of fresh air. The smoke has died down a lot, but it's still hard to breathe."

Steven walked a few paces from the far edge of rubble. He plunged his shovel blade into the soft ground and leaned on the handle. "I appreciate you coming. It doesn't look like there's much that survived."

"What happens now? Will the mine rebuild the cabins? I hope you didn't keep your savings here, and you can find somewhere to live. I wish there was a room open at the Jacobs' right now."

"Thankfully, I opened an account at the bank. I saved most of my money since we arrived last November, what with Ma rooming with Beth until the two of you married. Mrs. Roberts refused to accept help for the cost of the room, since she'd paid for herself and Beth several months in advance."

He twisted his lips to the side. "I'll probably find the cheapest room available in a hotel."

"And you'll be paying for yourself and your mother now that Beth and I are married. I imagine that's going to dip into your savings a bit. Maybe we can help. We've been thinking of finding a little place of our own. If it's big enough, we want to have Isabelle live with us there."

Steven tipped his head. "That's good of you, but she's my responsibility. Before we moved from La Grande, I sold three nice broodmares I'd kept from our farm, and I've set that money aside, hoping I can invest in land one day. You and Beth should start your married life on your own, if possible."

"Beth missed having a mother for so many years that I'm not sure she'll agree. She's of the opinion you've more than carried your share of responsibility, and now it's her turn. Besides, we love Isabelle, and she's not a burden at all. But since we haven't found a place to move to yet, I suppose it doesn't matter."

Steven walked forward and pitched a shovel of dirt onto a smoking pile, then kicked the embers around with the toe of his boot. Thank the Lord none of Ma's belongings were here. She'd be heartbroken if she'd lost her journal or any of the few things she'd retained from her old life. "Give me a hand with this mattress, will you?"

Jeffery gripped the end of the bedding and they heaved it out of the way. Sunlight flashed off a corner of an object that lay beneath, and Steven stuck his blade deeper and lifted.

Relief flooded through him. "My strongbox. I planned to take this to the bank weeks ago but never got around to it."

Jeffery squatted and examined it. "I hope you didn't keep paper money in there. It's apt to be singed from the heat."

"Only a few gold coins. Mostly it contains things I hold dear." At least nothing the world would see as valuable—but precious to him.

He took a handkerchief from his pocket and brushed aside the ashes and soot, testing it for heat. Taking the blade of his shovel, he lifted the lid and exhaled. Ten gold eagles lined one edge, and a thick bundle filled the balance of the box. It appeared the layers of cowhide he'd wrapped the papers in, as well as the mattress, protected it from the heat.

He unwrapped the long strip of leather and lifted out a tintype. Peering at the portrait of himself and Beth as children, he smiled, then laid it aside and extracted a knife—a gift from his father before his death.

His eyes lit on a paper scrawled in childish script. Why had he saved this? So much had changed since his youth, including his dreams and desires. He blew on the paper, sending bits of soot flying.

Jeffery leaned closer. "What you got there? Looks like it was written by a child. It wasn't Beth's, was it?"

Steven smiled. "No, she wasn't even four when she disappeared. I wrote this when I was seven. Our teacher asked us to write a short essay on what we were thankful for and what we hoped to do when we grew up."

He handed it to Jeffery. "I'm not sure why I kept this. Maybe because Beth disappeared not long after I wrote it."

Jeffery held it up and scanned it, then read it out loud.

"I am thankful for our cabin and my dog and my ma and my pa. My baby sister talks all the time, but I guess she is nice too. When I grow up, I am going to own a big farm and raise horses and tend the fields with Pa."

A grin formed on Jeffery's face. "She talked a lot, huh? I guess I'll have to tease her about that." He aimed a curious look at Steven. "It appears you decided to go a different direction than farming or ranching."

"I suppose a seven-year-old boy is too young to know what he wants. Besides, when Pa died, it was all Ma and I could do to keep food on the table. She remarried a few years later, and while my stepfather was a good-hearted man, he wasn't much of a money manager."

He shrugged. "I guess my hope of farming died along with my pa."

"What happened to the farm?" Jeffery handed the paper back to Steven.

"We lost it a couple of years after my stepfather passed away. I hunted for work in La Grande after that, and moved Ma to a little cabin on the outskirts of town."

"Sorry to hear that."

Steven placed the paper back in the metal box and closed the lid, praying he might find something else of value. At least he'd kept his savings in the bank and wasn't destitute, although he'd need to use some of this gold to purchase new clothing and boots.

His mind flew to Miss Carlson and her request for money to invest in her ranch. Rather, her father's ranch. Did the man even know what she was up to? Steven had a feeling he didn't, and that any money lent to her would be wasted. Not that she'd misuse it, but if Mr. Pape continued down the path he'd started to tread, no amount of money would pull him out of the looming quicksand. It would take a miracle to save the man if drink had as tight a hold on him as Steven assumed.

A shudder coursed through him. He hated the idea of anyone going through the loss he'd felt when the farm was sold to pay their debts, and he guessed Miss Carlson's love for her ranch ran even deeper than his had for their land.

Though it wasn't his concern, he dreaded telling Miss Carlson her request had been denied. Maybe he could talk to Mr. Hunt again. After all, the amount she wanted wouldn't create a problem for the bank, and surely her father would stand behind her. If he could be certain Miss Carlson managed the money and it would help improve the ranch profits, there would be little risk. If she got her father to sign for the loan, they might be able to manage.

He slapped Jeffery on the back. "Thanks for your help. I don't think there's much else to be gained here. I'm going to visit a few hotels and see what I can scare up for a room."

Jeffery grimaced. "I hate to see you do that. If you don't find accommodations soon, swing by the boardinghouse. I'm guessing Katherine would let you bunk in the parlor for at least one night."

Steven waved and turned away. He tucked the box under his arm and strode toward Front Street. Then he pulled up short. Maybe there was another way he could help Miss Carlson, even if he couldn't acquire a loan.

He'd have to think on it awhile and make sure she didn't get wind of what he was up to. In fact, if she thought she was aiding him, so much the better. From what he'd seen, the lady wouldn't take kindly to charity. He'd have to tread carefully or they'd be back where they began—squared off with mistrust on her part, and his hands tied.

Portland, Oregon
April 1, 1881
Thomas Pape inched the small wood box from under his bed and brushed away the cobwebs and dust. It had been a long time since he'd opened it. If he'd followed his first instinct, he'd have burned the thing years ago. He reached for a hammer and pried the two short boards off the top, trying to steady his shaking hands.

April was supposed to be a time for new beginnings, so perhaps he'd best deal with this now, although he doubted there could ever be anything new or good springing to life in his future. Every dream and desire he'd ever nurtured had withered and died these past few years.

He rocked back on his haunches, recalling Ma crying her heart out over her daughter. He clenched his teeth, forcing the roiling emotions back where they belonged. Didn't his sacrifice count? The contents of the wooden box taunted him, daring him to light a match as he'd yearned to do countless times in the past.

The only thing that stayed his hand was the pain it would have cost Ma. He wiped at his cheek and sniffed, ashamed of the moisture that traveled down it. Grown men didn't show their emotions, and having attained his twenty-first birthday, he was certainly a man.

But she wasn't here to care anymore, so why shouldn't he do as he desired? He sat on the dirty floor that would have shamed Ma, not caring that his trousers were stained.

Tom extracted a handkerchief from his pocket and blew his nose, then stuffed it back in his trousers. The dilemma of the box was all that mattered right now. He lifted one missive and stared at it, torn with the desire to rip it open and read what it contained. Just the thought of that action shot fire through him, and he dropped the thing back in the box as though he'd been scorched.

Maybe he was looking at this all wrong. There was something he could do that might put his life back to rights, although the work that it would involve didn't excite him.

No matter, he couldn't sit in this run-down excuse for a home much longer. He grabbed the lid and pressed it back on the crate, then pulled out his pocket watch—the only item he owned that had belonged to his father. The steamboat office didn't close for another hour … enough time to find out the cost of passage up the Columbia River. Everything within him fought against returning, but he could see no other recourse. Besides, Pa owed him, and if it was the last thing Tom did, he aimed to collect.

Chapter Six

Baker City, Oregon
April 4, 1881

Leah entered the bank and paused, allowing her eyes to adjust to the dimmer light. She'd wanted to come the day of the explosion but decided she should wait a few days. Somehow she doubted she'd find Mr. Harding at his place behind his desk tending to business the day his home was destroyed. Besides, as anxious as she was to obtain her loan, she wasn't callous to the man's loss, and she hadn't yet gathered the courage to approach her father about signing the papers.

It was probably a mistake coming here without Pa's approval, but a part of her hoped Mr. Harding was wrong. Maybe Mr. Hunt would agree to give her the money without Pa's endorsement. No matter what, she had to try.

Leah stepped into line at the teller window behind a woman she vaguely recognized—Mrs. Evans, if she remembered correctly, who occasionally filled in on the piano at church. They'd not had occasion to talk much in the past, and Leah cringed at the idea of doing so now. The older widow had a reputation of being a gossip and a busybody. Leah kept her face averted, hoping the woman wouldn't sense someone behind her.

Mrs. Evans pivoted and tapped her on the arm. "I say, aren't you Mr. Charles Pape's daughter?" She tipped her head to the side and the outrageously ornate hat teetered precariously. The gaudy assortment of flowers, butterflies, and birds danced as though working to right the creation.

Leah swallowed the giggle that threatened to erupt. "Yes, ma'am. I'm Leah Carlson."

Mrs. Evans nodded, and her double chin quivered. "I knew your mother. Too bad about her. And a real shame your father never attends church. I'm sure it would make a powerful difference in his life if he were to start."

"Yes, ma'am. I'm sure you're right."

The matron raised her brows. "So? Why doesn't he?"

Leah stiffened. The woman was certainly direct. "He has a lot to take care of on the ranch."

"As does every man who owns a business or farm, but most of them manage to find time for the Lord." She looked down an imperious nose at Leah. "But the majority of God-fearing men don't spend their evenings in the saloon, either, I suppose. He needs a woman to take him in hand."

Leah bit back a grin. "You seem to know quite a bit about my father, Mrs. Evans. Are you applying for that position?"

Mrs. Evans recoiled, her face blanching. "I should say not! It appears the teller is free, and I'm next. Have a good day, Miss Carlson." She rushed toward the teller's cage.

Someone touched Leah's shoulder, and she swiveled.

Steven Harding stood nearby, his lips twitching. He stepped a little closer and spoke in a conspiratorial whisper. "I came to rescue you, but from all appearances you did fine on your own."

This time Leah allowed a chuckle to escape. "I appreciate the sentiment, Mr. Harding. I wondered if I'd escape being crushed by that hat, but I managed to survive." She looked up into the man's warm gaze, suddenly noticing how close he stood. A spicy scent wafted to her, and her eyes strayed to his strong jaw and cleanly shaven cheeks. Her breath caught in her throat, and she took a half step back. "I hoped to speak to you, if you have time." She followed him, chagrined now that he'd overheard her comments to Mrs. Evans.

He stopped at his desk and held the chair for her as she sank into it. Leah waited for him to take his place on the other side. "I suppose I should apologize for my behavior with Mrs. Evans. It wasn't courteous to speak to an older woman in that manner."

"Actually, I rather enjoyed the exchange." He placed his elbows on the arms of his chair and laced his fingers together.

"I beg your pardon?" Leah's lips parted, and she snapped them shut before her mouth hung open.

He dropped his voice. "She gives no end of grief to my tellers, and it was a nice change, seeing someone else get the last word. I'm not sure how you managed it, but I applaud you for pulling it off."

Leah settled against the round spindles, amazed at the difference in the man when he smiled. His deep blue eyes gleamed with laughter, and his normally serious face encompassed her in warmth. She'd thought him handsome before, in a more austere fashion, but he was anything but severe now. In fact, she was having trouble corralling her galloping heart and runaway thoughts. That must change, and quickly. "Do you have word on my loan application, Mr. Harding?"

The smile faded. "Yes, but I'm afraid it may not be what you're hoping for."

Disappointment smote her, and she couldn't tell if it was due to his words, or the departure of that charming smile. "Mr. Hunt turned down my request."

"I'm afraid so. As I expected, he wants to speak to your father. If he were to come in, it's very possible Mr. Hunt would reconsider."

"Possible?" Her throat closed over the word, and she worked to breathe. "But I thought you said there would be no problem if Pa agreed."

Mr. Harding's eyes were sympathetic. "That is what I had hoped Mr. Hunt would agree to, and he still may. But I have another idea you could mull over, if you'll be so kind as to listen?"

"Of course. If there's another way of securing the funds, I'd love to hear it."

"Well, that's not exactly the case." He held up his hand as she started to speak. "Give me a moment, and I'm sure you'll understand. Then if you have more questions, I'll be happy to answer."

"All right." She placed her folded hands in her lap.

He hesitated. "I assume you heard about the explosion at the mine?"

Leah gave a brief nod, unsure what this had to do with her situation.

Mr. Harding kept his steady gaze on hers. "I'm not sure how to say this, so I'll get right to it. My cabin was destroyed, and I've moved into a hotel. An expensive one, I'm afraid. I'm looking for another place to live, and you need another hand at your ranch. You did say that's what part of the money would go for, correct?"

She scrunched her forehead. "Yes, but what does that ...?"

"I thought you might consider allowing me to live in your bunk-house for a while. It would be a great favor, and I would help with chores in the evenings and during my days off. That would save you from hiring someone right away, in case your father doesn't agree to the loan."

Leah was rarely at a loss for words, but she felt as though every last one had dried up in her brain—or gone to sleep and refused to awaken. She blinked a couple of times, trying to take in what he'd offered and what it would entail.

Finally, she managed, "I appreciate the offer, and I truly am sorry you lost your home, but I don't think it would work. I need a full-time, experienced ranch hand, not a banker with his roots in the city who probably doesn't know one end of a branding iron from the other."

A twinge of guilt tugged at her conscience, remembering how the women at church had prayed, but she pushed it away. She couldn't offer a home to every displaced man in Baker City, or she'd fill her bunkhouse ten times over.

"I may not be as uneducated about ranch life as you might think. I have some experience from childhood on a farm."

She smiled, hoping to soften her response. "It would be a long drive each day to and from town, and doing work you aren't accustomed to."

Gathering her reticule from the chair beside her, she got to her feet. "But thank you for trying to help. If you wouldn't mind talking to Mr. Hunt one more time, I'll see what I can do about getting my father's consent."

"Of course." He rose and held out his hand, grasping hers in a gentle but firm hold.

Her heart fluttered again, and she stepped away. "Would it be all right if I come back at the end of the week?"

"Yes, and if your father will sign the paper I gave you, and I can present it to Mr. Hunt, it may take care of the issue. Thank you for considering my suggestion, and I do understand why you don't care to accept it." His stiff smile said otherwise, but Leah didn't want to delve deeper.

She took a step backward and bumped into the low railing that separated his space from the rest of the bank. "Thank you. Good day." Right now she wanted nothing more than to escape the sadness in his eyes before she blurted out her willingness to give him a place to stay, even if he would be completely useless at the ranch. That wouldn't do at all. She didn't need a city man getting in the way.

Leah pushed through the gate and then paused, ashamed at how selfish she must appear. She straightened her spine. This was ridiculous! Why couldn't she do what she thought best without battling a guilty conscience?

Besides, Pa wouldn't be happy about her inviting a strange man onto the ranch. But did she really want to base her decision on what Pa would think, when he'd done so little to keep up his end of the work lately? Or was it more important that she at least attempt to please God, even if it meant going against what was comfortable?

She heaved a sigh and turned. "Mr. Harding, if you are unable to find new accommodations soon, let me know. Your sister is my friend, and I don't want to see Beth's brother living in an expensive hotel when I have an empty bed in the bunkhouse you could use for a few days."

Before he could reply, Leah bolted through the gate and headed for the front door of the bank. What had she done? If Steven Harding accepted her offer, he'd be more trouble than help. But for some reason she couldn't quite account for, the thought of having a handsome man on the ranch left her somewhat breathless.

Steven stared at the back of the intriguing, frustrating, beautiful woman as she all but ran from the bank. Leah Carlson lived up to her flaming red hair with her independent, albeit stubborn behavior and outspoken personality. *Intriguing* was the most apt word, however. Miss Carlson drew him in a way that set his heart racing whenever she was near.

He leaned back in his chair and clasped his hands behind his head, smiling to himself. He'd always wondered what type of woman would captivate his interest and never once thought it would be a feisty female rancher who preferred denim to calico. But, on the other hand, he couldn't imagine it being anyone *but* her.

It was no longer a matter of finances or the inconvenience of how far from the bank he must ride. He liked the idea of not having to go days—or weeks—at a time without seeing her. He'd find a way to change her mind about helping her at the ranch for his own sake, as much as for hers.

April 7, 1881

Three days had dragged by since Leah's visit to the bank, and she still hadn't corralled her father about the loan. She sloshed through the barnyard, which was heavy with mud from the recent downpour, and pushed open the door to the oversized barn. Pa had insisted on building it three years ago, even though the old one was adequate.

She glanced down the alleyway, appreciating anew the multiple stalls and tack room. Pa didn't do things halfway, and while she didn't agree with this expense, she couldn't help but admire it. But it was more evidence of their fragile financial state. If she didn't get a loan soon to purchase more cows and hire another ranch hand, it could all come crashing down.

"Pa? You in here?" She walked to the tack room and peeked inside but found it empty. Soft footfalls overhead and fine hay dust filtering through the ceiling boards alerted her. Heading to the ladder, she climbed up to the hayloft. "You want help feeding?" She stepped onto the upper floor, keeping one hand on the side rail of the ladder.

Her father brushed off his jeans and grimaced. "Naw, I'm about finished. You've done enough today without doin' my work too."

Leah's heart lifted. He hadn't been drinking and appeared to be in an affable mood. "Do you have a minute?"

"What for?" He stepped to the trap door in the floor and raised it. He pitched several forkfuls of hay into a feed trough in a stall below, then moved to the next trap door. "Need help with somethin' you didn't get done?"

"I was hoping to talk."

He propped the pitchfork against a wall and turned. "I told you I don't wanna hear any more about what you think I'm doin' wrong."

She gripped her hands together. "It's not that, Pa. It's about the ranch."

"What about it?" He glanced around. "The work is done for the day, and we had a fine crop of new calves this spring. Not sure what there is to talk about."

This wasn't going to be easy—in fact, from his expression she almost wished she hadn't approached him. But in for a penny, in for a pound, as Ma used to say. Her heart constricted at the thought of her mother. If only she were here. Ma always knew how to sweet-talk her father when things weren't going well.

"I rode out to check on the cattle yesterday, but that's not what I want to discuss."

"So spit it out, girl. Don't stand there wringin' your hands."

Why did he have this effect on her? Anyone else, she could stand up to without so much as twitching an eyelid. He always made her feel as though he were waiting for her to do something wrong and that she'd never measure up, no matter what choice she made. In fact, she'd been surprised when he'd said she'd done enough for the day. When he'd been drinking, he didn't have a problem foisting most of his chores off on her and never thinking about it again.

She dropped her arms to her side and kept them still. "I'm not wringing my hands. Fine, I'll say what I came to say. We must have more help, and if we're going to make a profit, we should add a couple of mares to our herd. The cattle are doing well, but it wouldn't hurt to buy a few young heifers, or at least not sell so many steers this fall and get more fat on them. If we don't sell them all, we'll need money to tide us over till next spring. Winter feeding isn't easy, and we'll need more hands to share the extra work."

He swiped the back of his hand across his forehead. "Money don't come easy, Daughter. Not sure what you expect me to do about it. You want me to go work in a mine and try to find some of that gold they're pullin' out of the hills?"

"No, Pa. I have another idea. We could get a loan at the bank. I talked to the banker, and he said—"

Her father erupted in a roar and smacked the palms of his hands together, making a crack so loud Leah jumped. "You talked to the banker about my business? You had no right to do that without talkin' to me first, Leah. No right at all."

"But I thought you'd be glad I cared enough to come up with an idea to help. All I did was ask if we could borrow a few hundred dollars. They have people coming in all the time asking for loans. I see no disgrace in that."

"And that's your problem. You didn't think, nor did you ask me before you traipsed in there talkin' about things that don't concern you. This is my ranch, not yours. I work it, and I pay for everything on it. I make the decisions here, and I don't appreciate you talkin' about our business to some banker. Next thing you know, he'll want to come out here and check everything over to see what we got and don't got that he can keep for himself, if we don't pay it all back." He wagged his head. "No sir, that won't do a'tall."

"But, Pa ..." She saw a dark cloud pass across his face. "I don't know how you plan to make this ranch work with the little bit of cash we have, or the lack of help, but I guess that's your business."

"You bet it is, and don't you be forgettin' it. 'Sides, I got enough cash to take care of what we need, when we need it."

Hope surged for a second and then faded. This was the same thing she'd heard in the past, but she knew very well where that money went—if he actually had any—and it wasn't into the ranch. "Millie is running tight on food supplies, and we could use another ranch hand. If you have plenty, how about giving Millie a bigger food allowance and seeing what you can do about hiring more help?"

"I'll do what I see fit, when I see fit. Now go along and leave me be. You're always naggin' me. I'm gettin' plumb tired of it." He stomped to the stairs and flung back at her, "And no more sneakin' off to talk to the banker without my say-so. John Hunt don't need any more reason to cause me trouble." Then he clamped his lips together and disappeared.

April 8, 1881

Charlie Pape swung off his horse in front of the saloon and looped his reins over the hitching rail. He placed his hands at the base of his back and stretched, hating it that he couldn't spend near as much time in the saddle as he'd done as a youngster. Of course, he'd put in nigh on to five hours out on the range, since Leah didn't seem of a mind to check on the cows after their spat yesterday up in the hayloft.

He turned toward his horse and stroked the gelding's face. "You'd never turn on me like that, would you, boy? You're thankful for the feed I give you and never complain. Don't know what's gotten into that girl of mine. Used to be she'd never complain. Followed me around like a puppy dog when she was young, always proud of her pa." He pivoted, then stepped up onto the boardwalk, steeling his thoughts and putting up barriers at the memories that tried to crowd in.

The past was dead and gone. Better if it stayed that way. What Leah didn't know wouldn't hurt her. At least he'd been able to keep her from knowing more than she needed to these past years. He grimaced and rubbed a hand across the stubble on his cheeks. His wife was gone, his son had run away, and the girl he'd loved and treated like his own flesh and blood looked to be turning against him. Nothing could change things or make life better.

Or maybe there was something that could help. This one more time, anyway. With a wry smile, he pushed open the batwing doors of the saloon and stepped inside.

Portland, Oregon
April 8, 1881
Tom Pape fingered the steamboat ticket in his pocket, not sure if elation or dread would win the battle. Maybe it wasn't a good idea to go home. Buying passage was probably a waste of his money. He removed the ticket and stared at it. Was it too late to cash it in and cancel the trip?

But Pa owed him, and he couldn't let any more time go by without claiming what was rightfully his. He'd spent the better part of the last six years nursing anger toward his father for the way he'd treated Ma. As far as Tom was concerned, the man had betrayed them all.

The ranch had never meant as much to Tom as it did to Leah, and he'd happily washed his hands of it all when he'd walked away. But things were different now. Even if he'd only been twelve, he still remembered hearing the arguments between his parents and the nights Ma cried herself to sleep. He'd stuck it out for three long years before he left, resenting his father every minute of every day.

Not once had he planned to return. He had made a life for himself here in Portland, but losing his job a few weeks ago had put him in poor straits. He'd sworn never to write to Pa again—the response he'd gotten the first time was bad enough. But four months ago circumstances beyond his control forced his hand.

He growled deep in his throat and spat, new anger rising to the surface when he remembered the terse reply. His father made it clear he'd shut the door on the past and had no intention of allowing anyone to open it now. Yeah, that had been a wonderful Christmas for sure. But Tom would kick open that door if it was the last thing he did, and make his father take back everything he had said or thought for the past nine years, since his ma …

He returned the ticket to his pocket and strode toward the hovel he called home. Time to pack his bag with the little he owned and make his way east. Baker City. How much had it changed? It had been a quiet town of only a couple hundred people when he'd left, but he imagined much had been altered by the discovery of gold.

Excitement quickened his pace. Gold. Maybe he wouldn't be forced to work the ranch. If things went as he planned, he might eventually sell the place and use the money to invest in a claim. He hadn't considered that possibility before. He didn't try to hold back his grin. Suddenly the future looked downright bright, in spite of the hurdles he'd have to jump across with Pa.

Chapter Seven

Baker City, Oregon
April 8, 1881

Frances Cooper picked her way around a puddle on Front Street and stepped onto the boardwalk leading to Snider's General Store. The crush of people appeared to be less today and traversing the streets easier than normal, other than the never-ending mud.

She'd wanted to purchase more yarn for her knitting and silk thread for her tatting, but it had rained too much the past few days to venture out. She drew in a deep lungful of air and exhaled slowly, loving the fresh-washed air. It cleared out all the foul odors of beast and man and left it smelling like spring. Well, it was April, after all.

In no time at all Katherine's baby would arrive. Frances could barely contain her exhilaration at the knowledge she would be by her daughter's side for this birth and continue helping for as many years as the good Lord gave her.

She had wasted so much precious time while Katherine grew up, as well as when her granddaughter Lucy was young. It was still hard to admit she had been a disgruntled, judgmental woman, but with God, and her friend Wilma's help, Frances was able to face her shortcomings more every day.

She passed a child clinging to her mother's hand and glanced over her shoulder at the sweet picture. How lovely it felt to be forgiven and finally have a relationship with her family. It was what she had always wanted but never knew how to attain. Why had she thought that bullying and controlling people would bring them over to her side of the fence? All it had done was chase them farther away.

All but her little Amanda, whose sunny personality and steady, loving acceptance had been a balm to Frances's soul. But in another couple of years, if she had stayed her course, even her younger grand-daughter would have recoiled at her presence.

Wilma would be a treasured friend for the rest of her life. Maybe someday Frances would mature to the point she could set aside her pride and openly admit how much the woman had changed her life. If it had not been for her plain talk and, of course, Lucy's revulsion at the way Frances had treated Lucy's mother, Frances would not be enjoying a friendship with Katherine now. Nor be shopping for material that would add to her store of baby clothes.

Frances increased her pace and began to smile as she wove through the milling people on the boardwalk. Just then her smile threatened to break into a grin. It probably wasn't wise, making outfits for a boy, but somehow she knew this child would be a son.

She pulled up short; she had walked too far. How had she missed the general store? She should have asked Wilma to accompany her, but her friend spent so much time with her new husband nowadays. Of course, who could fault her? If Frances had a handsome, conge-nial man who doted on her the way Caleb Marshall doted on Wilma, she probably would not leave his side either.

A foul odor permeated the air, and Frances wrinkled her nose. She hated the smell of spirits, whether it was rot-gut whiskey, beer, wine, or any other form of alcohol. Her first husband had occasionally imbibed, and it disgusted her then, the same as it did now. Somehow she had walked right past the saloon without even noticing.

The door burst open, and a man stumbled onto the boardwalk. Or had someone given him a not-so-gentle push? He landed on his knees but managed to grab a post to keep from sliding the rest of the way onto his belly. It was only two in the afternoon. Surely he couldn't be tipsy this early?

She stood riveted to the spot and stared as he struggled to his feet. Something about the man, taller than her by a head, lean, and dressed like a rancher, was familiar, but she couldn't quite place him. However, she didn't know any out-of-town men—in fact, knew very few men outside of the boardinghouse—so she must be mistaken.

She would have to cross the street to avoid passing the saloon door and that odious man. A glance at the street pulled her up short. Mud patches lined the broad expanse from one side to the other, and the wheels of heavily laden wagons had cut deep ruts in the road.

Heaving a sigh, she started back the way she had come. If the man tried to waylay her, she would simply put him in his place. She gripped the handle of her parasol, grinning as she remembered the way Wilma had clobbered that annoying man who had stooped to accost Beth in the café prior to her marriage. After that episode, Frances had taken to carrying a parasol as well.

Lifting her chin, she stepped around the man. He jerked forward and almost fell into her arms.

Frances shuddered and darted to the side.

The repulsive man weaved in the same direction and bumped into her, grasping her arm. "Sorry, ma'am. My eyes seem to be a mite on the blurry side, and I didn't see you."

She shook off his grip, which, surprisingly, was quite strong— not the mushy touch she would have expected from someone in his obvious condition. "You ought to be ashamed of yourself, sir."

He drew himself up. Sweeping off his hat and revealing a ring of gray hair around a bald top, he gave an awkward bow. Golden-brown eyes twinkled with merriment, and his finely chiseled mouth tipped up in a smile. "And why would that be, ma'am? I didn't hurt you, did I?"

"You did not, but you certainly could have. But that is not the question you should be asking."

His brows scrunched together as though his addled brain was working hard to decipher her words. "Huh?"

She tapped her foot. It was most assuredly her Christian duty to set this man on the straight and narrow and help him see the error of his ways. "What is your name, sir?"

He blinked a couple of times. "Why, do you want to ask me to dinner? Sorry, I don't got no fancy callin' card, ma'am." He smirked. "But I live outside of town on a big ranch if you care to find me. I always did enjoy spendin' a little time with a fine lady."

A grin stretched the corners of his mouth. "Pleased to meet you. Name's Pape. Charles Pape, but most everyone calls me Charlie."

"Well, Mr. Charles Pape, it would seem you could use a woman to whip you into shape, but it certainly will *not* be me."

She crossed her arms and scowled. "In fact, in your present condition I cannot imagine any woman in her right mind who would endeavor to undertake that abhorrent chore. What would prompt a man who appears sound of body, even if not of mind, to stagger along the boardwalk in a drunken state at this hour of the day? Or any hour, for that matter?"

His grin faded, and he threw back his shoulders. "That is none of your business, ma'am. And I've had about enough of dad-blamed women buttin' into my business and tellin' me what I oughta do. My daughter, Leah, is always yammerin' about me not gettin' my chores done, or grumblin' about the time and money I spend in town. It ain't her never-mind, and it ain't yours, neither."

"Your English is as atrocious as your manners, Mr. Pape." She narrowed her eyes as his words sank in. Could that be *her* Leah from the quilting group? It wasn't a common name, at least not that she'd heard in these parts. Come to think of it, the girl had asked for prayer for her father not terribly long ago. If this man was that father, Frances could see the poor girl had a difficult cross to bear. "I believe I am acquainted with your daughter, and I can unequivocally state that you do not deserve her."

His jaw sagged. "Un-e -what? I got no idea what you said, lady. I don't use fancy words or talk so highfalutin' as you, but I got my dignity and pride. I won't be talked down to, no matter if you use the King's English or speak Latin. I ain't drunk, and I'll have you know I *am* a gentleman."

He squared his shoulders. "I worked since early morning, then stopped here and had me a couple of drinks. There's no law against a man whettin' his whistle when it's dry, or stoppin' to chew the fat with the fellas at the bar."

"There might not be a law against it, but that does not make you a gentleman. You chose to imbibe in the middle of the day—and to make a spectacle of yourself in the process." She did not know why she persisted in conversing with this uncouth man. But she did not intend to give up, if for no other reason than for Leah's sake. Poor Leah. If she could talk some sense into the girl's father or try to help him see the error of his ways, it might ease the young woman's pain.

"And what you said about my daughter, that I don't deserve her?" He grimaced. "That ain't nothin' I don't already know." The words were low, barely above a whisper.

Frances held her breath. Had she heard him correctly? That smacked of contrition, not pride, and certainly was not what she had expected to hear. There was no sense in allowing a good opportunity to slip away. Jump on it while it was fresh, or whatever that saying might be. Regardless, she must push ahead. "If you believe that, Mr. Pape, why not change it?"

He turned sorrowful eyes in her direction. "What's that? Do what? Guess I missed what you said, ma'am."

She hesitated, suddenly unsure if it was wise to press the matter. Maybe taking a step back would be more productive. "Nothing important. But I think I might take you up on your offer one of these days, Mr. Pape."

He stared. "Sorry. I got no idea what you're talkin' about. Again."

"You told me you live on the edge of town on a ranch, and I might come calling someday. I will consider doing so—soon."

He grinned. "And when you come callin', who should I expect?"

She raised one brow and held it for several long seconds. "I do not have a calling card to give you, either, but I will tell you my name. Mrs. Cooper. Mrs. Frances Cooper, to be exact. It would do well for you to remember it, Mr. Pape, for when I call at your ranch.

Not that I have much faith you will remember, in your current state of inebriation."

"Now, ma'am." He held up his hand, panic widening his eyes. "I was only teasin'. You don't want to be seen visitin' the likes of me. Why, you got your reputation to consider, right?"

Frances gave him a mirthless smile. "My reputation will remain quite intact, thank you. It is yours we need to consider, Mr. Pape, and that of your daughter. Now, have a good day until we meet again—or until I choose to call at your home." She swept past him with a flourish, his expression of abject terror filling her with a deep satisfaction.

Charlie watched the woman stride along the boardwalk, her parasol swinging. What ailed her, anyway? The last thing he needed was another woman meddling in his life. The poor man who was married to *that* woman. If he were saddled with the likes of her, he'd hide in the saloon every day from sunrise to sunset.

If her husband was still alive, that is. She hadn't said she was Mrs. Horace Cooper, or some such, but Mrs. Frances Cooper. Probably killed the poor galoot by nagging him to death.

He stepped down onto the street next to the hitching rail, then aimed a fleeting look in her direction as she swung off at a brisk pace, skirts swishing around her ankles. She was a right pert gal, if he was pressed to speak his mind. Smart, sassy, and not bad looking for someone who must be riding high up into her fifties or even topping sixty. 'Course, he wasn't no spring chicken his own self, but he still had eyes and could appreciate a fine-looking woman when one came along.

He chuckled as he untied his gelding. Not that he expected she'd do what she said and show up at his ranch. No, sir, women like her stayed as far away from him as they could, and usually pulled their skirts back when they were forced to walk past—at least women who thought themselves too high and mighty to get their hands dirty or disdained a man having a nip now and then.

He mounted and settled onto the saddle with a groan. The ground looked as though it might rise up to meet him, and his head swam. Maybe that Mrs. Cooper was right. He'd had one or two drinks more than he ought. Sorrow trickled through his body like mud oozing off a pig. Maybe he'd hide out in the barn when he got home so Leah wouldn't see him. Having one woman chew him out was all he could handle in a day. Besides, he couldn't tolerate the disappointment that he knew would dim Leah's eyes when she saw him.

Chapter Eight

April 11, 1881

Steven had about given up hope that Leah Carlson would return to the bank. He pushed aside the stack of papers needing his signature and stretched, wishing he could get outside in the sun for even an hour. Maybe he should take a drive out in the country. He might encounter Miss Carlson and at least see how she'd fared.

For several days after she'd refused his offer to take up residence at her ranch and help out in his spare time, he'd smarted over the rejection. Then worry had set in. It had been a week with no word. While he didn't enjoy living at the Arlington Hotel and seeing his money disappear at the high rate they charged, he cared more that Miss Carlson might be having a rough go of things.

He stood and plucked his coat off the back of the chair. The morning had been spent visiting a mine, and he hadn't been able to concentrate on his work since returning. Sitting here much longer would drive him crazy. Perhaps his sister and mother would enjoy a visit.

He strode out of his office area and nodded at Mr. Parker. "I'll be back in an hour or so, if anyone inquires." Not waiting for a reply, he pushed through the door and onto the boardwalk, pausing only long enough to keep from running into a passerby.

The street was lined with wagons, buggies, and foot traffic, all seemingly intent on getting somewhere in a hurry. At times he found it difficult to adjust to the pace of Baker City. His job here was more challenging than the one in La Grande, but he'd settled into the routine without too many problems.

The brisk walk to the Jacobs' boardinghouse refreshed him in body and spirit, and he breezed through the front door, anticipating the welcome he'd receive from his family.

Stepping to the sitting room, he rapped on the door frame, not wanting to startle the ladies he glimpsed taking tea. "I'm sorry to bother you, but I'm looking for Beth or my mother."

Four heads turned his way, but none of the faces were the two he sought. His gaze traveled from Mrs. Frances Cooper, Beth's aunt Wilma, Mrs. Jacobs, and … his heart jolted. Leah Carlson. He'd not expected to see her here and hoped she wouldn't think he was trying to track her down when she hadn't returned to the bank. But that was nonsense. His family lived here, and Katherine had invited him to come and go as he pleased.

Mrs. Jacobs set her teacup on a saucer and beckoned. "Please come in, Steven. You know Miss Carlson, don't you?"

Leah gave a tight smile. "Hello, Mr. Harding. How good to see you again."

He removed his hat and dipped his head. "Thank you." He met her green eyes, and his tongue seemed to lock to the roof of his mouth. Finally tearing his gaze away, he focused on Mrs. Jacobs. "Is Beth here? I have a bit of time free and hoped to see her and Ma. Jeffery, too, if he's free."

Wilma shook her head. "I'm so sorry, but you've missed them.

They left an hour or so ago to have lunch in town. A celebration of a new contract for Jeffery's book. Didn't they tell you?"

Everything within Steven froze as he tried to take in what she'd said. Wouldn't his family have come by the bank and asked him to join them? Surely they'd want to share their joy. He mustered a smile. "It's likely they stopped at the bank and I was busy or absent, and the clerk forgot to give me the message. At any rate, I'm sorry I missed them. I won't trouble you ladies further."

He stepped toward the door, his heart pounding a dull thump in his chest. What he had said was possible, but he doubted the efficient Mr. Parker would have forgotten to alert him when he returned from the mine. Ma's time had been wrapped up in Beth since they'd moved to Baker City, but he couldn't believe they'd intentionally leave him out. No, there must be a good explanation.

Miss Carlson lifted her hand. "I wonder if you'd mind if I walk with you for a few minutes. I planned to stop by the bank later to talk. Of course, if you'd prefer to be alone on your time off and not talk business, I understand."

Warmth spread through Steven's chest, and he gave her a genuine smile. "I would enjoy the company. I don't mind talking business. Especially with someone as—" He bit off the compliment he'd almost allowed to escape his lips.

He didn't know her well enough to comment on her physical beauty and didn't care to appear shallow or flirtatious, even if it was the truth. "What I mean is, someone who's a good friend of my sister."

Leah wondered what in the world Steven Harding had almost blurted out. Someone as—what? Irritating as you? Stubborn or mule-headed as you? She'd heard those things from other men in the past when she hadn't fallen in with their plans. Maybe refusing Mr. Harding's offer to help at the ranch had angered him. If so, she might as well abandon her idea of obtaining the loan.

Frances touched her sleeve. "Leah? Are you going to keep Mr. Harding waiting?"

Leah gave a slight shake of her head and returned her attention to the man standing at the entrance to the sitting room. Earlier, he'd actually appeared worried and almost sad, when Wilma told him his family had departed. Maybe she should give him the benefit of the doubt. "I'm sorry. I suppose I was gathering wool."

She moved to the foyer and reached for her coat, but he plucked it from the hook and held it for her to slip into. His hands seemed to rest a second longer than necessary on her shoulders before he stepped away. She shivered at the pleasant sensation that stole through her body.

"Ready to go?" He moved to the door and held it open.

She passed him, and it took all her willpower not to stare. The man was too handsome for his own good, and she guessed he must be aware of the effect he had on women. "Thank you." The words held an air of breathlessness, and Leah worked to control her emotions. She walked down the path toward the road in silence as an uncommon reticence overcame her.

He moved beside her, matching her stride, and apparently understanding her desire for silence. But no matter how much she didn't want to talk, she'd best do so now or be forced back into sitting across from him at his desk.

Leah softly cleared her throat, unsure where to begin. "I appreciate you allowing me to accompany you." That wasn't at all what she'd planned to say. "I've been hoping you'd spoken to Mr. Hunt and gotten a different answer." She lifted her lashes and peeked his way, but his serious expression hadn't changed.

"I wish that were the case." He offered his arm as they came to the outskirts of town and readied to cross a busy thoroughfare.

She hesitated, then tucked her hand into the crook of his elbow, and another jolt shook her. Whatever was the matter? She'd held a man's arm while crossing the road a good many times and never reacted like this. "I see." Glancing ahead, she gathered her skirt with one hand and lifted it to the top of her boots, stepping carefully around the damp spots in the road. Somewhere ahead a man's voice broke into a rollicking song, and a child shouted in joyful approval.

Steven smiled before cocking his head toward her. "Is your father willing to sign for the loan? If so, I don't need Mr. Hunt's approval."

Her steps lagged, and he slowed his own. "He wants no part of it." The whispered words were more than she'd planned, and she wished she could take them back. "I suppose I'll have to make do without the money. We've managed in the past, and I'm sure God will make a way this time as well."

He halted and turned toward her, his warm gaze capturing her own. "And what if I'm part of God's answer?"

Prickles of shock and something more—awareness—darted across her skin. She slipped her hand from his arm and took a step back. "What do you mean?"

"You said God will make a way. Don't you suppose God has the ability to answer in a way that's not what you expected?"

"I asked for the loan, and He didn't see fit to let me get it, so I'm not sure what you're suggesting. I suppose if He wants to help me find the money another way, He could." She lifted a shoulder. "It's not up to me to question the Almighty."

He slipped his arm around her waist and quickly drew her onto the edge of the road, out of the path of a fast-moving wagon. "I apologize, but I didn't want to see your dress coated in mud."

He loosened his hold but didn't completely release her, turning to face her, his expressive face near. "But it is up to you to listen when He offers other provision."

She stepped out of his encircling arm, feeling the warmth dissipate from where his hand had so lightly rested. How foolish that a sense of loneliness took its place. She stiffened her spine, determined not to allow him to see her vulnerability. "Please stop talking in riddles. If you have something to say, I'm willing to listen."

"All right, I will. The last time you were at the bank you offered to let me stay in your bunkhouse for a few days until I found other accommodations. What I'm proposing goes a little further. Allow me to move out to your ranch. As I suggested before, I'll help with the chores. I'll gain a place to live, and you'll have part of the extra help you need. If you find it's not to your liking after a decent interval, I'll leave."

A smile begged to escape. "Are you certain you want to get your hands dirty with ranch chores, Mr. Harding?"

A strange look flitted across his face. "I'm no stranger to getting my hands dirty, Miss Carlson. I haven't always been a city boy. I spent a number of years on a farm, growing up."

"Really? Plowing fields is hardly the same as wrangling cattle, branding calves, or breaking horses." In spite of herself, a surge of hope came to the fore that his idea might work.

"I've dug my share of post holes, and we owned a few horses. Some rather nice stock, if I do say so myself, and not all totally broke when we purchased them. I'm not afraid of hard work or learning something new."

"And yet you left your farm and took a job in a bank." She stared at him. If she allowed him to come, would he stick it out for a week or two, then run back to town and the easier life he'd come to know? She and Buddy could use extra help, even if it was an occasional evening or Saturday, and if he stayed around only a few weeks that would be better than nothing.

She shoved down the feeling of joy that trembled somewhere inside her spirit at the thought of seeing this man on a regular basis. Was she foolish to allow him access to her world, or was she being even more foolish believing it mattered?

No man had ever looked at her seriously in the past—at least not one she gave a whit about— so there was certainly no reason to think this man would be any different. She met his gaze straight on. "Well then, you may be getting the best of the bargain, but if you're willing to do the chores I assign, I'll give it a try."

A grin broke out and then faded. "How about your father? What will he say?"

Leah lifted her chin. "I don't particularly care." The starch went out of her spine, and she looked away. "But you might. He could make it … difficult for you, if he takes a dislike to you being there. Maybe this isn't such a good idea."

He held out his arm. "You leave that to me. I've put up with worse characters than your father, and I'm guessing I can hold my own."

She slipped her hand in through the crook of his elbow again and moved forward, stepping onto the boardwalk that led to the center of town. "Let's hope so, for all our sakes." They wove around a cluster of men outside the hardware store and barely avoided a collision with a child rolling a hoop with a stick. "But I won't blame you if you decide to leave a day or two after you arrive."

He gave her a mysterious smile. "We may both learn something before it's over. But don't worry about it, Miss Carlson. Things have a way of working themselves out, and I'll try to be of help, even in my own bumbling fashion."

Leah peered at him. "I'm not sure what that comment is about, but I believe it's time we dispense with being so formal. If you're going to live and work on my ranch, you'd best call me Leah. Do you have any objection to me calling you Steven?"

He gently squeezed the fingers that lay on his arm. "Not in the least. And I must say I look forward to the challenge that lies ahead."

Steven walked Miss Carlson back to the boardinghouse and then returned to the bank, barely noticing the traffic as his thoughts stayed fixed on the lovely redhead. He grinned when he recalled her comments about him being a greenhorn.

She might be surprised at the amount of work he was capable of doing. Excitement swelled at the idea of seeing Leah every evening.

Getting blisters on his hands and toughening long-neglected muscles were small prices to pay to be in her company.

In spite of the delightful talk with the young lady, he was unable to shake the mounting disquiet he'd felt since the women at the boardinghouse informed him of the reason for his family's absence.

Striding briskly across the bank foyer, he stopped in front of Parker's barred window, thankful the bank was enjoying a brief respite from the normal brisk pace of business. Only the low murmur of voices across the lobby in Mr. Hunt's office broke the peace of the afternoon. He cleared his throat quietly.

Parker raised his eyes, then almost saluted. "Mr. Harding. I'm sorry, sir. I didn't see you. How can I help you?"

"It's nothing urgent, just a simple question. Did anyone stop by to see me earlier today?" He tapped his fingertips on the counter in front of the barred window.

"Yes, sir. Quite a number of people." Parker pushed his visor a little higher on his forehead. "You don't remember your appointments, sir?"

"Sorry, that's not what I meant. I was referring to a personal visit—possibly my mother or sister. Did they leave a message for me while I was away or talking to a client?"

Parker shook his head. "Not that I'm aware of, but I was busy most of the morning with long lines and had to run an errand for Mr. Hunt. It is payday at some of the mines, you know."

He scratched his chin. "It's possible one of the other employees could have taken a message, although I can't imagine any of them not setting it on your desk or giving it to me." He frowned and glanced around the room. "I'll make it my business to investigate and let you know. Is there anything else, Mr. Harding?"

Steven thought for a moment, then smiled. "I suppose not, but thank you for offering. Don't take too much of your time making inquiries."

The clerk shifted from one foot to the other. "Yes, sir. I'll keep that in mind."

Steven nodded and made his way to his desk. If his family hadn't stopped to invite him, how should he handle it? He hated to make his mother or sister feel bad that they'd forgotten to include him in Jeffery's good news. But the idea of being ignored, or at best, forgotten, rankled. He pushed it aside, ashamed of allowing anything so petty to clutter his mind. But the residue trickled into his heart and refused to be dislodged, no matter what he tried to tell himself.

Chapter Nine

April 15, 1881

Leah paced the front porch of her home, wondering for the hundredth time why she'd agreed to let Steven stay in the bunkhouse. She must have been captivated by those mesmerizing blue eyes and forgotten her good sense. A city man had no place on a ranch even if he had lived on a farm sometime in the distant past. He'd be more trouble than good.

If only he'd arrive while Pa was still in town. Four days ago when she spoke with Steven, they'd agreed he'd come that following weekend. She should have mustered the courage to send him a note with her regrets at making a poor decision, but she couldn't bring herself to turn him down. He'd been so eager and hopeful, and his confident air had stirred her resolve to stand up to her father and allow Steven to stay.

Pa would more than likely rail at her for allowing a banker access to his home, although Steven would be living in the bunkhouse, so he shouldn't be in the way. At least, she hoped not. She still wasn't certain how she felt about having him around every day. Then again, he worked at the bank and would probably want time with his family in the evening or the occasional weekend, so it was doubtful she'd see him much.

Millie poked her head out the door. "You're going to wear a hole in that floor if you keep on pacin'. What's got you in such a dither today? Your pa givin' you fits again?"

Leah halted and sighed. "Not so much, although I'll admit I'm a little anxious about what he'll think when he finds out I've offered a bed to a banker."

Millie's brows shot up. "You didn't tell Mr. Pape about Mr. Harding comin' here? Why ever not?"

"I suppose I thought it would avoid trouble, but I can see now it might make things worse."

Millie grunted. "Too late for that." She gestured to Leah's skirt. "Glad to see you at least put on a dress after doin' your chores. 'Twould be a shame to greet that nice banker man in your smelly barn clothes and boots."

Leah rolled her eyes. "After today that's what he'll see most of the time, so I'm not sure why it matters."

Millie snickered. "Musta mattered some, or you wouldn't a-gone to all the trouble to get gussied up." She rubbed her hands down her white apron. "Guess I'd best get to work and find a way to soften Charlie up when he gets home."

Leah grinned. "Are you planning to bake a treat?"

"Yep. That man has a special place in his heart, not to mention his stomach, for my molasses cookies. I'll get a batch in the oven right quick and make sure to have cold milk on hand. Might at least get his attention off'n Mr. Harding for a few minutes." She ducked inside and drew the door shut behind her.

The clip-clop of horse hooves approaching the house caught Leah's attention. Steven Harding reined a striking bay gelding to a stop at the hitching rail and dismounted.

Leah stared. She'd never seen the man in anything other than city clothes. But this time he wore a rugged pair of dark blue trousers, a plaid shirt with a scarf around his neck, and a hat tugged down over his striking eyes. Her heart stuttered, then jumped back into full flight.

He unfastened his saddle bag, turned, and grinned. "Did you think I wasn't coming?" The smile dimmed, and he stepped closer. "Miss Carlson—Leah—is anything wrong? I'm not late, am I?"

She shook her head. "Nothing like that. Let's get you settled. Is that all you brought with you?"

"I have another bag I left at the bank. I'll borrow my mother's buggy next time I go over and bring it back then. Where would you like me to put my horse?"

"In the barn. I have a stall ready with feed, and the outer door of the stall leads into pasture, if you'd prefer to turn him out." She hurried him along, suddenly anxious to get the horse and banker out of sight before Pa arrived. The longer she could delay—or at least until Millie's cookies could help work their magic—the better.

Steven followed Leah, struck anew over her grace and beauty. It wasn't often you met a woman who worked as many hours as she did who still looked fresh and rested with the day half over. Maybe she'd slept in this morning and had a leisurely day. He'd half expected her to be dressed like a farmhand instead of a lady.

But if he wasn't mistaken, Leah was troubled, and he guessed it had to do with her father. The one meeting he'd had with the man showed he might not be the easiest person to live with. In fact, Steven had racked his brain trying to think of a way to get on her father's good side. Not that he cared too much whether Mr. Pape liked him or not, but he hated to see Leah distressed.

She pushed the wide barn door to the side before he could spring forward and help. "You can unsaddle out here or bring your horse inside, if you'd rather."

"Inside is fine, thanks."

The next few minutes passed in silence as Steven made short work of stowing the saddle and the rest of his gear and stalling his gelding. He couldn't miss the tension in Leah's shoulders or the tightness in her voice. It might have been a mistake to move here, but he'd stick it out, at least for now.

Maybe her fears over her father's disapproval wouldn't be realized, and the transition would go smoothly. How bad could the man be, anyway? He looked to be at least in his midfifties, so he should have some common sense by this stage of life. Surely he'd see that having an extra hand on the place, even for a few hours a week, was a benefit, not an aggravation.

Leah silently beckoned and headed outside and around the barn. She walked with deliberate steps to a one-story clapboard structure with a stove pipe jutting from a shake-covered roof. A wide porch ran across the front and extended down one edge, with two rockers on each side of the door. A washbasin and pitcher perched on a shelf to the right, with a stack of firewood to the left.

It appeared neat and tidy and exuded an air of hominess. "This is where you'll bunk. You'll take your meals with our family."

He stopped short. It never occurred to him that he wouldn't do his own cooking. His pulse raced at the thought of eating a meal with Leah. He'd sat through any number of meals in polite company, but the idea of Leah Carlson sitting at the same table unnerved him. He wrenched his attention back to the bunkhouse. "How many ranch hands live here?"

She shrugged. "You're it. At least for now."

"You don't have any other help?"

"We do, but Buddy and his wife, Millie, have the room in the house that used to belong to my brother, Tom. Between Buddy, me, and Pa, we've done a decent job of keeping up with things, till lately."

She flung open the front door. "But it seems as if there's more and more to do all the time. The herd has increased—lots of new calves this spring and colts old enough to work, plus equipment in need of repair."

Steven heard the hesitation in her voice and sensed what she hadn't said. The ranch might be expanding, but he doubted Charlie Pape was doing much to pull his weight. "This looks fine. Did you do the decorating?"

A blush enhanced her cheeks. "Millie helped. It's not much, but we wanted it to be homey for—whoever came."

The neatly made bed to the right of the door had a clean pillow, a handmade quilt in bright colors, and a washstand near the foot.

Three other beds were devoid of bedding, but a stove in the back of
the room burned with a cheery blaze, and a coffeepot sat on the lid,
exuding a mouthwatering smell. Cream-colored curtains outlined
the front windows, and two braided rugs, one next to the bed and
another on the hearth, added more color. A rocker with a high
back and padded seat had been placed near a rustic bookcase with
several volumes on the top shelf.

He gave a low whistle. "It's a sight better than the cabin that
burned or my hotel room. I'm grateful, Miss Carlson."

Her face broke into a wide smile, a trait so rare that it made
him short of breath. "We agreed it would be Leah, remember?"

"Leah!" Boots thudded on the porch, and the door flew open.
"What's goin' on around here? I put my horse in the barn, and
there's a gelding I ain't never seen before. You'd better have a good
explanation, girl. I don't allow no tramp miners to bunk here, and
you know it."

Leah's smile disappeared, and a hard, tight expression took its
place. Steven's heart contracted at the raw pain he saw reflected there.

By the time she turned and faced her father, though, all signs of
anger were gone. "Hello, Pa. Millie should have a batch of cookies
out of the oven by now, so why don't we head into the house?" She
took a step toward the door, but Charlie Pape didn't budge.

"Cookies can come later." He gestured at Steven. "Who might
this rascal be, and what's he doin' in my bunkhouse?"

He scanned Steven head to foot. "Don't look like no down-
in-the-heels miner, but he ain't no seasoned cowhand or bronco
buster, neither. Those are new duds that ain't never been worked
in. Looks like he stepped outta some fancy store. Why's he here?"

Leah opened her mouth, but Steven stepped forward and offered his hand. "Pleased to meet you, Mr. Pape. I'm Steven Harding, and this clothing will get broken in soon enough, I'm sure."

Pape ignored the extended hand. "Don't really care if they do or not; it makes me no never-mind. But what you doin' in my bunkhouse?"

Steven exchanged a glance with Leah. He didn't care to stir up trouble between father and daughter, but he wanted to tell the truth. Funny, the man didn't recognize him from their encounter on the road, but he should have expected as much, considering the condition he'd been in.

"Your daughter was kind enough to offer me a place to stay for a short time. She's acquainted with my sister and knew my cabin was destroyed in the mine explosion."

Pape's brows rose. "You don't look like no miner."

"I'm not, sir. It was the only thing I found to rent when I moved to town last November."

"Why didn't you move in with your sister? She won't take you in for some reason?" His eyes narrowed.

"No, sir, nothing like that." Surely Leah had told her father about her friendship with Beth. "She recently married, and she and her husband live at the Jacobs' boardinghouse on the edge of town." He smiled, hoping the explanation would ease the tension building in the room.

Pape crossed his arms over his chest. "So move there."

"I would have done so, but they're full. Besides their normal boarders and three children, Mrs. Jacobs's mother, Mrs. Cooper, lives there. They've decided not to take any more boarders, as Mrs. Jacobs is in the family way and needs rest."

Pape took a half step back, and if Steven wasn't imagining it, his face lost a little of its ruddy color. "Cooper, you say?"

"That's right. Mrs. Frances Cooper."

"She a short, handsome woman?" Pape held his hand up to just above shoulder height. "And cantankerous—bossy like—always goin' on about somethin'?"

Steven bit his lip to keep from laughing, and Leah intervened. "Pa, that's not a kind thing to say about a lady."

The older man exhaled. "I bumped into her in town a while back, and I wouldn't call her a lady. Tyrant or dictator, maybe."

He scratched his chin. "All right. If you're only here for a short time till you find another place to live, I suppose I can tolerate it. But you'll pull your weight, you hear?"

"Yes, sir, I plan to."

"You got another job?"

"I do, sir. But I'll be happy to help with chores in the evenings and on weekends."

"Give me your hands." He reached out and grabbed Steven's wrists. "Ha. Just as I figured. Soft. Woman's hands. You'll be a blistered mess in no time. Can't see you amountin' to much help, that's for sure."

Steven gave a grim smile. "That's what gloves are for, sir. And I think you'll see I can hold my own."

Pape snorted and turned away. "Remains to be seen." He jerked his thumb at the door. "Leah, let the man get settled whilst we go have ourselves some of those cookies. And while you're at it, you'd better skin out of those fancy duds, as well. What possessed you to put that dress on 'stead of your trousers and boots?" He shook his head and disappeared outside.

Leah briefly closed her eyes, then met Steven's gaze. "Thank you."

"For what?"

"For not telling my father you work at the bank. It was enough for him to find you here. No telling what he'd done if he thought I brought you here to convince him to give us the loan." She picked up her skirt and fled through the door.

Steven stood in the middle of the room, his stomach growling over the thought of warm cookies, his hands already smarting from the blisters he knew were to come, and his heart hurting from the knowledge Leah's words had revealed.

Columbia River Gorge
April 18, 1881

Tom leaned over the rail of the steamer and stared at the awesome sights around him. He'd been only fifteen when he'd made this trip six years ago, and he'd been so frightened that his pa would follow and drag him home that he'd cowered below deck most of the time. Now he was headed home to face his father, and he would never cower again.

He squared his shoulders and concentrated on the magnificent Columbia River and the gorge it flowed through, cut between the state of Oregon to the south and Washington Territory to the north.

A little boy at the rail pointed. "Hey, mister, what's that waterfall?"

Tom dragged his gaze from the sight and smiled at the youngster. He'd been like that as a child, inquisitive and not afraid to approach a stranger. "Someone told me it's called Bridal Veil Falls, because that's what it looks like. Pretty, isn't it?"

"Uh-huh." The boy popped a peppermint stick in his mouth and sucked on it. "We haven't seen any houses for a long time. When we gonna get to a town?"

"I think we'll arrive at The Dalles by sundown. You stopping there or going on?"

"Pa is working in The Dalles, and we live there. We been visiting my grandparents in Portland for the past two months, but Pa's mighty lonely and said it's time to come back. I'm glad."

"Good for you." Tom nodded at a plain woman wearing a modest gown who moved close to the boy. "Ma'am. I hope you don't mind me visiting with your son."

"Not at all, but I was going to tell him not to bother you." She stroked the boy's tawny hair and smiled. "He tends to talk too much at times."

"I've enjoyed the visit. I haven't had anyone to talk to—" He bit off the last word and turned his gaze back to the river. "Sure is pretty here."

She nodded. "Wait till we get a couple of hours farther, when we pass the little town of Hood River. You'll be able to see Mt. Hood to the south. And there's another waterfall even bigger than this one another mile or two past here—it's called Multnomah."

"I remember that one." Tom gazed to the east as a hazy memory surfaced.

"Oh, so you've been this way before." She cocked her head.

"Yes, but it's been a number of years, and I spent a good amount of time inside."

"Ah, seasick." She nodded sagely, then offered her hand. "I'm Mrs. Cynthia Woodsmith, and we live in The Dalles."

"So your boy was saying." He nodded toward the child who'd edged down the rail. "What's his name?"

"Jonathan, after his father. You appear to be good with children. He took an immediate fancy to you."

He hunched a shoulder. "I like children, always have, I guess. I hope someday to have a houseful, if I ever find a woman who'll have me."

She studied him. "I can't imagine you'll have much trouble in that regard, a fine-looking young man who is kind to children. Are you stopping in one of the towns along the way, or continuing on past The Dalles?"

"Once I leave the steamboat I'll take the stage to Baker City."

"So it's the lure of gold taking you east?"

Tom hesitated, then nodded, not wanting to lie but loath to discuss his business with a stranger. Besides, only a few days ago he'd considered trying his hand at finding gold, so it wasn't exactly a lie.

"Well, I pray God will bless your endeavors and help you find what you're looking for." She moved away, following her son to the prow of the paddle wheeler.

Tom stood frozen as he tried to take in her blessing. Did he even know what he was looking for, really? He knew what he had to look forward to—a father who didn't care and a sister who more than likely had forgotten him. His gut twisted, and he felt sick inside.

The ranch should be his by birthright, but would Pa see it that way after he'd been gone so many years? In fact, would Pa even want him around? He fingered the letter in his pocket that he'd kept all these months. Only one of two his father had sent him in the six years he'd been gone. Not likely the man would welcome him as the prodigal son had been welcomed. Not likely at all.

The woman had spoken a blessing, but would God care enough to be involved in his life? He shook off the thought and fastened his gaze on the rugged bluffs to the south. It didn't matter. He knew what he must do, and God had no place in his plans. He hadn't for a long time, and especially not since God had let his mother die.

Chapter Ten

Baker City, Oregon
April 18, 1881

Steven set aside his pen and rotated his neck in the hope of work-ing the kinks out. He'd love to visit Ma, Beth, and Jeffery, but he'd stayed clear since learning they'd neglected to share Jeffery's news. Maybe he was being foolish. It had clearly slipped their minds.

After all, Beth and Jeffery were still newlyweds and couldn't be expected to invite extended family to every event that came along. He pushed away the reminder that his mother had accompanied the couple, plucked up his pen, and bent over his desk.

A brisk step alerted him before the gate to his enclosure swung open. Jeffery paused in the opening and smiled. "Would you have a minute? Your clerk said to come, but I don't want to take you from your work."

Steven hesitated. As much as he liked his brother-in-law, it still stung that he'd been cut out of a family gathering. But he couldn't allow something so insignificant to stand in the way of their rela-tionship. He straightened and offered a smile. "I'd appreciate a break. Please come in. Would you care for a cup of coffee?"

"Thanks, but I only have a couple of minutes." Jeffery eased through the gate and shut it carefully behind him, then crossed the space to the empty visitor's chair in one long stride. He sat and looked around. "I think this is the first time I've been in your office."

Steven gestured toward the open bank foyer. "I can't quite call it an office, but it does give me a bit of privacy, since customers aren't wont to walk through that gate without permission." He grinned. "Excepting family, of course. Is everything all right with Beth and Ma?"

"Sure, any reason you ask?" Jeffery leaned back, his long legs extended before him.

Steven shrugged. "Well, yes. As you said, you've never been here before, so it is rather unusual. I haven't seen much of my family of late." He shot a glance at Jeffery, wondering how far he should take this, then plunged ahead. "And I heard the three of you were celebrating a new book contract. Congratulations."

Jeffery's smile dimmed. "Thanks. We were sorry you weren't able to join us for dinner. Beth was disappointed."

Shock ripped through him like lightning. "What do you mean I wasn't able to join you?" From what he'd been able to discover, no invitation had been extended.

"We stopped by the bank, but you weren't here. I wanted to leave a message to see if you could meet us at the restaurant, but I was told you didn't have time."

Steven bristled. Parker had assured him there were no messages that day. He'd have to speak to the man as soon as Jeffery departed. "Did you ask Mr. Parker to give me the message, regardless?"

Jeffery shook his head. "We didn't speak to Mr. Parker. I didn't see him at his station, but Mr. Hunt was available. He's the one who informed us you were too busy."

Jeffery's brows drew together. "Don't tell me he didn't notify you that we came by? I'm sorry, Steven. I specifically asked him to. If we'd known you didn't get the message … Beth and your mother will be so upset when I tell them. You must have thought we didn't care to invite you."

"Then don't tell them. Please." Steven met Jeffery's clear gaze, which hid no pretense. "It's in the past and better left there. I was sorry to miss dining with you, but it's not your fault." He forced a smile, working hard to stifle growing anger at his boss. "Now, what did you come to see me about?"

"I know it won't make up for that day, but Beth and Ma hoped you'd come for dinner tomorrow."

"I wish I could, but Leah Carlson is expecting me to help with chores out at the Pape ranch. Maybe another time?"

Jeffery nodded and stood, but his smile didn't quite reach his eyes. "Of course. I'm certain Beth and Isabelle will understand." He stepped through the gate and strode toward the front door.

Steven's thoughts wavered, worried Jeffery would think him angry over the episode a few days before. He'd wanted to reach out more to his sister and spend time with his mother. He'd spent years praying his mother would find peace in regard to his sister. Now that she had, was he jeopardizing that new family relationship by spending time helping someone else?

Who was he kidding? Leah Carlson's plight tugged at his heart at a deep level, and she drew him in a way that was hard to resist. She seemed so confident at times, ready to take on the world and determined to come out on top; then, quick as a flash, he'd see a hint of vulnerability and sadness that left him wanting to fix whatever had hurt her.

He attempted to tuck the quandary in the back of his mind where it belonged. But no matter what he did, the memory of Leah Carlson's green eyes and sweet smile kept poking its head out and intruding, completely destroying his sense of peace.

Frances sank onto the divan in the Jacobs' sitting room across from Wilma and plucked her teacup off the saucer. "I declare, that Charles Pape is enough to give a person fits. I would like to teach him a lesson or two about manners."

Wilma gave her a blank stare. "Who is Charles Pape? I don't believe I'm familiar with the man."

Frances took a sip of the hot tea and set the cup onto the saucer. Sometimes it was easier to keep her thoughts to herself than try to explain to people who were a mite slow to understand. She grimaced. That was not kind in the least. It was not her friend's fault that she had done a poor job of explaining.

Wilma frowned. "Is the tea too hot?"

"No, no." Frances waved her hand in the air. "I was chastising myself for unkind thoughts."

"Toward me or this other person, Charles Pape?"

Frances worked to keep her eyes from rolling and almost succeeded. "It appears I am making a muddle of this entire conversation. Let me start over again, if I may?"

Wilma crossed her arms over her chest. "I wish you would. And if your aggravation was directed at me, I cannot conceive what I might have done to earn it."

"Not a thing, my dear. It is simply my deplorable personality rearing its head again."

"Ah." Wilma settled into her overstuffed chair. "Was that an apology or an explanation?"

This time Frances allowed her gaze to fix on the ceiling and a loud sigh to escape. "If I did not know better, Wilma Marshall, I would think you are purposely baiting me. You know it is difficult enough for me to admit when I am at fault. I would think you could take what I said and accept it."

Wilma reached across the intervening space and patted Frances's knee, her eyes twinkling. "I'm sorry, but sometimes it's delicious fun to tease you."

"Shame on you." Frances wagged her finger in Wilma's face, but try as hard as she could, she couldn't maintain her frown. Before she knew it, a chuckle broke forth and changed into a full-throated laugh.

Katherine paused on her way past the doorway. "Is everything all right in here?"

Frances clucked her tongue. "Fine, dear. Although I am sure you are not used to hearing your mother cackle like an old hen laying her first egg in months. But you can credit the mirth to Wilma." Her smile lessened. "Why are you up? I assumed you were taking a nap."

Katherine shrugged. "I wasn't overly tired, and this little one has been doing her best to kick her way out, so it's hard to sleep."

Wilma nodded. "He's eager to meet everyone."

"I don't think I've heard you ever refer to this babe as a girl. I'm more used to thinking in female terms, but between you and Mama, you almost have me convinced."

"Good. We've both been knitting booties and hats for a boy, so I certainly hope we're right."

"I'll leave you to your talk. Lucy and Zachary will be here soon to set the table and help start supper, but until then I plan to go to my room and read the most recent installment of Jeffery's book in *The Eastern Women's Magazine*."

Frances settled deeper into the divan, grateful beyond measure for the good relationship she now enjoyed with her family—and most of all, her daughter. She wasn't certain they'd attained a true friendship as yet, but it was no longer a cold, frustrating battle. God had done wonders in her life, and she could only pray their new bond grew into a warm, enduring friendship.

Wilma pulled her attention back to matters at hand. "You started to tell me about a Charles Pape. How do you know the man?"

"Thankfully I do not know him in any sense of the word. I had the misfortune to run into him, quite literally, the last time I ventured to town." She tsked. "I have never been able to abide a man who imbibes in alcohol, much less one who makes a spectacle of himself when he does. And, of all things, I discovered he is Leah Carlson's father."

"Beth mentioned Leah's father has caused her embarrassment in the past. I wonder if anything can be done to help him."

"My thoughts exactly." Pleasure coursed through Frances at her friend's astute question. "What I did not tell you is that he accosted me after he almost knocked me down."

Wilma gasped. "Accosted? Oh, my dear woman! Did he harm you in some way? Were you forced to call for help?"

Satisfaction swelled in Frances's chest that her friend should jump to her defense. "I should say not." Frances drew herself up, the satisfaction turning to indignation.

She filled Wilma in on the details of the episode, ending with a relish. "That is why I am determined to turn the man away from his slide into purgatory. I knew right then that something must be done, and I am the woman to do it."

Wilma leaned forward, eyes sparkling. "I have yet to see you set your mind that you don't end up in some type of excitement. Do you have a plan, and will you want help?"

Frances smiled. How perfectly gratifying that God had blessed her with such a friend as Wilma, even if they had started out at odds with one another. She sipped from her teacup and scowled. Tepid. "There is no one else I can think of that I would call on, should the need arise, but I believe I shall have it well in hand."

Wilma sipped from her own cup. "Splendid. But if nothing else, you must tell me all about it once you've brought the man to his senses."

Chapter Eleven

April 21, 1881

Steven stripped off his gloves and peered at his palms. If it were winter, he'd soak them in a snow bank to soothe the blisters. He'd better not let Leah or Mr. Pape see him standing idle, or he'd have more to worry about than sore hands. After five evenings of work on this ranch, his muscles shouted with every movement.

What had he been thinking when he volunteered to work here in exchange for lodging? Sure, he'd hoped to help Leah, but this was nothing like the farm where he'd been raised. He wasn't afraid of hard work. He'd done more than his share while growing up, but he'd never experienced anything quite like the work on the Pape ranch. He had always thought of himself as practical—thinking through a decision before he made it, and never doing anything on the spur of the moment. Had he really deliberated before coming here?

He'd thought so, but now he knew. It was those sparkling green eyes, that bewitching red hair, and the untiring spirit of Leah Carlson that had drawn him. The woman had captivated him and wouldn't let go.

Leah rounded the corner of the barn and bent to step through the corral bars. "Don't worry. There are only a few more posts to replace."

He tugged his gloves back on and grabbed the shovel. "I wasn't worried."

"No aches or pains or blisters, then?" She gave a slight smirk before rolling a post toward the newly dug hole with her boot.

He still wasn't used to seeing her in trousers, a man's shirt, and lace-up boots, but he had to admit she looked downright sweet, and she wouldn't be able to do much work in the full skirts women wore nowadays. "I'm not complaining. Let's get this done, all right?"

He hated himself for being testy, but Mr. Hunt had required he stay late the last couple of days and Charles Pape, or Charlie as he insisted on being called, had made it clear this holding pen must be finished before branding began this weekend.

Besides, the job would help him keep his mind off how adorable Leah looked in her men's trousers and boots—that is, if he could keep his eyes on the post holes he needed to dig instead of her.

"Certainly. No need to be irritated." She waited until he hoisted the post into the hole, then grabbed another shovel and used the end of the handle to tamp the dirt around the base. "Actually, I want to talk to you."

Steven stared at Leah but couldn't see any indication of her thoughts on her passive countenance. That look didn't bode well, and his muscles tightened in anticipation. Had her father complained and told her to send him packing? "I apologize. I'm listening."

She finished beating the soil in tight, then flipped the shovel around, sticking the blade into the ground. "I don't think you're cut out for ranch work. Your hands are soft, it's obvious your muscles are aching from the way you walk and move, and you don't seem particularly happy to be here. I haven't talked to Pa about it, but I think we need to call it quits at the end of the day. I can't imagine you'll want to get your hands dirty branding calves or deal with ornery cows bellowing for their babies."

A shock passed through Steven, and he jerked upright. "If you think I'm a quitter, you're wrong. I'll stick to our agreement, no matter what you throw at me."

"But you hate every minute of it," she fired back. "Why force yourself to do something when you're not cut out for it?"

He rested his hands on the shovel handle. At least she wasn't insisting he leave, but she didn't seem any too happy, either. His mind scrambled over the possibilities. Returning to live in town didn't entice him at all. Something deep in his chest wrenched at the thought of leaving the ranch—and Leah.

In the days since he'd arrived, he'd awakened each morning excited at the prospect of seeing her at breakfast and again after work. "Have I been any help at all, or am I only in the way?"

"You're a greenhorn when it comes to ranch work, but you're not lazy, I'll give you that." A saucy smile peeked out. "Not that I assumed you would be, of course. From my experience, which I'll admit has been scant, a lot of city men would prefer to sit at a desk than dig post holes." She sobered. "I know you said you lived on a farm years ago, but that's not helping you now. I meant it when I said you didn't have to stay on. There's no shame in admitting you aren't good at everything."

"I never said I hated ranching or that I wasn't cut out for it. Working at a bank doesn't make me unable to tackle other chores." He stuck the spade in the ground and flipped up a shovelful of dirt.

"Like I said, I have no intention of quitting. That is, unless you propose to throw me off the property."

The smile she tossed him was like meat thrown to a half-starved dog. He snatched it to his heart and prayed she'd realize his worth and not ask him to leave.

Leah didn't know whether to groan or laugh, although she did regret the teasing tone she'd used. Thankfully Steven hadn't seemed to notice, as she'd hate to have him assume she was flirting. What in the world kept the man here, anyway?

She'd been honest when she said he wasn't lazy—far from it. He flew at every job Pa or she gave him with a willingness that engendered a newfound respect on her part. But while she enjoyed his company more than she'd admit, she still couldn't help believing he didn't belong here. She was constantly torn where the man was concerned. Hearing his jaunty whistle as he went about his work lifted her spirits, and when Steven smiled at her—oh my—she wanted to melt into a puddle at his feet.

She grabbed another post and rolled it toward the fresh hole. As if she'd ever tell him to leave … but she would like to look him in the eyes without being addle-brained. She hadn't gotten nearly enough work done since the man had shown up.

Somehow Leah had to regain control of her life. "I don't think I'm strong enough to toss you out, but Pa might try, if he gets wind you're a banker. How's he been treating you the past couple of days?"

"Not bad, although he's barely spoken a word. I don't understand it. He does business at the bank, so why is my occupation a problem?"

Leah nibbled on her lip before replying. "I suppose because he's not happy I asked about a loan, although we could still use one. I'm sure he'd think I brought you here to talk him into something he doesn't care to do."

Steven placed the last shovelful of dirt close to the hole. "I see. I would have thought he'd want to improve the ranch."

"He believes we're doing fine." She hesitated, not sure how much to trust this man. Then again, he'd already seen Pa in bad shape. "It's no secret Pa likes his liquor, even though Millie, Buddy, and I have asked him to quit. He thinks he's in control."

She exhaled in disgust. "Sorry. I don't mean to be disrespectful."

When he continued to quietly work, Leah tossed him a smile. "So you really weren't drinking with him the day you brought him home?" In her heart she knew the truth. She'd never have allowed him on the place if he hadn't proved to be a man of his word. But the fear inside drove her to ask. She needed to hear him say the words ... needed to know his stand when it came to liquor.

"No, ma'am, I was not. I don't touch the stuff. Never have and never will."

Leah heaved a sigh, and her shoulders relaxed. "I guess I knew that."

He propped the shovel against the side of the barn and dusted off his hands. "I think we're about done here, aren't we?"

Leah stared at him, trying to probe his depths. Was he asking if they were done with the job—or the subject? Had he been too quick to deny her question, then changed the subject, or was he irritated she'd doubted him?

It had been unfair to ask. She knew very well he was telling the truth, and she'd had no business prying. "We've done more than I planned, and I appreciate all of your help. I've kept you long enough."

She grabbed the shovel and headed for the barn, but her feet dragged. It took all of her willpower not to look over her shoulder to see what he was doing. She wanted to race back and assure him she didn't mean what she said—had truly never thought the worst of him, even when he'd brought Pa home. She'd hate it if she'd upset him to the point where he decided to leave. This entire conversation had rattled her more than she cared to admit.

What if she started to fall for this man who'd been nothing but kind to her, and he failed her as Pa had done? And Tom. Her little brother had run away and left her alone as soon as he was old enough to care for himself.

Leah wanted to believe in Steven—to trust he would stick with the job, and that he'd be a true friend ... maybe even more, if God willed it. But terror filled her at the prospect of trusting any man. It would be easier if he decided to leave the ranch now, than for her to take the chance of being betrayed yet again.

Steven shoved his hands into his trouser pockets and rocked on his heels as Leah stomped around the corner of the barn. Maybe he'd been too abrupt in his reply, but her question had caught him off guard. She'd asked if he'd been drinking with her pa. Sure she'd smiled when she asked, but why had she invited him to live here if she still didn't trust him?

He'd come here praying he could help Leah—and not simply by digging post holes and fixing fences. He wanted to get to know this woman, to find out what drove her, what caused the sadness he'd seen flash across her expressive face more than once, and maybe even find a way to erase it. His heart twisted. Did she really look at him in the same light as her father? Had Charlie's actions soured her to such a degree that she would turn away from an offer of friendship from a man?

He headed across the barnyard, a deep sickness gnawing at his insides. He'd worked so hard to care for his mother and help find his sister, only to be shunted aside once they were reunited. Was it really worthwhile pouring time and energy into Leah's ranch—and life—in the hope of making a difference? And was he doing so because he wanted to feed a need of his own, hungry and raw, or because he cared about this young woman with the sad eyes and stormy expression?

Steven drew his gloves off again and peered at the raw blisters that had ruptured after digging the holes. Not that he'd been a lot of help either physically or emotionally since he'd arrived, but at least he'd taken some of the heavier chores off her hands.

Too many years away from the farm and soft living hadn't done him any favors. He hated discovering that about himself. He had always seen himself as the man of the family, someone who could get things done with ease. Now he discovered he could barely keep up with a woman.

He gave a rueful grin as he remembered Leah's sparkling eyes. A strong woman with a mind of her own, but one worth getting to know, if only she'd allow it.

Branding would start this weekend. While growing up he'd mostly followed a plow, helped cut and bring in the hay, and tended the animals. They'd had a milk cow that birthed a heifer each year, but they'd never needed to brand a calf.

No matter—he'd take whatever Leah and Charlie threw at him and not complain. He headed toward the bunkhouse, hands still stuffed in his pockets.

But it galled him that she'd compare him in any light to her father and his liquor. And in all fairness, other than the day he'd brought Charlie home, Steven hadn't seen the man under the influence. Was it possible Leah had become overly critical toward her father?

Not that Steven sanctioned the use of alcohol. He'd seen many a man who was mean and surly when he imbibed. But he'd hate to think Leah was unfairly misjudging her father based on one or two times he might have fallen from grace.

From now on he'd keep his own counsel, do his job, and stay out of everyone's way. He didn't want to raise Charlie's ire or cause trouble for Leah, but neither did he care to be an object of worry to a woman who apparently didn't completely trust him.

A dog whimpered, and he whirled around. The rangy brown mutt that Buddy called Rusty crept out of a stand of brush. "What's the matter, fella? You lonely?" He ran his fingers over the floppy cars and soft fur. "Hey, you can keep me company for a while." Moving toward the bunkhouse, he whistled, but the dog didn't budge. "Come on, Rusty. I'm not going to hurt you."

The dog's ears pricked at his name, but he backed away, whining and trotting toward the brush. He turned and gave a short bark.

"You want me to follow you?" Steven glanced back toward the barn, wondering if he should call Leah. No sense in alarming her when the dog probably simply wanted attention. "All right, I'm coming." He had to trot to keep up as the dog disappeared through the shrubbery beyond the newly rebuilt corral.

A prolonged whine came from the other side, somewhere in a stand of trees on the edge of a pasture. Steven broke through, stopping at a split-rail fence where the dog waited, staring into the middle of the field. Young calves frolicked a few hundred feet away and what looked like a pile of laundry was heaped under a lone tree. His gaze focused on it. Why would someone dump anything out here away from the house or barn?

He whistled to Rusty, but the dog darted past him, slipping under the rails and racing toward the tree. From the edge of his vision, Steven saw a dark, massive body move. He walked to the fence and surveyed the pasture, looking more closely. Some distance from the tree a bull pawed the ground, his head lowered and attention pinned to the pile of clothing that stirred and lifted what appeared to be an arm.

Vaulting over the top rail, Steven twisted his head back toward the barn. "Leah! Get out here. Hurry! There's someone in the pasture with the bull." He waved his arms and shouted, running as fast as his boots would allow, praying he could draw the animal's attention.

Chapter Twelve

Leah heard Steven's shout and came running. She skidded to a halt and took in the scene, then leaped forward, bounding over to the fence, her heart pounding and chest heaving. "Pa! That's Pa out there."

She struggled to breathe. Should she run back to the house and grab her rifle, or shout for Buddy and hope he'd hear and bring one? Never in her life had she felt so helpless.

Whirling around, she cupped her hands around her mouth and sucked in a deep breath. "Buddy! Bud—dy!"

Steven sprinted across the pasture, waving his arms and shouting at the bull.

The front door of the house flew open, and Buddy bolted outside. He shaded his eyes against the lowering sun. "What's wrong? Somebody hurt?"

Leah stepped onto the bottom rail of the fence and pointed toward the bull. It remained in the same position, head lowered and gaze trained on her pa, only a dozen yards or so away.

"Get the rifle. Pa is down, and the bull is in the pasture. He's not far from Pa." She waited only long enough to be sure Buddy had heard, then jumped down from the fence and raced across the grass, closing the distance toward Steven, who'd stopped between the bull and her pa.

Steven halted and spun. "Get back! I can handle this. I don't want you hurt as well."

Leah slowed her pace, anger surging. Who did he think he was, telling her to leave? That was her pa out there, hurt and in danger, not his. If anyone needed to be here, it was her. "I know cattle better than you do, and you're the one who ought to leave," she called. "That bull is going to charge if you keep running at him."

She'd been right all along. He was a city slicker who didn't know a thing about ranching, and she should have sent him packing. He'd get himself trampled, and then they'd have two people to rescue.

She pulled to a halt, her gaze darting from her father, to Steven, to the bull, and over to her father again. Pa sat slumped against the base of the tree, his arm lying at an odd angle by his side, his eyes closed and face drained of color.

The bull swung his head back and forth, froth flying from his open mouth, and a bellow rent the air. He pawed the ground and dropped his head, while his entire body shook with rage. What had set the bull off, and why was he in this pasture instead of in his own pen? And what in the world was Pa doing out here?

Steven pointed off to Leah's left but kept a wary eye on the bull. "Swing wide and come up on your pa as far away from the bull as possible. If you can get to Charlie, find out how bad he's hurt and help him to his feet, if he can walk."

Leah edged to the side, keeping her eyes riveted on the bull. "What about you?"

"Worry about yourself and your pa right now. I'll distract the bull, hopefully long enough for you to get Charlie out of danger."

Increasing her pace but not breaking into a jog again, Leah covered the distance between herself and her pa, keeping to the far side of the base of the tree where he lay. If nothing else, she could drag him behind the trunk if the bull decided to charge.

Her wild thoughts settled, and she forced herself to focus. The tree wouldn't do much good if the bull swung around and made another pass. She couldn't keep dragging a grown man from one side to the other, and Pa wasn't a lightweight. Not that he was heavy, but right now he was a dead weight. She balled her hands into fists. Why had she used that phrase? Pa would be fine. He had to be. It appeared he'd only injured an arm. But why wasn't he moving or opening his eyes?

Glancing up, she gauged the height to the lowest limb. An easy climb for her, but not likely if Pa was hurt bad, as she now assumed he must be. Otherwise, he'd surely be on his feet by now, running the other way or tossing epithets at the bull.

A slight smile formed at the picture. She squelched it and bent over, touching her father's shoulder and being careful not to move his arm. "Pa? Are you awake? Can you get up?"

Not even a groan answered her, and his eyes didn't open.

What was taking Buddy so long? She hazarded a look back at the house. He'd made it to the pasture fence, but his bad back must be giving him fits, as he appeared to be barely moving.

She dropped down onto her knees behind the tree and surveyed the scene before her. Pa lay quiet against the trunk, but she could see his chest rising and lowering, so he was alive.

Steven stood between Pa and the bull, his arms at his sides, but approaching the beast at a slow, steady pace. Rusty raced around in circles, barking and lunging at the bull, which swung his head and bellowed at the dog. Rusty would get himself trampled, and Buddy's heart would be broken. Besides, the dog wasn't used to taking orders from Steven and might get in the way.

"Rusty!" She placed her fingers to her lips and let fly the piercing whistle Buddy had taught her years ago—one Rusty knew better than to disobey. He gave one lingering look and a bark at the bull, then tucked his head and came to her side.

"You sit and be quiet." She stroked his silky ears, wondering if she should have called him off. Maybe he could keep the beast away long enough to allow her and Steven to get her father to safety.

She raised her head and focused on Steven, praying God would somehow deliver them from this madness. What a fool she'd been to allow a greenhorn like Steven to tackle the bull on his own, but there was no help for it now. She'd never forgive herself if he was seriously injured, but gratitude for his sacrifice and bravery swelled her heart nearly to bursting.

A loud snort broke the stillness of the late-spring evening. Leah's head jerked up from where she'd crept a few feet from her father's side.

The bull pawed the hard dirt beneath his hooves, stirring up dust, and shook his head, his fiery gaze riveted on Steven.

Leah jumped to her feet and screamed, sheer terror coursing through her body. "Run! He's going to charge! Get over here behind the tree before you get trampled!" Leah's insides bunched into a tight coil as Steven sprinted away from the bull—but not toward the tree as she'd instructed.

Steven heard a rifle shot ring out at the precise moment the bull plunged into action. The bull kept coming, so apparently the bullet missed its mark. Steven ran farther into the pasture, away from the tree protecting Leah and her father, and away from the fence.

He had to draw the bull away from Buddy. He'd seen the older man hobbling across the field toward Leah—no way could the man outrun the beast if he charged.

Steven's lungs emptied and screamed for air, and his legs, which were more used to sitting at a desk than plunging across an uneven pasture, cried for rest. Thundering hooves beat the ground not far behind, and new energy pumped through Steven's body. Would Buddy get off another shot before Steven reached the far side of the pasture—and the fence that seemed to recede with each succeeding step?

He zigzagged and jumped clumps of brush, praying his feet wouldn't tangle. The bull had no such concerns, as Steven heard the animal plunging through the brush at a steady pace.

He hated the thought of Leah and Charlie losing their prized bull to a bullet, but he didn't relish the pain and possible death that would come if the bull's horns hooked him or tossed him onto the ground. Being stomped by the animal could do as much damage as being gored by those wicked horns.

Finally, the crack of another bullet ripped the air, and the bull bellowed in rage. A second, then a third shot rang out. Another sound caught Steven's ear—the pounding of multiple hooves. He chanced a look over his shoulder, praying the brute had lost interest in him, but also dreading the thought the bull might turn his attention back on the injured man or his daughter.

A dozen cows and calves galloped across the pasture, straight toward the angry creature. As Steven veered to the left, the herd cut between him and the bull, slowing his pace and catching his attention. The bull's head lifted. He bellowed, then adjusted his gait and followed the last cow in the line, heading toward another pasture.

Steven stopped, placed his hands on his knees, and leaned over, trying to get his breath. Thanksgiving to God, as well as to Buddy for firing those shots, flowed through him.

Buddy lifted his rifle in the air. "Over here. You're safe now. Come help us get Charlie to the house."

Steven straightened and jogged across the intervening space, shaken from his close miss, but grateful to see Charlie sitting without assistance. He made his way to the older man's side and drew to a halt, wiping the sweat from his forehead with his sleeve. Thank the Lord Leah and Charlie had avoided serious injury. He grinned at Leah. "Everything all right now? How's your pa?"

Leah couldn't stop her hands from shaking—or her entire body, for that matter. She stared at the man who'd risked his life to lead the charging bull away from her father, wondering if she should throw her arms around him and kiss him, or chew him out for the risk he'd taken.

For the space of several long seconds she'd been certain the bull would trample him, leaving nothing but a bloody, limp rag of a man. A shudder shook her frame, and she choked back a sob. If their bull had injured or killed Steven, it would have been her fault for putting a tenderfoot in that position. And she'd have lost the first man who'd managed to touch her heart.

Fire raced along her skin. Leah ignored her father and turned her attention on the man who'd saved them. The fear inside hadn't subsided, but bubbled, threatening to pour out like a hot geyser. "What were you thinking, pulling a stunt like that, and against my orders?" She pushed to her feet, keeping her hands balled to control the tremors.

He simply stared at her, no comprehension lighting his eyes. "Orders?" He shook his head. "I have no idea what you're talking about."

"I yelled at you—told you to run toward us and get behind the tree to save yourself." She stamped her boot. If she had a rifle, she'd have dropped that bull. Of all the obtuse, stubborn, mule-headed men she'd ever met, Steven Harding won hands down. "You could have been killed!"

Slowly he shook his head, regret and disappointment vying for dominance on his face. "So you would rather I'd saved myself by hiding behind a tree like a coward? I was supposed to let you tend to your father and lead the bull back so he could trample you? What kind of man do you think I am? Forget it. You've already made that clear." He didn't wait for a reply but pivoted on his heel and stomped toward the bunkhouse.

"Hey! Come back here." Leah worked to calm herself enough to form another coherent sentence. Glancing down at her father, she almost spat. He'd been the cause of all of this. "Get up, Pa. Before I go get that bull and bring him back here to teach you a lesson."

She'd deserved that dressing-down from Steven, but the image of him lying bloody or dead under a raging beast still danced before her eyes. Why did the pain of her father's rotten decisions have to spill over into her life and color everything around her? There was no reason to snap at Steven, but she couldn't seem to contain all the roiling emotions screaming to be released.

Pa raised his head, and bloodshot eyes met hers. "I think I busted my arm." The words were slurred, but Leah had no trouble understanding.

"Good. Serves you right for getting drunk. What did you do? Leave the gate open, then try to climb the tree and fall out of it after you had too much to drink?"

She shook her head in disgust. "Your actions could have gotten all of us killed." Not to mention they could have lost their prized bull— one they needed if they hoped to grow their herd and improve their circumstances. "You are totally irresponsible when you're drinking, Pa. This has got to stop."

Buddy pulled to a halt, panting and wheezing. "Charlie? What's the matter with you?" He planted the butt of the rifle on the grass and peered at his boss, then straightened and sighed. "Uh-huh, I see." He held out his hand. "Give me your good arm, and let's see if we can get you to the house. Reckon you're still liquored up so the pain shouldn't be too bad."

Charlie grunted but let out a deep groan when Buddy heaved him to his feet. "Hurts. Need another drink."

Leah gave a sharp laugh that ended in a sob, then turned to Buddy. "Can you get him to the house? I need to open the gate to the next pasture and get the bull and cows out of here. Any idea how he got in?"

Buddy cast a knowing look at his boss.

Leah shut her eyes and sighed, then lowered her voice. "Right. I'll never understand him, Buddy. Never."

"Don't be too hard on him, sweetheart." Buddy grabbed Charlie's good arm and braced him. "He's a good man when he's sober; you know that."

"Yeah, but that's happening less often, and I've almost forgotten what it's like. I'm not sure I even like him anymore."

As soon as the words left her lips, she regretted them. Pa might be drunk, but he wasn't deaf. Fear rose inside and pummeled her, leaving her raw and defenseless. The last thing she wanted was for bitterness to burrow into her heart and take root, but the tendrils of resentment kept sprouting and spreading faster than she could cut them off.

Buddy peeked at his boss, then focused back on her. "You might need help with those cows. What if that bull decides to take a gander at you again?"

"I'll have my guard up, but he won't. He's got other things on his mind right now with the cows around. Besides, I imagine he got his mad out of his system, at least for today. Pa must have annoyed him. I've never seen him so ugly before."

"I'll get Charlie to the house, and Millie can look after him. Want me to go for the doc?"

Leah shook her head. "No, you stay and help Millie. Tell Steven to ride to town."

Buddy turned wise eyes on her. "That young man saved all our bacon with his quick thinking."

Leah shrugged, hating to admit it was true after the way she'd shouted. Why did she allow her emotions to get so tangled up that they caused her tongue to break out of the harness and run wild? "It was you shooting at the heels of the cows that sent them racing toward the bull. They caught his attention and slowed him down."

Buddy grinned. "You're fooling yourself, girl. You know right well if Harding hadn't took off running in front of that bull, he'd have charged you and your pa before you could say scat."

He tightened his grip on Charlie but kept his gaze fixed on Leah. "Now, go along with you. I'll take care of your pa and Harding, but you'd best get a grip on your temper and apologize to that young whippersnapper. That is, if you don't want to lose the only good worker you got around here now."

Her head jerked up, and she stared. "Huh?" Steven hadn't followed orders when she told him to stay clear of the bull. She'd had a right to lose her temper, hadn't she? The last thing she needed right now was a dressing-down from Buddy.

He nodded. "Your pa's going to be laid up with a busted arm, and my back is about to give out. You know I can't do no more heavy work. Don't know why you keep me around. Harding is the only healthy man we've got, so you'd best treat him right. Besides, that boy did you a favor when he came to work. Just because you're sweet on him don't mean you got to treat him bad."

Leah felt as if someone had poked her with a sharp stick and all the air had whooshed out, leaving her limp and shaken. "I'll think on it, Buddy."

She trudged away but turned for a second and gave him a weak smile. "And thanks for sticking around, bad back and all. I couldn't run this place without you and Millie."

Steven kicked a pinecone and sent it spinning across the barnyard. What was it about that woman that burrowed under his skin so easily? First, she'd accused him of drinking with her father, and now she treated him with less respect than the worst tenderfoot to hit the West.

Maybe he should find another place to live. She certainly didn't see much value in the things he'd accomplished. Even his effort to distract the bull while risking his own life had brought nothing but criticism.

He stepped onto the porch of the bunkhouse to be met by Rusty, tail wagging and tongue lolling to the side. "What's the matter? Did everybody desert you after the excitement?"

Steven lowered himself into a rocker and patted his leg. Rusty crept over and placed his head on his knee, emitting a gentle whine. "Why can't other people on this ranch be as friendly as you, huh, boy? I'm tempted to pack my bags and head to town."

At least he'd coaxed a thank-you from Leah when he'd brought the doctor back to the ranch a few minutes ago. Of course, she was still worried about her father, and Steven couldn't blame her. What was the man thinking, turning the bull loose in that pasture?

Steven stroked Rusty's soft coat. "Some people around this place don't use good sense, do they, boy?"

A thump on the walkway jerked him upright.

Buddy stood on the bottom step, leaning against the post. "You thinking about leaving us, boy? I heard what you said about packing your bags. Sure would hate to see you do that."

Steven stroked the dog's fur and met the older man's eyes. "Sorry you heard that, Buddy. I must sound like a complainer."

Buddy eased into a nearby chair with a grunt. "Naw, can't say as I blame you. Our girl can blister a man with her tongue when she gets riled. You shoulda heard what she said to her pa after she got him in bed. Whoo-wee!" He grinned and slapped his knee. "Not that Charlie didn't deserve every word of it. But I'm plumb sorry she took her fear out on you."

Steven's hand stilled, and he stared at the old cowpoke. "Fear? You mean about her pa getting hurt and being in danger?" He nodded. "I can understand that."

Buddy wagged his head and smiled. "That ain't what I'm talking about, at all. I meant Leah being a-feared for your life and how it almost made her sick, thinking you coulda been killed."

"She felt responsible, I know, since I live here and work for her part-time. I suppose I'd feel the same."

Buddy chuckled. "Fiddlesticks, boy—that ain't the only reason. But it's not my place to spell it out if you haven't seen it for your own self. But let me tell you, this ranch needs you. Leah needs you. If you go traipsin' back to town, she's gonna be plumb hard to live with."

"I can't say as I've been enough help since I arrived to make a lot of difference."

Steven hooked his arm around Rusty's neck and pulled the dog close, rubbing him behind the ears. What was all this talk about Leah's fear? What other reason would there be? From what he could tell she'd never noticed him as a man and seemed to disdain him as a worker—in fact, she'd made it quite clear she didn't think him capable of making good judgments. So clearly Buddy was mistaken in what he appeared to be hinting at.

A pang stabbed at Steven's heart. It would be nice if Leah did notice him in another regard, but that was highly unlikely after her behavior today.

"I'll think on what you've said, Buddy. I don't want to leave you or the ranch shorthanded, but I'm not convinced it would matter one way or the other to Miss Carlson."

Chapter Thirteen

April 22, 1881

Charlie lay on his bed and groaned, not over the pain that lanced through his arm as sharp as a dagger, but over his own stupidity. Why had he decided to drink while sitting out in that field?

Truth be told, he'd started drinking before he'd wandered into the pasture. He hated the look he'd seen on Leah's face when he'd come to, and he'd wanted to kick himself when she said she didn't know if she even liked him anymore. Where had he gone wrong? Why had his girl turned against him?

He'd seen the disappointment shining in her eyes, doing battle with anger and fear. But it wasn't his fault. None of it was. He drank because he had to, not because he liked the stuff.

Charlie shifted on the bed, trying to get comfortable, but no matter where he settled, his arm still throbbed. Doc said he'd be laid up for weeks without being able to use it. He'd already been lying here for twenty-four hours and hated the thought of being useless for so long. Stupid, that's what he was. Dad-blamed stupid.

A whine sounded nearby, and Charlie turned his head. Rusty stood in the open doorway, tail wagging and ears cocked, as though asking why Charlie was abed at this time of day.

He grunted. "Good question, fella. Come on in. Nobody else wants to keep me company."

The dog obediently trotted across to the bed, his nails clicking on the hardwood floor. He stuck his nose under Charlie's good hand and rooted, begging to have his glossy coat stroked.

"All right, guess I might as well talk to you as not. What d'you think about this business, huh?" He tried to shift his weight and groaned. The laudanum the doc gave him seemed to be wearing off.

He feebly rubbed the dog's fur. "I got myself hurt and made my girl mad all in the same day. You'd think if God cared about her at all, He'd not let things like this happen."

Rusty growled deep in his chest, and Charlie patted the dog's head. "You understand, doncha, fella. I only drink to ease the pain inside. Well, maybe to forget a little, too, I suppose. You ever had someone go off and leave you afore? Somebody you loved, and it hurt you so bad you thought you might die?"

Rusty's tail thumped against the mattress as he pressed in tighter, and his entire body quivered as though in response.

"Huh. Guess you ain't, at that. But let me tell you, it ain't no fun bein' all alone. No wife, no son, and a daughter who's got no use for you, no-how. I tried, boy. All those years, workin' so hard to keep the ranch goin'. A man has his pride, you know. What d'you think I should do about it, Rusty boy? Grab me another bottle and drink till I pass out, or tell Leah I'm sorry?"

Rusty stared up at him with soulful eyes but didn't offer a response.

"I'll tell you the truth—the bottle sounds almighty temptin'. I'm not so sure I could quit if I wanted to. Sometimes I want to ... so bad it about kills me. Other times I want to wallow in my misery with a whiskey clutched in my hand. Why is that, do you suppose? Wish I knew, Rusty boy. I wish I knew."

Leah walked toward the bunkhouse, her steps lagging the closer she came. The doctor had returned to check on Pa and she'd seen him off, but now her conscience pricked her until she could no longer stand it.

She swung around the corner of the barn and nearly collided with Buddy.

He reached out to steady her, grasping her upper arms. "Where you headed with such a glum face? Charlie having problems? You needing help?"

"No, I'm sorry, Buddy. Pa's settled and taking a nap." She stepped out of his grasp and kicked at a rock. "Millie's keeping an ear open in case he wakes, and I decided to get outside for some fresh air." She couldn't quite meet his gaze but saw him nod out of the corner of her eyes.

"You headed to see young Harding and apologize?"

Leah bristled and opened her lips to deny it, then closed them with a snap. She hunched one shoulder instead. "Maybe."

Buddy patted her arm. "Good. That's what I was hoping you'd do. And while you're at it, you might want to give that temper of yours over to the good Lord again, and ask Him to help you control it." He chuckled and moved away, launching into a jaunty whistle.

If she didn't love the man and been taught to respect her elders so much, she'd punch him. Leah blew out a breath of exasperation, then chuckled. Buddy was right. She could stand to have God's help when it came to her temper.

Why couldn't God have handed her a sweet, kind disposition like her friend Beth? Or Katherine? That woman had put up with more nonsense from her mother when she arrived in town than any woman Leah had ever seen and still managed to show respect at practically every turn.

Leah continued down the path toward the bunkhouse, sudden resolve driving her. Either friend was a wonderful example of what a Christian should be, and she'd be wise to follow their lead.

She stopped a few feet from the porch, taken aback to find Steven sitting in a rocker, Rusty at his feet. For some reason she'd expected to find him inside packing his bags. Maybe she hadn't angered him as much as she'd thought.

She hooked her thumbs in the pockets of her trousers as hope surged. It would be so nice if she could breeze on past this without having to eat too much crow. "Would you mind if we talk?"

Steven drew in a long breath and released it slowly. "Of course I don't mind. Please, come have a seat." He stood and waited for her to step onto the porch and head toward the closest rocker. "I've been thinking about some things as well. Maybe I should go first."

Rusty moved to Leah's side. She drew him close and whispered in his ear, then sat back. "All right. Go ahead."

He dropped into his rocker. "I've been going over what you said, and I've come to the conclusion you're right."

She straightened and laced her hands in her lap. Rusty whined and nudged her arm, but she ignored him. "About what?"

"Maybe I'm not cut out to work on a ranch. All I knew before moving to the city was working a farm, pushing a plow, and helping to feed a few cows. Obviously that wasn't enough to make me a good ranch hand. I want you to know I'll be moving on. As soon as I can find another place to stay, I'll be on my way."

Leah slumped in her seat, not sure she'd heard properly. He wanted to leave, after she'd made up her mind to apologize and ask him to stay? He couldn't leave. She had to find a way to convince him she hadn't meant what she'd said. Buddy was right. She'd made a complete mess of things with her poor behavior, but fear had pushed her to the edge. Now panic at the thought of losing Steven robbed her of speech.

She reached out and drew the dog close, finding comfort in his warmth and accepting gaze. Leah raised her eyes and met Steven's. It was time to get to the bottom of this. She needed to hear the truth. "Why?"

He met her gaze squarely without flinching. "I think it's clear you don't feel I can do a good job at the work you've given me. I would think you'd be happy to see me leave. You are the one who suggested I do so, if you remember, Miss Carlson."

She stiffened at his tone and the formal use of her name, then forced her body to relax. Hadn't she come here planning to set things right? She would not be drawn into an argument or say something hasty that she'd later regret.

What he'd said was true, after all, and Ma had always told her that honesty would serve her best. "Yes, I'm afraid I am guilty of saying that. But I won't continue this conversation if you insist on being so formal. I also recollect that you agreed to call me Leah, not Miss Carlson."

He gave a short nod. "I did, but that was before."

She quirked a brow. "Before ... what?"

"Before you made it clear that you weren't happy with some of my choices."

Leah ducked her head as warmth rushed into her cheeks. She deserved that rebuke and more. When had she gotten so callous? Had living with Pa all these years bequeathed on her the same rough edges that marred his personality? She had always wanted to be like her mother—warm, kind, and considerate. At least that was how she remembered Ma.

She lifted her head. "I shouldn't have said those things. I'm sorry." She wanted to blurt out so much more—to tell him how terrified she'd been, how seeing him in danger had opened her eyes to so many things that even now she found difficult to admit. That she was beginning to care about him ... no, care for him ... in a way that scared her, clear to the tips of her toes. She couldn't allow herself to care, couldn't become vulnerable to a man who might run off and abandon her.

This time it was Steven's turn to stare. At last he said, "Maybe I shouldn't have been so blunt. This is your ranch, and you have the right to run it however you see fit."

"But I don't have the right to be rude or disrespectful to anyone, whether or not they live or work here. If you don't mind my asking, what did you mean about being raised on a farm and pushing a plow? You mentioned that before you moved here. If you grew up on a farm, what made you leave?"

Leah waited, but Steven didn't reply. "You don't have to tell me." She got up. "I'll leave you and Rusty alone now. I'm sorry I bothered you, but I do hope you'll forgive me and consider staying."

Steven rose, making the rocker creak just as her boot hit the bottom step of his porch. "Please wait. You caught me off guard, but I'd like to answer your question."

Leah swiveled. Did he mean what he'd said, or was it simply his innate courtesy coming to the fore? "You're sure?"

He nodded. "Want to sit again?"

"Thanks." She made her way back to the rocker. This man unsettled her, made her question herself in too many ways. All this time she'd seen herself as a woman who could take the reins from her father and run things better than he did. Then along came Steven Harding—who one minute drew her like a hummingbird to nectar and the next minute left her bristling like a porcupine threatened by a bear—and she found herself stumbling over her feet and making repeated mistakes.

He leaned forward and propped his hands on his knees. The dog advanced and licked Steven's fingers.

Leah smiled, touched by the picture. "He's not typically so friendly except toward family." She'd often heard that dogs didn't give their affection to someone who couldn't be trusted, but was that really true? A tiny part of her felt irritated that Rusty had gone so readily to Steven, rather than to her, but another part rejoiced that the dog had accepted the man so completely.

"I've always loved dogs. So how's your father today?"

Her mind spun with the change of topic. She wanted to learn more about Steven, not talk about her father. "He's resting. After the

. . . numbness wore off, he's in worse pain than I expected, but the doctor gave him laudanum."

His eyes mirrored warmth. "I'm glad it was only a broken arm. It could have been so much worse."

"That's what I told him, but Pa seems to be hard of hearing when it comes to his actions lately." She bit her lip to keep from blurting out something she'd regret. From the look in Steven's eyes she knew he'd understood the cause of her father's accident. He scarcely could have missed the strong odor of alcohol on Pa.

"Maybe you're being too hard on him."

A lump rose in her throat, and she swallowed. What business did he have making a statement like that when he had no idea what her life had been like since her mother's death? "I thought you were going to tell me about being raised on a farm, not pass judgment on me."

His hand that had been stroking Rusty's head stilled. Then he slowly nodded. "You're right. It isn't my business, of course. I simply thought that, if anything specific caused your father's behavior, perhaps there might be a remedy."

She pushed to her feet, fighting angry tears. Why was she always the one who needed to understand Pa or make allowances? "You know nothing about my circumstances or what I've had to put up with for years. Pa drinks because he's still grieving my mother's death. What he doesn't recognize is that I lost both parents when she passed, not to mention my little brother, who left home three years later.

"Pa wallows in his grief and buries it in drink, while I'm supposed to remain strong and keep things running on the ranch—a ranch

I'll probably never own. And, all the while, I should understand his behavior and 'not be so hard on him.'"

Leah stomped off the porch, then pivoted back. "Come on, Rusty, let's go to the house. I need to check on Pa."

She leveled a steady gaze on Steven. "You might want to get some sleep. We start branding tomorrow, and I'll need you all day." She spun and headed toward the house, hoping Steven's time spent living on a farm had given him better skills with cattle than what he had with women.

Chapter Fourteen

April 26, 1881

Frances hobbled around the front of her buggy and tied the mare to the hitching rail. Two days ago at church she'd talked to Millie, Leah's housekeeper, and inquired as to Leah's absence. The good woman had informed her Mr. Pape had met with an accident and broken his arm.

Poor Millie had too much in her lap, caring for that irascible creature while Leah and Millie's husband, Buddy, were left with most of the work outdoors. Frances wondered if the man had been drinking while trying to ride his horse. It wouldn't surprise her at all.

She grimaced as she eased onto the first step leading up to the porch. Why did her ankles have to bother her at the most inopportune times? If only this gout would disappear once and for all, but it seemed she was destined to be plagued the rest of her days, unless the good Lord saw fit to remove it.

She raised her eyes toward heaven. "Well, what do You say, Lord? I would not mind a little help with my old joints, if You can spare the time." She grimaced. "I realize You have other things to keep You busy, like that stubborn old coot laid up with a broken arm."

She flicked her fingers toward the Pape ranch house. "Why You bother with that man, I am not sure. Of course, why I bother with him is a bigger mystery."

As she climbed up the steps to the porch, she clutched the railing, wondering yet again if this trip was a mistake. The last time she'd seen Charlie Pape, he'd burst from a saloon and nearly fallen on his face at her feet. Why she cared what happened to him mystified her still. But she did for Leah's sake, and that was the honest-to-goodness truth.

It was doubtful the old rascal was worth saving, but Frances had to try or she couldn't live with herself. It was her Christian duty to set the man's feet on the right road, before his drinking ways led him down a slick path straight to perdition.

She lifted her arm to rap on the door, but it opened before her knuckles met wood.

Millie stood in the doorway, a shawl around her shoulders, hat perched on her head, and handbag looped over her wrist. "Oh my! Pardon me, Mrs. Cooper. I didn't hear you knock."

"There is no need to apologize. I had not done so yet." Frances smiled. "I see you are on your way out. Would you be going to market?"

Millie bobbed her head. "Yes, ma'am. Were you here to see Miss Leah? She should be home anytime. I think she's out in the pasture checkin' on calves that were born last night."

Frances shifted her weight from one sore foot to the other. "I had hoped to see Leah, but I am calling on Mr. Pape to see how his arm is faring."

Millie's brows rose and touched the wisps of hair feathering her forehead. "You came to see Charlie? My word, I do declare." Her lips parted, and she stared, then shook herself as though waking from a startling dream.

Frances crossed her arms over her chest. "And why is that so disturbing, my good woman? I am here to do my Christian duty, nothing more. I heard he was injured and came to pay my respects, as well as have a word with Leah."

"I'm sorry, Mrs. Cooper. I didn't mean no disrespect. Forgive my poor manners." She swept open the door and ushered Frances inside. "I'll take my hat and shawl off and fix you a cup of coffee or tea." She plucked her straw hat from her gray curls and carefully hung it on a peg behind the door. "The coffeepot is on the stove and warm, and I can put a pot of tea to steep in a jiffy if you'd prefer."

Frances waved in dismissal. "Nonsense. Get along to your shopping. I do not require refreshment. A glass of water will suffice."

A pained look crossed Millie's face, and she wrung her hands. "But, Mrs. Cooper, what would people say if I left you and Charlie alone together before Miss Leah gets home? You don't want tongues to wag, do you?"

Frances stared at her, unable to decide if she should laugh at the woman or scold her for being so foolish. She would only offend the poor lady by uttering harsh or critical words, so she said instead, "I am not in the least worried about tongues wagging. How will anyone know Mr. Pape and I are alone until Leah returns unless you tell them? And I am sure you do not plan to do so. I am a mature matron, and Mr. Pape is an invalid, so there is nothing to be concerned about, in any event."

She plucked Millie's hat off the hook and held it out. "Please, go on to town. If you would let Mr. Pape know I have come to call before you leave, I would be most appreciative." She tilted her head. "I assume he is up to seeing callers by now?"

Millie accepted the hat with a hesitant look toward the stairs. "He came down for dinner at noon but went to take a nap. I can go see if he's up to receivin' you. But I don't mind stayin' till Miss Leah returns, truly I don't."

"Piffle. That is not necessary. I do not care to be responsible for you not getting your supplies before the stores close." She pulled off her gloves and placed them on a table beside the door.

Millie cast a wary glance at Frances, then sidled to the stairs. "All right. Give me a minute, and I'll tell Charlie you're here." She scurried away, her heavy shoes clomping on the wood steps.

Frances heaved a sigh. This was the right decision and hopefully would be a help to Leah, but would Charles Pape agree? Then again, did it matter what the man thought? It was apparent from what Leah had shared in the past that he didn't seem to care about his daughter's feelings or how his actions might embarrass her.

She gave a half shrug. It was not her concern whether he appreciated her visit or not. She would do what she believed to be best, and Mr. Pape would simply need to deal with it.

The tread of even heavier feet thudded down the hall upstairs. "Millie, you don't make a bit of sense." The crotchety voice of Charles Pape drifted downstairs. "If there's some church woman comin' to call, you should have sent her packin'. You know I don't cater to the likes of those women beggin' for handouts for their preacher or the folks who don't want to work."

"No, Charlie, she ain't a church lady. I mean, of course she attends church, but she's not here to ask for money." Millie's irritated words could be heard all the way to the first floor. "Suit yourself. Storm on down there and see what you get for your trouble. I'm goin' to town." Millie swept down the stairwell, her eyes stormy.

She paused at the bottom and smirked. "He's not in a good humor, ma'am, but I'm guessin' you're more than a match for him, even on his best day. I reckon Leah will be rescuin' him when she gets back, if I got my facts straight."

She gathered her shawl around her shoulders and refastened it with a large broach at the neck. "If he gives you too much trouble, speak your mind and don't back down."

Frances smiled. "I always do, Millie." She stared up the staircase at Charles Pape, whose face twisted into a fierce glower. "Are you going to stand up there all day grumbling, Mr. Pape, or come down here and greet me as you ought to? After all, you are the one who invited me to come to your ranch. Show some hospitality, for heaven's sake!"

Charles gaped, his mind unable to focus until he heard the click of the front door as Millie disappeared. Why had his faithful employee abandoned him to the wiles of this woman? And where was Leah when he needed her? "Leah!" He swiveled his head and stepped close to the banister, peering down to the first floor below.

Frances shook her head. "She is working, Mr. Pape, so there is no need to shout."

"I ain't shoutin', woman. If I wanted to shout, you'd know it, and that's a fact." He gripped the rail and leaned against it. "What are you doin' here, anyway, and why do you want to stay if Leah's not home?"

Frances planted her hands on her hips and huffed. "You sorry old galoot, I came to check on you. But I suppose that is hard to believe. I heard you were injured and thought to pay my respects. Now, are you coming downstairs, or do I need to get two mugs of coffee from the kitchen and take them up there?"

Shock galvanized Charlie into action, and he scooted down the stairs, still keeping a firm grip on the banister. No sense in taking another fall and breaking the other arm, or this woman might decide she'd need to plague him again. "No call to do that, Mrs. Cooper."

He halted on the landing at the bottom and scowled. "That is your name? I seem to remember meetin' you in town not long ago."

A pleased smile dawned, then vanished as quickly as it had come, making Charlie wonder if he'd seen it at all.

"So you do remember our earlier encounter." She gave a brisk nod. "Very good. I was hoping you were not so impaired that day to completely forget. As I recollect, you invited me to pay you a call. I would not have done so at all had you not had the misfortune to break your arm."

Charlie shuffled his feet, suddenly uncomfortable at the memory of the rash words he'd spilled that day. Impaired, she called it. Well, she was being polite, and he admired her for that, anyway. "I suppose I should thank you for your kindness, ma'am, but there was no call for you to drive clear out here. I'm gettin' along tolerable well, although my arm's painin' me some."

Compassion flooded her face, and her body relaxed from her stiff stance. "I am sorry to hear that. Would you care to sit in the parlor while I bring you a cup of coffee? Millie informed me she left a pot simmering on the back of the stove. I also brought a bottle of liniment for your arm. It will not heal a broken bone, but I know from experience that it can help when it aches badly."

For a moment, he considered her request. Once they'd finished, he could beg off any more talking and tell her he needed to rest. In fact, he'd probably want another nap by then, if this blamed arm kept throbbing. "Much obliged for the liniment, if I do say so. All right, then. Coffee don't sound half bad."

A brief smile softened her features, making her quite pretty. "Why, Mr. Pape, I see you are not entirely without manners." She clucked her tongue and gestured toward the parlor. "Now, go have a seat and rest that arm. I will be back straightaway."

He sank into the divan and tugged a pillow under his arm, heaving a sigh of relief, then leaned his head against the cushion and closed his eyes. He could go to sleep right here, if that woman hadn't invaded his home. Remorse tickled his thoughts as he remembered her smile and her offer to help. Maybe she wasn't as bossy as he'd thought at first meeting. Then again, that meeting was still a bit hazy, so he might not have been fair to the woman.

She swept back into the room, her full skirt swishing around her ankles, her hands clutching a tray with two steaming mugs. "I was not certain if you take yours black, but I did not know if you have milk or cream in the house. I do hope this will be suitable, Mr. Pape."

He reached for a mug as she brought the tray down in front of him. "It's fine, thank you. I always take it black." Charlie searched around in his head for something to say next but came up empty. Other than Leah and Millie, he had no experience talking to women—not since Mary. He took a sip and scowled at the memory.

Mrs. Cooper settled into a wingback chair and watched him. "Too hot or too strong?"

"No, it's fine. Guess my arm gave me a twinge there for a minute." The half-truth slipped out before he could stop it. His arm hadn't stopped hurting and throbbing since he'd come downstairs, but that wasn't what had caused his unease.

"What happened?" Frances leaned back and leveled him with a look.

Charlie squirmed, certain she must be reading his thoughts somehow about Mary, but maybe he'd better be sure before he blurted out something he couldn't undo. "I'm not sure what you're talkin' about. Maybe you'd best explain."

She motioned toward his arm. "How did it happen? Or is that another delicate subject?"

He reared back against the divan and spluttered, "Another? What are you implyin', woman?"

"My name is Mrs. Cooper, not 'woman,'" she replied in a feisty tone. "The last time we spoke I suggested you stop drinking, if for no other reason than it would be a mercy for your daughter, not to mention your own well-being. I assumed that was a delicate subject for you, as you did not care to continue the conversation. I am not a person who beats around the bush or plays parlor games like a child."

Charlie's head now pounded to the same rhythm as his arm, and he wondered if it might split wide open. He blinked. "I have no idea what you are talking about, wom—" He winced. "Mrs. Cooper. If you got a question, spit it out. Don't dance around like a man with hot coals down his britches."

Her lips formed an O. "Why would a man have … never mind. Did your unfortunate injury come about because you were drinking again, or did you meet with some other kind of accident?"

He rubbed his forehead, wishing the pounding would stop. "I'll have you know I didn't have a drop—"

He raised his eyes to meet hers and winced again, but this time at the disbelief and disappointment shining so clearly. "All right. The truth, then. I was angry about an incident from the past that I still ain't over. It was eatin' at me somethin' fierce, and I took to drinkin', hopin' to forget. I guess I wandered out into the field and left the gate open, not thinkin' about the bull bein' there, and he treed me. It was hard to hold on to the branch, and I fell out and busted my arm. There. You happy now?"

She gave him a saintly smile. "I imagine this is the first time you have confessed what actually happened, Mr. Pape. I should think you would feel better getting that off your conscience. I, for one, am quite proud of you for doing so. I realize you could as easily have prevaricated."

"Pervari—what? I got no idea what that means."

"Lied, Mr. Pape. You could have lied, but you chose to tell the truth. It takes a real man to do that, especially when it might cast you in a poor light."

"Oh. I suppose I did." Charlie's chest swelled, and he beamed. "Thank you, Mrs. Cooper." He bobbed his head, feeling better about himself and the world than he had in days. "I think I need to rest now, but I thank you for the company and the coffee. I suppose if you happen to be out this way, you can stop by again. If you have a mind to, that is."

She wobbled to her feet. "We shall see what transpires. But before I leave, let me say one more thing. It would profit you to consider your ways. Next time you might not be so blessed to have someone come to your rescue when drink causes you to fall, whether it be from a tree in front of a bull or onto a sidewalk in front of a lady."

Giving him a steady stare, she waited for a span of seconds before she continued. "And let me assure you, changing your ways would profit others around you, especially your daughter, as well as giving you a strong degree of self-respect."

He bristled and clenched his fingers. "I don't need you or anybody else tellin' me how to take care of my business, lady. I'll see you to the door."

Mrs. Cooper leveled him with a sorrowful gaze, then turned and walked toward the front of the house. "No need. I can easily see myself out. Take care of that arm, Mr. Pape."

Chapter Fifteen

April 30, 1881

Tom stepped off the stage at the station on the edge of Baker City's business district and gaped. This couldn't be the same town he'd left behind six years ago. At that time it had one main street with a couple of saloons, a general store, a church or two, a school, and not much else.

That was one of the reasons he'd skedaddled—that, and Ma. Would Pa and Leah be happy to see him? For that matter, would they know him? He'd changed a lot from a wet-behind-the-ears fifteen-year-old and become a man.

"Hey, mister." The stage driver thumped his knuckles against a bag lashed to the roof. "You want this now, or you gonna pick it up at the station later?"

All Tom had thought about was getting to town. For some reason, his plans hadn't extended much past his arrival. All he knew was he planned to make Pa pay for what he did to their family. He wasn't sure what he'd do yet, but once he arrived on the ranch he'd figure it out. He straightened his shoulders. "Leave it here."

"It'll cost you two bits extra if you leave it overnight." The driver unbuckled the straps over the load of luggage and tossed the first one to his partner.

"Then I'll take it now." Tom held out his arms and caught the heavy canvas bag, nearly landing in the dirt beside it. He grabbed the handles and heaved it off the ground. All his belongings in one container. Pathetic that he didn't have more to show for his life. That was Pa's fault as well. And even more wretched that he couldn't spare a two-bit piece to store his bag rather than lug it all the way to the ranch. A mile had never felt so far.

His stomach rumbled, reminding him it had been hours since they'd stopped for a bite to eat. Why hadn't he brought extra grub as the other passengers had? Everything always came back to money— or Pa's pride; Pa couldn't set that aside for a minute. Well, that would change soon, if he had anything to say about it.

Leah stuck the branding iron deep into the coals and wiped the sweat from her forehead with the back of her sleeve. They'd had to delay this chore for a week due to Buddy being laid up and to Pa's broken arm.

If Steven had more experience working with cattle, they probably could have managed alone, but she had to admit the man had been more help than she'd expected. Still, she was grateful Buddy's back was better. He'd kept the fire hot and shooed the calves back to their mamas when she and Steven finished.

Steven leaned over the water trough, splashed cold water on his face, then removed a soiled handkerchief from his pocket and passed it across his cheeks. "So what's next?"

She held back a grin. "You missed a little." Pointing at the streak of mud running from his forehead to his ear, she snickered. "I should have kept quiet. You don't look a bit like a banker today. I'd almost think you were raised around this kind of work, the way you've been catching on the past few hours."

He cast her a strange look. "I was. You don't remember me mentioning that a week ago?"

Leah withdrew her gloves and stuffed them in the hip pocket of her trousers. "I guess I do, now that you tax me about it. But you said it was a farm, not a ranch."

He kicked a loose coal back into the fire pit. "Yes. Most of my life until I was grown. I worked with my pa, then with my stepfather."

She shook her head. "I would never leave the ranch for any reason."

It was hard even for her to fathom such a thing. More than anything in the world Leah wanted to make this ranch a success, and if the good Lord willed it, live here until she died. She'd even had daydreams of marrying one day and working the ranch with her husband, unless he owned a neighboring ranch and they combined their spreads. But to walk away from the land and move to town? That didn't make sense at all.

Buddy hobbled over and patted Steven on the back. "Good job, son. You shore didn't act the greenhorn today."

"Thank you, sir."

"Don't sir me, boy. I've told you often enough, it's plain Buddy. Nothing fancy." He dipped his head once in Leah's direction. "I think I'll go see if Millie's got some food ready, and if she's done baking those molasses cookies. If you don't dawdle too long, I might even save one for the both of you." He winked at her, then limped toward the house.

Steven's lips twitched in an attractive smile. "He's a good man. I've had a few talks with him, and his faith in God runs deep."

Leah nodded. "So does Millie's." She beckoned toward the house. "I'm pretty hungry. Maybe we should head to the house. And by the way, I agree with you. Buddy and Millie have both been a godsend to me ever since Ma …"

She nibbled at her lip. "Sorry. You were starting to tell me why you hated your farm so much."

Steven stiffened and met her eyes. "I didn't say I hated it. I just—"

Rusty rose from where he'd been lying and growled, then bolted forward and barked, his hackles rising.

Leah took two long strides and laid a firm hand on the dog's neck. "What's wrong, boy?" She looked up the lane. A man toting a canvas bag on his shoulder walked slowly toward the house, his head twisting from right to left, as though trying to take in everything at once. Something about him seemed vaguely familiar. The way he walked or the tilt of his head?

He moved closer, and Rusty's growl deepened. The man looked young. His clothing was dirty but not torn or unkempt, and his hair needed a trim. The stubble on his face and the hat brim pulled over his eyes kept her from getting a good look at his face.

He stopped a few yards away and dropped the bag at his feet, then straightened and smiled. "Are you going to stand there staring, or are you going to tell your brother hello?"

Rusty's stance relaxed, and his head dropped.

Leah stared at the man and then glanced at Steven. Her breathing slowed, and she swayed. Steven took a step closer. "Leah? Do you know this man?"

She swung her gaze to him and, after several long seconds, nodded. "I think so. I mean, I recognize his voice, but I'm not sure ..."

Leah pivoted once more to the stranger. "Tom?" She passed her hand over her face. "It's been so many years. I can hardly believe ..." She choked on the last word, then took a tentative step forward. "Is it really you? Pa will be so happy to see you."

Rusty pressed against her leg, and his tail started to thump.

The young man lurched toward her, then stopped, the color in his face fading. "I couldn't stay here anymore—not with him here." He jerked his head toward the house. A scowl tightened his features. "I had to get away."

Six years since she last saw her brother, and he'd finally returned. He'd been good looking as a youngster, but now he was downright handsome, or he would be but for the scowl and the need of a bath and a shave. But Tom was different. The old, easy smile she remembered from their childhood had been replaced with a glower.

Yet, in spite of his expression, joy bubbled inside, and she held out her arms. "Come here and give me a hug. You have no idea how much I've missed you."

He turned his face away and gestured toward Steven. "Who's this guy? He your beau or your husband?"

Leah slowly lowered her arms to her side, wondering at her younger brother's tone. She shook her head, the braid swinging against her back. He seemed anything but happy to see her, so why had he returned?

Tom had rejected her welcome and turned away. Her lower lip trembled as pain knifed her heart. What could have happened to change him so much? They'd had spats when they were young as all siblings did, but he'd never been intentionally mean.

She collected her thoughts and mustered a smile. "I'm sorry. This is Steven Harding, and he's helping out around the ranch." She pressed her lips together, wondering if she should say more. But why should she? Tom wasn't owed any explanations, especially with his attitude. She looked at Steven. "This is my younger brother, Tom Pape."

Steven held out his hand. "Glad to meet you, Tom. So you're back for a visit? I'm sure your pa will be happy to see you."

The scowl deepened, and his arm stayed next to his side. "I doubt that. I wouldn't have come back now if it wasn't for Ma."

Tom hated what he was doing, but there was no help for it. He had to make his sister understand. Leah wasn't even Pa's real daughter, but all their life she'd stood up for the man—made excuses for him no matter how ornery he'd been. Tom couldn't tolerate that happening again. It was one of the reasons he'd run away and hadn't wanted to return.

What would happen if he gave in and hugged her? Let Leah know he'd missed her and wanted to come home? He'd never admit it to a soul, but he'd cried himself to sleep for a number of nights after leaving the ranch—and not once because he missed his father.

But Leah wouldn't believe him. He steeled his emotions and kept his elbows tight against his body. His sister always sided with their pa, and Ma loved Leah the best. Not a one of them put him first, and he'd never been able to set that thought aside. It rankled and grew like a thornbush watered by a spring rain and warmed by the sun.

If it was the last thing he did, he'd open Leah's eyes to the truth and prove that he mattered. That's all he'd ever wanted—to be as important to someone as Leah had been to Ma and Pa. But it was too late for Ma, and he didn't care about Pa. That only left Leah. He shook his head, trying to sort through the dizzying thoughts. Leah took all Ma's love, even if she hadn't meant to. The fact still stood, and he couldn't forgive her for that.

Steven narrowed his eyes. There was something going on here that he didn't understand. Leah's brother had seemed happy to see her at first, but the conversation had taken a decided turn as soon as Charlie's name came up. Very little had been said about this brother since Steven's arrival on the ranch, but if the animosity he saw in the man's face was an indication, the reason for his departure six years ago wasn't a pretty one.

"Tom!" Leah placed her fingers over her lips. "Pa has missed you something fierce since you left. And Steven is right. He'll be so happy you're home, especially now that he's laid up with a broken arm."

"I bet he will. Probably about as much as he missed Ma." Tom's top lip rose in a sneer. "The only time he was glad to have me around was when he needed an extra set of hands to do his work."

"That's not true, and you know it." The words dropped and hit the air, sizzling like drops of water on a branding iron. "You left us without even saying good-bye. I cried for weeks, worrying if you were safe and wondering where you'd gone. And how can you say that about Ma? Pa was heartbroken when she died."

The anger ebbed from Tom's face, but confusion flashed in his eyes. His gaze shifted away from Leah, then swung back. "I left a note. I didn't want you to fret over me."

She frowned. "That can't be right. Pa said there was nothing—that he had no idea where you went. He knew I was sick with fear. He wouldn't have lied when he knew the truth would've set my mind at ease."

Tom's eyes turned cold, cynical. "So he lied about that too. First he tells you Ma died. Then he doesn't tell you I left a note. Doesn't that make you wonder, Leah?"

Steven looked from brother to sister. "I think I'll excuse myself now. This is a family discussion, and I don't have any part in it. Good to meet you, Tom. I'll probably see you again soon, if you plan to stay." He jerked his head toward the bunkhouse. "I live here and help out in my spare time."

Tom held up his hand. "Wait. You might as well hear the truth right now, so you'll understand the kind of man your boss is." He barked out a sharp laugh before returning his attention to Leah.

Leah stared at her brother, and the back of her neck prickled. She couldn't get a grip on what was wrong. The look on Tom's face left her unsettled, not to mention his strange words. This wasn't the little brother she used to play tag with and race across the fields on their horses.

The man standing before her was a stranger. Why should she ask him anything about their mother? And what utter nonsense to say Pa lied when he told her Ma passed away! She died when Tom was twelve and Leah, fourteen—three years before her brother ran away—so there was nothing to tell.

Leah took a step back and almost bumped into Steven. He placed a reassuring hand on her shoulder and squeezed, then released her and stood close by.

She kept her attention on her brother. "Why would you come back if you despised it so much?"

Tom didn't waver. His gaze remained firm on hers. "I told you I came home because of Ma. Aren't you even a little curious what I'm talking about?"

Leah rubbed her arms, wanting to ease the chill of what she sensed might be coming. Tom had returned, and it should be a time of rejoicing, but instead he stood there like a block of granite.

She met her brother's eyes. "Ma's been gone a long time. I don't see why you'd say you came back because of her. Unless you want to honor her memory by reconciling with your family."

Tom snorted. "Now that's plumb funny, Sis. So Pa must have kept up the lies all these years."

"I don't know what you're getting at. All these ugly things you're saying about Pa ... I've heard enough." She reached out toward him.

"Let's go to the house and see Pa, Millie, and Buddy, all right? Why can't you be happy you're home? There's no need to dig up the past. It can only bring sorrow."

He stared at her. "You still don't get it, do you? Why do you keep sticking up for Pa? He's no good, Leah. He drove Ma off and caused her death."

Leah felt as though her heart were stuck in her throat. Pa didn't cause her mother's death. Fear swirled inside, warring with the confusion, and dread followed close on their heels.

She couldn't listen to these lies any longer … wouldn't listen. It wasn't fair to Pa. "Has living on your own for so long addled your brain? Ma died from a fever. Pa sent us to town to stay with friends when she took sick. I know you were only twelve, but surely you remember."

"Ha. You bet I do—that and a lot more." He shook his head from side to side in a slow, ponderous motion. "You never once wondered why she didn't have a funeral?"

Leah shrugged. "I asked Pa, and he said she didn't want one. That she asked him to lay her to rest in the big meadow behind the house and not make a fuss. She didn't want us children put through any more of an ordeal."

He laughed, but it came out hollow and lost. "I guess you wanted to believe that, but I knew the truth. Ma didn't die, Leah. She ran off and left Pa. She hated her life here, and she couldn't tolerate being married to him—or living here—another day."

Leah could only stare. She felt as though she'd been tossed into the air by the bull, then trampled. But even that kind of pain didn't cut as deep as Tom's words. This couldn't be true.

"You're lying." Her words cut like a knife honed to a fine edge. "I'm not going to listen to any more of this hateful talk." She fisted her hands on her hips. "Did you come home so you could stir up trouble and turn our family against one another? If that's the case, you can return to wherever you've been living."

Tom's face reddened, and he took a step toward her.

Leah felt Steven move forward to stand beside her. Gratitude enveloped her like a warm blanket, but an icy calm shoved the warmth aside. Steven's solid strength was comforting, but no amount of wishing for someone to rescue her would change what Tom said.

She stood and stared at her brother, disappointment churning her gut. Surely Tom would never be a threat to her physically, but there was no way she'd allow him to repeat those hideous words where her father could hear them. "So? What will it be?"

Tom glanced at Steven, then allowed his gaze to settle on her. "I'm not hiding behind a lie any longer. I did that for the three years before I left, and that was enough."

A shiver raced down Leah's back. "What lie? You know as well as I do that Ma is dead."

His eyes didn't soften. "She was very much alive when she left this ranch nine years ago."

Leah's stomach clenched to the point she thought she might be ill. She peered at Steven. What must he be thinking? More than likely, he wished he'd never moved to the ranch or met her family. She squared her shoulders—no more weakness or game playing. She glared at her brother. "You can't know anything about Ma. You disappeared and never came home. And if all of this were true, why wouldn't Pa have told me?"

Tom sneered. "Pa's pride has always been one of his biggest problems, other than the drinking and surly personality. But I'll admit that mostly got worse after Ma left. Sure, maybe Pa acts that way due to Ma leaving him, but he needs to get over it."

His mouth twisted. "Can you really see him admitting his wife deserted him? You asked how I know about Ma. Before she left, she told me what she was going to do. She gave me the choice of coming with her right then, and I almost did. I wish now I hadn't stayed here and wasted three years."

Leah's legs shook, and she swayed. Ma had been alive all these years? It couldn't be true. She refused to believe her mother would leave her behind. Her mother had loved her ... she'd proved it in so many ways before her death.

They'd picnicked together in a secluded place in the meadow where the daisies grew in wide clusters. Ma made daisy chains as garlands and placed them on Leah's head. They'd shared whispers and giggles and stories galore—secrets and precious things hidden where no one else would ever think to look. Leah had not returned to their special place since Ma died, never gone to their hidey-hole and uncovered their private box. She shivered and rubbed her hands over her arms.

But Tom said Ma hadn't died. She stared at her brother. "If Ma didn't die, where has she been all these years? Why would she leave without letting me know?"

He turned his head, but not before she saw a glint of sadness darken his eyes.

Her own pulse pounded. Ma had come to Tom and offered to take him away with her, but she hadn't so much as left Leah a note or kissed her good-bye? Why would Ma desert her own daughter?

A sense of desolation, deeper than any canyon she'd ever stared into, threatened to topple her. If Tom's claim was true, her mother had abandoned her without so much as a word. And nine years had passed without even a letter. Why? How could she do that to her own child?

Steven steadied her with a firm hand. "Why don't you sit on the porch?" He indicated one of the chairs.

She gazed up into his warm eyes and slowly shook her head. "Thank you. I'm fine now. A little dizzy for a moment, but it passed."

He gave a reluctant nod and released his gentle grip.

A cloud of loneliness swept over Leah. If only she could cling to Steven and draw on his quiet strength. Funny she hadn't seen him as strong until today, when she felt so weak.

She rounded on Tom as fury built, burning in her belly. "I don't believe you. Ma wouldn't have left without telling me. She would have asked me to go with her too. Ma wouldn't have left me here, alone"—she gestured toward the ranch house—"with him." What kind of woman would leave a fourteen-year-old girl with a man who wasn't even her natural father?

Guilt pricked at her thoughts. Pa had been the only father she'd ever known, since her own had died not long after she was born. But if Ma left the ranch out of anger or disgust with her own husband, why would she leave her defenseless daughter with the man? She gave a sharp shake of her head. It didn't make sense. None of this did.

Tom's firm mouth softened. "She knew you'd never want to leave the ranch. Ma knew how much you loved it here, and she didn't want to take that from you." His eyes darted away. "I can't tell you more. Ma refused to talk about it much."

Leah shook her head, still not able to fully comprehend the awful truth. Her mother had abandoned her. Willingly. Knowingly. Without so much as a backward glance. She swung her attention to her brother, suddenly certain he wasn't telling the full truth. What was he hiding? He'd never been able to tell a lie while looking her square in the eyes. "And why would she do that? What else are you hiding?"

Her brother shot a malevolent look at the house. "You weren't that young when Ma left. You should remember the fights between her and Pa, and how unhappy she was living here."

"No, I don't. Ma loved the ranch, the same as me."

"You're fooling yourself, Leah. That might be what you want to remember, but it's not true. Ma hated living in the country. She was raised in a city and begged to move, but Pa wouldn't have it." His lip curled. "All he cared about was this ranch. It meant more to him than any of us, and it still does."

She wrapped her arms around herself, hating what she was hearing. Ma hadn't hated it here; she was sure of it. A vague memory of raised voices and Ma's face streaked with tears intruded on her thoughts, but she pushed it away. "How do you know? You can't convince me Ma revealed her deepest emotions to a twelve-year-old boy before she deserted her family."

"She didn't tell me then, but I learned it bit by bit over the past few years."

"What do you mean?" Leah hadn't thought Tom could tell her anything that would hurt her worse than what he'd already shared, but she cringed at what she sensed coming.

"I've been living with Ma for the past six years. Right before I left the ranch, I wrote to her that I was leaving."

"You wrote to her?" The words felt like heavy mud on her tongue, and she barely pushed them out into the air. "You knew her address for three years and didn't tell me? Why would you keep it a secret?"

Tom shook his head but again didn't meet her eyes. "Before she left she said she was moving to Portland—back to where she lived when she was a girl. I sent a letter general delivery and told her I'd be arriving in a few weeks."

"So is she coming back after all this time? Is that why you came, to prepare me and Pa for her arrival?" Leah stiffened. "I don't know if I want to see her, even if she's at a hotel in town right now."

Her brother stared at her for several long moments. "I told you, Leah, Ma's dead. She passed away not long before Christmas. That's one of the reasons I came back."

Leah blinked, unable to comprehend the import of his words. Dead? But Tom said he'd been living with her all these years. Ma left her alone on the ranch with a father who turned into a drunk. She never wrote or tried to contact her before she died.

Pain pierced Leah's heart, as deep and dark as a mine shaft cut all the way to cold bedrock. She'd already lost her mother once, nine years ago—only to discover now that her mother hadn't wanted her. Why would God force her to endure her mother's death all over again now? He could have stopped her from leaving, could have made Ma stay and care for her.

A shadow passed over her vision, and she shivered. She pivoted and started toward the bunkhouse that sat a few yards from the corrals. She had to get away from Tom and think. Leah took another step, but the heaviness and darkness increased. She stumbled, and the last thing she saw was the ground rising toward her and the strong arms that wrapped around her.

Chapter Sixteen

Tom stared at the limp form of his sister as the stranger gathered her to his chest and strode the short distance to the bunkhouse. Horror swept through Tom at the realization that he'd caused her to faint. Leah had never been weak. She'd never carried on like other girls no matter how afraid.

A memory of his mother's pale face leaped to the forefront. Leah couldn't be sick like Ma, could she? Why did this have to happen? He hadn't wanted to return, but Ma had wheedled and begged before she died. She'd made him promise.

He gritted his teeth. As far as he was concerned, he'd come back to get what was rightfully his. A shiver ran across his skin. But he'd made a deathbed promise— the kind a man should never break.

He grabbed his bag from the ground and tucked it under his arm. He didn't belong here—had never belonged here, even as a child. Ma had loved him in her own way, but he'd never been able to please his father, no matter how hard he tried. He turned and walked toward the rutted road that led back to town. There was no way he could face his father right now, not with Leah lying unconscious in the bunkhouse and all of it his fault.

Steven smoothed a red curl from Leah's cheek, marveling at the softness of her hair and skin. He straightened and took a step back. She was his landlord, if not his boss, and he was suddenly ashamed for taking such liberties. Pulling a handkerchief from the pocket of his trousers, he hurried across the room and then dipped it in a basin of cool water. He strode back to the bed and gently placed it across her forehead.

Leah's lashes quivered; then her eyes slowly opened, revealing depths of confusion and pain that stirred Steven to the bottom of his soul. He hadn't completely figured out the conversation between Leah and her brother—at least, not to the point of understanding how Leah's mother could leave her family—but he'd heard enough to know he wanted to protect her from another verbal assault from that man.

"Steven?" Leah rolled her head to the side. "What am I doing in the bunkhouse?" She pushed herself up on one elbow. "And on your bed." A wave of red flooded her cheeks, and she swung her feet onto the rag rug covering a space on the board floor. "What happened?"

Steven's heartbeat increased, but he threw a loop over his thoughts and hauled them back where they belonged. Relief flooded him that Leah appeared to be all right. He'd truly worried when she'd collapsed in his arms.

He stepped away from the bed. "I'm not sure. One minute you were standing outside locking horns with your brother and the next you fainted. Maybe you shouldn't get up too fast. How are you feeling now?"

"I'm fine," she said swiftly. "We worked so long branding calves that we missed dinner." She avoided his eyes. "I was light-headed earlier from not eating; then, before I knew it, everything got black. How long was I out?" Her eyes flew back to his. "Where's Tom?"

"You've only been unconscious a few minutes. We need to get you to the house so you can eat." He tried to stem the flood of concern at the sight of her pale skin and shaking hands. It was certainly possible she'd fainted because of the hard work, hot sun, and lack of food, but even more probable her collapse was tied to her brother's arrival and startling declaration. "And I have no idea where your brother is. Taking care of you was my first priority."

Her cheeks flushed rosy. She smoothed a few stray strands of hair off her face that had loosened from her braid, then took his hand to assist her in getting up. "Thank you."

They stood face-to-face without moving while Steven's heart nearly pounded out of his chest. He released her hand and didn't move. Clamping down on his emotions, he kept his arms pinned to his sides, barely able to breathe.

Several heartbeats passed before Leah shifted her gaze. She took a step around him, then moved toward the open door. "Do you suppose Tom went to the house? I'd better get up there. Pa will be fit to be tied when he sees him."

Steven frowned, still finding it difficult to shake free of the need to touch her. "Why? I'd think he'd be happy to welcome his son after so many years."

Leah gave a harsh laugh. "I'd have thought so too, until Tom spouted all that rubbish about Ma. I don't believe for a minute that she wanted to leave the ranch." Her lips quivered, and she turned her head, but Steven still heard the faint whisper. "Or me." She headed across the porch and down the steps. "You coming?"

Steven wanted to race forward and wrap his arms around her. She'd sounded so ... fragile ... not at all like the strong woman he'd come to know. He kept a tight rein on his emotions. A hug from him was the last thing Leah would want. "Sure. I could stand some of Millie's good cooking. So you don't believe Tom?"

He kept a close eye on Leah, ready to jump and catch her if she so much as stumbled over a stone on the path. He didn't care for the effect Tom Pape had had on Leah. She was usually clear and decisive, knowing what she wanted and stating what she believed, but the arrival of her brother seemed to have changed things somehow.

"Believe him about what?" She turned quizzical eyes his way.

"Your brother. He said he's been living with your mother, and she recently passed. You think he was lying?"

Charlie hitched himself up against the pillows, being careful not to bump his arm. He reached for the mug of coffee Buddy had brought in. "Thanks. Hate to have you waitin' on me like this. You have enough to do keepin' up with extra ranch chores."

"I don't mind helping Millie out. She's baking bread for dinner, and since my stomach thinks my throat's been cut, I'm more'n happy to help out." He grinned and placed a folded towel on the bedside table and set a tin coffeepot atop it. "Besides, Millie said you had a restless night and needed to sleep late this morning. I don't argue with the missus."

Charlie cradled his arm and cut loose with a groan. "Dinged arm's hurtin' worse today." He shifted around on the bed, but nothing helped. "Can't say as I blame you. I like to stay on Millie's good side my own self. How's the work goin'? That Harding fella pullin' his weight?"

Buddy hitched a chair close and straddled it. "Yup. I gotta say, boss, he's a good worker. I wasn't sure what to expect when he showed up, but he does a decent job." He pointed at Charlie's splinted arm wrapped in a bandage and done up in a sling. "You'd probably have a lot worse than a busted wing if he hadn't been there. That bull mighta got Leah, too, if it weren't for Harding. If you ask me, you owe him, boss."

Charlie carefully lowered his mug of coffee and stared at his old friend. "She never told me she was in danger."

"The doc was here, then you took a nap, and it's been busy ever since. Guess she didn't have time." The man didn't quite meet Charlie's eyes.

"What you not tellin' me, Buddy? Out with it. Leah didn't get hurt and then hide it from me, did she?"

Buddy met Charlie's gaze square on. "No, sir. Nothing like that, at all. Sorry I made you worry. I think her hurt is more inside, like."

Charlie's heart skipped a beat, then plunged ahead, seeming to gather speed as it went. "What do you mean, hurt inside? That don't make a lick of sense."

"I'll try to explain. The way I see it, she's worried about you and don't know her own mind about Harding. I think the worry and confusion has her plumb flummoxed, if you get my meaning."

"No, Buddy, I don't, so quit skippin' around what you're tryin' to say. I know you well enough to know there's more, so spit it out."

"Fine." Buddy leaned back in his chair. "Your drinking has been a trial to your girl. You almost got yourself and everyone else hurt, if not killed, with that stunt in the pasture. Then Harding put himself in danger to draw the bull away from Leah so she could get you out of harm's way. That like to scared ten years off her life, 'cause she's starting to care for the boy. Leastwise, I think she is from what I've been able to tell."

Charlie's stomach plummeted until he thought he'd be sick. His actions had put his girl in real danger? Somewhere inside he'd known that, but he hadn't wanted to face it. If it had been anyone but Buddy telling him this, he'd have spat the words back and turned aside. But his foreman and friend was a straight shooter and not one who embroidered the truth. He gave a slow nod. "All right. I'll think on what you've said about the liquor. I've knowed for a while that I've let it get out of hand. But what's this about Leah takin' a shine to Harding? I ain't seen no proof of that, and I'm not sure I'm happy about the idea."

"You haven't been watching, boss. I've seen little signs from the girl. She got overly irate when he put himself in danger, and she watches him when she thinks he's not looking." Buddy hunched a shoulder. "Nothing big, but Millie's noticed too. I'm not sure Leah even knows it her own self, yet."

Charlie's hand shook as he gripped his coffee mug. It had never occurred to him that his girl would fall in love and leave him. He'd be alone if she married, and he'd hate that. She belonged here, not with some man who didn't deserve her, even if he had saved her life. "How about Harding? You think he feels the same?"

Buddy hesitated. "Not certain, but I wouldn't be surprised. She's said a couple of things to him lately that set him back a mite, so it's hard to say. But Leah's a beautiful girl and more than that, she's good clear through. Any man would be right proud to have her care for him. It's a wonder to me she's not been snapped up before this."

Charlie settled into his pillows propped up against the headboard. "Huh. I'm glad she hasn't been snapped up. I don't want her to leave the ranch. Not ever. Guess I'll have to keep an eye on Harding. We've got enough to deal with without some city man comin' in and hurtin' my girl. I'll run him out on a rail if he does anything to hurt her."

Buddy peered at him over the rim of his mug. "Boss, I reckon it might be wise to look to your own self in that regard as well."

Charlie stiffened, and a hot retort sprang to his lips, but he bit it back as the memory returned of lying under the tree hearing the bellow of the bull. He'd been more than a little stupid that day, and if Buddy was right, his actions had gone a long way to hurting Leah more than anything Harding could do. Besides, there was also the matter of Leah's ma. He suppressed a shudder and shoved that incident to the back of his mind. He couldn't think about that right now. Tackling one issue at a time was the best he could do.

Leah kicked a rock out of the way. "I'm not sure what to believe. All these years of being so certain of facts—it's a lot to take in."

Her gaze traveled to Steven's hands, remembering the seconds before she'd opened her eyes in the bunkhouse. She had felt his light touch as he'd brushed a strand of hair from her face, but she'd kept her eyes closed for several long heartbeats, trying to control her breathing.

No man had ever touched her with such tenderness, and no man had ever stirred her senses the way Steven did. Strange that this was the first thing she thought of, rather than the gibberish her brother spewed.

She wrenched her thoughts away. This was no time for sentimental foolishness, no matter how kind and handsome the man.

What would have made Tom say all those things? Leah wanted to believe it was all a lie. She had even accused Tom of purposely causing trouble in their family. But hearing Steven voice the question made her reconsider.

She'd never known her brother to deliberately lie, but she hadn't seen him for six years. A lot could change in that time. He'd grown from a boy to a man, and she suddenly realized she didn't have an inkling what kind of man he'd become.

"You asked if my brother might have lied. Honestly, it would be so much easier to believe that than to accept what he had to say. But no matter what, I'll get to the bottom of this."

"I hope you won't be offended if I ask, but you believed your mother died when you were fourteen?"

Sadness mingled with bitterness, and she nodded. "There's a grave site up on a knoll with her name on a marker. I've sat there for hours and hours these past nine years. I can't believe it's all been a lie."

Steven walked silently beside her, his presence bringing a quiet comfort.

"I shouldn't burden you with this. I'm sorry."

"It's not a burden. I wish I could help in some way." He waited for her to precede him up the porch steps to the house.

"It's been a help having someone else to talk to." She mustered a smile. "Now we need to find something to eat and see if I can talk some sense into my brother before he wreaks havoc with Pa."

Tom wilted under the weight of the heavy rucksack. Why hadn't he taken the time to fill his canteen from the springhouse before stomping away from the ranch? Or, better yet, he should have put aside his guilt-ridden feelings and stormed to the house to confront his father. It shouldn't surprise him that the man had continued feeding Leah a lie all these years.

But something else hurt almost as much. His sister had called him a liar. He'd hoped she, at least, would be happy to see him and understand what he'd been through. That she might stand beside him and put the ghosts of their past to rest. Anger drove spiked tendrils deeper into his heart. He didn't need her. In fact, he didn't need anybody. Even when he lived with Ma, he'd still been second-best. She'd spent so much of her time talking about Leah that Ma barely noticed him.

And all those letters. His gut twisted in shame. He needed to hold on to his anger. Feed it so he'd remember that Leah came first in everyone's life, and he hadn't mattered.

Leah. Always the perfect daughter who could do no wrong. He'd often wondered what the real reason was that Ma had left

Leah behind. Every time he'd tried to ask she'd shut him up or changed the subject, as though she had something to hide. Was it possible there was more than her guilt over abandoning her first-born? And why hadn't she returned to the ranch to get Leah if it troubled her so?

After she'd extracted the promise from him, she'd mumbled a few words he couldn't quite catch—words that didn't make sense no matter what direction he turned them. "Don't forget ... Leah ... box ..."

It wasn't possible she could know about the box of letters he'd hidden. His heart felt as though it had shriveled inside his chest. He'd been so careful to keep them hidden. The one time he'd caught her starting to sweep under his bed he'd asked that she never enter his bedroom again. A man needed his privacy. He hadn't quit shaking for hours after she'd left.

A resonating bark somewhere behind him slowed Tom's steps. Rusty hadn't been even two years old when Tom had left for Portland, but he'd hoped the dog would remember him. Funny that he'd felt such a sense of loss and almost betrayal when the dog had growled at his arrival. No one cared that he'd returned home.

It would've been better to stay in the city and shut the door on this life completely. But that wouldn't satisfy his need. Only return-ing and making Pa see that he mattered would do that.

His gut twisted yet again as more memories rushed in. But these went farther back, to a time when life was uncomplicated and their family intact. To a time when he still believed in loyalty and love. He pushed them away, annoyed that his brief contact with his sister would raise so many tender emotions.

Another bark, closer this time, brought him to a stop. Slowly Tom pivoted, his heart thumping. Rusty stood a few yards away, poised and attentive, his head cocked to one side.

Tom placed his bag carefully on the ground, not wanting to startle the dog. He puckered his lips and gave a soft whistle, two short and one long, a signal he'd taught the pup over six years ago. "Rusty? Don't you remember me, boy?" Once more, he tried the whistle, and the dog's tail moved, then started to wag with a vengeance. "Come on, Rusty." Tom patted his thigh and whistled again.

The dog bolted forward and leaped at Tom, his body quivering. Rusty jumped up and placed his paws on Tom's chest, then licked his face.

"All right, all right. Down, boy." Tom chortled with joy, his hands shaking as he dug them deep into the dog's fur. "I'm glad to see you, too."

He looked at his bag and then back toward the house, far enough down the road to only be a speck in the distance. "I can't believe you trailed me all the way out here. What do I do now?"

Rusty whined and trotted toward the ranch, then stopped and looked back, ears on the alert. He whined again and took another step, then gave a gentle yip.

Tom grimaced and shook his head. "I'm not so sure that's a good idea, fella. You're the only one who wants me there. I was going to stay in town." He stuffed his hand in his pocket and pulled out a small wad of bills, then shoved them back into his trousers. "Although I'm not crazy about wasting what little money I have on a hotel when I have a perfectly good room at the house."

He emitted a sharp laugh. "Although I can't see anyone chomping at the bit to offer it to me." He moved forward and stroked Rusty's head, trying to muster a smile. "All right. Let's go home—or at least, let's go visit what used to be home."

Chapter Seventeen

Leah set her empty milk glass on the table, content with the sandwiches and canned applesauce Millie had served, but still mystified at where her brother might have gone. "Thanks so much, Millie. I appreciate you putting something together for Steven and me."

"Anytime. I already fed Buddy and Charlie. I've got fresh gingerbread hot out of the oven. Soon as Buddy gets here, I'll serve it." She stepped to the window and pushed aside the curtains, then lowered her voice. "I'm sorrowin' that Tom hasn't come to the house yet. What do you think is keepin' him?" She shot a look toward the stairwell. "You told your pa about Tom?"

Leah shook her head. She didn't blame Millie for whispering. She was almost ashamed of the relief she'd felt when they'd walked in and discovered her brother hadn't arrived. "I figured Tom would let Pa know, and I wouldn't need to. I haven't seen Pa for the last few hours. How's his arm doing? Still paining him a lot?"

Millie nodded. "Don't seem to be much better. I wonder if that doc set it proper." She turned to Steven. "You get enough to eat, Mr. Harding?"

Steven leaned back in his chair and grinned. "Plenty, Millie. And please call me Steven. I get enough of that Mr. Harding business at the bank. It's nice to be less formal out here."

"Sure enough works for me." She removed the plates and glasses from the table and set them next to the sink.

Footsteps thudded down the inner staircase at the same time someone tapped at the front door. Leah stiffened, then bolted from her seat and raced down the hall. She had to get to the door ahead of her father. The hinges creaked as the door opened. She froze a few steps from the base of the staircase, waiting for the roar she knew was coming.

"What in tarnation!" Her father's bellow from several feet behind Leah filled the house and sent a shiver down her spine. "What you doin' here, boy?"

"Hello, Pa. Happy to see me?" Tom's booming voice echoed through the house.

Millie let out a shriek. "Thomas Pape! Is that you, boy? Let me get my hands on you."

Leah stopped at the edge of the entry, sensing Steven behind her. Millie dashed past them, tears rolling down her weathered cheeks. She skidded to a halt.

Tom turned his gaze from his father, and his frown evolved into a wide grin. "Millie! Do I get a hug?"

She huffed. "Now that you tax me about it, I'm not so sure if I'm goin' to hug you or spank you." She looked him up and down, and her face softened. "Guess you're too big to spank, so it'll have to be a hug." Opening her arms wide, she stepped forward, and Tom almost flew into them.

Leah swallowed a hard knot in her throat before glancing at her father. Not a scrap of delight on his face. If anything, the glower deepened.

Steven touched her shoulder, and Leah jumped. "Sorry to startle you. It's nice to see Millie give him such a welcome."

Leah pivoted and tried not to glare. "You're implying I didn't?" She ground the words out between clenched teeth.

"I'm not saying anything of the kind," he murmured. "It's obvious your father isn't too happy, and I know your brother has been contrary. I'm simply glad to see Millie happy he's here."

Leah tried to relax as irritation prickled her skin. "If you'll remember, I tried to give him the same welcome, but he couldn't bother to receive it." She dropped her voice to a whisper, not caring to have Pa hear. "I have no idea why he's so standoffish with me. But I'll admit Millie always had a special place in her heart for Tom. She attended my mother at his birth."

Apprehensive, she peered at her silent father. Pa was even more dangerous when quiet than when he roared. Reaching out, she tugged at his sleeve. "Pa? Want to come in the kitchen for coffee?"

He shook her hand off. "When Millie's done blubberin', I'll speak my mind."

Millie's head turned, and she swiped at her damp cheeks with the corner of her apron. "I'm not blubberin', Charlie Pape. I got the right to spill a few tears over the prodigal son comin' home, don't I?"

Charlie cradled his arm in the sling. "He ain't no prodigal returnin' home. And don't you go gettin' any notions about killin' a calf and fixin' up a fancy meal."

Millie cocked a brow. "You know about the prodigal son? I didn't think you ever read the Bible."

"Of course I do. I ain't a complete heathen, if you all think I am. But it don't matter, 'cause I ain't plannin' on changin' my mind."

Their cook scowled. "It's your calf, so I guess I got no say in whether you want to butcher one or not. But it's my kitchen, and I've got hot coffee perkin'. No sense in the entire family standin' here when we could sit."

She motioned toward the back of the house. "Come on." She pivoted and clomped down the hall.

Mirth welled from the pit of Leah's stomach, but she knew better than to let it escape. Millie was the only person she knew who could stand up to Pa like this and get away with it. But Pa was in no mood to be trifled with. She could only pray he'd come to his senses and allow Tom to stay.

Strange that she'd feel that way after all the things Tom spouted earlier. She didn't doubt that Ma was dead, but she still couldn't believe what he'd said. But one thing she knew. She planned to learn the truth now that he was home, and not even Pa would stop her.

Steven edged toward the door. It was time he got out of here and back to the bunkhouse. He gripped the knob and inched open the door, hoping Leah wouldn't try to stop him. Stepping outside, he almost collided with Buddy. He attempted to sidestep, but the older man grabbed his arm.

"Hold on there, son. What's the hurry? Thought I saw someone coming up the lane with a bag slung across his back, but my old eyes aren't what they used to be. He stop at the house?"

Steven nodded. "He did, at that, and your wife informed everyone they should come to the kitchen for coffee."

Buddy peered at him. "Then why you slipping away instead of joining us? And who was the feller?"

"It was Tom Pape, Leah's brother."

Buddy jerked as if shot. "I know who Tom is. You say he came home?"

"Uh-huh."

"That don't answer why you're leaving." Buddy clamped a firm grip on Steven's elbow and propelled him across the threshold and into the entry, then drew the door shut behind him.

"Guess I figured this is time for the family to get reacquainted," Steven hedged. "I'm not family."

"Sure you are. You live here, eat your meals with us, and work side by side with us when you aren't at the bank. That makes you family. If Millie said everyone should come for coffee, that includes you. Let's go."

Steven wasn't sure if he should duck out of the man's grip and dash for the door or go quietly into what he knew had the potential to be a difficult scene. All of a sudden, he knew. How could he abandon Leah after she'd collapsed in his arms less than an hour ago, especially after he'd seen her expression of horror as her father had bellowed at Tom? "All right. Another cup of coffee sounds good."

They trekked down the hall and paused in the doorway to the roomy kitchen, which held a round table and six chairs off to the side. The larger dining table was in the next room, but Millie often served the meals or snacks and coffee here when the group was small. Leah, Tom, and Charlie all sat at the table, avoiding one another's gaze, while Millie puttered between the stove and the table, carrying over mugs of steaming coffee.

Leah swiveled in her chair, her face showing relief. "Buddy, Steven, come take a seat. Millie's got fresh gingerbread."

Charlie glared at the two of them. "Don't you have work to do?"

Buddy grunted as he dropped into the chair. "'Course we do, but a man's got to take a break once in a while. I'm not passing up Millie's gingerbread. Besides, I wanted to say howdy to young Tom." He leaned across the table with his hand extended and his face solemn. "You've grown up some, young man."

Tom hesitated, then reached across and gripped Buddy's hand. "I suppose I have. Good to see you, Buddy."

"Same to you. What brings you home after six years? Or have you already hashed that out?"

Charlie thumped his palm on the table, making the coffee mugs rattle. "Nothin's been hashed out." He leveled his glare on Tom. "What you got to say for yourself, troopin' in like you belonged here?"

Steven winced at the harsh tone and cold words. Both his own father and his stepfather had been kind men, and it was hard to imagine what Tom must be feeling. Steven glanced at Leah, but she had her eyes fixed on her father.

Millie thumped a pitcher of cream down and sat. "I say we pray before we speak another ornery word."

Steven blinked at the blunt pronouncement, then hid a smile with his hand. He bowed his head but noticed Charlie still had his eyes open, shooting baleful looks at his son. Steven offered a silent prayer that God would bring reconciliation to this broken family.

After several moments Charlie cleared his throat. "All right, enough of this foolishness. It's not like we're eatin' a meal and need to bless it. Millie's gingerbread is good without a blessing."

Steven raised his head and met Leah's eyes. He gave her an encouraging smile, wondering what might be going through her mind. An answering smile flickered for an instant. If only there was something he could do to comfort her and help bring good out of this situation.

Millie hoisted the pitcher of cream. "It's fresh from the cow this mornin', and we got plenty, so help yourself."

The next several minutes passed in silence as the gingerbread was consumed and coffee was sipped. Steven didn't sense a hint of peace or comradeship settling over the family, but he wasn't going to try to escape again. Leah and Millie deserved that much. He planned to stay and ride this out whatever might come. And from the anger on Charlie's face and his untouched plate, he guessed that a storm was brewing.

"Let's have it. What you want comin' back here, boy?" Charlie settled stiffly back against his chair.

Tom shrugged and didn't meet his father's eyes. "Guess I figured I've been gone long enough."

"I'll say you have, but I didn't invite you. You figurin' on stayin' in town while you're here?"

"Pa!" Leah gaped at the man. "How can you suggest that?"

"Easy enough. Tom didn't give a fig what it would do to anyone when he took off. He did it without so much as a by-your-leave. I won't have him think he can waltz in like he ain't never been gone."

"But he's your son and my brother."

"He was once. He chucked his life here like it weren't any account. That don't set well with me, and it shouldn't with you, neither. That's not what family does, Daughter."

Tom pushed back his chair with a scrape of the legs against the wood floor. "What do you know about family? You drove Ma off and didn't care if I left or not. All you cared about was your ranch."

Charlie stared at his son, and Steven could see beads of sweat break out across the man's forehead. "Your mother is dead."

Steven shifted in his seat at the table. He didn't belong here. Going back to the hotel would be preferable to living on the ranch and being caught in the middle of this family war. He chanced a look at Leah. Her lips were firm, but tears shimmered on the edge of her lashes. His heart softened. Maybe, for Leah's sake, he could tolerate the situation for a few more days, anyway.

Leah's stare slid from her father to her brother, wanting to throttle them both. If what Tom claimed was true, she'd heard too many lies over the years, and she wanted it to end. "Pa, Tom told me about Ma, and it's different from what you've said."

Tom nodded. "She's dead now, but Ma was very much alive when she left this ranch nine years ago. You lied to Leah and everyone in town. You lied to Buddy and Millie. Ma left and you didn't care enough to stop her—for sure you didn't care enough to change."

Millie gasped and placed her fingers over her mouth, and Buddy muttered low under his breath.

Charlie sprang to his feet, then winced and grabbed his arm resting in the sling. "Enough! I refuse to discuss your mother." Red spread from his neck into his cheeks, leaving them splotched.

"Pa?" Leah touched his sleeve as dread roiled in her stomach, making her wish she hadn't eaten that piece of gingerbread. Still reeling from the revelations about her mother, she couldn't stand the thought that her father had lied to her. If only Pa would refute it all. Take them up to the knoll and somehow prove Ma was buried there.

Somehow, dealing with Tom telling untruths seemed easier than facing her mother's abandonment and her father's deception. "Please tell me the truth. I want to believe what you've told me for the past nine years. But what Tom said makes me wonder. Is it true that Ma didn't die, and she's not buried up on the knoll?"

He backed away, his eyes darting from Leah to Tom and back but refusing to meet Leah's gaze. "I ain't answerin' no more fool questions." He pointed Tom toward the door. "Now git on out of here! You didn't care to stay and help run this ranch, and I don't intend to give you a part of it now just because you decide to come crawlin' back home."

Tom stood and picked up his bag, but Leah dashed around the table and grabbed him. There had been too much loss—too much pain. As hard as it was to hear the things Tom had shared, she knew in her heart they must be true.

Leah still didn't understand his coldness toward her or why he'd chosen to return, but it didn't matter. He was her brother—her only blood relative still living. "I'm not going to lose you again. I don't care how hateful you're being to us, I still want you to stay." She didn't care that defiance toward her father's wishes oozed out of every word she'd spoken.

Tom studied her for a minute, then gave a slow nod.

Pa rocked on his heels. His eyes narrowed, and all Leah could hear was the ticking of the clock in the living room. "Fine, but he sleeps in the bunkhouse."

Millie shook her head. "We'll move out of his old room. He should be in the house where he belongs."

"I said the bunkhouse or nothin' at all." Charlie spit the words. "Don't you stand against me on this one, Millicent. I won't have it. You and Buddy belong in that room, and you will not give it up. Is that understood?"

"It is." She eyed Tom. "I'll take some clean beddin' out to the bunkhouse and make up a bed. There are plenty of towels and extra covers."

"Thanks, Millie," Tom murmured.

Leah looked from one to the other, not sure exactly how she felt about the arrangement. She'd blurted out that she wanted her brother to stay, then almost immediately regretted the words. He'd been cold and ornery, and she was certain he was keeping a secret.

She wasn't sure she could tolerate more poor treatment, but maybe having him stay wouldn't be such a bad idea, after all. She might be able to discover more about Ma's disappearance and why she'd left without saying a word.

"I think I'll go to my room now, if you'll all excuse me." She dipped her head toward Steven and barely acknowledged her brother or father. "Millie, call me if you need help, will you?" Turning, she worked to control her steps to keep from dashing up the stairs. She couldn't allow Pa or Tom to see the pain that was ripping her heart in two.

Charlie stood his ground, his eyes swiveling from his daughter disappearing up the steps to the son he'd given up as lost or dead—until some months ago when he'd gotten the letter from Tom. Mary was sick, and Tom wanted his help.

Charlie had grabbed a sheet of paper and dunked the pen in the ink pot so fast he'd almost spilled it, as cold fury gripped his innards. Help the woman who'd run off and left him, then lured his son to follow? His body ached, and sweat poured off his forehead as he penned the words. She could find someone else to nurse her. She'd made it clear it was no longer his job.

How was he to know she was dying? The boy hadn't told him. He'd never said how bad it was until after she'd died. Charlie had figured Mary was trying to work him, hoping to get back in his good graces and worm her way home. He wouldn't allow that, no sir. Not after the way she'd treated him.

Now a flood of remorse hit him that he'd not known how sick she'd been. If Tom had told him, things might have been different. He would have gone to her, tried to set things right. But the boy had waited until she'd died to send him another letter. Charlie straightened his shoulders and tried to shake off the guilt. He hadn't done anything wrong—at least, not knowingly. If he could go back and change the past, he would, in several places along the way, but that wasn't possible.

He pivoted toward his son, who'd stood silent these several long minutes. "You goin' to take a bed in the bunkhouse, boy? Or maybe you'd rather head back where you been livin'. You don't look fit to work a ranch. You're plumb soft."

Tom bristled as red suffused his face. "I worked to pay for my keep—and Ma's—for the past two years. When she took sick, she had to quit waiting tables at the restaurant, so I stepped in and took over her care." He reached for the doorknob. "As much as I'd love to go back to Portland, I think it might bring more satisfaction to stay right here." He turned his gaze on Buddy. "You mind going out with me?"

Steven stepped forward. "I need to head that way. I'll walk with you, if you don't mind. Of course, Buddy's more than welcome."

Buddy gave a curt nod. "Don't mind if I do. Millie, you might as well stay here and get your work done. Me and the fellas can make up the bunk for Tom." He waited while Millie handed him a stack of linens, grabbed his hat off a peg behind the door, and shoved it onto his head. He swung open the door and stalked out, the other two men on his heels.

The click of the door echoed in the quiet entry as Millie's footsteps receded down the hall. Had this whole blasted family turned against him? What had he done to deserve this kind of treatment? He was the one who'd been wronged. Mary had deserted their family. It wasn't any fault of his.

Sure, she hadn't been happy here, and she'd admitted she wasn't in love with him when he'd offered his hand in marriage. She'd been open about the fact that she still loved her dead husband, Leah's daddy, but that didn't give her the right to disappear out of their lives, did it? 'Course not. No good woman would do a thing like that.

But he'd spun a tale to the children, even to Buddy and Millie, hoping to spare them all the gossip and pain of her betrayal. No one in town knew Mary hadn't died and been buried in the family plot, and he was happy to let them keep thinking as much.

And if he'd had his way, they still wouldn't know. His pride had smarted enough when Mary informed him she wanted to leave— had never loved him, even when he'd tried so hard to please her over the years.

He'd worked to keep his temper and never to drink, knowing it worried her. Why, he'd even attended church with her when the children were young, before the ranch kept him so busy. A man who worked hard to provide for his family had earned the right to a bit of pride. But nothing he'd done seemed to soften her heart or draw her closer. Not even the birth of their son.

Charlie's arm throbbed as he walked into the sitting room and settled into a chair. Tom. He loved the boy. Always had. But he could tell Tom didn't feel the same. A man deserved to hold on to his pride, didn't he? Why should it be his job to make things right between them? The boy had chosen to traipse off after his mother, not once caring that his pa might need him, might want him, might even love him.

Charlie leaned his head against the chair and closed his eyes. Maybe it was too late for happiness. Too late for forgiveness or making things right. He'd tried so many times to say the right words to Leah, but they always got stuck in his throat.

Vaguely he recalled things the preacher had said in church so many years ago. He'd talked a lot about forgiveness and the necessity to repent, but Charlie had never felt like much of a sinner with a need for God. Wasn't it mostly people who stole or cheated or killed who required forgiveness? He was like most men, from what he could tell—decent, hardworking, and honest, with a few things he'd done wrong over the years, but not what he'd call sins.

Would the hurt he'd caused his children qualify as a sin in God's sight? He hadn't intended to hurt them; it just seemed to happen. Surely God wouldn't fault him for that, would He, when it was Mary who deserted the family and left them all in a bad way? Tom had gone his own way, but Leah … he'd seen the confusion and pain in his girl's face.

Charlie maneuvered himself to his feet and paced across the room, the unhappiness within making it hard to settle. He didn't know what God thought or if He'd fault him or not. In fact, Charlie guessed he didn't rightly know much about God, one way or the other.

Charlie shivered, thinking about how close he'd come to meeting his Maker when that bull was about to charge. If it hadn't been for Leah, Buddy, and Harding, he'd be making his excuses to the Almighty before he was ready.

He gritted his teeth and rubbed his injured arm, wishing the throbbing would subside, but thankful he was alive and able to feel pain. Maybe he'd best think this repentance-and-forgiveness business through a little more. That is, if God or Leah were at all interested in hearing about it.

Steven walked beside Buddy but kept an eye on Tom Pape as he trudged ahead of them toward the bunkhouse, every inch of his frame exuding anger and frustration. Steven's emotions were divided where the young man was concerned. Part of him felt sorry for Tom after he'd seen the way Charlie had treated him, but another part wanted to shake some sense into him for upsetting Leah.

Buddy leaned close and dropped his voice. "You going to be all right rooming with the boy? He's lugging around a mighty big pile of anger and hurt right now. Might not make it too pleasant for you."

Steven shrugged. "I've dealt with worse. I'd like to see if I can help him, although I'm not sure he'd listen to me."

"I reckon that would make Leah happy." He wagged his head. "She's had a lot to deal with the past few months, what with Charlie's drinking and then him getting hurt." He shot a sly glance at Steven. "I've noticed she perks up right smart when you're around."

Steven wanted to laugh at the absurdity of the notion. Perks up? Not hardly. More like she found reasons to bristle or run whenever he came around.

But there was no point in belaboring the point. "I'll tell you, Buddy. I'd do about anything in my power to make Leah's life easier and take some of the stress off her shoulders, but I'm not certain she'd welcome my interference. Of course I'll be kind to Tom and help if I can, but I doubt Leah will notice."

"If you think that, you're not as smart as I figured you for." Buddy picked up the pace as Tom stepped onto the porch of the bunkhouse and opened the door. "Come on, let's see if we can calm the boy down and mend some fences."

He tossed a grin at Steven. "I'd also suggest you open your eyes and ears when you're around Leah. Sometimes you got to wade through her redheaded stubbornness, but once you do, you'll find a treasure trove of caring beneath her prickly exterior."

Steven stifled a laugh, not wanting to hurt the older man's feelings. Prickly he could attest to, but caring? Sure, where her family was concerned. He'd keep his eyes open, but as much as he might long for it, somehow he doubted that the affection Buddy alluded to would spill over to include him anytime soon.

Chapter Eighteen

May 3, 1881

Frances pulled Katherine's buggy to a stop in front of the Pape home-stead. She had not spoken idly when she'd threatened to visit the man again after he'd broken his arm, but she hadn't planned on letting a week pass before returning. She set the brake on the buggy and stepped down, thankful her feet and ankles were doing so much better today.

She reached inside the buggy for the covered dish of apple dump-lings she'd baked that morning. It was the least she could do to help lighten the load for Millie. No doubt Charles Pape kept her scurrying from one thing to another, trying to keep up with his demands, leav-ing her little time for baking. Of course, she didn't really know the man, but from what she had seen of his testy personality, she surmised he'd be a difficult patient.

Frances knocked on the door and waited, then rapped again, harder this time. No answering footsteps inside, and the door remained closed. Surely Millie was home, or Leah would be about? It would be a shame to waste this fresh-baked dessert, and Katherine had plenty at home.

Frances twisted the knob and poked her head inside as she pushed the door open. "Hello? Is anyone at home?"

She stepped in and looked around. Everything was as neat and tidy as she'd expected. Not a speck of dust rested on the floor or furnishings in the entry or the living area beyond. Everything glowed.

What a nice, roomy house. The parlor opened from the entry, and Frances glimpsed a colorful rug at the far end of the room. Comfortable furnishings were tastefully placed, and artwork adorned the walls. She'd been so irritated with Charles Pape the last time she'd visited that she'd barely noticed her surroundings. She hadn't realized Leah had such an eye for color and design, although the girl had shown evidence of her cleverness when working on the quilts at the church.

If memory served her right, the kitchen was at the back of the house. She'd tiptoe back there in case Millie were resting and leave the dish for her to find. Moving past the staircase and down the short hall, she glimpsed two closed doors that must be bedrooms, then stepped into an attractive dining room with the kitchen beyond. "Millie? Leah?"

Frances waited a minute before slowly crossing the wood floor to stop beside the workspace next to the stove.

She placed the covered dish on the table, then scanned the room again. No fire burned in the kitchen stove, and there didn't appear to be any food waiting to be prepared for the evening meal. Where had everyone gone?

A deep-throated growl somewhere behind her made her heart jump nearly into her throat, and she whirled, wishing she'd brought her parasol to defend her from whatever beast might be ready to attack.

Charles Pape stood in the doorway, his good hand clinging to the door frame, and his eyes staring from his ashen face as though she'd walked straight out of the graveyard. "Where's my gun when I need it?" His roar ricocheted in the room.

Frances narrowed her eyes at the man. "Now, there is a nice welcome for you. Is that how you greet all of your guests?"

"You ain't a guest. You're an intruder come without permission or an invite." He drew back a half step. "What are you doin' here again?"

She smirked. "So you have your wits about you, I see—at least enough to remember me from my last visit. I must say I am gratified. As to what I am doing here, I brought Millie a pan of fresh apple dumplings. I might even allow you to have a serving if you behave yourself and stop shouting. I know Steven is visiting his family in town, but where are Millie and Leah, Mr. Pape?"

His nose wrinkled, and he shook his head. "It's Millie and Buddy's day off, but I'll be hanged if I know why Leah's not back."

"Mr. Pape! You will control your vulgar tongue in my presence, if you please. I do not hold with that kind of talk."

He scratched the patch of thinning hair above his ear. "What vulgar talk? I didn't say anything sinful. Besides, it's my house, and I'll say what I blasted—" He gave a deep sigh. "Beggin' your pardon, ma'am. My arm's been hurtin' somethin' fierce today. I didn't sleep much last night, either. I think Leah's takin' a walk." He glanced out the window above the sink. "How'd you get here, anyway, and how'd you get in the house without Rusty barkin'?"

"I assume Rusty is your dog? I did not see any animals other than the cattle and horses in the pasture when I arrived."

"Well, tarnation!" He shot her a glare. "And that ain't a bad word, neither. My pa used to say it all the time."

She tapped her foot on the floor. It had been a long time since she'd met a man with such ill manners as well as a poor vocabulary, but she would not dignify his remark with a reply.

He grunted. "Fine. It might not be the best word to use around a lady, but Leah and Millie don't complain. Why should you?"

"More than likely they have both given up trying to reform you. Would you stop speaking that way if they complained?"

He stared at her, then slowly shook his head.

"I did not think so. More is the pity that some men were not taught any manners as children." She stepped closer and motioned at his arm. "I am sorry your arm is giving you such trouble, Mr. Pape."

"Why do you have to keep callin' me 'mister'? I'm guessin' we're both of an age, so it's not like you're talkin' to an older gent. Nobody calls me Mr. Pape. Everyone calls me Charlie, other than Leah. Can't you say Charlie?"

Frances rolled her eyes. "Did you fall on your head as well as your arm? I am a lady, Mr. Pape, and I am not accustomed to calling a strange man by his Christian name. Besides, why should it bother you so much? We are not liable to form any type of friendship, so it will not be an issue for long."

His shoulders slumped, and his eyes darted to the side.

Frances stared, certain she had seen a glimmer of disappointment and … what? Sadness had surely been reflected there before Mr. Pape had shifted his gaze. Could the man actually want a friend, as she had when Wilma chose to befriend her, in spite of her prickliness?

Maybe she should test the waters before shutting the door entirely to the idea. "Or are we?"

His head jerked around. "Are we what? I got no idea what you're talkin' about. And I'll have you know, my head is fine."

"I think you do know, Mr. Pape. I was referring to the comment I made that we are not liable to form any kind of friendship. I believe in being blunt and speaking the truth, but I may have spoken too soon."

She tapped the toe of her shoe again. "Is your request that I use your Christian name an indication you would like me to visit again? If so, I would insist you watch your language and converse with the respect and dignity I am sure a man of your age and station can muster."

His words came out in a sputter before he formed anything intelligible. "My station? What in tarna—" A wave of pure frustration washed over his features. "I got no idea what you're yammerin' about, woman."

"Your station is your place in society. You are the owner of a large ranch and, I would assume, respected in the community." Her gaze intensified. "Or at least, I would think you might have been at one time in the past, before you took up with the cursed bottle. A man of your station should care how others perceive him. And if you want to completely ignore my original question, then so be it. I will not remain where I am not wanted. Good day, sir. I hope you enjoy the apple dumplings. Please give my regards to Millie and Leah."

She planted the tip of her boot on the floor and pivoted toward the door. The man was too mule-headed to listen to anything she had to say, no matter if it was designed to help elevate him in the community or in his own estimation. She would wash her hands of any efforts to reach out to him and make her way home.

"Wait." The word was almost a growl, but clear and distinct.

Frances hesitated, then slowly turned. "Yes, Mr. Pape?"

He winced but didn't squabble this time. "All right. You win. The fellas at the saloon respect me well enough, but most of them are idiots. I suppose it might be nice to carry on a decent conversation with a lady occasionally. If I promise to watch my language—or try to watch it—would you call me Charlie? 'Course, you could visit one more time if you'd have a mind to, but it's all the same either way."

She peered at him, trying to gauge his sincerity. He intrigued her. She had already been surprised twice while conversing with the man. It might be worth the effort to befriend him and see if there were more depths to be plumbed. "I suppose I could stop by one more time while you are recuperating, but I will not call you Charlie."

His face scrunched into a scowl.

She held up her hand. "Before you launch into some rambling harangue that you might regret, allow me to finish. I agree to call you Charles, and that will have to suffice. I am not in the habit of calling men, even friends, by their Christian names, but I will do so when visiting you during your convalescence. For that is what I will be doing, Charles—coming to offer comfort and companionship while you are unable to work. And I will come a third time and possibly a fourth, if all goes well."

Charles's eyes lit. "Can't make any promises about bein' a perfect gentleman, ma'am, but I'll surely work on it." He cocked his head to the side. "So what do you want me to call you?"

Frances startled and blinked. It had never occurred to her that he might want to call her anything but her surname. "Why, Mrs. Cooper, of course."

"So you don't claim a Christian name?" His smirk belied his innocent question. "Or maybe you think you're too good for the likes of me." The question was flat, almost without emotion, and he turned his head away.

"Not at all, Charles. I am sorry if it appears that way. But I think those types of liberties must be earned. You are the one insisting I call you Charles. I did not request that privilege, if you recall. Let us see what happens as time passes, shall we? And as you already know, my name is Frances."

He nodded. "All right, Mrs. Cooper. I'll abide by your terms, and we'll see how this thing goes. Now let's shake on it to seal the bargain." He wiped his hand on the front of his trousers and grinned, then extended it again. "And I didn't so much as spit on it before I offered to shake. Shows I'm tryin', don't it?"

She rolled her eyes but took his hand, giving it a firm shake. "That will remain to be seen, Charles; that truly remains to be seen."

Chapter Nineteen

May 4, 1881

Leah walked briskly up the path to the church, thankful this was quilting day, but battling guilt for deserting her family with so much turmoil going on at home. She eased inside the door, letting the gentle tranquility wash over her spirit.

Ever since Tom had arrived at the ranch, her nerves had been jumpy. Leah knew if she had stayed there trying to keep the peace between her father and brother for one more hour, she'd have happily throttled them both.

She walked the width of the sanctuary and entered the side room, glad everyone had arrived. Leah smiled as each expectant face turned in her direction. "Hello, ladies." She hung her shawl on a peg behind the door, then stood, drinking in the sight of her dearest friends, along with an infrequent visitor, Wilma Marshall. "How nice to see you, Mrs. Marshall."

The woman looked up from her work. "Frances told me I need to get out more, but I think she's just lonely for my company since I married Caleb."

Frances scowled. "You think too highly of yourself, my dear. Lonely, indeed. Why, I have plenty to keep me busy with Amanda,

Lucy, and Zachary, as well as helping with the household chores since Katherine is resting more."

Wilma rolled her eyes. "That's what you say, but we both know the truth."

Katherine smiled. "This is what I get to hear every day at home." She shot a look at her mother and Wilma, working side by side on the quilt. "But I wouldn't change it for the world."

Leah walked toward Katherine. "I'm surprised to see you. It looks like that baby could arrive any day."

"I wish. The doctor says it could be another week or two." Katherine rubbed her protruding abdomen. "I wouldn't be opposed to an earlier arrival, though, if she's eager to join us."

"Still claiming it's a girl, hmm?" Leah grinned. "I'm voting with your mother that it's a boy."

Frances snorted her approval from the far side of the quilting frame. "Exactly what I have been trying to tell her. I think my daughter is simply unwilling to get her hopes up that she might have a son."

Katherine sighed. "At this point I won't be disappointed no matter what. I'm more than ready to meet this little one."

Ella shifted Missy to her hip. "As long as it's healthy, that's what matters. Missy is sleepin' through the night now. Matt and me are so grateful."

Hester Sue nodded. "That's right." She plunged her needle through the quilt fabric before glancing up. "Speaking of staying healthy, we need to pray for Virginia. She's been fighting a cold for the past couple of weeks and feeling right poorly."

Leah moved to her place beside the quilting frame. "I'm sorry to hear that. I'll try to run by and see her one day this week, if you think she's up to it?"

"I'm guessing she'd be mighty pleased ta have the company. I took her a pot of stew the other day and some baked goods. She thought she might try to come today, but I told her she'd best stay home and rest. Neither Katherine nor Missy should be around someone what's sick."

Katherine got awkwardly to her feet and shuffled to a stool beside Leah. "I'll work for a few minutes, but if this little one starts kicking too hard, I might stop. I've had more energy today, but my back's been aching more than normal."

Hester Sue peered at Leah from the far end of the quilt. "Heard tell your brother came home. How's your pa taking it, and how you holding up?"

A lump formed in Leah's throat at the sympathetic tone. "Pa's not any happier about it now than he was the day Tom returned. I try to stay clear of both of them, but it's not easy." She ran her needle through a brightly colored square and started to edge it. How much should she say? She trusted these women completely, but would it dishonor her father to speak her concerns? It had been so hard these past few days, not having anyone to talk to. Millie would understand, she was sure of it, but she didn't want to put the older woman in the middle.

"Can I ask you all a question?"

Heads nodded. Frances broke the silence. "Of course, we cannot promise to have all the answers, but we will certainly listen."

Leah smiled, suddenly glad that Katherine's mother had joined their quilting group. The woman could be stern and opinionated, but she had a caring heart. "That's more than enough, although I wouldn't mind if you pray for the situation as well. I'm wondering if any of you knew my mother well?"

Frances pursed her lips. "I cannot help you there. Wilma and I both arrived in town within the past year." She directed her attention to the rest of the group. "Ella, you're too young to have known her well, but, Hester Sue, you've been in Baker City the longest. Were the two of you friends?"

Hester Sue shook her head. "Sorry to say, we weren't. I seen her at church from time to time, but we weren't friendly. Virginia was, though. I think she and your ma spent time together once in a while. What you hoping to find out, hon?"

Leah sucked in air, needing to fortify herself. She wasn't even sure she should tell these friends, but the pressure of bearing so much alone had become too hard to handle. "Tom claims Ma didn't die when Pa said she did." There. Relief flooded her heart. The words were out, even if they had almost choked her to speak them.

Wilma snipped off another length of thread and held her needle up to the light, squinting at the tiny hole. "You mean he got the date wrong?"

"No. Pa told me and Tom nine years ago that Ma died, and that she's buried up on the knoll behind our house. Tom says that's not true, and she died just before last Christmas."

Stunned silence blanketed the room, and all eyes fixed on Leah. She moistened her lips and waited, unsure what else she should add.

Frances took off her thimble and tossed it into the nearby basket, her hands trembling. "And how would your brother know this?"

"He's been living with her since he ran away from the ranch six years ago—or so he says."

Katherine touched Leah's arm, and concern shone from her eyes. "Do you believe him? Is there a chance he's lying? And if not, why would your father lie to you all these years?"

Leah pushed the pain aside, not willing to give in to the emotions assaulting her. "I'm not sure. Tom hints at Pa driving Ma away, then keeping it hidden because of his pride. I'm not sure what to think."

Her friend gave her a hug. "Did you ask your father about it?"

"He refuses to discuss it. When I tried, he got angry and stomped out of the house. That's why I hoped one of you might have known her well and be able to tell me more."

Frances tapped her toe, making a soft clicking noise. "I've noticed your father's pride often manifests itself in boastful talking. Are you certain your brother is telling the truth? It is hard to believe your father would tell you an outright lie."

Leah threw up her hands. "At this point I'm not certain about much of anything, but I want to know what happened. It's so hard not knowing if Ma deserted us and lured Tom away—and, if so, why Pa kept it a secret."

Frances looked thoughtful. "Might he have been hoping to protect you from the pain of learning the truth?"

"I wish I knew, Mrs. Cooper. He won't answer any questions."

"You oughta talk to Virginia," Hester Sue urged her kindly. "I can't say for sure, but she probably knows more than the rest of us."

Leah poked her needle into the fabric and left it there. "Good idea. Maybe I'll stop by on the way home and see if she feels well enough to chat. I'm not sure I want to go home and face Tom and Pa without a better understanding of what's going on."

Katherine suddenly clutched Leah's arm and gasped. Her grip tightened. "Oh dear." Her other hand pressed itself low to her belly, and she moaned.

Leah wrapped her arm around Katherine's shoulders, her heart racing. "What's wrong? Is it the baby? Do you need the doctor?"

Katherine nodded. "I guess I should have stayed home today. I think this baby has decided she's going to make an appearance sooner than I expected."

Leah walked down the hall of the first floor of Katherine's boardinghouse, tired but incredibly happy. She'd witnessed the birth of dozens of calves and colts over the years, but that paled in comparison to the miracle of the birth of Katherine and Micah's baby. Of course, Katherine and the doctor did all of the work, but Leah had toted water basins and towels and been available for whatever the doctor might need.

Longing swept her as she continued to hear Micah's quiet voice murmuring words of affection to his wife. The look of joy and love on the man's face when he'd stepped into the room all but caved Leah's resolve not to cry.

She yearned for that kind of tenderness, and maybe even a child of her own one day. An image of Steven's caring eyes swam before her blurred vision, and she curled her fingers into her palm. What she wouldn't give to have him look at her the same way Micah looked at Katherine.

But why would he? All she'd done was to show him her bristly side since he'd arrived at the ranch, and now she knew exactly what caused her to do so. The trust on Katherine's face when she looked at Micah was absolute. She knew without a doubt that her husband would always be there for her—would cherish her and care for her no matter what came their way.

With all the turmoil hitting Leah these past few weeks—coming from her father, and then her brother, and now discovering her own mother might have betrayed her—she didn't feel as though she could fully trust anyone ever again.

With a mighty effort she shook free of the depressing thoughts and pasted on a pleasant expression, determined to drive Steven from her mind. Even if he were interested in her, it wouldn't be fair to ask him to step into the muddle her life had become.

As she halted in the doorway of the parlor, a sea of faces turned her way. Katherine and Micah's three children, Lucy, Mandy, and Zachary, along with Wilma and Caleb Marshall and Beth and Jeffery Tucker, all moved toward her at once. She held up a hand and smiled. "Hold on. I don't have much energy left, and I don't care to be trampled. If you'll all sit down, I'll answer your questions."

Mandy tugged on her skirt and looked up with wide eyes. "Do I have a baby sister? When can I hold her?"

Lucy reached out and drew her sister onto her lap. "Shh, let Miss Carlson talk."

Leah smiled at the eager young faces. "You'll get to hold your baby brother instead, Mandy. Is that all right?"

A whoop exploded from Zachary as he shot to his feet. "I have a brother! Pa and I won't have to be the only men in the family anymore."

Lucy glared at him. "And what exactly is wrong with women?"

He opened his mouth to reply, but Leah shook her head. "Hold it, you two. How about being happy the baby is here, and he and your ma are healthy? As far as when you can hold him, that will be up to your parents." She glanced around the room. "I can tell you that he has a bit of blond fluff for hair, his face is red, and he's about yea long." She held her hands apart about the width of her shoulders. "He's strong and has a good set of lungs, and your mother is feeding him. But we'll all need to be quiet so your mother can rest."

Wilma nodded. "I agree. Beth, Lucy, and I will take care of preparing the meal. I know we pay to live here, but Katherine will want Frances and Mr. Jacobs with her for the next few hours." She raised her brows at the two young women. "Shall we head to the kitchen, girls?"

Lucy set Mandy off her lap and stood. "Sure, but I'm going upstairs first to see if Pa will bring the baby to the door so we can see him." She looked at Zachary and her little sister. "I'll call you if he says it's all right."

Zachary spun toward Leah. "What's his name?"

Leah shook her head. "They need to tell you that, not me." She stood in the parlor as each person headed in various directions. A sense of loss replaced the earlier excitement. This wasn't her home or her family. Hers were all at the ranch, probably still bickering or, worse yet, refusing to talk to one another.

As happy as she was for Katherine and Micah, she longed for a husband and child of her own. Ever since her mother had died—or left, as the case may be—Leah had poured her heart and life into the ranch. Seeing Katherine holding her new baby boy only emphasized Leah's loneliness.

Would she ever get the chance to experience holding a child in her arms who belonged to her? And would she be a good mother if it happened? She still found it hard to take in that her own mother had deserted her at a time when Leah had needed her most.

A shudder shook her body. What if she lost interest in her son or daughter before they were grown? Had she disappointed Ma somehow and made her want to leave? Tom claimed that Pa had been the cause, but what if her behavior as a child contributed to her mother's desertion? Her heart turned over at the idea, but she could think of no other reason Ma would leave her behind.

Someone touched her arm, and Leah jumped. "Oh, Beth, I didn't hear you come back in."

The young woman smiled and took a step back. "Forgive me. Were you thinking about Katherine and the baby?"

"I suppose I was, in a way." Leah shook off the last remnants of melancholy. "I would venture to guess you'll be a wonderful mother when it's your turn."

Beth's cheeks colored, almost matching the deep rose of her gown. "Jeffery and I are hoping that might happen, but it's early yet. Will you stay for supper?"

Leah smiled. "I'm afraid not. When I left the ranch for the quilting meeting, I assumed I'd be home in time for dinner. Millie is probably fit to be tied that I haven't shown up. I'm surprised they haven't come looking."

A movement out the parlor window caught Leah's attention. "It looks like I spoke too soon."

Beth peered in the direction Leah pointed, then clapped her hands. "It's Steven! It's been too long since he's visited." Her smile dimmed. "Are you upset that he came?"

Leah worked to produce another smile. She wasn't exactly upset. But Steven's appearance simply emphasized her feelings of being alone. More than once since he'd arrived at the ranch she'd allowed her thoughts to swing to him, wondering if they might have a chance at a real friendship. Now she realized how much more she wanted than friendship.

But as kind and helpful as Steven had been, he was a city man at heart. He worked in a bank and enjoyed being around people. He'd even admitted he'd grown up on a farm, but from what she could discern, he'd chosen to leave.

No matter how much her heart was drawn to him, she couldn't allow herself to become interested in someone who didn't share the same goals and desires she had—or who might leave when he tired of working the land. Look what had happened when Pa had tried to keep Ma tied to their ranch.

"Leah?" Beth touched her hand. "Is anything wrong?"

"I'm sorry." Leah worked to corral her thoughts. "I must have been gathering wool again."

The hearty cry from the baby drifted down the hall, interrupting her need to answer Beth's inquiry further. "It sounds like Baby Jacobs is awake."

Beth nodded. "Can you share his name with me?"

Leah bobbed her head. "I don't think Katherine would mind. They wanted to tell the children themselves. They named him Trent, after Katherine's father. Trent Micah Jacobs. A good, strong name, don't you think?"

"Indeed it is." Beth slipped her fingers through the crook of Leah's elbow. "Now let's welcome my brother and see if we can convince him to stay for supper. There's no need to rush back to the ranch now that he knows you're safe."

But it was difficult for Leah to even enjoy this moment with her new friend. Her entire world had tipped sideways with Tom's arrival, the revelation of her mother's betrayal, and her father's lies. She clenched her hands in the folds of her skirt, wondering if she'd ever feel safe from betrayal again, even with Steven.

Chapter Twenty

May 5, 1881

Leah strode up the path to Virginia's inviting cottage as the memory of the women's comments from yesterday's quilting session beat in her ears. Virginia had known her mother years ago, and if anyone would have information, it would be the older woman.

More than one young woman had gone to Virginia for wisdom and advice over the years, and it was very possible Ma had as well. Leah's stomach felt queasy that she might learn something to confirm that her mother hadn't cared and purposely left her and Pa alone.

She shifted the package of freshly baked bread to the crook of her elbow and rapped on the door.

Virginia swung wide the door, every hair in place and looking her normal tranquil self, although her eyes appeared tired. "Leah, how good to see you, dear. Can you come in and stay for a chat?" She stepped aside and moved back a pace.

Leah held out the bread. "Yes, thank you. I heard from the ladies that you've been feeling poorly, and Millie and I thought you might enjoy fresh bread." She moved into the cozy living area, noting the clean, tidy appearance of the hardwood floors and colorful rugs gracing the center of the room.

Virginia stopped beside her. "The bread smells lovely. Thank you. May I cut you a slice and bring you a cup of tea? The kettle is on, and it's ready to pour."

Leah nodded. "That would be nice, but I don't want to put you to any trouble."

"Nonsense. I'm much better today, and my eyes are tired of reading, anyway. I'm ready for a nice chat. Please, take a seat, and I'll be back in a moment."

She waited until Leah sat in a chair near the one she'd vacated and then hurried from the room, returning a short time later with a tray of cups, a teapot, a plate of sliced bread, and what appeared to be a honey pot. After setting the tray on the low table near Leah's knees, Virginia poured the tea and handed a cup to Leah.

"Thank you. I must be honest. There's a personal reason I came to see you." She took a sip of the tea.

Virginia inclined her head but didn't speak. A grandfather clock struck the hour.

Leah set her cup on the tray and sighed. "I want to ask what you remember about my mother. You knew her well, didn't you? Hester Sue thought Ma visited you years ago."

"She did occasionally."

"Were you close?"

Virginia's forehead wrinkled; then she gave a slight shrug. "Not terribly. I'm not sure anyone was close to your mother. She didn't share her heart much, I'm afraid."

"I thought maybe …" Leah hesitated, then rushed forward. "Maybe she might have told you the truth, about why she left us."

Virginia peered at Leah before setting her cup carefully on her saucer. "Left you? Child, it's my understanding your mother died. Whatever do you mean?"

Leah blew her breath out, relief surging through her and almost leaving her weak. "So you didn't know all these years that she was alive? You haven't been keeping it from me?"

"I'm afraid I don't know what you're talking about, but believe me when I tell you that there's nothing I've been keeping from you concerning your mother. Now what is this all about?"

Leah's hands shook. Finally, she poured out the story of what she'd learned from Tom.

Virginia sat quietly and listened, her face creasing in sorrow and then in sympathy as Leah concluded. "I'm so sorry, dear. I wish I had known. Maybe I could have talked to her and helped her find peace in the midst of her struggles. Barring that, I would have tried to keep in touch with her and urged her to return, to give your father another chance. Do you have any idea why she left him—and you? Did Tom give you any hint?"

Leah shook her head. "Not really. He implied that Pa had driven her away, but that could be due to his own anger toward Pa."

"What does your father have to say?"

"He refuses to discuss it or answer any of my questions."

"I'm not surprised."

Leah tensed, her attention riveted on the older woman's face. "Why do you say that?"

"Mary, your mother, didn't talk much about Charlie or their relationship, but I remember her mentioning that his pride was all he had when they married—that he was a hard worker and mighty proud of the fact. I'm not sure exactly what she meant, but it's very possible that her leaving wounded him deeply. If his pride is involved, I can understand how he might not want to discuss it."

"What do you think she meant by 'all he had'?"

"I assume that he had few worldly goods when they married. I know he was a very hard worker after they married. I didn't know him before that time."

Leah leaned back in her chair. "That doesn't make sense. They had the ranch when they married. I've lived there for as long as I can remember."

"I wish I could tell you more, dear. I didn't meet your mother until you were several years old. I know she married Charlie when you were still a baby, but beyond that, I'm unsure."

Leah nodded. "Yes, I knew that, but I guess I never thought to ask for details. Thank you for sharing what you have, even if it's not what I hoped to learn."

She scooted forward, onto the edge of the chair. "And there's something you might not have heard yet that I can tell you. Katherine just had her baby—a boy! It appears Mrs. Cooper was right in her guess after all."

Virginia chortled, and the skin around her eyes crinkled. "I'm happy for Katherine, but I'm guessing Mrs. Cooper won't let her daughter forget that she guessed right any too soon. Tell me all about it, and don't leave out a single detail."

Steven stepped into the stirrup and settled onto the saddle on his gelding, but his mind wasn't on the cattle he needed to move. It was on the look of dismay he'd seen on Leah's face when he'd walked into the Jacobs' boardinghouse parlor, day before yesterday.

She'd done a masterful job cloaking it but not quickly enough. Why would his arrival evoke such a response? Could he have upset Leah and not realized it, or did it have to do with her brother?

Trotting hoofbeats thudded off to his right, and he turned his head, almost dreading who he'd see. Tom hadn't been the easiest person to bunk with since he'd arrived, although the younger man spent most of his evenings in town. It was all right with Steven, as they didn't have much in common beyond the work they accomplished.

The mare Tom sat astride slowed to a walk. "Thought you might be able to use a little help bringing them in." He gestured toward the acres of pasture that ended a half mile away at the base of a foothill and then frowned. "That is, if you want my help."

Steven forced a smile. He was a bigger man than this. There was no need to get worked up over having a little company on the ride, even if he was looking forward to time alone to think. "Sure. It'll speed things up if we work together."

They rode in silence for a while, trotting their horses side by side. Cattle dotted the expanse of green, and contentment warmed Steven's heart. How he'd missed the land. This wasn't the farming he'd grown up with, but he was away from the city and the constant barrage of people. He hadn't realized how much he'd longed for the solitude until recently.

"So why are you here, anyway? You after my sister?" Tom's blunt question jerked Steven out of his reflection.

He swiveled to face Tom, the blood pulsing through his ears. "I beg your pardon?"

Tom lifted a shoulder. "She's a good girl, and I care about her. I don't want to see any man fool with her heart if he doesn't mean to do right by her."

Steven opened his mouth to reply, then snapped it shut. Nothing but anger would escape if he didn't take a minute to cool down first. He drew in a long breath and allowed it to flow out through his nostrils. "I suppose I have a difficult time believing that, after the way you treated her when you arrived."

The young man bristled. "What's that supposed to mean?"

Steven pulled his horse to a stop and reined around to face Tom. "That you were downright unkind in the things you said about her mother—your mother—and wounded Leah deeply."

Tom's face paled. "That's not true. I was telling her about Pa. How he drove Ma off with his behavior and ornery ways. What call do you have to say I spoke unkindly to my sister? I love my sister and don't want to hurt her. I was telling her things about Pa—things she needs to know."

"You can't be that dense, Pape. You think it's all right to spill your guts about your mother leaving the ranch without so much as talking to her daughter or leaving a note? You truly believe that wouldn't hurt your sister?"

Tom fiddled with his reins. "She's seemed all right the past few days. Besides, she told Pa she wanted me to stay, so she couldn't be too mad, could she?"

Anger roiled through Steven's chest. He wanted to punch this cocky young rooster and then rub his face in the dirt until he understood what he'd done. After lifting a silent prayer heavenward for patience, he returned his attention to Tom. Could he really be that thickheaded, or was he simply insensitive to others' feelings?

"Why did you come back? So you could tell Leah all the hurtful things about her mother's past, or to get even with your pa somehow? Are you planning on running off and disappearing again once you've accomplished that goal?"

Tom stared at him, his face working. Whether with grief or anger, Steven couldn't tell. He pulled his hat off and slapped his leg, making the dust fly, then shoved it back onto his head. "Who are you to question me? You're not my pa or my boss, and I don't have to listen to this. I guess you're on your own with the cattle."

Steven sat his mount without moving and kept his eyes on the receding rider as he cantered across the meadow. Not toward home, but straight for town. He shook his head and clucked to his gelding. He probably should have kept quiet and not stirred things up, but he certainly wouldn't stay silent any longer. Charlie had simmered in his own stew of emotions since his son arrived and didn't seem to notice the hurt his daughter waded through. Somebody needed to care, and Steven guessed it ought to be him.

Leah had about all she could tolerate of her wishy-washy brother. First Tom arrived all cold and standoffish. Then he decided to stay and make her life miserable. Every time she thought he was starting to thaw and treat as like he had when they were children, he presented another side of his personality—cold, silent, morose, or all three.

Then there was the occasional smile that seemed to escape without his permission or the laughter that rang out when he thought she wasn't close by.

Thankfully, he'd ridden out after Steven to help gather cattle, so she had a couple of hours to herself. She should be with them, but it wasn't a big job. Only a handful of cows with their calves remained unbranded, and those had been sighted not far from the ranch.

She gathered her skirt above her ankles and struck out across the meadow, intent on getting as far from the menfolk as possible. Pa wasn't much easier to get along with, although she had to admit he'd slowed down on his drinking since Frances Cooper had come to visit.

Leah hopped over a rabbit hole and skirted around a stand of brush. Why Mrs. Cooper bothered with Pa, she couldn't understand. The last time she came she'd spoken about doing her Christian duty, but she couldn't imagine what good Mrs. Cooper would do.

A bird sang from a branch overhead, trilling with almost exuberant joy. Leah stopped under the tree and looked up, but the bird flew to a higher limb and commenced to scold her for trespassing. Stripping a willowy branch off the tree, she absently flicked at the tips of the long grass as she waded toward the top of the knoll. If only her life could be so simple and basic.

But then there was Steven Harding. She still hadn't figured him out. One day she was certain he was ready to hightail it back to town and wash his hands of ranching. The next, he was excelling at the work she gave him and doing it with a smile.

Why were men so hard to understand—or, more to the point, so hard to live with? And men complained about women. Ha! She swung her slender whip and clipped off the top of a weed, feeling quite satisfied with the action.

Leah trudged up the hill until she reached the crest. She slowed her steps and allowed her eyes to roam over the countryside ahead of her. It had been years since she'd been up here. Nine, as a matter of fact. It had been summer, and the wild daisies were in full bloom.

A week before Ma died.

She drew in a long breath and blew it out hard.

Before Ma ran away.

Everything in her life came back to that one pivotal point. She still found it hard to believe. Ma had loved her. She'd been sure of it. She had counted on the memory of that love to get her through so many difficult times with Pa and the lonely days without Tom. Couldn't God have left her at least one anchor to hold on to? Did everything have to be stripped away?

Leah shaded her eyes and studied the wide expanse of the ranch. She'd almost waited and asked Steven if he wanted to accompany her to the top of the hill. He could have seen the beautiful view and maybe come to better appreciate the ranch.

But she'd decided against it. This first trip must be made alone. She'd avoided this hilltop for years, but now she had to face the memories.

Not much had changed—but everything had changed.

Everything that mattered.

It was the same hillside, the same view looking down toward town, with the towering Wallowa Mountains as a backdrop. But nothing had ever been the same since the day Ma had gone. The sun shone in a cloudless sky, and a warm breeze stirred the wisps of red curls that escaped the bow at the base of her neck.

She looked around, half expecting to see the white daisies with the rich yellow centers dotting the hillside, but it was still early. Memories threatened to swamp her. She'd sat near here, holding a special box in her hands, one that Pa had carved for her seventh birthday. Only very special things were to go in that box, he'd told her. Then he tickled her belly, kissed her cheek, and called her his precious little girl.

When had that affection and sparkle in his eyes disappeared? When had Pa grown morose and turned to the bottle instead of to his children's love?

When Ma died.

It was like something inside him had shriveled up and died as well.

She shuddered and shook her head, angry that she'd allowed herself to slip back into that lie. She'd never imagined her pa or ma as a liar, but that's what they were. Pa lied when he told them Ma had died.

Ma lied by running away and only telling Tom.

And Tom lied when he kept the secret for three long years before he, too, left without a word. Then he returned and tried to claim he'd left a note. She didn't believe it.

A pang rent Leah's heart, leaving it sore and throbbing. If Ma was still alive and she could talk to her, would Leah want to listen to whatever she might have to say? Maybe, if she could be assured her mother spoke the truth. Longing rose in her chest and threatened to choke her. She fought against the pain, but it wouldn't subside.

How could she still ache for a woman who'd deserted her without so much as a word? She should hate her—never want to hear her name or think of her mother again. But she couldn't stem the tide of loneliness that threatened to drown her. It was worse now than when Ma left, if that were possible.

She turned in a slow circle, staring at the ground. How could she find the exact spot where she and Ma had buried the box, after so many years? It had been near the base of a tree.

She glanced over her shoulder and smiled. The single towering pine was only a dozen paces away. Leah moved in that direction, keeping her gaze trained a short distance before her, every step deliberate. She still didn't understand why she'd awakened this morning with such an urgent desire to see this place again—her and Ma's special place.

But there was no denying or escaping that desire.

One pace from the base of the tree, she tripped over a slight rise in the ground. She stopped, her heart thudding. The spot was no longer bare of weeds, and a number of new trees had sprouted in the vicinity, but she could still see the barely discernible rectangular outline under the surface of the dirt. Falling to her knees, Leah tugged at the grass and weeds, easily plucking them from their shallow home.

Leah's fingers touched the lid of the wooden crate her mother had used to house the keepsake box, then carefully removed the lid. She grasped the oilcloth wrapped around a smaller box and lifted it from the depths. Excitement stirred as she felt the firm outline of the carved treasure box beneath the folds of oilcloth.

She clearly remembered the last time Ma and she had sat here, looking at the items they'd placed in her memory box over a span of seven years. A curl from her first haircut. The first tooth she'd lost. A note a boy had given her at school. A faded ribbon she'd worn so many times it was ready to fall apart, but she couldn't stand to throw it away. Her favorite set of spurs that she'd outgrown as a young child.

Ma had gently wrapped the box in the thick folds of oilcloth and smiled. "You'll be a woman soon, Leah," she'd said. "I want you to come back here every birthday and look in this box. It will remind you of your life and those who love you. But I want you to be sure and come on your sixteenth birthday. No matter what happens between now and then, I want you to come. Will you do that for me, sweet girl?"

Leah had nodded, loving the cadence of her mother's voice. Ma was so beautiful, but that day her beauty had been marred by sadness. A shadow chased itself across her face and dimmed the bright light that usually shone in her eyes when they spent time alone.

But after Ma died—after she ran away—Leah hadn't come back. She'd been afraid to stir up the past, afraid of the pain that swamped her every time she thought about losing her mother. The box and its contents would only bring that rush of pain to the surface again.

So she'd stayed away.

Until now.

Slowly she unwrapped the box and stared at the ornate carving of a horse on the lid, wanting to delay the tide of emotion. Maybe she'd been foolish to come here again after such a long absence.

She traced the outline of the box with her fingertips. Somehow she'd forgotten how lovely it was. What a fine gift her father had given her so many years ago. She hadn't appreciated the craftsmanship as a child, hadn't realized the hours of love he'd poured into it, just for her.

Where had that father gone? The one who laughed and loved and cared? And why couldn't she get him back? Was Tom right? Was Pa bitter because his pride had been wounded? He'd pushed everyone away, drowning himself in liquor.

If only she could help. At times she got so frustrated she wanted to shake the man, but beneath his gruff exterior and drunken binges she still glimpsed a father who yearned to be what he had been in the past. He was the only father she'd ever known, even if they weren't related by blood. She prayed she could break through the walls he'd erected and show him the unconditional love that God spilled out on her.

She should have retrieved this box years ago and not left it so long. What a blessing that the heavy folds of oilcloth had protected it from moisture, as the outer container was beginning to rot. Leah lifted the lid, almost forgetting to breathe. A heavy sheet of folded parchment paper sat on top of the other items.

Leah plucked it out of the box and turned it over. Her name was written in her mother's clear, decisive script. Leah gasped and dropped the missive. When had Ma returned and placed this inside? And why had Leah waited so long to discover it?

Charlie grunted as Buddy halted the wagon in front of the board-inghouse where Frances Cooper lived, not sure he'd made the right decision in coming here. What if she thought he was sweet on her? Worse yet, what if she told him to skedaddle and leave her alone?

He ran his finger under his collar, trying to loosen the blamed thing before it choked him. "I changed my mind. Let's go home."

Buddy stared at him, then shook his head. "Can't go home now, boss. You know I got to go to the store for supplies. Millie will have my hide if I come back without everything on her list."

Charlie slumped against the high backboard. "I'll go along and help you load the wagon."

"Don't reckon that's a good idea either. Not with that busted wing you're still coddling."

Charlie almost wished he were a praying man. He could use the good Lord's help to get out of this spot.

The front door of the house opened, and a woman stepped out, clutching a large braided rug in one hand and a broom in the other. She took in the wagon and its occupants and stepped to the front of the porch. "Why, Charles Pape. I declare. What brings you out our way? Might you be here to talk to Micah or Jeffery?"

Buddy grinned and nudged him in the side. "Guess you oughta get out and go help the lady with her rug, boss. I'll pick you up soon as I finish Millie's shopping."

It seemed there was no help for it. Charlie climbed down from the wagon, panting from the pain that shot up his arm when he bumped it against the wheel. Keeping his head low, he trudged up the path toward the waiting woman.

What would she think when she discovered he'd come to see her, not one of the men? Maybe he'd visit with Jacobs or Tucker until Buddy got back, and she'd be none the wiser.

Mrs. Cooper stepped aside as his foot touched the landing at the top of the steps. "So, who have you come to see, Micah or Jeffery?"

Charlie raised his eyes to meet hers and froze. He couldn't lie to this woman. There'd been too many lies the past few years. Wasn't that what he'd decided as he lay in bed most of last night? But here he was again, considering spewing a passel of lies before the sun was three hours in the sky. He removed his hat and tucked it under his arm. "Neither, ma'am."

"Oh? Do you have a message for Beth from Leah or Steven? I can get her for you. Is everything all right with your daughter?" She half turned and reached for the doorknob.

"Wait. Please." The air whistled between his teeth as he searched his mind for something more to say. "I ain't here to see none of those people. I came to see you." He ran his hand over his bare head. "I was hopin' you might be able to spare a few minutes to talk some."

He glanced at the rug and the broom. "Maybe it ain't such a good idea. I can see I'm interferin' with your work. I'll mosey on toward town and sit in the wagon till Buddy's ready to head home."

She dropped the broom and rug to the floor. "You will do no such thing. That rug can be beat in an hour as easily as now. Would you care to sit out here or come into the parlor and have a cup of coffee?"

He gripped the rim of his hat, feeling it crinkle beneath his fingers. "Coffee sounds right good, ma'am, but I don't think I'd care to sit in the parlor." A bead of sweat trickled down the side of his face. "Thank you kindly for the offer, though."

She waved toward one of the rockers positioned off to the side. "Please take a seat. I will return in a moment."

He edged toward the steps, wondering if he should bolt. More than likely Mrs. Cooper would run him down and drag him back by the ear if he tried. He sagged into the rocker. Why had he thought this woman could help him? It wasn't like he really knew her—beyond the few visits she'd paid to the ranch when he was abed and ailing.

He scratched his head. In all fairness, though, he had to admit she had a sight more sense than most women he'd met.

She pushed through the door, carrying a heavily laden tray. Two mugs of steaming coffee and a plate heaped high with cookies made Charlie's mouth water.

He jumped to his feet and strode forward. "Let me help you with that, ma'am."

Mrs. Cooper almost yanked the tray out of his reach. "No, sir. You certainly will not juggle a heavy tray with a broken arm."

She placed it on a low table between their two chairs, then stood erect and leveled him with a no-nonsense look. "All right, out with it, Charles. Why are you being so polite and continuing to call me 'ma'am'? This is not like you at all. Have you done something for which you are feeling guilty and have come to confess, or are you planning some dire deed and hoping I will give my blessing?"

Charlie sat bolt upright, his growling stomach forgotten as his ire crept to the fore like a coyote on the hunt. "Woman, what kind of talk is that? I got nothin' to confess or feel bad about—leastwise if I did, I'd not be blabbin' about it to you." He got up from his chair.

Mrs. Cooper huffed. "There is no need to get in a lather, Mr. Pape. I meant no offense. I simply wondered why you are being so polite. It is not like you."

She waved him back toward the chair and settled into her own. "Sit down and stop pouting. Your coffee is getting cold, and the cookies need to be eaten."

Charlie glared, but the enticing aroma of freshly baked molasses cookies drew him back to his seat. "All right. I suppose I can manage to eat one or two before Buddy returns."

They munched in silence, and Charlie downed three cookies and half of his coffee before Mrs. Cooper leaned forward. "Now, out with it. What brought you by today? Are Leah and Millie well?"

He plunked his mug onto the tray. "You do beat all. I've never in all my born days seen someone who can ask so many questions. Can't a man stop by for a little socializin' without somethin' havin' to be wrong?"

She stared at him so long he thought she'd bore a hole clear through his brain and out the back of his head. "Maybe, maybe not. Socializing, is it? Are you implying that you have come calling on me and are considering asking to court me?"

He reared back in his seat, his mind awhirl, and almost choked on his last cookie. "Courtin' you? Me?" The last word came out in a high-pitched squeak, and he ran his finger under his suddenly too-tight collar. "Weren't it you who suggested we be friends?"

He held up his hand. "No, ma'am. I don't wanna court nobody, nohow!"

She sighed and raised her gaze to the sky. "I do declare. You have the worst manners and grammar of anyone I know." Turning her attention back on him, she spoke in a frosty tone. "And, might I ask, what would be so terrible about courting a woman? You are all alone in the world except for your children, and they are not apt to live with you forever. I would imagine you must get lonely."

One corner of her mouth tipped up. "And lest it might have slipped your notice, I did not say I would be willing to let you court me even if you were to inquire."

He groaned and placed his face in his hand. Why had he sought out this opinionated, rude woman instead of heading to the saloon to chew the fat with some of his old cronies? He raised his head. "Well, I ain't askin', so you can get that worry out of your head. And I won't ask you why you wouldn't because you'd probably start naggin' again."

She arched her brows. "Now that we have that subject out of the way, what is on your mind?"

He grabbed one arm of the rocker and maneuvered to his feet. "I reckon that whatever it was has been scared right out of me. Thanks for the cookies and coffee, Mrs. Cooper. I'd best be on my way."

Gaping, she started to rise, then sank back into her chair. "It is not an easy thing for me to say, Charles, but I beg your pardon for offending you. It was not my intention at all. I bid you a good day."

Charles slapped his hat onto his head and strode down the steps and along the walkway to the dirt road, suddenly at a loss as to why he'd come in the first place. He'd worried over matters concerning the ranch, and guilt over his wife's passing and Leah's feelings of loss, but he'd be ding-blasted if he could put his finger on it any closer than that.

Court her? Where would she have gotten such a tomfool idea? If she were the last woman on earth …

His thoughts drew up short, and he almost stumbled as he remembered her kindness in the past. He had to admit he'd enjoyed their bantering exchanges and matching wits with the woman, even if she did irritate him at times.

He headed toward the center of town, one thing on his mind—getting a good, long drink. A few minutes later he skirted around the end of a wagon parked in front of the general store and stepped onto the boardwalk in front of the saloon.

His steps slowed as he drew closer. Frances Cooper's face flashed in his recollection—her disapproval and disgust the time she'd encountered him in this very spot.

Then Buddy's rebuke about Leah's hurt and disillusionment rose to the surface. He halted abruptly and winced. How much more pain could his daughter take and still tolerate having him around? He'd been the cause of too much sorrow already.

Slowly, with a longing look at the batwing doors, he turned. Then he picked up his pace and almost ran, feeling as though the hounds of hell were nipping at his heels. And maybe they were—he couldn't be sure. All he knew was he must get away from the sight and odor of that building, before the evil sucked him back into the darkness once again.

Frances sat on the porch, her coffee forgotten, and stared down the empty path toward the road. What was wrong with her that she couldn't keep her comments to herself? Why did she think it necessary to blurt out everything? That had almost destroyed her relationship with her daughter and oldest grandchild, and she thought she had learned. Apparently not.

She slipped out of the rocker and gathered the tray, suddenly feeling every one of her sixty years. Nonsense. It wasn't in her nature to give up or back down. She straightened her spine.

Something was plaguing Charles Pape, and she intended to get to the bottom of it. Although holding her tongue to some degree while she did so might be a wise idea, it wouldn't be easy. But, with God's help, maybe she could manage—a chuckle broke from her lips—as long as the irritating man didn't drive her to blurt out anything more or cause her to take a rolled-up newspaper to his thick head.

Chapter Twenty-One

Steven unsaddled his horse in the barn and turned him out to pasture, anxious to finish the chore and find Leah. He hadn't had more than a minute to call his own in days, and it felt even longer since he'd spoken more than an occasional sentence to her. He sauntered to the house and rapped on the kitchen door, then poked his head inside. "Millie? Is Leah here?"

The older woman stepped into sight, wiping flour-caked hands on her apron. "No, sir, she's not."

Steven's exuberant spirits slipped a notch. He'd been so certain he'd find her at the house, as she hadn't been in the barn or out in the pasture gathering cattle. "You wouldn't happen to know where I can find her?"

Millie gazed at him, as though considering whether she should answer. "Reckon I might."

"Uh-huh." Steven stepped into the kitchen and settled his head against the doorjamb. "Are you willing to tell me, or do I have to guess?"

"Depends." She dipped her hands back into the bowl of dough and smiled.

He grinned. "On what?"

Her face turned serious. "On whether whatever you aim to say to her will bring her more grief. The girl's had more than her share of worries since Tom arrived, and I don't care to see any more heaped on her shoulders."

Steven straightened from his position against the door. "Then you needn't worry. I have no intention of causing Leah more stress. In fact, I'd like to alleviate some of it, if I only knew how."

Millie peered closely at his face. "Are you startin' to care for my gal?"

Steven jerked in surprise. He hadn't been willing to face that question too deeply. "She's a very special woman, but I can't seem to get close. Leah keeps me at a distance, and I'm not sure why."

"And you haven't figured that out?" She scattered flour onto the breadboard and slapped the lump of dough onto the surface. Her fingers dug into the dough, flipping it over and scrunching it into itself.

Steven stared for a minute, fascinated by the movements of her hands, then raised his eyes and met hers. "I suppose not."

She gave a lopsided grimace. "The girl's been hurt too many times. First her ma dying." Her eyes darkened. "Runnin' off, is more like it. I still find that hard to believe. Her pa takin' to drink and lyin' to Leah all these years. He might as well have left her when her ma did, as much good he's been as a pa. Then Tom disappearin'. The girl is scared to let anyone get close. I reckon she figures they'll up and walk off if'n she does."

The truth of her words sank in. Of course. Why hadn't he realized all this on his own? Leah was an amazing woman to have stayed as strong as she had and not crumble under the pain.

He breathed a quick prayer for wisdom. "I promise you that I'm not going to do or say anything to upset her, Millie. I believe I am coming to care for Leah, but I have things to sort out. I'm not ready to tell her that yet. I do want to talk and spend some time with her, if you're willing to share where she might be."

"All right. Guess you'll do." She jerked her chin toward the kitchen window. "She has a favorite place on top of that hill, yonder. Hasn't gone up there in years but I saw her trudging up there maybe an hour ago. Surprised me she hasn't come home yet."

A shadow passed over her face. "Leah and her ma used to go up there together and talk. I'm not sure what all they done up there, but Leah always came back happy. Hope she will this time too, but I'm afraid it might stir up hurtful memories. Maybe you can help. I surely do hope someone can, and that's a fact."

Steven tipped his head. "Thank you for trusting me, Millie. I can't promise, but I'll do my best. At least I'll listen, if she wants to talk. That is, if she doesn't send me packing."

"You go on and give it a try, son. My ma always used to say, nothin' ventured, nothin' gained." She flashed him a saucy smile. "You never know, she might decide to take a shine to you."

Heat seeped into his face, and he backed toward the door, not wanting to prolong this conversation until he sorted out his own turbulent thoughts. But as he drew the door shut behind him and headed toward the pasture, hope for the future surged in his heart.

Leah sat perfectly still, her hands clasped on top of the box still resting in her lap. The sight of her mother's handwriting had prompted warm recollections for several minutes. She hadn't yet opened the missive to see what it contained.

Now, with trembling fingers, she plucked at the wax seal and pried the pages apart. She smoothed the deep fold and saw what appeared to be a letter, then took a deep breath before she read.

My dearest Leah,

My heart is breaking as I sit here in the meadow and write this, knowing you might not read it for a year or two. I pray you'll remember my wish that you return to our special place on your sixteenth birthday.

You are a woman now and entering a time when you'll make your own decisions. I don't know what your pa has told you about my departure, but I hope he spoke the truth—that staying here with him any longer wasn't working.

I wanted to come to you, to ask you to leave with me, but Charles begged me not to. I agreed that you were too young to be put in a position to choose between your mother and the ranch you loved and where you wanted to live the rest of your life. I will never put you in that position, my darling.

But I want you to know how much I love you. Should you decide to do so, I'd love to have you join me in Portland. If not to live there permanently, then at least I hope you might visit once a year or so. I've agreed not to put pressure on you. It shall be up to you to write to me, but my heart will be longing to hear from you.

Leah's shaking fingers could no longer retain their tentative grip on the paper, and it fluttered to the ground beside her. Ma wanted her to come live with her in Portland? She hadn't forgotten her or totally abandoned her? Sorrow mixed with rage at her father and brother threatened to choke her, and she tried to stem the tears.

What would her life have been like if she'd been given a choice? She raised her eyes and stared across the expanse of meadow rolling down the hill toward the ranch house in the distance. Could she have left this for more than a visit, even if she'd known? Or would she have traveled to Portland, unwavering in her youthful eagerness to convince her mother and brother to return, only to have her heart break anew if they refused?

She plucked the letter from the grass, determined to somehow finish this disturbing and revealing missive.

I'm so sorry that I couldn't stay with Charles on the ranch. To be brutally honest, I never loved him the way he loved me. I was a very young widow with a baby when we met, and I agreed to marry to protect you from a life of poverty and possibly worse. In short order, I realized I'd made a mistake.

Then Tom came along, and I decided to stay. But as the years continued, my unhappiness grew. I missed the city. I missed the companionship I'd known by having people close by. I saw myself growing old and bent, and never having the life I'd dreamed of.

And even more than that, living on the ranch was a constant, painful reminder of Aaron, your father, the only man I've ever loved. I saw him everywhere, in everything—the house he built with such love and care before we married, which I now live in with a man I don't love—and it cut me to the quick.

It is horribly selfish, I know that, and that troubles me more than I can say. A part of me is selfish, I suppose, or I wouldn't be running away. I would force myself to continue in this life that I hate (or I should say, dislike, for you and Tom have made it endurable, even joyous at times), but it is no longer enough. At this point all I can do is hope you will forgive me, and that someday soon you and Tom will come to live with me.

Your brother doesn't care for the ranch as you do, and I'm considering telling him my plan. He is a child, but he has the same love of adventure and hunger for companionship as I do. Please don't blame him for not telling you anything beyond what your father tells you, for I will swear him to secrecy.

One more thing you must know. When I pledged to marry Charles, I told him he must promise to care for you like his own, no matter what might befall me in the future. One thing I'll say, he fell in love with you when you were a baby, and that love has endured to this day. He might be gruff at times, and rough around the edges, but he truly adores you. He would have cared for you even without his promise.

But I wanted to be sure. And in exchange, I told him I would consider giving him the deed to the ranch someday. I didn't change your name to Pape, out of respect for your real father, and because I wanted the ranch to remain in the Carlson family.

We've never told you, but the ranch belonged to Aaron, your father. I loved him, and that made living so far from others bearable. Baker City is so tiny, so dirty, so quiet. Now that I'm leaving, I'm not certain it's the right thing to put the deed in Charles's name. I'm sorry for him, and I know I'm not doing right by him by leaving. He married me and has taken care of his family, the best way he knew how. But it's not enough.

I must make a decision, even though I know it will hurt and possibly anger Charles. Your father lived long enough to see you, and he wanted the ranch to be your inheritance. So I've put the deed in your name. It's enclosed in this box. When you're old enough, you will need to make the decision to keep the ranch or sell it.

When Aaron died, a part of me died as well. I want to take you and Tom with me, but I've promised Charles two years with you both, before you decide whether to join me or not. It is the least I can do. Please write to me, Leah. Tell me you forgive me for leaving you and that you'll visit. And, please, promise you won't hate me.

Your loving mother,
Mary Carlson Pape

Leah dropped the letter into her lap, her fingers numb and cold, her heart unable to take in all that she'd read. She picked it up again, fumbling with the pages, her eyes blurred. Fighting to keep the tears from falling, she rubbed her sleeve across her eyes, then forced herself to focus on the flowing script once again.

Hope, fear, joy, pain, anger, and, finally incredulity, all dipped and soared, each taking their turn raging through her heart. At times the sorrow was so deep she thought she'd be ill. She wrapped her arms around herself, rocking and crying.

Her mother hadn't hated her. She hadn't walked away without caring or thinking of her. Ma had left a letter, had left the ranch to her, had wanted Leah to come live with her. She hadn't told her of the decision to leave to be fair to Pa—to give him time with her and

Tom, to allow Leah to grow up and make decisions for herself. But she'd still chosen to leave. Couldn't she have stayed a few more years, until Tom and she were both grown?

Pa had never told her the truth. The pain of that fact was almost her undoing, and a fierce anger grew. It had been bad enough when she'd heard the facts from Tom. But to hear that same truth from her mother—that cut deep.

Pa was supposed to tell her that Ma wanted her to visit or live with her in Portland. Ma thought he would tell her. Why had he lied? Why had he allowed her to think her mother had died? And once Tom returned and revealed the truth, why hadn't Pa explained? Didn't he know she'd figure it out?

He had to know she'd despise him for letting her think Ma died when she could have been in touch with her all these years. Leah could have visited her, been there for her when she took sick, maybe cared for her and kept her from dying.

Sobs racked her body, and her shoulders shook. Her fists clenched, and the paper crumpled within her grasp. It didn't matter. None of it mattered. Since Tom's return, she'd believed her mother a liar—believed she hadn't loved her, and Pa let her continue to think that. But it wasn't true.

Well, maybe a little bit. Ma admitted she was selfish to leave, and Leah had to agree. What could be so awful that she couldn't stay a few more years? She'd never seen her mother as shallow or self-centered, and it hurt to do so now, but the truth was there, all the same. But better that than to believe Ma didn't care.

Leah scrubbed at her tears again, hot and wet beneath her fingers. A hiccup took the place of the sobs. She pulled a handkerchief from her skirt pocket and blew her nose, then folded it and tucked it back. It was time to look at the situation squarely. She was an adult now.

A pang hit her. An adult. She hadn't kept her word to Ma when she'd asked her to come back here on her sixteenth birthday. The pain of her mother's loss had been too deep even then. This field where the daisies bloomed had been their special place. After Ma left, and Leah believed she'd died, keeping her promise no longer seemed important.

If only she had. She'd have found the letter, confronted her father, and written to her mother. At the least, Leah would have gone to see Ma. Maybe a trip to Portland with Tom would have kept him from running away.

Leah glanced down at the open box and tentatively reached in, setting aside the dried daisy chain Ma had made for her hair. She pulled out another paper, her heart pounding, and her mouth going dry. It had to be the deed.

What would Pa say when he discovered Ma put it in Leah's name instead of his? Should she tell him, or let him go on thinking Ma had kept her word? Would that be any worse than what he'd done? But Ma said she hadn't promised. She'd only said she'd consider it, and Pa probably assumed she'd follow through.

A twig snapped in the distance, faint but distinct in the calm air, and Leah's hands stilled. Animals rarely made noise while traveling, unless pursued and not paying attention to where they were running.

A sense of dread pushed aside all her other tumultuous emotions. The last person she wanted to see right now was Pa. Or Tom. She hadn't come close to sorting through the feelings stirred by her mother's revelation. She didn't care to face either of them and have to explain her swollen eyes, red nose, or the letter strewn across her skirt.

She shuffled the pages back into a neat pile and folded them, then turned her head, peering over her shoulder. Steven Harding stood a dozen yards away, warm eyes pinned on her. Concern shone clearly on his handsome face.

Steven stuffed his hands in his pockets and rocked on his heels, indecision rooting him to the spot. Leah sat at the base of a tree, her skirts spread around her and clutching a sheaf of papers. He'd have made his way forward with a cheerful word but for her red-rimmed eyes and sad countenance. From all appearances she'd been crying. The last thing he wanted to do was impose on a woman dealing with some kind of grief, but he longed to rush forward, gather her in his arms, and comfort her.

Millie's warning echoed in his mind. Leah had enough to deal with. She didn't need anything more. He hadn't planned on bringing unhappiness or anxiety, but it was very possible that intruding would do so, even if he wasn't delivering bad tidings.

He could face down a charging bull in a pasture or a grumpy boss at the bank, but the prospect of facing Leah's tears unnerved him. Not that he hadn't dealt with plenty of his mother's tears over the years, but this situation was different. He'd worked to accept Ma's sorrow—he had his own to deal with after his sister's disappearance—and somehow learned to comfort her.

But his mother wasn't this young woman who made his heart rate increase each time he was around her and at other times raised his ire and made him want to stomp back to town. He had yet to figure out how he could be attracted to someone who could so easily frustrate him.

He started to swing away when Leah beckoned. All indecision disappeared. Steven strode toward her, his heart lifting at her slight smile. She had to be grieving the passing of her mother, but after her initial start at seeing him here, she'd offered a welcome. He couldn't ask any more.

Steven stopped a stride from the edge of Leah's skirt and bowed his head in a brief greeting. "I'm sorry to intrude. I planned to return to the ranch as soon as I realized ..." He wanted to kick himself for calling attention to her tears. "That is, I didn't mean to imply ..."

Leah shook her head. "It's all right. I'm sure I look a sight, so there's no need to pretend you didn't notice. Has something happened at home to bring you out here?"

He removed his hat, ran his hand over his hair, then stuffed it back on, jamming it hard over his forehead, all thoughts fleeing of why he'd come. Why did her eyes have that effect on him? "Everything is fine."

"Oh? So you were out for a walk and stumbled across me?" She gave a pointed look at his boots. "I thought cowboys—or bankers, for that matter—didn't much care for walking."

Steven grimaced. "Millie mentioned you might be up here, and it wasn't far enough to merit saddling my horse."

Leah leaned back, her hands braced in the deep grass near the base of the tree. "You asked Millie where I'd gone? If everything is fine at the ranch, why would you?"

He held a tight rein on his emotions. She wasn't making this easy.

A hawk flew over, then folded its wings and dived toward a spot on the knoll a hundred feet or so away. Quick as a flash his talons extended and he snatched a field mouse from the grass, then winged his way back into the sky.

Steven stared after the magnificent creature. "What would it be like to soar on the wind, without any cares?"

Leah smiled. "He has plenty of cares. More than likely a full nest of babies and a wife that chases him away every time he tries to land and relax. You might also ask, what would it be like to be the field mouse?"

She cocked her head to the side. "What kind of cares do you have, Steven?" She patted the grass beside her. "You're here. You might as well rest those feet and sit awhile."

He looked askance at the spot Leah indicated, then back at her. "You're sure you don't mind?"

"I wouldn't have invited you if I did." The words had a hint of sadness, but the curve of her mouth softened it. "Please."

He lowered himself onto the springy grass. "Thanks. I should be asking you that question, as you appear troubled." He glanced at the box in her lap and the folded paper now tucked beneath it. "Not bad news, I hope?"

"A ghost from the past." The words escaped on a sigh. "One that might better have stayed buried."

He hesitated, uncertain how to respond, and not sure she'd want him to speak, even if he knew what to say. The statement didn't seem to require a response, and her sad expression didn't invite more questions. He sat quietly and silently prayed, asking the Lord to heal her heart and give her peace.

They had both lost a sibling for a number of years—had both experienced the pain of a mother who was no longer there to meet their needs. He'd gotten his sister and mother back, only to feel as though he'd lost his mother again. Leah's brother had returned, to disclose that Leah's mother had deserted her years ago, then died before they could make peace.

Pain rippled through Steven's heart. The minutes stretched on and he heard her gentle sigh. He clasped her hand, drawing it toward him. Somehow he needed to help this wonderful woman find a way to deal with her pain and forgive those who had hurt her, as he realized he must do in his own life.

He'd waited too long and allowed resentment to build in his heart toward his mother—and even his sister—and now he understood what God wanted him to do.

Forgive. Let it go.

Understand that his mother had given all she had to give while he was growing up, and Beth wasn't at fault for disappearing and holding his mother's heart captive.

Finally, Leah bowed her head and squeezed his hand.

He returned the gesture, then slowly released her, not certain how much liberty was appropriate. She was obviously hurting, and he hoped to bring comfort, but the last thing he wanted was to take unfair advantage.

During these few minutes, he'd never felt closer to a person, never felt such a flood of peace and ... love. But this wasn't the proper time to speak. Leah needed to walk through whatever was troubling her, whatever had brought her to this place and etched the sadness in her face.

She turned and looked him directly in the eyes. "Thank you."

"For what?"

"Your kindness. Your silence. For taking the time to care and sit with me."

He gave a slow nod. "It's the least I can do. But if you want to talk …"

Leah smiled, but her eyes were like dark pools, reflecting her sorrow. "It's not like you came to listen to my troubles."

Steven squared his shoulders. "Actually, I did."

Her fingers went to her throat. "Excuse me?"

"Millie told me you've been dealing with a lot lately, between the problems with your pa and Tom and things needing to be done on the ranch. I thought you might appreciate a sympathetic ear."

He held up a hand, suddenly aware she might not understand. "Not that you have to share anything, mind you. I can continue to sit quietly, if that's what you prefer. Sometimes having a friend nearby who cares is enough."

Chapter Twenty-Two

Leah could only stare, not sure she'd heard correctly. She'd never known a man this sensitive, who could feel her mood and be willing to do what was best for her. Even on his good days before Ma left, Pa hadn't known how to deal with Leah's emotions or outbursts. "Thank you for that sweet offer. But if you don't mind, I'd prefer to talk."

Steven silently gave a nod of assent, his gaze trained on her.

Leah tried to think. Where to begin? How much should she tell this man? She felt that she'd only scratched the surface on getting to know him, but what she'd seen so far she liked—and trusted. Would he understand the tug-of-war she felt concerning her mother and father, and all the inner turmoil this letter had stirred? There was only one way to find out.

She slipped the letter from under the box and handed it to Steven. "I think this will explain better than anything I can say. Would you mind reading it?"

He took it reverently but didn't open it. "Are you sure?"

Again amazement quieted her thoughts. Most people would be more than willing to read a private letter and possibly discover some secret they could pass along to their friends. "If you don't mind."

He opened the letter and bent over it, taking his time and perusing each page carefully, before moving on to the next. After several minutes, and returning at least once to a page, he folded it and placed it back in Leah's hands. "That must have been very hard for you to read."

Leah closed her eyes, only now realizing how much she'd hoped for such a response. "Yes."

"I'm so sorry, Leah. Sorry that your father put you in this position, and that your mother didn't tell you the truth before she left."

His words soothed the turmoil inside. The confusion and anger began to subside, and calm took their place. "That's the thing I find the hardest to understand. Why didn't she tell me herself? Why leave a letter and hope that I'd find it?" She turned to face him, searching deep within his expression, praying he'd have the answers she so desperately sought.

"You feel that she deserted you." Steven didn't ask, he stated it as a fact. "And I suppose to some degree, she did." He plucked a blade of grass and examined it, then tossed it aside. "May I speak plainly?"

The question took her by surprise, but she nodded. "Of course."

His eyes met hers. "Parents can desert you even if they never leave."

She frowned, not certain what he was saying. She flicked a finger against the letter. "I beg your pardon? My mother left."

"I know. But do you think she'd have been the kind of mother you needed if she had stayed?" He waited a moment, then plunged forward. "Let me explain by giving you an example. My father died, and at the same time, my little sister, Beth, disappeared. The grief almost killed Ma. I knew, deep in my heart, that I wasn't enough to keep her going. She pushed through and lived because of her determination to find Beth—not because I needed her.

"I lost both my parents that day. Ma withdrew inside herself for years. I became the caretaker in some respects, even though she married again a few years later. When my stepfather died, she crawled back into the black hole of despair."

Leah mulled over his words, then leaned forward. "But she didn't leave you. She stayed. She didn't run off trying to find Beth."

"She would have if she'd known where to go and if we'd have had the funds to travel. Please don't misunderstand. I love my mother, but as surely as if she had run down the trail after Beth or curled up in the grave beside my pa, I lost her. I didn't get her back until the day we found Beth." He hesitated and turned his eyes away.

Leah touched his fingers, sensing his unease. "But you're still not happy. There's more?" She withdrew her hand, longing to keep it there to comfort him, but afraid if she grasped it, she'd not let go.

"Yes." He gave a harsh laugh. "It sounds weak, coming from a grown man. I got her back, only to lose her again. To Beth."

Leah gasped. "But you love your sister! I thought you were happy to find her. Are you bitter she came back into your life?"

He shook his head. "I'm sorry if I gave you that impression. I do love her, very much. God worked a miracle when He returned her to our family, and I'm grateful. But it's like Ma is almost afraid to let her out of her sight for fear she'll disappear again.

"Maybe I should be grateful that I no longer have to care for Ma all the time, or be responsible to rouse her from her melancholy moods. But somehow I thought once we found Beth, life would become normal for all of us."

He grimaced and gave a wry chuckle. "I'm not so sure I know what normal is anymore." He turned toward Leah. "I didn't mean to talk about myself. I told you that to say, although you have a parent in the house, it doesn't mean they aren't absent in other ways. Your ma left you behind, but the words she wrote tell me she did it because she thought it was best for you—she truly loved you."

"Then why didn't she take me with her?" Leah whispered the words.

"Could you have been happy living in Portland, away from the ranch and the life that you loved? Even if you were with your mother, wouldn't you have resented her for taking you away?"

Surprise coursed through Leah. Would she have come to resent Ma if she'd forced her to move? "But what if she hadn't made me go—if she'd let me make the choice?"

"You were fourteen. Could you have chosen between your mother, and the ranch, and your pa? And if you'd gone with her, how long would it have been before you begged to come home, then grew bitter if she refused to come with you?"

Leah scooted back against the tree trunk, stunned. Was it possible her mother had understood her that well, had known that the choice would have cut her heart in half? "But what about Pa? He lied. He should have told me Ma was alive, not let me think she'd died.

"That was wrong. It was cruel! He could have at least told me after the two years were up. There's no excuse for him to keep the knowledge to himself, and then to start drinking and abandon me as well."

"I agree. He shouldn't have lied, as your mother shouldn't have. But do you think it's possible that both of them were trying to protect you in their own way?"

She stared at him, not quite taking in his words. "No, that doesn't make sense. Lying doesn't protect someone. It hurts them."

"It does, but that's not always the way our minds work." Steven reached out an inch or two and touched her, then withdrew, resting his hand on the grass near hers.

It took all of Leah's willpower to sit still and not move her hand sideways. When he'd released his hold earlier, she'd wanted to snatch it back and never let go. This time Steven's slight movement had seemed involuntary, but was it really an accident that his fingers were so close she could feel sparks jumping between them?

Almost as though he sensed her thoughts, Steven enclosed her hand in his again.

Warmth coursed through Leah, and she closed her eyes, savoring the sensation. Oh, to feel like this all the time. To have the comfort of a man's touch … no, not any man. Steven. She didn't want this to end. Not ever.

Steven gave her fingers a gentle squeeze, then released her, placing his elbows in the grass and leaning back. "Your pa might have understood how much it would hurt you to know your ma left. I'm sure he worried that you'd want to run after her and knew how unhappy you'd be if you did. And I'm guessing his own heart was hurting from his wife leaving him. He might have been afraid of losing his entire family."

Leah blinked a couple of times, her own sense of loss accentuated by the emptiness she felt as she linked her fingers together in her lap. Had Steven once again held her hand only to bring comfort? Did it not mean anything more to him?

She worked to remember what he'd said. Pa afraid? Pa hurting and unhappy? Sure, she'd seen him drunk plenty of times. Anger and bitterness were common emotions, but fear or pain? She'd never even considered those as a possibility for Pa. "When I thought Ma had died, I knew Pa was upset, but I never saw him cry for her. I always wondered why he didn't."

"I imagine he's like most men. If he loved her, he'd be hurt, and his pride would be smashed to bits." Steven scratched his cheek. "In fact, I wonder if that's why he drinks so much. If he loved her, he'd think himself a failure as a man, because he couldn't keep his wife happy and at home."

"Ma said he loved her, and she never loved him." She turned and looked at him, realization dawning. "Her letter said she told Pa she'd consider putting the deed to the ranch in his name. He worked hard all these years, caring for the land. Pa thinks the ranch belongs to him."

Steven pursed his lips, then let out a long whistle.

Leah stared at the ground for a minute. Finally, she lifted her head and tried to keep her voice steady. "When he finds out, he'll drink even more. Maybe he was trying to protect me when I was young, but I'm a woman now, and I haven't seen anything change. I'm sorry, Steven, but I don't believe Pa cares more about me than about the ranch, or he wouldn't have lied."

She gathered her skirts around her and pushed to her knees. "I appreciate you coming to check on me, and especially for taking time to share your thoughts, but it's probably best that we get back. I've left enough things undone today."

Steven stood and extended his arm. "Let me help you up."

His warm fingers gripped hers again with a gentle firmness that sent her heart pounding. When was the last time a man had touched her this way? With deference, kindness, and even—dare she allow herself to dream—a touch of personal interest? But it went even further, beyond the physical.

Somehow Steven had managed to reach into her soul. She felt it starting to open, starting to trust for the first time in years. He was someone she could share her heart with.

And maybe, just maybe, someone she could trust not to leave her and walk away, as so many others had done.

He helped her to her feet and retained his hold. Her heart continued to hammer, and she smiled up at him, willing him to kiss her. Praying he was starting to care in the same way that she was.

"Thank you. I've gotten out of the habit of wearing dresses and hardly know how to walk in one anymore."

Those were not the words she wanted to say. She longed to pour out her heart—to ask if he'd sought her out because Millie had urged him to or because he'd been drawn to her. Instead, all she could manage was to prattle about her clothing.

He took a step back and released her. "What now?"

"I beg your pardon?" All she could think of was losing the warmth of his touch and the security it had brought for those few moments. "Now? I don't understand."

"As you said, Charlie assumes the ranch belongs to him, but it is legally yours. What will you do? Tell him the truth?"

Her heart stuttered and jerked before it accelerated to almost twice its normal pace. Tell Pa the truth? She had a pretty good idea what it would do to Pa when he discovered Ma had left the ranch to her. It might be the final blow. No doubt he'd drink more than ever, but how would he treat her? But if she didn't tell him, she would be guilty of keeping a secret from Pa, as he'd done with her.

A secret that had the power to wound him, possibly almost as much as when Ma left. Maybe her father had feared the same thing would happen if he told her the truth about Ma leaving—that Leah would be hurt beyond repair. By revealing this secret, would she lose her father as well as her mother?

Chapter Twenty-Three

Tom stalked across the barnyard and yanked on the barn door. "Pa? You in here?" He stepped into the cool, dimly lit interior and looked around, frustration building in his chest like steam in a teakettle. "Pa!" He strode from one stall door to another, peering inside, then over to the stack of loose hay piled against the back wall, giving the edges a kick. He figured he'd find his father sleeping off another drinking binge.

He hurried out to the wagon yard and stopped short. The buggy was gone. Had Pa driven himself to town with a broken arm? More likely Buddy took him. He hustled to the house and pushed through the kitchen door, ready to holler for Millie.

She stood a few feet away, a scowl on her face. "Not another step inside this kitchen, Thomas Pape. You hustle and back up."

She pointed at his feet. "I don't know what you stepped in, but it looks like you've been walkin' through somethin' unpleasant and more'n likely stinky to boot. Out!" Millie thrust her hands toward him. "Clean up before you traipse across my kitchen floor."

Tom gritted his teeth. He loved Millie almost as much as he'd loved Ma, but he didn't have time to be scolded right now. "Fine, I'll leave. But where's Pa? He's not in the barn, and the buggy's gone."

"Yep. Him and Buddy headed to town. We're gettin' low on sup-plies, and I sent a list. Somethin' troublin' you?" She peered at him with alert, piercing eyes.

"I'm sorry about the floor. I'll get out of your way," he said half-heartedly. He'd started to shut the door behind him before she could question him further when another thought occurred.

He poked his head into the room, careful to keep his muddy boots outside. "Millie?"

She swiveled, a damp rag in one hand and a bucket of water in the other. "What you needin' now?"

"Did Leah go with Pa and Buddy?"

"Nope." Millie clamped her lips together as though fearful a secret might escape.

Tom narrowed his eyes. He knew that look. He'd seen it often enough when he was young, but he also knew that no amount of prying would soften Millie once she decided to keep her own coun-sel. "Any idea where she might be?"

She shrugged and dipped the rag in the bucket. "Around. Since it's nigh on to supper time, I'm sure everybody will be home soon, includin' your sister."

She scowled again. "Now, get on out of here and let me get my work done so's I can get supper on the table. Your pa and Buddy should be rollin' in anytime."

Tom turned away, wondering at her brusque tone and evasive reply. What was she hiding? The crunch of wheels on rock and the clop of hooves alerted him that Pa and Buddy must be home. He'd waited too long for this talk with his father, and he didn't intend to wait any longer.

Buddy reined the horse to a stop in front of the barn and set the brake, then swung down. "I'll unhitch, boss. You might want to head into the house and rest that arm. Seems like it's been paining you all the way home."

Tom winced. If Pa was in pain, he might not be in the mood for what Tom planned to say. He almost let out a laugh. Pa would probably never be in the mood to listen. He strode over as his father awkwardly clambered to the ground. "Pa? You got a minute before you go inside?"

Buddy shot him a look, then grasped the horse by the bridle and led him through the open barn doors.

Pa, shoulders hunched, eyed him. "I'm wantin' a cup of coffee pretty bad right now, so don't take long. Or you can follow me to the kitchen and speak your piece there. It's up to you."

Tom shook his head. "I'll hurry, but I'd rather talk here if it's all the same to you." He motioned his father away from the barn. His courage faltered, and he almost changed his mind.

No, this was important. Besides, it was his due. He straightened his shoulders. "I've been doing a lot of work since I arrived."

His pa grunted but didn't reply.

"I haven't gotten paid a nickel."

Charlie rounded on him. "You got a free place to live and food in your belly, doncha?"

Tom's gut tightened. This was exactly what he'd expected, although deep in his heart he'd hoped for more. "Yeah, I do. But I'm your son, and this place will be mine someday. I don't mind working every day if it's needed, but it would be nice to have you appreciate it sometimes."

He bit his lip, wishing he could take back that last part. He'd only planned on asking for money, not approval or appreciation. He stuffed his hands in his pockets. "Not that I expect it."

"Why should you? You're my son, but that didn't stop you from walkin' away from this ranch years ago."

Tom grimaced. "I was young, Pa. And I was missing Ma. She was alone and—" He stopped as anger blossomed in his father's cheeks.

"You sure as the dickens didn't stay young all these years. You coulda come back anytime once you growed up. It weren't like your ma needed you to keep her company every minute. You ever once think maybe Leah and I needed you here? That Buddy was gettin' up in years, and we could use another set of hands on the ranch? You never so much as wrote to see if any of us was alive."

Pa's voice choked on the last word, and his face contorted. "Now you come back thinkin' you can waltz right in and get all sorts of smiles and a big thank-you-kindly. It don't work that way, boy. Not now and not ever."

Tom fisted his hands by his sides. "Ma needed me. I told you that."

"Yeah, so you said. But so did I. And she wasn't sick when you took off and left us."

"But all you wanted me for was work. It's not like you cared about me. Ma got sick. Bad sick. It was cancer. I couldn't leave her to ..." He turned his head and choked back a sob.

The picture exploded in his mind—his mother lying on her bed, wasting away from the cancer that killed her one day at a time. As he'd sat by her bed helpless to take away the disease, he'd hated his pa. Hated that the man hadn't followed his wife and convinced her to return home years ago.

Maybe she wouldn't have come, but he didn't so much as try. "Why, Pa? You never tried to see her after she left. You never wrote to her, not once. Why didn't you care enough to come when she was dying? Why did you ignore my letter and stay away?"

Gravel crunched behind him, and Tom turned. Leah stood a few yards away, her fingers to her throat and her face white, Steven Harding one pace behind. Leah extended her hand toward their father. "Pa?"

Charles Pape's face turned as red as a man whose head was stuck in a noose. "I don't have to answer to you, boy. You run outta here and never looked back. You didn't care about your sister, who nigh worried herself sick, or Millie, who looked like walkin' death for months after you left. As for your ma ..."

His face went from red to deathly pale as the blood drained from it. "I'm sorry she suffered, truly I am. But I won't talk to you about her, or to anyone else. And that's the end of it." He stalked onto the porch, bolting through the front door and pulling it closed behind him with a decisive click.

Leah stared after her father, then turned her eyes to Tom. "Is it true, little brother? Did she suffer for months with only you to tend her?" She brushed her palm across her cheeks, swiping at tears that she couldn't control. She'd gotten the first glimpse into her mother's heart since she'd become an adult, and now this new pain was added to the rest of her troubles.

Cancer. The dread disease that doctors still didn't understand or know how to treat. Only that the patient wasted away—sometimes lasting weeks, other times months, or even beyond—often in excruciating pain.

She wouldn't wish that on anyone, and especially her mother. "Did Pa really know she was sick and refuse to come?"

Tom shot a look at Steven. "I don't want to talk about it in front of strangers."

Steven jerked as though suddenly awakened and took a step back. "You are right, of course. I have some things to take care of in the bunkhouse." He bowed his head toward Leah. "If you need me for anything …"

Leah wanted to grab Steven's hands and hold on tight, drawing from his gentle strength. She'd always seen herself as a strong, capable woman—sometimes more competent than her father—but right now she felt as weak as a newborn calf. "I want you to stay. Please," she murmured to him.

Tom glared, not trying to hide his displeasure.

Leah glared back, then thought to soften her expression. "He's not a stranger, Tom. He's my friend, and I think if you'd let him, he'd be yours, too."

Steven gave her an encouraging smile. "I'm not sure there's any way I can help, but I'll certainly listen and try."

"Thank you." She touched Steven's arm, her other hand still clutching her wood box.

Tom curled his lip. "All people do is walk away when you need them. But I won't fight you about it. I don't really care."

Tom kicked at a rock. "Nobody can help, mister. Not you, or Leah, or Pa. Ma's dead and gone. There's nothing to be done about it now."

Steven arched his brows but didn't respond.

Leah shifted the box to a spot deeper under her arm.

Tom lifted his head and jerked a thumb toward the box. "What's that?"

She averted her eyes, unwilling to let him see too deeply into her heart. She allowed several moments to pass before she replied, "Some things I collected as a child. Ma and I put various objects in it when I was growing up."

Her brother gave a dismissive wave. "Girls and their play-pretties. Truth be told, Leah, I'm about done with this place. It's clear that old man in there doesn't care about me at all."

Distress coursed through Leah. "Tom! That's no way to talk about Pa. Can't you show some respect?"

"Why should I? He doesn't care about either of us."

She rounded on him, sorrow warring with anger in her heart. "I don't know the details about what happened to Ma, or what happened between her and Pa. But I do know that you didn't write to me when she got sick. You didn't give me a chance to care for her or to say good-bye. So don't point a finger at Pa."

Tom hung his head. Finally, he lifted it, and his stormy eyes met hers. "I didn't write because she told me not to."

Leah felt as though she'd been pitched from a rank horse and landed flat on her stomach. "I don't understand." She gazed from Tom to Steven and back again, hoping one of them might have an explanation. "Why would she say that?"

Tom shook his head. "It wasn't only you. She didn't want me to write to Pa or Millie, either. I think she hated having anyone see her toward the end, once she knew she wasn't going to make it."

Leah's lips parted. "But you did write to Pa. You didn't heed what Ma said, and you wrote anyway." It wasn't a question. She'd heard what Tom had tossed at their father and Pa's less-than-charitable reply.

Tom squared his shoulders. "I did."

"Then I don't understand why you couldn't have done the same for me. Pa might have been able to ignore your request, but I would have come." She wrapped her arms around herself to contain a shiver, hating the image that wouldn't leave her mind of Ma lying sick and dying.

His gaze shifted away, and his body tensed. "It doesn't matter now."

"Yes, it does! It matters to me. You and Pa both kept me from knowing about Ma from the time she left until she died. That wasn't kind, and it wasn't fair, and I want to know the reason."

Steven touched her shoulder in a warm, comforting way. Leah moved closer. Steven placed his arm across her shoulder and, suddenly, all felt settled and steady once more.

Tom took a step closer, his breathing ragged. "You want to know why? I'll tell you. Because I left home to take care of Ma. I abandoned the ranch and everything I knew to follow her. And you know what happened? She cried and carried on because it was you she wanted. Not me. I fetched and carried for her when she got sick because she was my ma and I loved her.

"And all she could talk about was you. 'Leah is such a sweet girl,' she said. 'I miss her so much.' And, 'Why doesn't Leah write to me?' It wasn't fair, that's what. If I'd written to you and you had come, she would have forgotten me completely." His red-rimmed eyes glimmered with unshed tears.

Leah could only stare, barely able to believe what she was hearing. "I can't accept that, Tom. I'm sure Ma appreciated everything you did for her, and she loved you very much. You were there every day, but I was gone. That's the only reason she spoke of me so much. It would have been the same for you, if I'd gone with her and you stayed here."

He backed up a couple of steps, his eyes wild and his body shaking. "No, she loved you and didn't care about me. I saw it for six years. Nothing you can say will change that. Nothing." He turned and bolted for the bunkhouse.

Leah took a step, slipping out of Steven's embrace, intent on following and trying to bring her brother some kind of comfort.

Steven grasped her hand. "No. Let him be, Leah. He needs time alone. If you go to him now, he'll only resent you more."

"I don't understand why he resents me at all." She pulled free, irritation at Steven's comment overcoming the earlier warmth she'd felt at his touch. "I've done nothing wrong. I'm the one who was lied to and left behind, not Tom. He had our mother for years while I stayed on the ranch and put up with Pa."

She crossed her arms. "Fine. I won't talk to him now, but this business needs to get settled. Pa has to face some things about the past as well as the present, and Tom had better do the same."

She turned and headed up the steps to the house, then pivoted to face Steven. "Forgive me, Steven. It's not your fault either, but I find it hard to accept that you seem to have so much compassion for Tom after the way he's behaved."

He opened his mouth, but she was suddenly too weary to hear more. "We'll talk another time, if you don't mind. Right now I need to go to my room, read my mother's letter again, and figure out what I'm going to do. Thank you for staying with me when I talked to Tom, and forgive me for my frustration. I meant what I said about you being a good friend and hoping you might be to Tom, as well, even if I don't completely understand your reasoning."

Chapter Twenty-Four

May 18, 1881

Steven settled behind his desk at the bank with a quiet groan, wishing he were back at the ranch. It was getting harder and harder coming to work each day, leaving Leah behind with her troubles and facing his own challenges, both at work and in his family life. His relationship was getting smoother with his sister and mother, and he thanked the Lord for that.

But he needed to make some important decisions. His job no longer held the thrill it once had or offered the same stimulating challenges. He'd hoped that the move to Baker City would bring contentment, but he realized anew that his position in La Grande had been eminently more satisfactory.

Was it because he was stuck in an office day after day at this new position, and he'd been able to travel while working in La Grande? Or had the discontent with his job come after living at the ranch and the fulfillment he'd found working with his hands? Whatever the case, he couldn't continue this way much longer, disliking his job and praying the hours would pass quickly until time to close.

The gate set in the wood rail moved soundlessly, but the motion caught Steven's eye, and he glanced up. He rose to his feet as his boss carefully closed the gate behind him. "Mr. Hunt. Did I miss an appointment with you, sir?" He peered at the clock sitting on a nearby shelf and racked his memory, but nothing came to mind.

His boss shook his head. His suit, as always, was impeccable, and his eyes sharp as he surveyed Steven's office, then refocused his attention on his employee. "Getting along all right, Harding? Any troubling customers lately?"

Steven tried to contain his surprise and cover his unease, wondering where this was leading. "None to speak of. The usual requests for loans and an occasional extension, but nothing of consequence."

He gestured to a chair. "Would you care to have a seat, sir?" He waited until the older man sat, then took his place behind his desk. Why had Mr. Hunt come in here instead of calling him into his office?

"I'm happy to hear that." Mr. Hunt smoothed an imaginary wrinkle on the front of his lapel, then looked up. "Are you happy working here, Mr. Harding?"

"I, uh—certainly, sir. Why do you ask?" Steven straightened, praying his boss wouldn't pick up on his hesitation and press the matter. "Is my performance of concern, sir?"

"Not at all, Mr. Harding." He cast a look over his shoulder at the empty bank and lowered his voice. "By the way, I would have asked you to my office, but Mr. Parker is setting up in there for a meeting with some of the mine owners in an hour or so."

He leaned his forearms on the front edge of Steven's desk. "This is a bit confidential, which is why I came first thing this morning before we open the door to customers."

"I see." Steven didn't, but he had no idea what else was expected. "How can I help, Mr. Hunt?"

"By giving me a satisfactory answer to what I'm going to propose."

Steven's mind scrambled over the possibilities and came up blank. "I'll certainly try to be accommodating, sir."

Hunt rapped his knuckles on the desk. "Good, good. That's what I like to hear from my men." A broad smile creased his face, a rarity except when in the company of large investors. "Here's the situation. You remember Mr. Marvin Riddle at the La Grande bank, I assume?"

Steven gave a slow nod. "Of course. He was the vice president while I was there. A good man, as I recall."

"I'm sure he is, but that's not the issue. He's been promoted and will be heading up a branch in Pendleton in two months' time. The bank makes a number of substantial loans to farmers and ranchers in the area."

Steven listened closely but still couldn't decipher where he fit into this. "I'm happy for Mr. Riddle. He's a hard worker and deserving man."

"Quite so." Mr. Hunt scooted his chair closer to the desk. "The board that governs all three banks, which I happen to sit on, met recently to decide on a replacement. We are offering the position to you, Mr. Harding, assuming you care to accept. I am aware that your mother and sister both live in Baker City now, but since La Grande was your mother's home for a number of years, I imagine she would be content to return."

Steven fumbled for words, but none came. He gave his head a slight shake, hoping to clear it. "Me, sir? The vice president?"

"It's quite an honor, and of course, comes with a sizable salary increase. I can't imagine anyone turning down an opportunity like this, but it's your choice. You have one month to give me your decision, unless you feel you can tell me now?"

"No, sir. I mean, thank you, sir." He forced a smile. "I'm quite honored, and I do appreciate the time to mull it over. You are correct. I have family to think about, as well as other considerations."

"Certainly, Mr. Harding." Hunt frowned and tapped his fingers on the desktop. "And if by chance you come to a decision sooner than thirty days, let me know. The board has another man in mind who already lives in La Grande, but you were at the top of our list. Other than family responsibilities, I can conceive of nothing that should cause a conflict."

He pushed to his feet and towered over Steven's desk. "Of course, we'll be sorry to see you leave us here in Baker City. You've done an admirable job since you arrived, but I imagine you'll want to accept the board's offer."

Steven stiffened but kept his smile firm. "As I mentioned, there are other considerations, but that doesn't mean I'll turn it down. Thank you again, sir, for your generous recommendation. You've given me much to think about."

Hunt's frown deepened, but he smoothed out the scowl as he spotted the owner of one of the mines.

Steven waited until his boss exited his office and disappeared inside his own door before sinking back into his chair. What had happened? Had the past ten minutes been real, or had he imagined it all?

Steven looked out over the main lobby of the bank as a line of customers formed at the first teller's window and another two prominent businessmen strode toward Mr. Hunt's office. Mr. Parker stood nearby, balancing a tray of coffee like a butler instead of a bank clerk. Business as usual.

Leave Baker City and move back to La Grande? Would his mother even consider such a thing now that she'd found Beth? Probably not. In fact, he knew she wouldn't. Maybe Beth and Jeffery would think about moving to La Grande. His career as a writer and hers as an illustrator didn't depend on the town where they lived. But somehow he doubted it. Beth seemed to have made friends at the boardinghouse, as well as the church, and Jeffery appeared quite content in Baker City. Besides, it appeared Beth's adopted aunt intended to settle here as well.

Where did that leave him? The opportunity to take a vice presidency, which of course was only a stepping-stone to running a bank of his own, was immense.

Leah. Why hadn't he thought of her first? The offer had hit him so hard and come so unexpectedly that he was surprised he'd even thought of his family. But it wasn't as if he had any ties to Leah beyond friendship, although he'd change that if it were up to him.

There had been times recently when he'd touched her that she'd responded in a way that made his heart leap, but other times she puffed up like a startled porcupine.

He blew out a frustrated breath as another memory surfaced. Yesterday she'd appeared upset at his suggestion that she leave Tom alone and allow him to think through the turmoil assailing him. Somehow she'd seen that as taking her brother's side rather than how Steven meant it—a warning that pushing Tom could result in more hurt for her.

He'd hoped that explaining his struggles with his own family would help Leah understand her brother a little better. But in all fairness, Tom wasn't an easy person to be around. He hadn't helped his case by keeping the truth from Leah all these years, no matter his excuse.

Steven dipped his pen in the ink pot and drew a blank sheet of paper from a stack. Time to get to work and put personal issues aside. Mr. Hunt would want this report by the time his meeting ended, and he'd better have it ready, or the offer of a new position, or keeping this one, might not be something that need trouble him any longer.

Chapter Twenty-Five

May 25, 1881

Steven hitched sideways in his saddle and peered across the brush-covered ground at Leah riding her gelding nearby. A week had passed since Mr. Hunt's offer, and he still hadn't told a soul. He'd planned on talking to Beth and his mother, and possibly Leah, but something held him back—more than likely, his own indecision, or possibly, concern over the various reactions of the women he cared for.

Leah brushed a strand of wayward hair from her eyes, then tugged her hat farther down on her forehead, but she didn't turn his way or seem to notice his regard. Steven shrugged, content not to break the silence, even if he wasn't enjoying his thoughts. They had another couple of miles to go, pushing the cattle to a grassy meadow.

He shifted to the fore again, keeping his focus on a cow and calf that kept trying to wander off the trail. What would his sister think of his proposed move? Would it bother Beth to lose her brother so soon, after so recently reuniting? Or was she so wrapped up in her new marriage that she'd barely notice?

He grimaced, ashamed of his thoughts. It probably was no more Beth's fault than his own that they hadn't spent time together lately, since he'd been burning the candle at both ends between his job at the bank and his work at the ranch. He hadn't even visited the boardinghouse to see his mother as often as he should.

Ma would likely be torn between happiness for her son and grief that she might lose touch with him. But La Grande was only a two-day ride from Baker City, and he would assure her he'd visit. Ma would never move back with him, Steven knew without asking. Beth had become her world, and even his leaving wouldn't change that.

He reined his horse sharply to the right and bumped him with his spur, urging the gelding after the rogue cow. She darted around a tree and ducked into a stand of brush, her calf galloping close behind.

Leah's horse broke into a canter and headed toward them. "Need help?"

He waved a gloved hand. "No, thanks. You've probably got enough ornery critters on your side of the herd."

She nodded and moved in a wide arc, returning to the outside flank of the couple of dozen head still moving forward.

Steven pushed his mount a little harder, and they reached the stand of brush at the same time the cow and calf broke through. "Aha! I got you now." He uncoiled his rope and swung it, dropping the loop over the cow's horns, then looped his end around his saddle horn. The bawling cow dug in and pulled, but only wrestled for a moment before she dropped in behind Steven's gelding. She swung her head and bellowed for her calf, then trotted along behind.

Steven moved closer to the cow as they neared the herd, shaking out his rope and flipping the loop over her head. "Go on now and don't run off again."

He slowed his gelding to a walk and fell in along the flank opposite Leah. What would she think if he told her about the possible move to La Grande? Would she be sorry to see him go, or shrug it off, figuring it nothing more than an inconvenience that she'd need to find another cowhand to take his place?

Truth be told, she'd be better off to find someone steady who could help her and Charlie and give a full week's work, since Tom didn't pull his weight as many hours as they needed. Maybe he shouldn't mention it until he'd made up his mind whether to take the job.

But why stay? The vice presidency would give him a solid financial foundation, and it wouldn't be long before he could purchase his own home.

He looked around him at the mountains in the distance and the broad expanse of lush pastureland that stretched clear to the base of the foothills. La Grande was beautiful too, but this place was special. Was it only the beauty of the landscape that drew him?

His gaze drifted to the woman sitting on her horse as though she belonged there. Leah was born to the land and loved it with every fiber of her being. If only he believed she could come to care for him, as well.

She chose that moment to shout and wave, jerking him back to his immediate surroundings. "We're here. Let the herd settle."

Steven reined to a halt and rested his hands on the pommel. A spring-fed pond about twice the size of a large settler's cabin glistened in the sunshine. A creek ran out the end closest to them and wended its way through the meadow. The cattle drifted toward the water, dipping their heads as they neared and stopping to drink their fill.

Leah trotted her horse around the rear of the herd and slowed as she neared him. "We made good time and didn't lose a single head."

Steven chuckled. "Not for a lack of trying on the part of that spotted cow and her calf."

Leah's laughter rang out, clear and full of quiet joy. "There always has to be one." She dropped her reins on her horse's neck. "I love this life! The blue sky, the green grass, the feel of a horse under me. I even love these ornery cattle."

He grinned, her joy contagious. "I'm not sure I agree with the cattle, but the rest sounds good. I'll miss it all if I leave." The words slipped out before he'd realized it.

Shock swept across Leah's features. Her arms fell to her sides, and then she reached for the reins and pivoted her horse to face him. "What do you mean? Are you planning to leave?"

If only he could take the words back—return to the earlier happiness. He'd ruined a perfect moment and caused her worry. But maybe it was better this way. It wouldn't be fair to spring it on her if he should decide to take the position. "I don't think so."

"You don't think so? What, exactly, does that mean?" Leah stared at him, her gaze steady, her eyes bright. Her smile trembled a bit. "You're scaring me, Steven. What are you hiding?"

"Nothing. I'm simply working through some things and trying to make a wise decision."

Her smile faded. "About leaving the ranch." The words were flat, almost without expression, as though waiting for more and not sure how to process it.

Now Steven really wished he'd kept quiet, but he was in it too far to back out now. He couldn't lie to Leah—wouldn't lie to her. She deserved to know the truth, whatever it cost him. "Actually, possibly leaving the area."

"Really. I see." Her eyes met his for several seconds and then swung away. "I'd hoped that you and I—" Her voice choked. "I need to get back. We'll talk on the way to the ranch." She urged the animal into a fast walk.

Steven closed his eyes for an instant, then followed. "Will you let me explain?"

She kept her gaze trained straight ahead. "What is there to say? You're moving away. I should have expected as much. When do you leave?"

He nudged his horse forward and bent over, grabbing her reins and hauling her horse to a stop. Somehow he must break through the frozen reserve she'd built and make her understand. "I didn't say I was leaving, only that it's a possibility."

Leah yanked on her reins. "Let go of my horse, Steven."

He tightened his grip. "Not until you listen to me. If I have to, I'll haul you off that horse and hold on to you until you do."

Her eyes widened. "You wouldn't dare."

Frustration boiled in Steven's chest, and he released his hold on her reins and swung his leg over his saddle. "Won't I, though?" His boots thudded as he landed. He dropped his horse's reins on the ground and stalked around to where Leah sat unmoving.

Leah stared at him, then backed her horse a few paces. "All right. I'll listen. You needn't get so riled."

He stopped one stride from her leg, his fingers itching to pull her from her horse and kiss her until she collapsed in his arms. If only he could tell her how he felt, but that wasn't an option now.

Leah had just discovered she owned this ranch, and the last thing he wanted was for her to think he'd set his cap for her as a result. He'd be in the same position as Charlie. Living on a ranch that his wife owned and not having brought a thing to the marriage.

He needed to make something of himself—and that could only happen by accepting the promotion in La Grande. Even if he gave her the money he'd saved, would he ever be sure she valued him as much as the ranch?

He stood stiffly, legs spread shoulder width apart. "Fine, if you're willing to actually listen. But how about you step down off that horse first?"

She hesitated for several long heartbeats, then slowly swung her leg over the saddle and stood by her horse, gripping the reins.

Steven wished this conversation had never started. Why hadn't he kept quiet and left things as they were? He'd upset Leah before he'd made a firm decision about his future. "I've been offered a new position at the bank in La Grande. The vice president has been promoted to a bank in Pendleton, and the board asked me to take his place. It's an opportunity for me to get ahead financially and an honor to be asked."

There, he'd said it, but his mind went back to the six words she'd said moments ago. "I should have expected as much." Why? What had he done to make her believe he'd leave?

Her silence almost unnerved him. "Leah?" He shifted his position so he could better see her expression. "Why did you say that earlier?"

She still didn't look at him, but her lips pressed tight together before she finally spoke. "What?"

"That you should have expected as much. And what you said about hoping you and I … I'd like to know what you meant. Besides,

I'm still thinking and praying about the job. What have I done to make you assume I'd leave?"

She kept her face averted. "Everybody leaves. I suppose I'd hoped you might be—" Her voice broke, and the silence lingered between them. "I care for you, Steven, but I guess I was wrong to allow myself to do so."

Steven's heart felt as though a lance had been plunged through it. It hadn't occurred to him that she'd feel this way—that she'd lump him in the same camp as her mother and brother—even her father, for that matter, since the man had never really been there for Leah after her mother's desertion.

Or that she might care for him. He'd never dared to hope, never thought he had a chance. Somehow he must help her to understand that he could never live off her inheritance.

"But it's not the same thing, Leah. It's a job offer. It's not personal against you. In fact, if I go, it's because I care about the future and want so much more for us both." He shut his eyes and clenched his jaw as the words fell into the silence.

Not personal? Was that really true? If he took this job, wasn't he trying to run to his future, hoping to make it more than it was now? Or was he running away from things that hurt or worried him, the same as her family had done? Wasn't that being as much of a coward as the people who'd left a young girl to fend for herself?

She turned her head and met his gaze. Sorrow and confusion shone from her expression. "Your future." She nodded slowly. "Then you should take the job and go. I'm sure that would be best."

He held out his hand, willing her to take it, willing her to truly listen with her heart.

Leah backed away. She gripped the saddle horn and swung aboard. Keeping her face averted, she kicked her gelding in the side, taking off down the trail at a hard gallop, leaving only the sound of hoofbeats ringing in Steven's ears.

Leah didn't know whether to cry or scream, or maybe do both, one after the other. Why was she surprised by Steven's news? She'd meant it when she'd said she expected as much. Nobody in her life could truly be counted on. They all had their own selfish needs that excluded her, and the sooner she came to accept that, the better off she'd be.

Except for Millie and Buddy. Those two dear people had never let her down. A shiver ran across her skin. If anything ever happened to either of them, she wasn't sure how she'd live through it.

But Steven … she'd come to believe he appreciated the ranch, that he'd settled in and wanted to be her friend, maybe even more than a friend. She'd been foolish to allow her heart to dream where Steven was concerned. Dreaming only opened a person's heart to hurt and loss.

She leaned over her gelding's mane, relishing the wind in her face and the rhythm of the horse's body beneath her. If it were possible and it wouldn't kill her horse, she'd let him run like this for hours, until some of the tension eased from her muscles.

But too many other dangers lurked, like gopher holes that could snap a horse's leg and send her sailing through the air. She slowed to a controlled canter, wondering if Steven had followed her fast pace but refusing to look. She truly hoped not. All she wanted was to figure out what she really felt and what, if any, course of action to take.

Leah let out a shuddering breath. This situation was out of her hands. If Steven chose to leave, there was nothing she could do to stop him. And if he stayed, she'd always wonder if the next opportunity that presented itself would lure him away.

Charlie shaded his eyes against the late afternoon sun, wondering at the fast pace of the rider racing toward the ranch. It appeared to be Leah's horse, and his heart jumped to his throat. Had an accident befallen the girl, or Tom or Harding? He strode toward the barn. Time to saddle up. He peered toward the rider again only to see her slow her mount, then in another dozen yards or so, pull down to a walk.

He heaved a sigh, then stopped and waited. She'd be here soon enough—at least before he could throw a saddle and bridle on his horse one-handed. Maybe she was simply enjoying the thrill of a fast horse, but somehow he didn't think so. He could make out her face now, and she didn't look happy. Hadn't she taken a herd of cattle to the pasture near the spring with Harding's help? What happened to the man? That fella better not have laid a hand on his girl.

He walked back to the house and climbed the steps to the porch, shading his eyes again. Looked like Harding was bringing up the rear, far behind Leah, at least by a quarter mile. She had a bee in her bonnet, or he wasn't Charlie Pape.

That Harding fella had turned into a right good worker, even if he was a banker. Leah and Harding had never said a word about the man's occupation, but Charlie saw him ride his horse out of here every morning in his fancy duds and decided to follow him one day. Charlie considered giving the man his walking papers after that, but then he broke his arm and thought better of it.

Besides, he'd come to realize Harding was nothing at all like old man Hunt, who ran the bank with an iron rod. He'd quarreled with the bank president a few years ago when he'd asked for a loan. The skinflint knew Charlie owned the ranch, but he wouldn't loan him a dime without seeing the deed.

Charlie had stormed out, swearing he'd never darken the door of that place again. That's why he'd been so irate when Leah asked about a loan. He'd never take money from that bank even if he could find the deed.

He sure wished Mary had told him where she'd put it afore she went off and left him. She'd promised him she'd give it to him and make sure it was in his name. Many a time he'd wanted to make this place better. He'd smarted with shame when Leah asked if he'd sign the loan papers, and he had to say no.

But he couldn't bring himself to tell her the truth—that her ma owned the ranch and didn't love him enough to share it with him. Even after he'd loved and cared for her child like she was his own. Not that he'd change that part of his life. Leah was his girl. He loved her so much it liked to kill him to turn her down when he knew she was right. The ranch needed help—and a man committed to work, not one who drank himself under the table.

He waited, watching Leah ride closer and studying her face.

Yep, shore enough, she looked upset. He leaned against a porch post. Just like her ma in that regard. Her emotions showed bright as a summer day and no mistake.

As she walked her horse past the house toward the barn with no sign of slowing or speaking, Charlie straightened from his position and took a step forward. "What happened to Harding?"

The big sorrel gelding took three more strides before Leah pulled him to a halt, her shoulders stiff and her back rigid. "I have no idea." She didn't turn her head, but her words were clear as spring water.

"Uh-huh. So you left him behind, that it?"

"He knows the way home. There's no reason for me to drag along beside him."

"You were in some kind of hurry to get here. Runnin' that horse pretty hard for a distance. You coulda broke his leg or taken a bad fall. We can't afford to lose any stock due to carelessness."

She half turned in her saddle, her voice soft. "It's my horse, Pa, and I know what I'm doing."

Irritation flared, and Charlie stepped to the edge of the porch. "I ain't gonna argue about this, Daughter. The stock on this ranch are my responsibility. That one happens to be a valuable cow horse, and we don't need him lamed by bein' foolish."

Leah yanked the horse's head and booted him in the flank, bringing him around to face Charlie. "You got that wrong, Pa. The stock on this ranch are my responsibility. I know what I'm doing and don't need to be lectured."

Charlie gaped and blinked, working to understand what she'd said. "Since when do you speak to your father that-a way, missy?"

His voice rose a notch, but he didn't care. Leah had better change her tone and show some respect.

The door behind him banged open, and Tom strode out of the house. "What's all the yelling about?"

Leah ignored her brother and fixed her gaze square on Charlie. "Since I found out I'm the legal owner of this ranch, that's when."

Chapter Twenty-Six

Tom felt as though he'd been caught in some kind of bad dream that suddenly turned into a comedy. And wouldn't you know it, that Harding fella had to ride up and butt in again, right when he wasn't wanted. What had his sister said about owning the ranch?

"What's wrong with you, Leah? You know this ranch belongs to Pa." Tom stared at his father's stony face, wondering why he hadn't replied. "And someday it's going to be mine. Right, Pa?"

His father's eyes were fixed on Leah, and the color had drained from his face.

Leah didn't so much as look at Steven Harding as he drew to a halt nearby.

Tom took a step closer to Pa and touched his shoulder. "Pa? Why aren't you saying anything? Tell her what I said is true."

Pa gave a slow shake of his head and brushed Tom off like he was some kind of pesky fly. "Leave me be, boy. This is between me and your sister."

Tom crossed his arms over his chest. "No, sir, it is not. I am part of this family even if you seem to keep forgetting that fact. And someday this ranch will belong to me. As your only son and your heir, I got the right to know what she's talking about."

Pa laughed—a cold, dead sound. "Somehow I don't think you're gonna like what she has to say."

Steven backed his horse a step but didn't turn and leave. Tom wanted to toss the man off the property, but whatever was wrong with Leah would probably come out where everyone would know, anyway.

The door creaked again. Millie stood in the opening, smiling and beckoning, with Buddy looking over her shoulder. "Supper's about ready. Why don't you two put your horses in the barn and get washed up?"

Tom's stomach chose that moment to grumble, but he ignored it. Something was going on here that he didn't understand. He intended to get to the bottom of it, and the sooner the better.

Leah shook her head. "Not yet, Millie. I've got something to say, and you might as well stick around and listen. This isn't how I wanted it to happen"—she sucked in a sharp breath—"but things don't always happen the way we wish."

Deep frown lines formed around Millie's lips. "What you talkin' about, girl? How you wanted what to happen? What did I miss?"

Leah looked at Tom. "This will probably hurt you, Tom, and I'm sorry. I found a letter a few days ago that Ma left for me. She said the ranch belonged to my pa—Aaron, her first husband—and she put the deed in my name. I own the ranch, not you or Pa."

Tom felt shaky and sick. "You found Ma's letters? What were you doing going through my things?"

Leah stared at her brother, all thought of what she'd been about to say blowing away like a tumbleweed in a stiff wind. "Letters? Your things? What are you talking about?" She clenched the reins tightly, quieting her restless mount, her short-clipped nails digging into her palms. "You said 'Ma's letters' ... 'in my things.' You have letters Ma wrote? Who did she write them to?"

Panic showed clear in Tom's eyes; then a veil dropped over them. "Nothing. Letters Ma wrote to me, that's all."

Her father's head snapped up, and he grabbed Tom's arm with his good hand, yanking her brother toward him. "I always could tell when you were lyin', boy. There'd be no reason for your ma to write letters to you with you livin' with her. Tell the truth now. Why'd you go all white and sickly when Leah asked you that question? What are you hidin'?"

Leah looked from one to the other as dread formed in the pit of her stomach. "Tom?" She urged her horse forward a few steps until he was almost to the edge of the porch. "Do you have letters Ma wrote to me?"

He didn't speak, and her father shook him like an angry child with a rag doll. "Tell her the truth! She's been lied to for enough years by both of us. It's time to come clean, boy."

Tom's head whipped back and forth as though he had no strength or will to hold it steady. Finally, Charlie dropped his hand and stepped back, but he kept his hands balled. Tom stood there, rocking and shivering, but no sound came from his lips.

Leah dismounted and looped the reins over the hitching rail, then walked toward her brother. "Tom?" She touched him on the shoulder. "Please tell me what you meant about Ma's letters."

The sadness in his eyes as he turned toward her was so unexpected it shook Leah hard. She'd anticipated anger from Tom after

Pa's harsh treatment and words, not despair that cried for understanding. While she tensed at what might be coming, she wished she
could wrap her arms around her little brother and hold him tight as
she had when he was a baby.

But this wasn't the time to coddle him. Tom needed to 'fess up
to whatever he'd done wrong, and she wouldn't do him any favors by
trying to protect him.

He gave his head a half shake as though attempting to wake
himself from a bad dream. "I'm sorry, Leah. Truly I am."

"For what, Tom? Tell me." She reached out to touch him again,
but the pain in his eyes stopped her. "Please?"

He nodded. "I stole the letters Ma wrote you. I was so jealous.
I knew she'd promised Pa not to contact you for two years after she
left. When I arrived in Portland, she asked me to mail the first letter
to you. I wanted her all to myself. You were always her favorite. If
you came, I'd be pushed aside again."

Leah heard Steven's harsh intake of breath and her father's low
rumble of anger, but she paid them no heed. "How long did this go
on, Tom? How many letters?"

He spread his hands in a wide arc. "I'm not sure. I never counted.
I was only going to keep the first three or four, to give her time to
want me there, as much as she wanted you. Then she started worrying and wondering why you didn't answer, and she sent another one
asking if you'd gotten her letters."

Leah nodded, understanding dawning. "You knew if I got that
one, I'd write and tell her I hadn't gotten any of them. So you had to
keep taking them."

Tom lowered his head until his chin almost touched his chest. "Yeah."

"But you didn't throw them away? You said you thought I was rummaging in your room. Did you keep some of them?" Leah's emotions galloped wildly back and forth between anger, pity, and hope.

Was it possible her mother hadn't walked off and completely forgotten her after writing the letter she'd found in the box? All this time she'd grieved her mother's death, only to find out she had deserted her, and now to discover Ma might have cared after all ... it was almost more than Leah could grasp.

"I kept them all." Tom lifted his head, his voice hoarse and hollow. "Wait here. I'll get them for you." He turned and walked away like a man whose will had been broken.

A lifetime of thoughts and memories flew through Leah's mind. A deep, profound silence hovered as they all waited for Tom's return. Leah looked first at her pa, then at Millie and Buddy, standing with arms entwined near the still-open front door, and finally at Steven, compassion showing clearly on his face. Her heart twisted as she remembered his words. He was leaving her too.

Footfalls on the hard ground behind Leah alerted her, and she pivoted.

Tom's normal swagger was gone, and he all but shuffled up to her, clutching a crudely handcrafted box. He stopped in front of her and thrust it forward as though anxious to run, as she knew he must be. "Take it. They're all there."

He waited until she had a firm grip on the box, then sidled backward toward the bunkhouse. "I'll be going now. The ranch is yours. I'm sure you and Pa hate me for what I've done."

Leah stared, not comprehending. "I don't hate you, Tom. I'm disappointed and even angry, but I could never hate you. Give Pa some time to get past all of this, and me, too."

He shook his head. "I'm not so sure, Leah. I think I need time by myself." He pivoted and walked toward the bunkhouse without looking back.

Pa lunged forward as though finally waking from a stupor. "You come back here, boy. We're not finished!"

Leah leaped toward him and grasped his arm. "Leave him be, Pa. It's not going to help to yell at him right now. He said he was sorry, and I believe he meant it. That's enough for now. There's time for more talk later." She cradled the box against her chest. "I'm going to my room, but promise me you won't say anything more to Tom tonight, all right?"

He stared at her for several long seconds, then nodded. "I suppose I can leave him be until tomorrow. Then he and I are goin' to have us a long talk." He narrowed his eyes. "Now, what was it you started to say about that deed, girl? Somethin' about your ma leavin' the ranch to you, is that what I heard?"

She bit her lip, hating to add any more tension to the situation. But she didn't want to dance around the truth. There had been far too much of that over the years. "Yes. Ma left me a letter in the box you made for me when I was a girl. She said the ranch is mine—that my pa wanted me to have it—but that she'd told you she might put it in your name if you cared for me. I'm not sure how I feel about it yet, but I was planning on talking to you about it. Just not like this. I'm sorry."

Steven stepped forward and cleared his throat. "I'll be excusing myself now and go check on Tom." He smiled at Millie. "I'd love to have some of your delicious supper later, if you don't mind holding it for me." He waited for her assent, then headed for the bunkhouse.

Millie stared at Steven, then grabbed Buddy's arm and dragged him inside. Leah could hear her hissing unintelligible words as they closed the door behind them.

Leah faced her father—or, at least, the man she'd called Pa for as long as she could remember. They stood alone near the hitching rail, and the silence felt like a smothering blanket, making it hard to breathe. "Pa? I need answers. Not tomorrow. Now."

He shook his head like an old dog struggling to wake from a deep sleep, his eyes clouded and sad. "I got no idea what to say to you, girl. You got the say-so around here from now on, according to the paper your ma left. Guess that's all you need to know, ain't it?"

Anguish rose inside Leah, and she wanted to wail. "No, it's not all, Pa. There's a whole lot more I want to know, and you are the only one who can give me the answers. You. Not Tom, or Millie, or Buddy, or Steven."

He kicked a loose rock, and it bounced a few feet and struck the bottom step of the porch. "I don't got any answers that would make you happy, Leah. Nary a one."

She gripped his arm tightly above the elbow. "I didn't ask you to make me happy. I asked you to give me answers."

Pa raised his eyes and met hers, and Leah felt a dart of pain as she read the deep struggle in his own. A war raged in her father's heart, almost too terrible to comprehend.

She released her hold and took a step back. "Is it all true, what Ma said in her letter? She left because she hated it here, and you convinced her not to tell me, and to pretend to be dead, so I wouldn't leave too? But you were supposed to tell me the truth. You promised her you'd tell me after a couple of years went by and allow me to make my own decision. You never told me at all, Pa. You lied."

He jerked as though a whip had struck him across the face. His lips formed words but nothing escaped.

Leah held out her hands, desperate to understand. "Why, Pa?"

"I wish I could tell you somethin' that would ease your mind, but I can't. There ain't nothin' that can take back what I did or undo the pain I caused. I got no excuse, girl. None at all."

"I'm not asking for excuses. I want reasons!" She flung the words at him as though they were daggers. She only wished they could pierce the thick hide of resistance that shrouded the man standing bent and stoop-shouldered before her.

"I couldn't lose you, Leah girl. You were all I had left. I couldn't stand the thought I might be all alone," he whispered. "I guess that's all there was to it. I'd lost your ma. She threw me away like I was a no-account critter, and then Tom ran off too."

He stiffened. "But now the ranch is yours to do with as you want. That's the way it ought to be, I guess. It's fair, after what I done. I hope someday you can find it in your heart to forgive me, but I won't fault you if you can't."

He plucked his hat from his head, wiped his perspiring forehead, and jammed the hat back down over his balding crown. "I got chores to do, and there ain't nothin' more to say." He stalked across the clearing to the barn without a backward glance.

Steven had no idea what he planned to do, but he couldn't stand around any longer listening to a conversation that had nothing to do with him. He pushed open the bunkhouse door and halted. "What are you doing?"

Tom swung around and glared. "What does it look like?" He gestured toward the bed, which was littered with clothes. "Packing. Didn't you hear me say I want some time by myself?" He turned back and stuffed a shirt into his bag.

"I didn't realize that meant you'd be leaving. Are you headed to town?" Steven rested his shoulder against the door frame.

Tom kept his back turned. "What's it to you?"

Steven didn't miss the husky note in Tom's voice. He straightened and stepped closer. "I hate to see you leave the ranch with things unresolved between you and your father. It's going to hurt Leah, you know."

Tom's movements stilled. "It always comes back to Leah, doesn't it?" The words were soft but clear. He shifted into action again, snatching at a pair of trousers and cramming them into his bag without folding them.

Steven hesitated, not sure he had any business speaking his mind. This wasn't his family, or his problem, but somehow he couldn't let it go. "She's your sister, Tom. Shouldn't you care about her as well?"

Tom laughed, but it came out strangled and choked. "I spent the past six years listening to my mother care about Leah. Isn't that enough?" He flipped the top closed on the bag and secured the buckles, then half pivoted. "Why does everything have to be about Pa or my sister? Don't I matter?"

Steven's heart hurt for the young man, but Tom didn't need pity, he needed direction. "Of course you do, but I think you're looking at things a little off-kilter."

"Yes? And how's that, exactly?" Tom sneered, but his eyes still reflected his pain.

"Your sister loves you. And I'm guessing Charlie does too, but he has a harder time showing it."

"Ha! Then you don't know my pa very well. The only thing he loves is this ranch and the saloon. Why do you think my mother left?"

Steven tipped his head to one side. "From what I've heard, she left because she never really loved him, even though he loved her. As for loving the ranch and the saloon more than you, I doubt it. I've noticed he's not been drinking much, if at all, since his accident."

Tom emitted a hollow laugh and sat on the edge of the bed. "So he hasn't felt up to going to town. That doesn't prove anything."

"He's been to town at least once that I know of, and probably more. And do you think someone who loves to drink does it all in a saloon?" Steven wagged his head. "That's not been my experience with the people I've known who love their liquor. They keep it stashed close. If Charlie wanted to drink, he'd be doing it straightaway here on the ranch. His broken arm wouldn't stop him."

Tom didn't meet Steven's eyes. "That's nothing to me, either way. It doesn't prove he cares about me."

"I think it does." Steven sat on the bunk across from Tom. "I think your father is struggling with remorse over his actions. He might be trying to change his ways—maybe in the hope of earning your respect."

This time Tom threw back his head and laughed in earnest. He wiped his eyes and looked at Steven. "That's the craziest thing I've ever heard. Pa doesn't care about earning anyone's respect. He has so much pride he figures everyone sees him the same way he sees himself."

"It's too bad you feel that way. You're missing out by not spending time with your pa. You think you know all about him, but I'm guessing there are things you don't understand. And then there's Leah. She's been grieving your disappearance for years and is pretty happy you came home. Why take your anger at your parents out on her?"

"You don't understand anything, mister, and it's not really your business." Tom got up, grabbed his bag, and slung it over his shoulder. "I'm headed to town, and I'd appreciate it if you keep that information to yourself. At least for tonight. I don't want Leah or anyone following me and trying to talk me into returning. I want to be left alone. Think you can do that?" He towered over Steven, who sat on the bed without moving. Tom's eyes smoldered with frustration.

Steven stood and forced himself to relax. He'd love to throttle some sense into this young man, but he doubted much that he said or did would make an impact. "I can."

"Good." Tom strode through the open doorway without looking back.

Steven moved to the porch, wondering what it would take for Tom to find his way out of the darkness that surrounded him. He lifted his eyes toward heaven and sent up a silent prayer on the young man's behalf. At this point in Tom's life, God was probably the only One who could reach him, and even God might have to put some thought into how He'd bring that to pass.

Chapter Twenty-Seven

May 26, 1881

Early the next morning Tom swung his bag up to the top of the stage heading out of Baker City, then opened the door and plunked onto the hard seat. He was more than happy to put the town behind him. The stage couldn't leave too soon for him.

As the driver cracked his whip and the team surged forward, Tom put his elbow on the window opening and looked outside. Would Pa or Leah show up and try to stop him? Or maybe Buddy or that banker Steven Harding would ride in at the last minute, in hopes of talking him out of his decision.

The streets were congested with early morning shoppers, miners heading to their work, and wagons carting cargo to and from the mines, but Tom didn't see a single face he recognized as the stage rolled through town. Disappointment hit him hard, but he pushed it aside. It wasn't as if he'd told anyone he planned to take the stage to La Grande. Harding assumed he would spend a night or two in town, and it was possible Leah and Pa didn't know he'd left the ranch, since he'd made the banker promise not to tell last night.

Part of him had hoped the man would break his word, rush to the house, and spill the beans. He sagged against the seat and stared at the opposite wall, thankful he was the only passenger. Apparently most travelers were coming to Baker City rather than leaving.

So Harding had kept his own counsel. Fine. He didn't need anyone in his life interfering. No sir, he'd gotten along fine and dandy for six years, and he'd continue no matter where he landed. He clenched his jaws to keep them from quivering. If only Ma were still alive, he'd go back home.

He sat up straight. He wasn't a baby; he was a man. Maybe he'd find a good paying job in a mine, or better yet, he'd do some prospecting and strike it rich. Dust rolled in through the open window and Tom coughed, then hitched over to the middle of the seat. If he struck gold or even a good vein of silver, he could go back and show them all how successful he'd become. He wouldn't be the son or brother who'd been forgotten by his mother when she deeded the ranch to her daughter.

He couldn't believe Ma did that. Even if the land belonged to Leah's real pa, his mother could have given him a share. The ranch was left to her by her husband, and it would only be fair for her to divide it between her children. He remembered the look on his father's face when Leah made the announcement. At least Tom had the satisfaction that Ma didn't leave it to Pa, either.

Settling back against the seat, he tried not to draw in deep breaths of the dust-laden air. He pulled his hat over his eyes and his bandana up over his nose. Time to sleep and forget the pain of the past. Today was a new day, and if all went well, tomorrow might be even better.

Frances slipped into the door of the café situated inside the Arlington Hotel and surveyed the room, wondering why in the world Charles Pape had sent her word to meet him here. Couldn't the man have simply come to the house like any decent person if he wanted to talk? She touched the hair that framed her face and straightened her hat, wondering again if she appeared presentable. The last time she'd looked in the mirror she was certain she'd found another half dozen wrinkles scattered across her face. Before long she'd be a shriveled-up mess that no man would care to spend time with. She'd better enjoy this outing while she could.

She snorted a half laugh, annoyed at her penchant for vanity. She'd not battled that in the past, so why it reared its troublesome head for Charles Pape, she couldn't understand. A twinge of guilt smote her at her dishonesty. She knew exactly why vanity plagued her now, but she simply did not care to face it.

A waiter stopped and bowed. "Good morning, ma'am. A table for one?"

She straightened to her full height. "Do I look like someone who dines alone, young man? Of course not. I am meeting a friend, if he is not here already." Her gaze swept the room again, but she didn't spot Charles. She nodded toward a table on the far side of the dining area but directly across from the entrance. "Is that table reserved?"

"No, ma'am. If you will follow me, I will be happy to seat you." The waiter led the way to the table and held her chair.

"Thank you, young man. And I am sorry if I spoke sharply earlier." She sank into the seat and leaned back, closing her eyes and feeling her age more than she had in some time.

A step near her table alerted Frances, and she opened her eyes. "Charles. How are you today?" She peered at the man and started. He looked worse than she did, if that were possible. He appeared to have aged considerably from the last time she'd seen him. She motioned toward the chair across the round table. "Sit. You look terrible. Whatever is the matter?"

He pulled out the chair and plopped into it. "As blunt as always, I see."

She waved in dismissal. "I am not blind, and I am certainly not in the habit of prevaricating when the truth will do as well. Set your pride aside and tell me why you asked me here. I am guessing it has to do with the trouble carved all over your face."

He fiddled with the spoon that lay next to the cup and saucer.

The waiter glided up to their table holding a pot of coffee. "Would either of you care for a cup?"

Both of them nodded. They waited until he'd filled their cups and went on his way before Charles picked up the conversation. "Some terrible things have happened, Frances."

A little shock coursed through her at the familiar use of her Christian name, but she decided to let it go. She had formed a liking for this man even though he irritated her at times. Maybe it was all right to allow him this small familiarity, especially in light of his troubled tone. "Tell me all about it. Do not leave a single thing out if you expect to feel better. Talking often cleanses the soul." She laced her hands in her lap and waited.

Charlie took a sip of the hot coffee, allowing the heat to trickle its way down his throat and land in his belly. He'd wondered if Frances would come or if she'd add to the disappointment that weighed like a boulder on his soul. One more boulder would most likely smash him flat and leave him to dry in the sun where the buzzards could pick his bones.

He shook himself free of the gloomy thoughts. Frances had said that talking often helped cleanse the soul. If that were the case, she should be high up on God's list of saints. *Now, that weren't at all nice, Charlie Pape.* This lovely lady had agreed to give him some of her time, and he'd do well to show his appreciation by answering her question.

He leaned forward, his fingers tightly grasping his cup. "I sure do hate to spoil the afternoon. Shouldn't we talk about somethin' pleasant instead?"

"Certainly not." She shook her head quite emphatically. "I am here to help in whatever capacity possible. The least I can do is listen, and then we shall decide if there is anything more to be done. You talk, and I will try not to interrupt."

Charlie relaxed his grip and rotated his head, hoping to ease the kinks out of his neck. "All right, then. It's my children. I'm afraid I've done somethin' terrible to them."

Her eyes widened, and she sat upright. "Oh dear. You have not harmed them, have you?"

He stared at her, unsure what to reply. Harmed them? In so many ways he didn't know where to start. "I'm afraid so. And I think I've done sent Tom packin'."

Her brows drew together. "I beg your pardon? Sent him ... packing?"

"He skedaddled out of town two days ago on the stage. We didn't find out until he'd been gone a few hours, and it was too late to bring him back."

Frances held up her hand. "Maybe you should start at the beginning. I know I said I would not interrupt, but I am afraid I have no idea what you are talking about, Charles. If you would humor me, please, and explain why Tom would leave and what you did to expedite his departure, I would greatly appreciate it."

Charlie nodded. "I guess I'd best start with Leah, then, or you won't understand about Tom."

"Leah? Oh my. You sent her packing? Oh dear!" She placed her hand over her heart.

"No, no. She's still at the ranch. Although I ain't sure how long I'll be there, at the rate things are goin'."

Frances shook her head, the confusion evident on her face. "This is all a big muddle. You are leaving the ranch as well? Who will care for it? Have you taken leave of your senses?"

"I think I might have, Frances, for sure and for certain. Hard to tell, since it seems I've been makin' mistakes right along for some time now." He scratched the stubble on his chin and winced. He'd been so preoccupied this morning he'd forgotten to shave.

"Charles." She reached across and touched him, her fingertips light and soft. "Slow down and try to speak clearly. I have no idea what you are saying."

"I know, I know. I'm makin' a mess of this, too." He clutched her hand, not caring one whit what others might think. Right now he needed hope to cling to.

Frances didn't pull away, so maybe he hadn't scared her too bad.

"I thought I owned the ranch. I always believed it would be mine, anyway, since Mary told me she planned on puttin' the deed in my name. I've worked it for years, cared for it, and planned that Tom and Leah would share in it if they wanted to make a home there permanent like."

She squeezed his fingers. "That makes complete sense. Go on."

"Mary left Leah a letter, and she found it a few days ago. She left the ranch to Leah, not to me. I don't care so much about that anymore, not after what I done. Tom, he's been talkin' all angry and hateful since he came home. Said I drove his ma off, and he hated me for it. She died, you know."

Frances looked at him without moving. "Yes. From what I understood, that happened a number of years ago when the children were young. But you said Tom thinks you drove his mother off?"

Misery spread through Charlie's chest like one of those twisters he'd seen when crossing the plains. Huge, swirling, and angry, consuming everything in its path. "No, ma'am. I let them think that she died then."

He grimaced, ashamed that once again he'd slanted the truth to make himself look better. "That's not exactly true, either. I outright lied to them, Frances. I told them their ma died. But all the time Tom was home, he knew the truth. Mary told him she was leavin' before she walked away. I made her promise not to tell Leah she was alive. I hurt my children, Frances. Hurt them bad, and now I don't know what to do to fix it."

He shook his head, ashamed to continue. "The girl loved the ranch so much, but she loved her ma, too. I knew Tom would hate me, and place the blame on me, and he did. I couldn't stand to lose both of those children.

"I begged Mary to wait two years until Leah turned sixteen before she told her she was alive and livin' in Portland. Tom came home after bein' gone for six years and told Leah what I'd done. He threw it all in my face, then walked out again. I got no idea where he went this time, or if he'll ever come back." A part of him felt like wailing the words, while another part deep down simmered with an anger he couldn't explain.

Frances slowly withdrew and slumped into her chair, the color fading from her cheeks. "And Mary did that? She did not tell Leah? She allowed her daughter to think her dead all those years, and you encouraged that lie?"

Charlie sagged and hung his head, shame flooding him as it had never done before. The look on Frances's face was nearly his undoing. She must hate him too. "I'm ashamed to admit that's the awful truth."

"But why, Charles? Why did you choose to tell your children a lie? Why hurt them by allowing them to think their mother died? And Tom? He knew and never told his sister?"

She shook her head. "I do not understand that at all. It makes no sense. Then to come home and blame you for his mother's death."

"She passed last year. Doctor told Tom it was some kind of disease. I didn't know about it until it was too late. Tom sent me a letter sayin' she was sick. Then a few months later I got another letter sayin' she died." He worked to hold in his roiling emotions. "I didn't want my children to leave me alone."

"No, I do not believe that, Charles." She peered at him closely, her intent gaze unwavering. "There must have been another reason. I cannot perceive of any man telling his children their mother was dead simply because he hoped they wouldn't leave him."

Charles squirmed under her scrutiny and shrugged.

"You are a man with an overabundance of pride, from what I can make out since meeting you." She cocked her head to the side. "I would guess that you had a difficult time admitting your wife would leave you for any reason, and you did not want your children—or your neighbors or friends—to know the truth, as it might cast you in a poor light."

He groaned and placed his face in his hand, leaning his good elbow on the table and rocking back and forth. More than anything, he wanted to bolt from this table and sprint for the saloon—to drown the pain and loss in whiskey until it didn't hurt anymore. "I need a drink."

Frances desired nothing more than to take the man by the ear and slap him, good and hard. First he'd held her hand and acted all humble and sorry; then he'd admitted to a bald-faced lie that must have broken his children's hearts. And now he planned to run to the saloon and get drunk. Maybe a hard shake until his teeth rattled would be a better idea. If only the café wasn't filling with patrons, she'd do it.

She leaned across the table and hissed between pursed lips, although at this point she didn't really care who overheard. "Stop your blubbering, Mr. Pape, and act like a man."

He dropped his hands from his face and scowled. "I am not blubberin', Mrs. Cooper. I will have you know I'm full of sorrow for what I done to my children."

"Ha." She allowed one lip to curl in disgust. "So full of sorrow that a trip to the saloon seems in order?"

His face reddened, and his cheeks hollowed. He looked as though all the air had oozed from his body. "I reckon that wasn't the best idea, huh?"

"Not in the least, Mr. Pape. Not … in … the … least. In fact, I would have to say it might be one of the worst ideas I have had the misfortune to hear in a long time. Why in the world do you think drowning yourself in alcohol is going to solve your problems at home? Can you not see that doing so will only further grieve your daughter, if not your son?"

He lowered his head and refused to meet her eyes. "They've already been grieved so much I can't imagine seein' their pa drunk one more time will make much difference. 'Course, Tom's long gone, so he won't care."

She rapped her knuckles on the table, and his head snapped up. "I beg to differ with you, sir. Your daughter has been hurt enough and does not deserve any more ill treatment. I was going to tell you that I was proud of you. I will admit that I had heard a portion of this from Leah some time ago. Not the part about the deed or much detail about you or your wife, but Leah mentioned the allegation from Tom that his mother had been alive all this time.

"I had hoped you would come to me and share the truth. That you would trust me enough to help you. I appreciate that you finally did so now. I am very pleased you have told the truth, even at your own expense.

"But I am quite disappointed. I must emphasize *quite disappointed* that you would regress in such a manner, and at the first sign of trouble, assume that drinking would solve your problems."

She fingered her napkin in her lap. "I had thought, hoped, imagined that you had given up the evils of drink after we had started talking and formed a friendship of sorts."

His eyes widened. "I did. Truly I did. I don't know why, but I didn't feel the need for it anymore. Until now, that is." His gaze fell, but not before she'd spotted the raw pain and confusion.

"How will whiskey solve your problems, Charles?" She softened her voice. "Will drink bring Tom back or earn Leah's love? Will it give you back your self-respect or your standing in the community?"

"I suppose not, but I don't know anythin' else that will, either." He mumbled the words, but Frances caught each one as they tumbled from his lips.

"You remind me of someone. More than I care to admit, I'm afraid."

A tiny shred of interest lit his eyes. "Who might that be?"

"Myself a few months ago."

His jaw slackened. "You used to drink?"

A chuckle escaped before Frances could stop it. "Hardly. But I am afraid I had the same problem with pride as plagues you. I believed I had all the answers and everyone needed to fall into line the way I demanded. What I did not understand was that my actions were driving those I loved farther and farther away every day."

"Who said anythin' about pride, woman?" Charles reared back in his chair.

"You did, by your response right now. You admit you hurt your children one minute, then fight against anyone trying to help you see the error of your ways the next. You are not God, Charles. He is the only perfect One in His creation, as much as you might disagree with that fact. And He is the only One able to turn this situation around before it grows worse."

Stubbornness firmed the lines of his jaw. "God don't want nothin' to do with me. Him and me parted ways when Mary left. I wasn't good enough to keep her love, and I'm not good enough for Him, neither."

"Hogwash. If your wife did not love you, that was her loss. She was a fool to leave you and your children, no matter what her excuse. I assume you were not beating her or the children?"

"Of course not! I never laid a hand on any of them, and I done my best to show her how much I loved her, every day." He wagged his head. "She still had feelin's for her dead husband, Leah's pa. I think she couldn't stand bein' on the ranch anymore, with everythin' remindin' her of him. It was too hard, I suppose."

Charles rubbed his chin. "But I got to admit, it stung somethin' fierce when she left me."

Frances nodded, her heart filled with sympathy toward this man and ire at his wife. "I can only imagine. But you spoke correctly when you said you were not good enough to keep God's love."

Charles gaped. "Huh?"

"None of us are, although I tried to tell myself that I was a good person and others did not understand me. I suppose I still feel that way at times, but it is not true, you know. We aren't good enough to earn God's love. He gives it to us as a gift of grace, not because we did anything to earn it. He loves us as much as He loves His Son, Jesus. When you understand that, you will have a different outlook on love."

He hung his head. "I'm a low-down polecat who's done little good in this life, so that's hard for me to accept, but I'll have to take your word for it. I never knowed you to lie, Frances."

His eyes looked up, and he reached across the table, palm up. "I'd like to know more about that kind of love, truly I would. You make it sound like somethin' worth havin'. But I'm not sure I can do it all alone. Would you make an old man happy and be my friend while I try to figure all this out?"

She slipped her hand into his and gave his fingers a soft squeeze, her mind returning to the offer of friendship given to her by Wilma a few months before. Gratitude welled in her heart like a spring of clean water rinsing out the grime and grit of the world.

Frances smiled. "It is the least I can do, Charles. I would be proud to help you learn how to stand strong and depend on God's love instead of your own pride. I will admit, it is not an easy lesson, and you may take more steps backward than forward, but if you continue the journey, you will be more than happy with the results at its completion."

Chapter Twenty-Eight

May 30, 1881

The day had dragged with Steven gone to the bank. Leah hated becoming emotionally dependent on anyone, especially a man—and particularly since she knew Steven was considering moving to La Grande. Her father and brother had both failed her in the past, and there was no guarantee Steven wouldn't end up being cut from the same cloth.

She'd told herself repeatedly that Steven would stand by her. After all, he'd declared he wanted to have some kind of future together. Any betrayal by him couldn't be true. But years ago she'd thought the best of Pa, Ma, and Tom, as well.

Leah glanced at the sun, well past its zenith, and smiled. Steven would be home in the next hour or so. Most of the pressing chores were done, and Buddy was turning the horses they'd used today out to pasture. Maybe she should find her father and have the talk she'd been dreading since finding her mother's letter. But what would he say that hadn't already been said?

She'd waited, worried he might hit the bottle again when he learned the truth. For some reason that she still didn't understand, he'd been strangely sober for over three weeks—or possibly longer—and she hated doing anything that might tip the balance in the other direction.

Well, there was no help for it. The longer she put it off, the harder it would become. Pa had been quiet and withdrawn since Tom left the ranch, and she'd not had an opportunity to talk with him since that awful day she'd confronted them both.

A chill chased across her skin, and she rubbed her arms in spite of the warm sun. Tom had always assumed the ranch would be his someday. When he'd walked away six years ago without looking back, Leah figured he'd lost all interest. But when he returned, seeming to think that the ranch was his right, she wasn't so sure anymore.

Truth be told, she had expected him to rear up on his hind legs and scream long and loud. Instead, he'd left on the stage for parts unknown. But maybe he'd come back soon and do just that, once the shock of their mother's revelation faded.

She pushed open the barn door and stepped into the cool, dim interior, thankful Pa was here rather than in the house. Not that she didn't trust Millie or Buddy, but this was between Pa and her. "Pa? You still in here?"

"I'm in the tack room, cleanin' the saddles. Come keep me company while I finish up." There was a cheerful note in his voice that she hadn't heard in months—or had it been years?

Leah stopped in the open doorway and smiled, loving the sight of her father standing relaxed and easy in the late afternoon sunlight streaming through the window. "Looks like you're almost finished."

She stepped into the spacious room and glanced around. "The shelves are dusted! Oh my. And all the bridles are clean and bits shining." She turned amazed eyes on her father. He hadn't done anything like this in years; it had always fallen on her shoulders. "I've been meaning to take care of this for some time now."

He growled low in his throat. "Wasn't nothin'. I reckon you've had more than your share of work. Thought you might like things all spiffed up and purty."

She wanted to race across the open space and throw her arms around his neck and hug him, but she stood rooted to the ground. This was not in character. Who was this man, and why the sudden change? Was it possible he hoped she'd feel sorry for him and return control of the ranch?

Shame washed over her mere seconds later. That was unkind and certainly without foundation. Had she become so hardened by her father's past actions that she couldn't take his current kindness at face value? She moved closer and touched his shoulder. "Thank you, Pa. I know Ma always appreciated it too."

He ducked his head and kicked at a rock embedded in the hard-packed dirt floor. "I'm doin' it for you." He raised watery eyes and smiled. "But don't you go to repeatin' that, or I'll have to deny it. I don't want Tom comin' back and thinkin' I'm gettin' soft."

Leah tipped her head to the side. "Tom wouldn't think worse of you, Pa."

"Maybe so, maybe not. But I don't aim to give him the satisfaction. He's been plumb ornery since he got home. The boy needs to be put in his place and not be so cocky. When he gets back, if he comes back, I'm goin' to tell him so. See if I don't."

Leah sighed. She'd started to hope Pa was softening, and he had to toss this out. "Have you considered he might not be as ornery if he thought you weren't against him?"

He dropped the cleaning rag onto the saddle and swiveled toward her. "I ain't against him at all. I don't like his attitude since he got back, thinkin' he can spout off and speak his mind without carin' whose feelin's he might be trompin' on."

"Have you told him he's hurt your feelings, Pa?"

He jerked and gaped at her. "Me? I wasn't talkin' about myself; I meant you. All that talk about your ma and her not writin' to you or askin' you to come see her. I saw how much it cut you, and I'm plumb sorry. You didn't deserve to be caught in the middle of this mess."

Leah hesitated, unsure what to say. It was rare for her father to apologize, and it meant even more since he still seemed wounded by her mother's desertion. But she knew him well enough to know he wouldn't appreciate her camping on what he'd said and sifting through his words. "Thanks, Pa. I'm sorry too."

"'Bout what? You didn't do nothin' wrong that I can remember." He scratched his head. "Somethin' you need to tell your pa?"

"I meant I'm sorry it's been hard for you, too." She hesitated a moment, then plunged forward. "Actually, there is. I know you must be upset about Ma leaving the ranch to me. You've thought it would be yours all these years, and you've worked hard to make it a success."

She winced. "I'm not going to lie to you, Pa. You've let a lot of things go, what with your drinking and all, but I think I'm starting to understand that more than I used to."

He bent over the saddle, rubbing with renewed vigor. "Maybe, maybe not. Guess I have been drinkin' a mite more than I oughta."

He lifted his head and stared straight into her eyes. "Truth be told, I shouldn't have been drinkin' at all. It hasn't done a blasted thing but make me miserable. I hate myself the next day, and even more when I see how it hurts you. Me and God talked about it, and I decided to give it up. With His help, if He's willin'."

Leah wanted to hug him but wasn't sure he'd receive it. "I'm glad, Pa. More than I can say. And I'm proud of you too."

A wave of red suffused his cheeks. "What you think of Mrs. Cooper?"

Leah struggled to take in his declaration about drinking, much less his mention of Mrs. Cooper. "Uh, I suppose she's a nice-enough woman. A bit outspoken and blunt, but she seems to have a good heart."

"Uh-huh. My thoughts exactly." He commenced to scrubbing the leather again.

Leah touched his arm. "Pa? I'm very happy about what you said—about not drinking anymore. It's wonderful. But why did you ask me about Mrs. Cooper?"

He mumbled under his breath.

"What did you say?"

He kept his eyes cast down, and his fingers kept moving. "I'm thinkin' of callin' on her, is all. Didn't know what you might think. But I don't got nothin' to offer a woman, especially now. Guess it was a poor idea all around. Forget I asked about her, all right?"

Leah's heart hammered in her chest. Mrs. Cooper and Pa? She shook her head, not sure if she should shout with laughter or groan with despair. "All right, then. Pa, about the ranch, I was thinking—"

He dropped the rag and his head snapped up. "Don't you go to sayin' what I think you're going to. I won't take no charity, even from my daughter. I ought not to have expected anything different from your ma."

Leah opened her lips to protest, but the words died before they were born. Stubborn pride shone on Pa's face, as well as something else. Sadness. Grief. A yearning she'd not seen before.

"Pa? We haven't really talked about Ma leaving, but it had to cut deep. Did you love her when you married, or were you mostly trying to give her security and a man to help around the ranch?" She worded it that way intentionally, praying he'd finally open up and tell her the truth. There'd been too many half-truths and outright lies over the years, and she wanted that part of their life to change.

He stared out the window without responding, then turned and picked up the rag. Leaning over the old saddle, he scrubbed at the leather as though trying to restore it to its former self. "Guess I loved her, all right. When I told her I'd care for you, I done it because I fell for you hard. I never hoped for anything more from either of you than you both might love me."

Leah's heart took wing at the revelation. Her father had never been this forthcoming about his feelings or his past before. Ma had clearly stated she'd never been in love with Pa. She'd only ever loved Leah's real father … the one Leah didn't remember. She decided to change to a less painful question. "How did you meet Ma?"

He peered at her beneath hunkered brows. "Why all the questions, girl?"

She lifted a shoulder. "I suppose because I've never asked but always wondered. Neither of you talked about meeting or getting married. Did you know her long?"

"Your birth pa was a good friend. I used to come out here and help Aaron do chores. Got to know Mary before Aaron passed. Good man, a hard worker and steady, with a gentle heart. The kind of man your ma needed in her life." He turned his head away.

Leah waited, praying he'd continue but hating to push. This might be all he'd share, and if so, that was all right. It was more than he'd ever been willing to say. She wanted to tell him he was kind too, had been when she was young, and that it was the drink that made him surly and mean. But this wasn't the time.

He'd made a declaration that he wanted to change, and she'd stand beside him in his battle to stay sober. No, it was better to be silent and allow him to say as much or as little as he wanted for now.

He glanced back at her. "I thought a lot of her even then. I could tell it was hard on her, livin' on this ranch and doin' work she wasn't used to. She and your pa met in the city and fell in love. He told me once he offered to move away from here, but she wouldn't hear of it. His heart was in the land, and she loved him so much she promised to stay with him, help him become a success."

He rested his weight on the pommel of the saddle and gave a sad smile. "I guess when your pa died, I thought I was helpin' by offerin' to marry her and give you a father. You were the prettiest little thing. Bushels of red hair even when you were a tyke, with bright eyes and a winsome smile that wrapped all the cowboys around your finger."

Leah smiled at the picture he'd painted. "And Ma agreed to marry you? So soon after my father died?"

"I waited as long as I could—three months I think it were—but she was strugglin' to boss the cowboys and get the work done. Buddy and Millie hadn't come along yet, and Mary didn't know the first thing about ranch work." He shook his head. "I knew she didn't love me, but I always hoped she'd learn to, one day. I saw how loyal she was to your pa, and I guess I thought …"

Leah winced at the pain that laced Pa's words. He'd thought Ma would fall in love with him and want to stay on the ranch, be his helpmeet, the same as she'd promised to do for her first husband. But it never happened. Ma never fell in love with Charlie Pape, and the ranch became her prison. "I'm sorry, Pa. I never knew."

He straightened and turned with a smile. "Guess it don't matter now. She did two good things for me, that's for sure and for certain."

"What were they?" Leah returned the smile, happy he'd been able to pull away from his gloomy memories.

"She birthed Tom, and she let me keep you when she left. I made her swear she wouldn't try to convince you to move to the city. If she was gonna leave me, she had to promise to give you a chance at happiness on the ranch you loved so much. I think she got to the point where she couldn't abide the sight of me."

He choked on the last word and coughed. "It woulda tore my heart out if she'd taken you away with her. It was hard enough when Tom decided to leave. I'm not sure what I'd a done if you'd left too."

Leah wrapped her arms around his neck and gave him a fierce hug, placing her lips close to his ear. "I love you, Pa." She didn't know what had softened her father's heart so much, but whatever it was, she was grateful. And there was no way she'd say anything more about the ranch today. No, sir, she wouldn't risk ruining this rare time of love and companionship for all the ranches in Oregon.

Chapter Twenty-Nine

June 9, 1881

Steven settled his hat tighter on his head, wondering if this was a good time to talk to Charlie. He'd hung around the bunkhouse, hoping he'd get a chance before he headed to La Grande. He didn't want to tell Leah of his plans and worry her, but he couldn't simply disappear, as that would certainly cause her concern. Maybe telling Buddy would be a better choice.

Steven had hoped to have some kind of a relationship with Charlie, but he'd never quite figured out how to get close to the man. But lately, Leah's pa seemed different. He was mellower, not so belligerent, and more approachable somehow. Perhaps the departure of his son, two weeks ago, had made him rethink his choices.

A jaunty whistle split the air outside the bunkhouse. Rusty barked and rushed across the porch, his tail thumping against the post next to the steps. Steven stopped in the open doorway and stared, unable to believe the whistle came from Charlie.

He strode up the path toward the cabin, carrying a tray containing a plate heaped with doughnuts and two mugs. "Hey there, Harding. Millie baked some bear sign, and they go mighty good with coffee. Want some?"

Steven grinned, remembering his father calling doughnuts by the same name, but it still created a not-so-pleasant image in his mind. He sniffed and closed his eyes as the fragrance of warm doughnuts and hot coffee surrounded him. "Don't mind if I do. I was hoping I'd find you today, anyway."

Charlie plunked himself into a chair on the porch and shoved the tray toward Steven. "Help yourself." He waved at Rusty, who crept forward, his tongue hanging out. "These ain't for you, fella."

He peeked at Steven, then broke off a chunk and tossed it to the dog. "Well, maybe it won't hurt to share a bite. Never could stand that sorrowful look when he wants somethin'."

Steven bit into a sugar-coated doughnut and sighed. "Millie's got to be the best cook in the county."

Charlie grunted and polished off another sweet treat. "The whole blasted state if you ask me."

"Right."

Silence fell between them, and the plate emptied. Rusty crept a little closer, and Steven tossed him a bite, careful not to look directly at Charlie, who pretended to study a bird strutting and screeching on a tree branch nearby.

Steven stretched his legs in front of him, enjoying the warmth of the sunlight filtering through the leaves and slanting under the porch roof. "I've got a question for you, if you aren't in a hurry."

Charlie turned toward Steven. "No rush at all. The morning chores are done, Leah's in town at her quiltin' meetin', so she's not apt to thump me with a broom for lazyin' around, and Buddy's at the house eatin' his fill of bear sign. He won't be in no hurry to roust me out. What's on your mind?"

Now that the time had come, Steven wasn't sure what to say. He could tell Charlie about his trip, but should he go beyond that? One step at a time. "I'll be away for a few days. I don't want anyone to worry."

Charlie stared. "You tell Leah?"

"No, I didn't see her before she left. I thought I'd talk to you or Buddy. I'm going to stop by the boardinghouse to see my sister and mother, and I'll leave from there for La Grande." He shifted his gaze away from Charlie, not sure how to proceed.

Charlie narrowed his eyes. "What you tryin' to hide, young man?"

Steven winced. "I imagine you deserve to know the truth since you're Leah's father."

"Uh-huh." His bushy brows bunched close together. "That I am. Spill whatever you got to say, boy, without varnishin' it."

Steven sat straighter. "Yes, sir. Well, it's this way." He brushed a patch of dust off his trousers, then looked up. "I care for your daughter, Mr. Pape, but I've been offered a promotion that would take me to La Grande. I'm still considering what I ought to do."

"Charlie." The older man growled the word. "You takin' a shine to my girl don't mean you got to call me Mr. Pape, even if you are a banker." He scratched his head. "We never did have us a talk about that, neither—you sneakin' out here and workin' on my ranch and all the while you were a banker."

Steven stared at the man, confused at the turn in the conversation. "I beg your pardon? I didn't sneak. Your daughter offered me a place to live after my cabin burned. What does my being a banker have to do with anything?"

Charlie held up his hand. "Hold on. I didn't mean no offense, although I can see why you'd take it that way. Guess I'd best start over. When you first showed up, I tried to find out who you were and what you were doin', but Leah shied away from my questions like a young colt runnin' from a scary critter. That set me to wonderin', so I followed you to town one mornin' and seen you go in that bank and sit in your fancy office. Been wonderin' ever since why you'd bother with us ranch folks.

"First, I figured Mr. Hunt sent you to spy on me. I never have trusted that fella since he turned me down for a loan." He shook his head. "I reckon my thinkin' was partly due to the whiskey. But I still didn't understand why an educated man like you would want to spend his time diggin' post holes and brandin' calves—until I seen the way you look at Leah."

He hunched forward. "Now, that brings us around the barn and back to the open door where you let the horse outta the stall. You said somethin' about carin' for my girl, but now you're thinkin' about movin' on. You playin' with her affections?"

Steven stiffened at the brusque tone. "No, sir, I am not. I am quite serious in my intentions, but I can't say she feels the same about me."

Charlie spat off to the side. "Then you're blind, mister." He shoved his feet against the floor planks and set his chair to rocking.

A flash of hope tore through Steven's chest, then as quickly died. "There's something else. I hope you won't be offended."

"Uh-huh. Out with it."

"I've been concerned about Tom taking off two weeks ago. I feel partly responsible, as I might have stopped him if I'd realized he was leaving town."

He kept his gaze trained on Charlie's face, praying the man would listen. "I did some digging and discovered he's in La Grande. I'm hoping to convince him to come home."

Charlie's boots hit the floor and the chair came to an abrupt halt. His nostrils flared; then he leaned forward, his face illumined by the dim light of hope. "Why would you do a thing like that? You think he'd listen to you?"

Steven gripped the arms of his chair. "Partly because it would make Leah happy." He plunged forward, praying Charlie would understand. "And partly due to the unhappiness I've seen in you since Tom left. I know what it's like not having a father in my life and losing a sister. From what I could see before he left, Tom was hurting pretty bad. And no, I'm not sure he'd listen to me."

Charlie laced his arms across his chest. "I don't see what this has to do with me."

"Come with me to La Grande. Help me find Tom. Talk to him. I doubt he'd return if I asked him, but he might if you do."

Charlie shook his head, then turned his face away.

Steven looked closely. Was that a tear trickling down the older man's weathered cheek? "He's your son. He loves you, even if he's hurt and doesn't know how to show it. I know he's hurt and angered you as well, but you're his father. Won't you give it a chance?"

Charlie's hands shook so hard he couldn't control them. What was this young whippersnapper thinking, asking him to go with him to

La Grande? He was plumb loony, that's what. Tom didn't give a fig what his father thought.

In fact, he'd run the other way if Charlie so much as showed his face in town. "It won't work, mister. Tom won't listen to me. He never has. He hates me. You musta seen that when he was here."

Steven's direct gaze didn't waver. "I agree. It seemed like that at first. But the more I listened and watched, the more I talked to Tom, the more I saw little bits of myself in him. I went through some of the same confusion and fear when I lost my pa, and my ma retreated so far inside herself. Then when we found my sister after so many years, I figured it would all work out right. When Ma turned all her attention on Beth, I started getting bitter all over again."

Charlie's chest hurt. He wanted this to stop. He didn't want to relive the pain of the past, over and over. Not Steven's past, or Tom's, or his own. "Young fella, that's got nothin' to do with me." He started to get up from his chair, but Steven's expression gave him pause.

"Please, sir. Don't leave. This might be your last chance to find your son and truly understand him. Don't throw that away. At least listen—for Leah's sake."

Charlie plopped into the chair, pain swirling so deep he reckoned he'd be sick. All he thought about anymore was Leah and Tom, and the ways he'd hurt his youngsters. He'd driven Tom away, but he had no idea how to make it right.

Leah seemed like she was on the trail to forgiving him, but would it make a difference to her, or to Tom, if he followed this foolish scheme Steven suggested? "All right. I'll listen. But I ain't makin' no promises."

"Thank you. What I'm trying to say is, Tom is a lot like me. I understand him. He lost his mother and came back with a gut full of anger and resentment, believing it to all be your fault. As time passed, he may have seen it was partly his mother's responsibility as well, and that was hard to take. Just like it was hard for me to find fault with my mother, since I was used to being her protector and support."

Charlie nodded but couldn't bring himself to speak. The images Steven's words evoked were too strong, too hard to deal with. Finally, he cleared his throat. "Like I said before. The boy hates me for what he thinks I done to his mother. I wasn't there when she died, and he blames me."

Steven nodded. "Yes, but she's the one who left you and Leah. And part of him is angry at Leah because she held his mother's love for so many years. What he doesn't see yet is that his mother loved him as well. But just as I was always there for my mother, Tom was there for his. She poured all of her time and emotions into bewailing the daughter she'd left behind, instead of appreciating the son who stayed by her side. At some point Tom will need to forgive his mother, as I've had to do. But right now he needs to know he has a father who loves him and won't desert him."

The walls around Charlie's heart began to crumble—slowly, like a trickle of water eating away at an earthen dam—until finally the crack widened and the flow of cleansing water increased and broke the dam wide open. He buried his face in his hands, and silent sobs shook his shoulders. Several long minutes ticked by while he worked to get himself under control. Finally, the sobs subsided and the shivering stopped.

He raised his head and looked Steven square in the eyes. "I love him more than life itself. I'll go with you to La Grande." Tears trickled down his cheeks, but he no longer cared. All these years he'd thought that by working hard to be a good provider, he'd done enough, but now he knew different. His pride had destroyed his family once, and somehow—maybe with God's help—he could humble himself and try to salvage what was left of his family.

Chapter Thirty

Leah shut the church door and headed for her buggy, her skirts swishing with each step. The ladies had decided to work on the quilt again, as a local family was in need. It felt as though life had finally started to settle back into its normal routine after Tom's departure over two weeks ago.

But for one thing.

Pa hadn't touched a drop of liquor from what she could tell. The big row Pa and Tom had and Tom's second disappearance should have pushed her father through the door of the saloon at a full gallop. He'd headed to town and she'd been positive he'd come home drunk, but he'd returned as sober and meek as a church mouse.

Then he'd shared his decision to stop drinking and try to trust in God. She'd worried that it wouldn't last, but he seemed to be sticking to his decision.

She walked to the side of the buggy and wrestled her skirt as she climbed to the seat, annoyed yet again that she couldn't wear trousers in town. Picking up the reins, her thoughts turned back to her brother. Tom was another thing worrying her of late. When she'd tried to approach Pa about finding Tom, he simply shook his head and turned away, but not before Leah noticed the sadness shadowing his eyes. She had no idea how to help her father or what to do about Tom.

Part of her believed her brother would come dragging back to the ranch with his tail between his legs, asking forgiveness and ready to settle down. But another part worried he'd disappear, and they might never see him again.

Then there was the ranch. Pa had never wanted advice, and she doubted his pride would allow him to accept anything from her. Leah's excitement over inheriting the ranch had dimmed in the days since first reading her mother's letter. Pa's grief weighed on her mind, in spite of the day he'd opened up and shared his heart.

Then Leah shook off her doldrums and smiled. Her father had made more than one trip to visit Frances Cooper lately. Could Pa actually be interested in a woman after being alone so many years? If he could find real love after so many lonely years, she'd be happy for him, but she hadn't yet sorted out her feelings about it being Mrs. Cooper.

It didn't matter right now. She'd talk to him later, but first she needed to pay a visit to Steven at the bank.

She traversed the busy streets from the outskirts where the church was situated, enjoying the warmth of the sun in her face as the mare trotted sedately up the road. The minutes sped by as a nervous excitement at seeing Steven held her in its grip.

She slowed her mare to a walk as the buggy wove its way through the busy, late afternoon traffic. Another block brought her to a stop in front of the bank. Leah placed her hand over her beating heart, trying to still the pounding. When had the man come to mean so much to her? She heaved a sigh, wound the reins around the brake handle, and stepped to the ground.

Leah marched into the bank and straight for Steven's office. She seriously doubted he'd turn her away, as long as he wasn't busy with another customer.

Mr. Parker hurried toward her as she crossed the foyer, bypassing the teller windows. "May I help you, miss?"

Leah wanted to roll her eyes, but she kept her composure. Surely this man knew by now who she was and that Steven boarded at her ranch. "I'm here to see Mr. Harding. Is he in?"

"No, miss. He's not. May I take a message?"

Disappointment left her feeling almost weak, after the anticipation she'd felt. "I'll wait for him, if you think it won't be too long."

"He left town a few hours ago, headed to La Grande. I would have thought you'd know that, Miss Carlson."

Embarrassment at her earlier critical thoughts brought a rush of color to her cheeks. Then it dawned on her what the clerk had said, and her heart felt as though it had stopped beating. "La Grande? Do you know when he'll return?"

"I have no idea. However, I believe he went to accept the position he's been offered. A fine job, and one any man would be proud to have. I'm sure he'll make an excellent vice president."

She barely heard the clerk's last few words as she turned and made her way out of the bank, fighting a wave of dizziness. Steven had gone to La Grande to accept the job and hadn't told her. She'd begun to hope he'd decided against accepting it—that he'd see how much she cared and decide to stay on the ranch.

Leah stepped up on the running board of her buggy and almost vaulted into the seat, trying to quiet her shaking hands.

Steven had done the unthinkable—he'd abandoned her, same as her mother, father, and brother had done.

She whipped the reins over her horse's back and urged her into a fast trot, wishing she could outrun her thoughts as easily. It couldn't be true. Steven would be at the ranch when she returned. He had to be.

The drive to the ranch passed almost without coherent thought. A swirl of emotions pursued her like imps, effortlessly keeping up with the brisk pace of her horse. Her insides were quivering when she arrived at the house and jumped from the buggy, barely taking time to secure the mare. She raced up the steps and burst through the door, then moved down the hall to the kitchen.

Millie gasped. "My lands, child. You liked to scare me half to death, bangin' through that door and racin' in here. What's come over you? Someone sick or hurt?" She wiped her hands on her apron. "I'll come and help, whatever it is."

Leah worked to get the words out past the lump in her throat. "Where's Steven? Did he come back?"

"Whoa there, girl, slow down." Millie placed her arm around Leah's shoulder and drew her to the table. "Sit. I'll get you a cup of hot tea. The pot's fresh."

"Thank you, but no." Leah pulled from her grip. "I don't need tea. I need answers."

Millie shook her head. "I figured you'd know by now. Your pa came in before he headed to town with Steven and said they was goin' to stop at the boardinghouse and see the folks there." She sucked in her breath. "But then ..."

Leah's shoulders slumped. "How silly of me. I'm sorry for being such a goose, Millie. And forgive me for interrupting. Maybe I'll drive back to town and visit Katherine and Beth."

Millie frowned. "You didn't give me a chance to finish, girl. They was only goin' to stay a short time to say good-bye to Steven's family. Not sure why your pa went along, but he said to tell you he's headed to La Grande with Steven. He was in an all-fired hurry, and his voice was all choked up. If I didn't know better, I'd think he'd been cryin'."

Millie shrugged and continued. "But that don't make a lick of sense. I've been here since you were a little tyke and never seen Charlie Pape cry. When I asked when they was comin' home and what they were doin' there, he said he didn't have time to talk. He lugged a bag downstairs and tossed it into his old buggy, tied Steven's horse to the back, and jumped on board. He said to tell you he'd be back as soon as he could and not to worry."

Leah sank into a chair, her stomach growing tighter at each word. "Pa said 'he' would be back, not he and Steven? What do you think is going on? If Pa took his horse, that means Steven might not plan to return."

"I'm not rightly sure. I think that's what he said, but I didn't pay much mind. I'm sure he meant they'd both be comin' home soon, though."

Leah placed her head in her hands and groaned. She had no idea why her father would be going to La Grande with Steven, but one thing she knew. Steven hadn't left word for her, and Pa spoke the truth even more than he or Millie realized. Steven Harding would not be returning with her father. He'd decided to take the job in La Grande, and she'd probably never see him again.

Chapter Thirty-One

June 15, 1881

Leah sat on the knoll near the large tree and smoothed the last of her mother's letters. She'd spent three hours rereading every one of the missives Ma had asked Tom to mail but he had kept. Those hours had been some of the hardest of her life, as she'd dug deep into her mother's heart and tried to understand what drove her—and then worked to accept and believe the affirmations of love written over and over again.

She laid it carefully in the box and lifted the bouquet of white daisies she'd picked. The flowers covered the crest of the meadow, the clumps and stands cascading down over the hillside. Ma had loved this view. It seemed to be a place that had soothed her spirit and brought her peace.

Leah prayed that same peace would visit her now.

Steven had been gone for six days, and Pa hadn't returned, either. It took two days to travel to La Grande, unless they'd pushed well into the night. Allowing four days for travel and at least one to take care of whatever business took them, Pa could easily be home today.

Every night she'd tossed and turned, unable to sleep more than a few hours, the pendulum of her emotions swinging from one

extreme to the other. Anger that Steven would leave without so
much as a word, as her mother had done, veering to grief that she
hadn't shown him the depth of her feelings. If she'd done so, would
he still have gone?

Her mother did, and she claimed to have loved her.

Deep in her heart Leah knew Ma's love to be true. But now Leah
realized her ma was a woman of shallow, selfish character who hadn't
denied her own desires to escape a life she saw as intolerable. Was
it possible Steven was that kind of man? Had he viewed life on the
ranch as unbearable and, like her mother, decided city life was best?

But he'd seemed so honest, kind, and caring that she found it
difficult to accept he could be that way. He'd stood beside her when
she was hurting. He'd sat on this hilltop, holding her hand and offering silent support. He'd spoken hard things to her, as well—made
suggestions that angered her—but they'd finally made her think.
That wasn't the kind of thing a shallow, selfish man would do.

She took a handful of daisies and braided them together in a long
chain, then twisted the final stem around the first, creating a loop.
Ma had done this for her countless times as a girl. They'd pretended
it was a crown for a princess, and if she wore it, she could summon
her prince and go live in a castle.

Leah had always believed her mother was thinking of Pa when
Ma allowed Leah to place it on her head. She had closed her eyes
and whispered words Leah couldn't understand. But now she knew.
Ma was dreaming of the man who'd given Leah life—the man Leah
couldn't remember, but who had forever held her mother's heart.

Steven almost vaulted from his horse as he came to a halt at the hitching rail in front of the Pape ranch house, only vaguely aware of the buggy containing Tom and Charlie behind him. He lashed the reins to the rail and bolted to the door, then gave a hard rap and waited. His palms were damp with sweat, and he wiped them down the side of his trousers. If someone didn't open the door soon, he might break it down. This had been the longest six days of his life. He'd wanted to get back yesterday, but it took longer than they'd expected to find Tom.

The door swung open, and Millie broke into a huge grin, with Buddy behind her peeking over her shoulder. "Steven! It's so good to see you." She reached out and enveloped him in a warm hug.

Steven's heart swelled. This was exactly the kind of welcome he'd hoped for, just not from the person he'd anticipated. He released Millie and returned her smile. "It's great to be back. Is Leah …?"

Millie's shriek almost split his eardrums as she raced past him and plummeted down the steps. "Tom! Charlie … you brought him home?"

Steven turned, his joy almost complete as he watched the young man wrap Millie in a hug that seemed to go on forever.

Tom finally let go, only to be met by a hearty slap on the shoulder by Buddy. "About time you got yourself back here, boy. What took you so long?" He turned to Charlie and gripped the man's shoulder. "This your doing, boss? If so, I'm right proud to be your friend."

Tom brushed his knuckles across his eyes. "Pa came to get me, Buddy. Him and Steven. All the way to La Grande. They talked me into coming back." He looked around, and his tentative smile faded. "Where's Leah?"

Millie sobered, then gestured to the hill beyond the house. "She's up there. Took her ma's letters you gave her. I thought she'd be back by now, but I don't plan to rush her. Don't think you should either."

She gave Tom and Charlie a stern look before turning to Steven. "But I got me a feelin' she's hankerin' to talk to you, young man. And if you know what's good for you, you'd best hightail it up there. You've got some explainin' to do."

Charlie scowled. "Why him? I'm her pa. I oughta go up there and make sure she's all right."

Buddy laid a firm hand on Charlie's shoulder. "No, sir, you oughtn't." He nodded at Steven. "Millie's right. Harding needs to explain why he lit a shuck outta here without so much as a by-your-leave to Leah."

Steven felt as though a giant had slammed him in the gut and knocked out every bit of wind. "What do you mean, without a word? Charlie, you told her we were going to La Grande, right? And how long we'd be gone, and why we were going?"

Charlie scratched his head. "Well now, Leah weren't here when I come to the house to get my things, so I left word with Millie. You gave her my message, didn't you?"

Millie harrumphed and laced her arms over her chest. "What scant bit there was, I did. But there wasn't nothin' about Steven comin' back, nor anything about findin' Tom. We was all worried and tryin' to figure out what took you both outta here in such a hurry."

She beamed a smile at Tom. "'Course, I'm right happy it turned out like it did."

Then she rounded on Charlie. "But you got some explainin' to do, your own self." She reached out and grabbed him. "You come in, eat, and tell me how you found this boy and what happened."

She jerked her head at Steven. "While he goes up on that hill and makes his peace with Leah."

Leah placed the wreath on her head and closed her eyes. Wishing for her prince to arrive wouldn't bring any more results than it had for her mother. She could do something else, even more important. "I want to forgive you, Mama." She whispered the words over a lump in her throat. She'd known for a long time this must be done, and it was fitting it be here—and now.

But it was hard. So very hard to let the anger go and, even harder, to part with the hurt. But maybe she didn't have to deal with all of the hurt right now. Maybe all God expected of her was to give Him the anger, and He'd take care of the rest.

"Mama, I missed you for so many years. Then I found out you hadn't died but deserted me. I think for a while I hated you, because I didn't understand. Part of me still doesn't, but I don't hate you anymore." The tears rolled. She couldn't stop now. She didn't dare open her eyes, or she'd lose her courage.

"I think I understand, a little. If you loved my real father as much as I love Steven, I see why your heart was broken. Why you found it impossible to love again. Maybe a part of you wasn't selfish—you might have thought you were sacrificing—to give me the life my father loved so much and would want me to have. Maybe you didn't want to make me choose when I was young."

A tear dripped, but she no longer cared. Nor did she care about the sobs that ripped open her heart. She covered her face and rocked back and forth. "Oh, God, please help me let go of this once and for all."

She drew in a shuddering breath and released it slowly, keeping her head bowed. "I forgive you, Mama. With all my heart." The hardness inside cracked, and a flood of healing cascaded over her spirit.

She sat without moving for several long minutes, drinking in the peace that enveloped her. Somehow Leah caught a glimpse of the future. She might have to forgive her mother again and again, as new hurts and memories surfaced. The pain of the past wasn't all washed away with a few simple words, but the door to restoration had finally opened. With God's help, she didn't intend to enter that dark place again.

"Thank You." Leah whispered the words to the Father who would never forsake her, would never betray her. Leah sat with her head bowed and eyes closed, basking in the gentle tranquility that wrapped her in a cocoon of warmth.

All this time, she'd thought the most important thing in her life was the ranch. It was what she'd lived for, worked for, dreamed about improving.

Now she realized how wrong she'd been. People mattered so much more than things. Her father. Tom. Millie. Buddy.

And Steven.

She'd fought her feelings for him long enough. It was time to fully admit she was in love with the man. Time to give her fear of the future to God and allow Him to make of her future what He willed.

"I choose to trust You, Lord. With Pa, and the ranch, and Tom. Somehow, some way, I'm going to trust You about Steven, no matter what the circumstances look like right now. I love him, Father, and I'm asking You to bring him home.

"I'm going to make things right with Pa, and I want to find Tom and forgive him. Please, please help me put my pride aside where the people I love are concerned. I've blamed Pa for having too much pride, but I'm like him. Thank You for choosing to love me in spite of all that I've done."

She lifted her head and opened her eyes.

And gasped.

Steven stood a few paces away, his hat removed and head bowed. How long had he been there, and how much had he heard? Leah wanted to jump up and race to him, throw her arms around his neck and hold on for all she was worth.

But what if he'd heard her asking God to help her to trust Him about Steven? What if he'd heard her say she loved him, and he didn't feel the same way? Another thought hit her and left her insides quaking. Had he returned to get the rest of his things from the bunkhouse and tell her good-bye?

"Steven? What's wrong? Are you all right?"

His eyes snapped open. "I'm absolutely perfect. But it appears I've once again interrupted you at a bad time. Would you like me to leave you alone? I can talk to you when you come to the house."

"No!" Leah almost choked on the word. "I mean, please stay. I have so much to tell you, ask you—"

A slow, glowing smile lit his face and sent a delicious shiver clear to Leah's toes.

"I'd like that. May I sit?" He motioned toward the grassy area nearby and waited for her approval. Lowering himself onto the grass, he glanced at the wreath of flowers on her head. "Is this a special occasion?"

She reached up and touched the daisies as warmth stole into her cheeks. She'd placed the garland there when remembering her mother and completely forgotten to remove it. It probably looked silly—something a child would do, not a grown woman. "My mother and I used to make them, then pretend … it doesn't matter." She pulled off the wreath and placed it carefully in her lap.

Steven captured her hand in his. "It matters very much to me. Everything about you matters. Will you tell me about it?"

Her fingers felt so alive, vibrant, tingling. Excitement flooded her as he rubbed his thumb over her knuckles. She wasn't sure she could even respond, much less keep her mind clear enough to answer.

Finally, she smiled. "I'd rather hear what you have to say first. You were gone a long time. I know it was only six days, but it felt like so much more."

Leah looked down at their entwined fingers. "I thought—I assumed—you'd gone to La Grande to take the job. Have you come back to gather your things? Will you be leaving again?" She worked to keep her voice steady, not wanting him to sense the fear and anxiety hovering below the surface.

His hold tightened, and the silence lengthened. Finally, Steven leaned forward. "I'm so sorry, Leah. I thought Charlie had told you … or at least that he asked Millie to tell you I was coming back in a few days. We didn't plan on staying so long, but I had to wrap up the business at the bank, and it took longer than we expected to bring Tom home."

Leah's heart catapulted into her throat, and she thought she might choke. She jumped to her feet. "Tom? Wrapping up the job? What? How ..." She pressed her palm against her chest, trying to still the wild beating. Tom was home? Had her father come too? Of course he had. There would be no reason for him to stay in La Grande.

But the two of them together ... maybe she should return and make sure everything was all right. "I don't want Tom and Pa fighting again. I have to convince Tom to stay this time. He needs to know that Ma wrote about him in her letters—how much she loved and appreciated him."

He stood, then gently, quietly captured her hand and drew her close. "Wait. Remember what you told God a few minutes ago? That you were going to trust Him with Tom and your father?" A glint lit his eyes, and he gave her a teasing grin. "And maybe even me, if you could."

Once again warmth flooded Leah's cheeks, and she twisted her head, embarrassed that he'd heard her prayer—and her confession.

Steven tenderly touched her chin with his fingers and turned her to face him. "Leah, I didn't take the job. I told them I have too much here that I care for."

Leah's chest constricted. "Of course. Beth and your mother."

His grip tightened, and he leaned closer. "I care very much for my family. But that wasn't all I was talking about. Do you remember once that you asked why I left our farm and moved to the city? We ended up in an argument, and I never explained."

She nodded, remembering all too clearly that she'd been the cause of that upset.

Steven gave a sad smile. "I've always loved the land, but my step-father was a poor money manager. I wasn't old enough to advise him, and I don't know that he would have listened, regardless. He was a good man, but like your father, he had a proud spirit.

"My mother and I had to sell the farm for less than it was worth. We purchased a cabin on the outskirts of La Grande with enough land for a garden and a milk cow. All I salvaged from the farm were three valuable mares that I sold. Ma insisted I keep the money for the future, as she knew how much I wanted to buy my own land."

Leah's pulse raced, and she lifted her face and met his eyes. "Truly?"

"Yes. I'll admit I was tired of struggling and thankful for the job at the bank, due to the steady income. But it didn't take many months after moving to Baker City to decide I wasn't cut out for city life and being a banker."

Steven caressed Leah's cheek with his fingertips. "Then I met you. I no longer cared about anything but trying to make you happy." His face came within inches of hers and stopped.

Leah could feel his warm breath, and she closed her eyes. His fingers trailed down the side of her face, stopping to cup her cheek.

"Leah? May I kiss you?" The words were breathless and heavy with meaning.

She didn't reply but lifted her face and leaned toward him. His lips met hers, and everything within her danced. Sizzling arcs raced through her veins. Steven's arms came around her, and his kiss deep-ened until she thought she would swoon.

After several glorious moments he lifted his head and laid his face against her hair. "I love you, Leah."

She pulled back a few inches, but he didn't release his hold. "What did you say?"

"I love you. With all my heart and soul. For as long as I live." He captured her lips again.

This time she clung to him, drinking in his scent, the feel of his lips, and the strength of his arms drawing her close.

Too soon he released his tight hold but rested his forehead against hers. "Did you hear me that time?"

She nodded, barely able to breathe.

"Do you have anything to say in return?"

"I think you heard me earlier."

He barely moved in assent. "But I'd very much like to hear it again. Only this time, please say it to me, instead of to God?"

"I love you, Steven, and I trust you. Completely." She raised her eyes and met his. Somehow she must help him understand what she'd battled for so long. "I'm so sorry I've not shown you before—that I didn't open my heart to you. I was so afraid to let you in, so frightened to trust—so sure I'd be betrayed again by someone I cared for."

"Shh." He drew back and placed his fingertips against her lips. "No more sorrow or regret. You've endured enough for a lifetime. I want to spend the rest of my life bringing you happiness and, I hope, security. If you'll have me, that is? Will you marry me, Leah? Soon?"

She nodded and did what she'd wanted to do for so long. She threw her arms around his neck and hugged him, laughing and crying at the same time. "Yes. The sooner the better. But we still need to deal with Tom and Pa and the ranch."

He shook his head. "Tom and your pa are at peace with one another. When Charlie found Tom in La Grande, he was so happy and relieved. He told your brother he loved him, was sorry he'd wronged him, and wanted him to return home."

Leah gasped and blinked. "Pa said he was sorry and told Tom he loves him? Really?" It was almost too much to take in. Steven loved her, Pa loved her, and Tom was home. Then another thought struck. "What did Tom say? Did he accept Pa's apology? He didn't say anything cruel to him, did he?"

Steven stroked her face, keeping his eyes on hers. "Not at all. In fact, your little brother broke. He cried and hugged Charlie and asked if he could come home, then admitted he'd wronged you too. I think he'll have plenty to say when you go to the house."

She closed her eyes as joy bubbled inside. Pa and Tom. Both home. Both at peace. Her world was finally fitting together again. "Now there's one more thing I must take care of."

He tipped her face up. "Whatever it is, can we get married after it's done?"

She smiled and gave him another kiss. "Yes, Mr. Harding, we can."

"Will you tell me?"

"I'm going to give the ranch to Pa."

He stared. "Leah, the ranch is what you've wanted all your life. I can't believe now that you know it's yours that you'd give it up." He bent and pressed a warm kiss on her lips. "But I'll support whatever you decide. We'll buy our own ranch in the future and start over. I'll do whatever I can to make you happy."

Leah shook her head. "It doesn't matter anymore. You are what matters. Wherever you go, wherever you want to live, will be my home." She leaned into him again, her lips lingering, and realized the dream she'd been so afraid to dream had finally come true. Only instead of a prince, God had sent her a man who could be trusted—a godly man who would stand beside her, love her, and guard her heart with all the love that his own contained.

Epilogue

A month later

Leah stood in the side room of the church where the quilting group had gathered, while Beth and Katherine settled the ivory-colored dress over her head and shook out the skirt. Leah ran her hand over the heavy lace edging on the square neck, still amazed that Millie had finished sewing this gown in only a month.

Of course, Virginia, Katherine, and Beth had all helped in various ways. Frances had donated the handmade lace she'd saved over the years, and Wilma, not wanting to be bested by her friend, had urged Leah to accept the bolt of ivory silk she'd had shipped from back east. Leah had to giggle at the two women, both so proud of her while fiercely competitive at the same time.

The fitted bodice hugged Leah's curves and dropped down to a point over the skirt. The satin skirt widened slightly, and a flowing train was attached at the back of the bodice, flounced with a small bustle. She felt like a princess as she looked in the mirror, barely recognizing the green-eyed redhead who stared back.

Katherine fastened the last pearl button on Leah's bodice and then moved to the front. "You are positively stunning. I'm guessing Steven is going to faint dead away when he sees you, since you almost always wear trousers around him." She touched a curl swept up on Leah's head.

A tap at the door halted their discussion, and Beth glanced at Leah. Her eyes twinkled, and she shot Katherine a wicked grin. "Steven isn't allowed to see Leah before the ceremony, so he'd better not try to sneak in here. If he does, I'll have to use my sisterly charm on him and chase him down the hall."

Leah giggled. "I have no idea who it is, but I do not want Steven to see me. Can you check?"

Beth eased the door open. "Oh, Mr. Pape. Frances. Did you want to see Leah? She's all dressed and ready. Is it time for her to go?" She opened the door the rest of the way, and her father came in, Frances Cooper on his arm.

Leah looked at them both, and tears brimmed in her eyes. Pa wore a dapper black suit with a white shirt and string tie, and a black hat was tucked under his arm, although he looked a bit uncomfortable if she read him right. Frances was elegant as always in a deep blue gown with a high neck, modest ruffles at her wrists, and a straight skirt that fell to the floor. "You both look wonderful."

He came to her, his eyes swimming. He dug at his tight collar. "So do you, Leah girl. I just hope I live long enough to see you married. Frances made me wear this ding-blasted—" He shot her a look and pressed his lips together.

Frances's mouth relaxed in a full smile. "I will not say anything about your language, Charles, since you have every right to be excited—and a bit forgetful of your manners. And you are correct. Leah is more than lovely. She is truly a treasure to behold."

Pa placed his arm around Leah. "We brung you somethin' that I'm hopin' you'll accept. Two things, actually." He met Frances's eyes and gave a slight nod.

The woman opened her large bag. She drew out a beautiful wreath of freshly woven daisies, fitted with a sheer veil, and gave it to Pa. "You do the honors, Charles. She is your daughter, and this is important to you."

He accepted the wreath and smiled. "Your ma always loved these flowers, and I know you do too. Would you wear it as your bridal wreath as you walk down the aisle?"

Leah's throat closed. She'd never been so thankful that she'd forgiven her mother as she was at this moment. "Yes, I will. It's lovely, Pa." She tipped her head forward and allowed him to place it gently on her hair. The room grew still as she looked at her father. "Is it all right?"

A lone tear trickled down his weathered cheek, but he didn't brush it away. "It's perfect, Leah—as are you." He stepped closer and wrapped his arms around her in a warm hug. "I love you as much as if you'd been born to me. And I got one other thing for you."

He released her before she could speak and dug in an inside pocket of his jacket. "Where is the dad-blamed—" He aimed another look at Frances, who simply rolled her eyes and smiled. "Ah, here it is." Pa withdrew a folded paper and pressed it into Leah's hand.

"What is this?" She knew before she opened it, and she shook so hard she could barely hang on to the document.

"It's the deed to the ranch that you give me the day I come back from La Grande. I couldn't go through with it. I ain't gonna put it in my name, Daughter. It's yours, fair and square. Your pa started this ranch, and your ma gave it to you. I ain't gonna take it."

She held out her hand. "You are my father. You've worked your entire life for that piece of land. Steven is my future now."

He took a step back and folded his arms. "I done talked to him about it already. He wants to stay on at the ranch if you do. Says he meant to give you a weddin' present of some money he's been savin'. Wants to invest it in the ranch to bring things back to rights. So the deed is yours. Yours and his. And that's final."

"I'll take it under one condition." Leah looked him square in the eyes. "That you come in as a full partner and work it with me. Steven and I can build you another home, or we can build a cabin for Millie and Buddy, and you can live in the house with us. I'll tell Tom we want him to stay and have a part in the ranch."

"I'll accept that, but I won't live in that house. I got other plans for my future." Pa wiggled his brows at Frances, who colored under his gaze. Then he turned his attention back to Leah. "You can let Buddy and Millie keep livin' there if you want, or we can build 'em a cabin so you have more room free for a family someday."

He drew her into a close embrace. "But that ain't got to be decided now. I accept your offer, little girl. I'm proud to partner with you in the ranch and to know my son will be there as well." He planted a kiss on her cheek and held out his arm. "Now let's walk down the aisle and put that poor man out of his misery before he falls dead on the floor."

Leah tucked her fingers through the crook of his elbow and smiled, then reached for the bouquet of daisies Katherine held. Leah bit back a giggle at the still blushing Frances. Since seeing the changes in her father after he'd started calling on Frances

Cooper, Leah couldn't be happier. She knew exactly who was going to catch her carefully aimed bouquet once the ceremony ended.

Steven waited for her at the front of the church to start a new life together, and all was finally right in her world. She knew problems would come in the future, but with God and Steven by her side, as well as Pa, Tom, and apparently Frances, too, she could face that future with strength and peace, knowing that love would conquer anything life might bring.

... a little more ...

When a delightful concert comes to an end,

the orchestra might offer an encore.

When a fine meal comes to an end,

it's always nice to savor a bit of dessert.

When a great story comes to an end,

we think you may want to linger.

And so, we offer ...

AfterWords—just a little something more after you

have finished a David C Cook novel.

We invite you to stay awhile in the story.

Thanks for reading!

Turn the page for ...

- **Author's Note**
- **Great Questions for Individual Reflection and/or Group Discussion**
- **About the Author**
- **Other Books by Miralee Ferrell**

Author's Note

Why I Wrote This Story

A question many authors are asked is, "What prompted you to write this particular book?" Naturally I hoped to find a story line that would entertain readers, and I wanted to continue with the characters created in the first three books of this series. But each book needs a theme. I don't ever want to write a simple romance without something that drives it. In this case, it was a young woman who's been emotionally damaged by a father who turned to alcohol and abandoned her emotionally, and a mother who abandoned her physically.

In my years of counseling women, I've discovered that alcoholism, abandonment, and depression impact even the strongest Christian families, leaving deep scars that can linger for a lifetime. My hope is that women who have encountered a similar situation might find some aspect of the story that would minister to their heart. Jesus is our Great Physician and is able and willing to heal every broken and wounded heart that's brought to Him.

I dedicated this book to my father, Curtis Gould, who was nothing at all like Charlie, Leah's father, except that he loved his children. Daddy was old-fashioned in many ways, including not caring for the use of "Dad," but he was comfortable showing appreciation and love and enjoyed receiving it in return. He passed away when I was in my late thirties, and I still miss him and think of him often. I'm so thankful I had him in my life.

I created Charlie Pape after a conversation with my publisher, Don Pape. I had used my copy editor's last name, Carlson, for my heroine, and Don wanted to know who I planned to name after him. I responded that I was working on another book that contained a gambler, and would that be all right? He chuckled and said as long as he was a three-dimensional bad guy, that was fine. It got me thinking and digging, as I'd not planned to give Charlie Pape a different name from Leah's, or his own point of view, but suddenly, I knew he needed both, as well as some deep issues that only God could resolve.

Don Pape is about as far removed from Charlie Pape as two men could be, so I hope he'll forgive me as I wandered into areas of pride and overindulgence—and I hope he'll get a chuckle or two from the romance between the two most stubborn and opinionated people in this series, Charlie and Frances. Thank you, Don, for challenging me to dig deeper without even realizing you did.

I hope you've enjoyed this fourth book in the Love Blossoms in Oregon series and will join me again in the novella I hope to write about Tom and Mei Lee, the young Chinese woman befriended by Julia McKenzie in *Forget Me Not*, my other novella in this series.

Great Questions

for Individual Reflection and/or Group Discussion

1. Have you, like Leah, ever been on the receiving end of empty promises from someone you love and count on? If so, when? In what way(s) can you identify with Leah's emotions?

2. How has that situation in the past influenced your current relationships and the way you perceive other people in general?

3. When Steven meets Leah, he is judged wrongly by her as being her father's drinking buddy. How does he choose to handle the misunderstanding? Would you have handled it differently? And, if so, how?

4. Charlie believes no one has a "right to tell him what to do or how to live his life. It is his business if he drinks, and nobody else's." Do you agree? Why or why not?

5. What qualities of Leah's do you consider admirable? What traits cause her trouble? In what ways are you like Leah? Unlike Leah?

6. Have you ever found yourself working in a job you originally thought you'd love, but didn't fit your personality long term, as

the bank job was for Steven? If so, how have you handled that situation?

7. All around Leah, her friends seem to be getting married and having babies. She admits sometimes she feels envy, wishing for what they had, but she continues to involve herself in the lives of her friends. When have you found yourself jealous of what a friend has? How have you dealt with that envy? Has it changed anything in your relationship, and, if so, what?

8. Why does Leah fight the attraction she feels for Steven Harding? Are her feelings based on facts, feelings, fears, or a combination of those three things? Explain.

9. Steven feels lost, ignored, forgotten, and petty now that his mother has found her daughter again. Do you think his feelings are valid? Why or why not? Imagine you are Steven for a minute. How would you relate to your now-reconciled mother and sister?

10. Leah can stand up to just about anyone without batting an eyelash, but her father always makes her feel as though he is waiting for her to do something wrong and that she can never measure up, no matter what choice she makes. What was your relationship with your father like when you were growing up? In what way(s) can you identify with Leah's experience? In what way(s) is your experience with your father different?

11. Which character in the book did you feel the most empathy for? Why? What about this character resonates with your personality and life experience?

12. Why do you think Steven Harding has a soft spot in his heart for Tom Pape that makes him want to go the second mile to reconcile him with his family? How might looking through Steven's or Tom's eyes give you perspective for a family situation you're facing right now?

13. Why do you think it took someone like Frances Cooper to break through Charlie Pape's tough shell? What qualities is he drawn to in her? What qualities is she drawn to in him? What makes their highly unusual relationship—between two prickly personalities—"work"?

14. Frances Cooper uses life lessons she's learned—even recently—to try to make a difference in someone else's life who is hurting. How might you use the unique life lessons you've learned to help others?

15. When Leah tells Steven that "God will make a way," he responds, "Don't you suppose God has the ability to answer in a way that's not what you expected?" Has God ever answered a prayer of yours in a way you didn't expect? If so, share the story.

About the Author

Miralee and her husband, Allen, live on eleven acres in the beautiful Columbia River Gorge in southern Washington State, where they love to garden, play with their dogs, take walks, and spend time with family. She is also able to combine two other passions—horseback riding and spending time with her grown children—since her married daughter lives nearby, and they often ride together on the wooded trails near their home. In early 2013 the family welcomed a baby granddaughter, and Miralee is totally in love with being a grandmother to Baby Kate, who will be close to two years old when this book releases.

Ironically, Miralee, now the author of eleven novels and novellas and a contributor in four compilations, never had a burning desire to write—at least more than her own memoirs for her children. So she was shocked when God called her to start writing after she turned fifty. To Miralee, writing is a ministry she hopes will impact hearts, and she looks forward with anticipation to see how God will use each of her books to bless and change lives.

An avid reader, Miralee has a large collection of first-edition Zane Grey books that she started collecting as a young teen. Her love for his storytelling ability inspired her desire to write fiction set in the Old West. "But I started writing historical fiction without even meaning to," Miralee says, laughing. She'd always planned on writing contemporary women's fiction, but God had other ideas. After signing her first contract for the novel *Love Finds You in Last Chance, California* she decided to research the town and area. To her dismay, she discovered the town no longer existed and hadn't since the 1960s. Though it had been a booming town in the late 1880s, it had pretty much died out in the 1930s. So her editor suggested switching to a historical version, and Miralee agreed, although she'd never even considered that era.

It didn't take long to discover she had a natural flair for that time period, having read and watched so many Western stories while growing up. From that point on she was hooked. Her 1880s stories continue to grow in acclaim each year. Her novel *Love Finds You in Sundance, Wyoming* won the Will Rogers Medallion Award for Western Fiction. *Blowing on Dandelions*, the first book in the Love Blossoms in Oregon series, achieved bestseller status on the ECPA list in early 2014.

Universal Studios requested a copy of her debut novel, *The Other Daughter*, for a potential family movie. Another movie production company is currently considering her book *Love Finds You in Sundance, Wyoming* as a made-for-TV family movie as well.

Aside from writing and her outdoor activities, Miralee has lived a varied life. She and her husband have been deeply involved in building two of their own homes over the years, as well as doing a full remodel on a one-hundred-year-old Craftsman style home they owned and loved for four years. They also owned a sawmill at the time and were able to provide much of the interior wood products. Miralee has done everything from driving a forklift, to stoking the huge, 120-year-old boiler, and off-bearing lumber, to running a small planer and staking boards in the dry kiln.

Besides their horse friends, Miralee and her husband have owned
cats, dogs (a six-pound, long-haired Chihuahua named Lacey was
often curled up on her lap as she wrote this book), rabbits, and, yes,
even two cougars, Spunky and Sierra, rescued from breeders who
didn't have the ability or means to care for them properly.

Miralee and Allen have lived in Alaska and the San Juan Islands
for just under a year each, where she became actively involved in
women's ministry. Later, she took a counseling course and earned her
accreditation with the American Association of Christian Counselors.

After serving five years as the president of the Portland/Vancouver
chapter of ACFW (American Christian Fiction Writers), Miralee
now volunteers as a board member and belongs to a number of writers' groups. She also speaks at women's groups, libraries, historical
societies, and churches about her writing journey.

www.miraleeferrell.com
www.twitter.com/miraleeferrell
www.facebook.com/miraleeferrell

Books by Miralee Ferrell

Love Blossoms in Oregon Series
Blowing on Dandelions
Forget Me Not
Wishing on Buttercups
Dreaming on Daisies

Novellas
Forget Me Not
(part of the Love Blossoms in Oregon series)
The Nativity Bride
(part of the 12 Brides of Christmas series)

Love Finds You Series
Love Finds You in Bridal Veil, Oregon
Love Finds You in Sundance, Wyoming
Love Finds You in Last Chance, California
Love Finds You in Tombstone, Arizona
(sequel to Love Finds You in Last Chance, California)

Other Titles
The Other Daughter
Finding Jeena
(sequel to The Other Daughter)

Other Contributions/Compilations
A Cup of Comfort for Cat Lovers
Fighting Fear: Winning the War at Home
Faith & Finances: In God We Trust
Faith & Family: Daily Family Devotions